The

UNFORTUNATES

The

UNFORTUNATES

Sophie McManus

FARRAR, STRAUS AND GIROUX

NEW YORK

Farrar, Straus and Giroux
18 West 18th Street, New York 10011

Library of Congress Cataloging-in-Publication Data
McManus, Sophie, 1977–
    The unfortunates / Sophie McManus. — First edition.
        pages   cm
    ISBN 978-0-374-11450-3 (hardback) — ISBN 978-0-374-70974-7 (e-book)
    I. Title.

PS3613.C58533 U54 2015
813'.6—dc23

                                                                    2014031272

Designed by Abby Kagan

Farrar, Straus and Giroux books may be purchased for educational, business,
or promotional use. For information on bulk purchases, please contact the Macmillan
Corporate and Premium Sales Department at 1-800-221-7945, extension 5442,
or write to specialmarkets@macmillan.com.

www.fsgbooks.com
www.twitter.com/fsgbooks • www.facebook.com/fsgbooks

1   3   5   7   9   10   8   6   4   2

For my parents
And for E.H.M.

Behind every great fortune there is a great crime.

—HONORÉ DE BALZAC

The

UNFORTUNATES

It began with a house. It was the property next to her own, a half mile up the road. One afternoon driving to town, she noticed the blue-lettered FOR SALE sign nailed to a post, set back in the trees. When that same day her son called to say he was engaged, Cecilia Somner decided it was too lucky a coincidence to ignore. What better gift for the start of a new life? A home for George and Iris. She bought the place at asking. Later that month, at the end of an otherwise ordinary lunch in the city, she plunked the keys down among the half-emptied coffee cups in front of George, repeated the address as Iris fumbled for a pen, and concluded, "—but the wedding will be at Booth Hill. Your house is too small."

When the day arrived, the bright lawn rolled down to a tent beside the sea. Cecilia kissed the guests hello and sent them down to the water in twos and fours, their cars left in a jumble for the valet, the sun already flaring off the fenders and their sunglasses and off the windows of her house, a house that for a century the Somners had called the

Cottage, despite its forty rooms. A dog barked from behind a downstairs window, its shoulder a red blur against the glass, startling each group of passing guests. The women laughed as they picked their way along the gravel, careful of their shoes.

You could see even from the top of the hill how George was trying to win over the Nelsons. Iris's grizzled uncles and aunts, the only guests already seated, squinted up at George from the first row at the lawn-edge of the Atlantic. Being so few, they had room to put their bags beside them. George stood in front of the sun asking them friendly questions, his face turned a little away. A good face, under a wave of bright copper hair tossed out of his eyes. His fingers remained loosely in his pocket, unless he was raking his hair, elbow aloft, or flicking a gnat out of his drink. Something about his easy manner and the mean, charming way his eyes—green like his mother's, for there was no mistaking them for anything but mother and son—narrowed to some little eternity in the manner of a cologne advertisement, made those in his presence feel they were their most interesting selves.

Still, the Nelsons could not be put at ease. When George asked how the trip from Nova Scotia had been and whether they landed at LaGuardia or JFK, they circled their chairs and argued until one answered, "No, Kennedy." When a cousin of Cecilia's, a Gifford, joined them and offered that his family used to vacation in Chester, and wasn't that in Nova Scotia?—they said they'd never been. The mood didn't improve when George snuck away and the Nelsons, finding themselves among strangers, asked, "Where do you work?" instead of "What do you do?" and the Somners' people answered, "Oh—in the city."

So many violins and George had to be found. He was in an upstairs bedroom, listening to the muffled flurry of Iris being dressed on the other side of the wall. From the window he watched his mother—CeCe to all—on the lawn below, slender and silver, directing the ushers as they balanced out the aisles, moving the more peripheral of the Somners' guests to the empty seats on the Nelson side like load on a small plane before takeoff. Then it was time—George and the minister at the long grass bordering the sea. Iris, alone down the aisle, looking neither left nor right. *Beautiful*, everyone said. Iris, the ceremony, the house rising above the water, dinner under the low sun.

At dusk, the sea was gray. It made a picture, the younger people straying down as if it were a great magnet, their shoes in their hands. There was drinking and dancing into the night. Iris and George— even from the shadows leaping up the far end of the candlelit tent, you could tell it was the real thing. When the hour came for them to say goodbye, they stood and waved, not beside a car but at an opening in the trees, for a path had been cut to connect Booth Hill to the house they were to make their own. The path was lined with lanterns. Lanterns hung in the trees.

I

SOMNER'S REST

(Summer)

1

On the same lawn, in the dark before sunrise—ink horizon, ink sea, the grass now blue in the dark—George takes his mother's hand and leads her stumbling down the dewy slope and through her garden to a small, private dock on their private patch of beach. Holding his mother's hot, bony hand, he misses Iris. How excellent to miss her still. Love-struck as he ever was. A year since the wedding and they've fallen into the pattern of their days—their new home, her new job, mornings and evenings together—and all is right with the world. At the office, he still sits and thinks of her with the childish rapture of the blessed, picturing her mouth, picturing he is inside the tiny, pink cathedral of her mouth, in one way or another, as he fiddles with the ivory letter opener or the silver box on his desk, a box engraved *J. Stepney Somner*, a box that on another desk might hold paper clips or stamps, but on George's holds only a fine dust he likes to think is the residue of his great-grandfather's snuff.

"Almost there," he says, tugging his mother down the last of the dank lawn to the dock. He pulls the orange life vest over her head, catching his phone as it falls from his pocket. He rolls his trousers but neglects to take off his shoes and curses as he stands in the shallows. The soles of his loafers burp in the mud as he hoists her into the motorboat. Seaweed swells around the hull. She's easier to lift than he expected— her feather-frailty, her diminishing density, the air in her bones.

How brave he is! Yes, *brave* is the word. And honest. Honesty keeping step with bravery. Brave how he doesn't look away from his mother and honest to admit he misses Iris. Honest to see that missing his wife, missing what he has, is impossible and is the case; brave enough to follow this thought to the next—that missing Iris has something to do with his no longer being twenty. Not twenty, but forty! That each day he wakes again and sits down to breakfast *again*, and still he isn't anybody. And the years are piling on. And yet, to keep hope, to have faith. What harder courage can any man possess?

He steadies the prow and climbs in. They scrape rock. A final push takes them off the bottom, and the boat putts out into the dark, lapping water of the Sound. George points them toward the *Matador*, the five-masted clipper they've rented and staffed for the day, several hundred yards out, in deeper water.

"I forgot this peapod belongs to me," CeCe says, looking disapprovingly around the motorboat. The previous afternoon, George had dragged it from underneath a blue tarp in a long-neglected shed in the woods behind the house, the shed's walls lined floor to thatch with rusted license plates, a collection of the late groundskeeper, a man known to George only as Pete; the concrete under the boat a damp ecosystem of brown leaves and slugs. He'd checked the motor and gotten oil and sweat up the white insides of his arms and decided himself the victor.

He *does* want breakfast. Being awake so early doesn't suit him, and he commends himself for doing all he has for his mother, who is saying she will never again have a party up at the house. Not after the strain of the wedding. Though yes it was a great success and nothing had been stolen. She's asking if he's paying attention—for only she knows how George's expression doesn't convey his mind, how no indication of boredom will hold in the natural intensity of his face. Only she can tell when he isn't listening.

"This jacket stinks of mildew," she concludes, tugging the clasp.

"But," he answers, adjusting the strap, "doesn't the Cottage look nice from here? See what your guests will see?"

The house on the shoreline has become gray and small as a photograph. The hill he'd been married on looks steeper in the indigo than by day. The house is set farther back from the shore, more splendid, but less obviously so, than its new-built neighbors. They watch as Esme—it must be Esme—passes from room to room, throwing on the lights, fading the slim morning moon. They can see the wide wrap of the stone veranda and the red glow of two of the sitting rooms and the warm shine of the coppery kitchen and the willow trees that flank the house reaching in silver assurance up to the gabled top windows, glowing from within.

"Where are you going, please," CeCe says. "With your navigational skills, we'll be found bumping in the reeds down current, dead of dehydration and leathered as jerky."

A plane crosses the dawn sky, its green and red lights blinking; another plane soon follows. CeCe knows this should be pretty to her, and not a menace. She should also like the water on her hands. She does not. The flesh too is made of water and needs no reminder. Her mind—why, she can't guess—finds its way to George at age eight, home early from school with a consonant-drunkening cold, singing, *Glory, glory hallelujah, by teacher hid me wid a ruler, and we all began to laugh whed da ruler broke id half . . .* Her back where it is leaned against his strong arm slips a little, and the next part of the song falls away. Something about marching, and in the inch her ribs collapse forward and will not be pulled right again, she is reminded that unless her luck turns, the next years will be a series of quotidian humiliations increasing in frequency and severity until the days blend into one ugly noon, and at that shadowless hour she will have to answer to her child. If she can answer at all.

"You forgot to shave," she says. "Take care of it before we start the day. Don't forget."

What *had* she been thinking? She'd scheduled this event so long ago—was talked into it at the wedding, in fact—a fund-raiser on a boat for a youth program in oceanography, and why had she said yes? So many parties and all the same. And boat people, not her kind. "Not my kind," she always said. Noisy. Tourists and fishermen and her arrogant new neighbors with their captain's hats and their glowing tablets and their children screaming down to the dock to man the jib. For many summers she's complained about these children. The penetrating problem of noise pollution—how their high choral voices skipped along the water and pierced the glass of her front windows—did they not have mothers who taught them manners? She'd written to the town's community board to ban boat traffic past her house. Her lawyer reviewed a draft of the letter and agreed it was reasonable. When the board didn't respond, she invited the mayor and the district's most prominent judge over for tea. She took them out onto the veranda and handed them the binoculars and showed them how the boats might avoid the cove. The community board sent an apology attached to a basket of poppy-seed cake and Meyer lemons with the leaves still attached but said they could do no more. The mayor called in a favor at the Historical Preservation Society and had her house granted landmark status, as if she were dead.

"Should have gotten around to it years ago, no excuse," he said.

She'd thanked the mayor and the board and without notice stopped payment on a check to the County Development Foundation for the restoration of the town's second, older marina, ensuring the jetty remain a dilapidated grave of rotting posts rising out of the water, cleaved from the body of the dock by a chain-link fence, which the kids who are townbound and time idle still scale with beers jammed down their pants, to swim the water slick with oil, and after, under the idiot moon, to lie on the dock in the dark, listening for the cruiser on night patrol rolling past with its lights off.

Thus, the Stockport locals among the sixty-five to receive the Somners' invitation, which read *A Day at Sea!* in royal-blue cursive across heavy card stock, were surprised.

CeCe lifts her feet to avoid a pool of water rolling at the bottom of the motorboat.

"Insecure tub! George, go faster. If I drown out here, they'll call it you-know-what."

He gives the cord another yank. They putt along the curve of the cove out toward the Sound. A modest blue house comes into view where the land opens to ocean, a figure by the door.

"Mrs. Barnes, smoking," George says.

"No, the time! Who smokes at dawn?"

"Dana Barnes, I guess."

"Cigarettes are disgusting."

"Isn't a cigarette."

"Ah." CeCe laughs. "We invited her, didn't we? Do you think she'll be stoned on the boat? Now I'm looking forward to this brunch." But her face bunches into sadness. "So drive already."

Javier sees them coming and readies himself on the metal steps, unfolded into the water.

They board and take breakfast on the stern because the captain advises that from there they can watch the sunrise. It's pink and blue. They descend belowdecks to change. Ridiculous, George feels, to be on board so early, to dress so early, and then do nothing for hours but bicker and look at the sky. But she'd insisted: to supervise. He does his mother the courtesy of putting on a jacket he knows she won't like, asking her opinion, and descending again to shave and change into the poplin laid out on the bed.

CeCe puts on a sleeveless sheath of cerulean crepe. Bending carefully, she puts on the ballet flats of soft, blue leather with white soles she had ordered for the day, dark soles and heels being unacceptable on a boat, though she doesn't expect her guests to know the old rules. At the top of each of her flats is a gold sailor's knot with two tiny pearls-of-the-sea, a gold anchor nestled into the knot, too much whimsy for her taste, but discreet enough. Shopping, that demoralizing endeavor. Especially once she crossed into her seventies, five years ago. With increasing regularity, her shopper at Bergdorf urges her toward items of themed exuberance, clothing with pictures, as if she were a toddler, as if older women and toddlers are alone together in having so little of interest or coherence to say that instead they might point to their shoes or their chests with cheer. She feels tired. Don't think about it, she thinks, as she struggles to clasp the pearls at her neck. She wills herself, schools herself, so often it's almost a mantra: she'll not indulge the shake in her hands, the shake in her legs. They are *not* invited. She will not invite the most humiliating, the aerobic shake of her neck: a tiny, smiling quiver as friendless as a match fired on a hill. She's learned to play a trick on herself this last year, which sometimes works—she imagines herself inside a kind of farmyard pen, encircled by a strong wire fence. The world outside the fence is sonic, an earthquake, but she is still.

The shakes, when they do come, are preceded by an unnerving sensation and sound inside her ears like the metal hum of a train track before the train appears—her ties, her spine; their rattle—a minute, alien music—her neck. As if she is agreeing, agreeing forever, with some small point. And what point might this be? She will not use the wheelchair, refused George's plea to bring it on board—the absurd comedy of a wheelchair on a boat! She pretended, and he pretended with her, that the crawl down the lawn had been easy, that she was playing a game as quaint as—what is its name? The one where you must move sideways to move forward.

"Good morning," says a young woman in a white apron, passing with a tray of juice glasses. Chaos, CeCe thinks, for the server's hair is down. No time to ruminate. She must round up the staff, remind them how to comport themselves. The micromanaging one must do to have it right.

George shaves. If he were home right now, he'd be by the pool, drinking coffee and reading the paper, watching Iris swim. Across the deck he sees Javier, assembling the catering staff for CeCe. They make a checkerboard of black and white. George could mark the passage of his life in speeches he's heard his mother give to caterers. As she surveys the brunch buffet—"Dears. You are all dear to me today—" he escapes to the other end of the boat. Still, he can hear:

"—and you are to do more than pass around the food and keep tidy.

You are in control. Do you know you must be in control? Of the very mood. The enjoyment of the guests is yours to bear. I can see from here—is there mustard somewhere to go with the lamb? Cold meat? Mustard? If I see but one wilting lily draped over the rail with nothing to drink—have these—star fruit?—been sliced neatly enough? Daisy, is it? Daisy, go get a knife and tidy them. If anyone drinks too quickly, you will forget to pour every other time, and if they look slighted, pour half as much as usual. We know how to pour for me, nothing but air or water and stand directly in front of the glass so this goes unnoticed—those oysters—that one, that one, look where I am pointing. Women do not like to swallow oysters as large as these! Your thumb, no longer than your thumb."

George leans as far over the water as he can. He dares himself to jump. He contemplates the authenticity of his sadness. An hour ago he was full of the courage and pleasure of Iris, of all their life to come. How is it he's now so low? His mother, pretending to be frail, only to cause him grief. He could jump. He could! Debating an act so serious and miserable binds a dark delight to his sorrow. He waves a waiter over, requests a Bloody Mary. He doesn't want to die. However, there is the pleasant vision of them weeping at his funeral. He checks his watch, his hand over the blue. It has a crack across its face he's certain wasn't there the day before—could it be from when he tugged the throttle of the motorboat? Had he not noticed, in the dark with the roar of the outboard? Next week he'll take it to the repairman on Lexington. He can't let his mother see—an heirloom, not John Stepney Somner's but John's son, CeCe's father, Edward George, and George's namesake. Once more he's overcome by the child's dream of witnessing them mourn at his funeral, and he knows, though he can't say it to himself so directly, that for a man of middle age some other dream should long have replaced this one. His mother's voice returns to him on the wind.

"—And don't be afraid to give a compliment. There's a story underneath or behind every hat or brooch a lady wears. Dress the greens there only at the last minute! But never speak in a way that forces a guest to indulge *your* interests—Blue Point? Kumamoto? To indulge the tastes of others you must reveal no tastes of your own. I hope the eggs, over there, are underpoached to account for the heat of the sun? *Madame* is a forbidden address. It's old-fashioned! Fruit should not be next to salmon tartare. Try not to fret if a guest takes out some frustration on you. It may not be pleasant, but you are a repository. George? Young miss, please set yourself to extracting those Brazil nuts from the mix. No one ever wants a Brazil nut. Perhaps the cheese is oozing out of the figs and overpowering the surrounding dishes because someone's put that plate in the sunniest spot on the table? Find and use the shade! When the boat turns, find it again. For the vegetarians—should tomato consommé be next to carpaccio? We shall all be clean, clean and invisible, yes? Invisible, but you must watch with an intimacy that allows you to foresee each desire. Try to abstain from using the restroom—edible flowers? Is this a luau? Javier, toss—yes, overboard is fine—*smile*, I'm *teasing*—but if you must use the restroom take a clean towel so that if anyone sees you going in, they will assume you are improving it for their benefit. Bartenders, we will not serve anything with a straw. Mr. Antonopoulos. I am glad to see we no longer have the scuffed-shoe problem of our last engagement. I know there is a tendency to let off steam when you think you are amongst yourselves. I am not a fool. This is absolutely forbidden. It is always possible we are being heard or seen without our knowledge. This is good life-advice, dears, not just for today."

Well, George thinks, that's one point she's got right. He can tell she's finished and rejoins her, sewing on the warm smile that says, *What's that?*—his hands amiably pocketed, his chin and eyebrows up like a birder on a walk full of ordinary sparrows.

Thank you, the staff says. They disband to their stations. Javier nods in the direction of the shore. The first load of guests is shuttling over from the dock.

2

Iris's dog is first out of the shuttle, which bounces against the starboard of the *Matador* as it's tethered for ascent. He's part Akita or mastiff, an unlikely red—dried blood or old iron, with a long, solemn face, the flesh drawn toward the jowls and loosening around the neck as if tied with butcher's string. He has big mutt paws, long, yellow teeth. Barrel ribs, and the kind of attenuated belly that tapers and disappears into the top of the hindquarters. Tie-dyed by the devil, Esme said when she first saw 3D. A strange name for such a serious creature.

George respects but does not like the dog. His frank gaze, his dark eyes, unnerve George. The dog has known Iris longer than George has known Iris, has witnessed versions of her that will forever remain unknown to George. There she is, he thinks, when he looks into 3D's face. Younger, hotter, a million moving pictures of Iris suspended in the spinning web of dumb-dog neurotransmission, forever doing whatever 3D watched her do from the threshold of her darkened bedroom door. Her past is the vaulted property of 3D. Though dogs, George knows, can't tell time, at least not the way men can.

3D scrabbles up the metal stairs and pushes past George, who is standing at the top, smiling and waving over the water.

"Champagne?" he calls. "Wet shoes? Everyone's shoes stay dry?"

"My feet got wet, and so did 3D's, but he doesn't care, and neither do I," Iris says, her voice low and full of cheer, the dog racing back down to accompany her as she climbs the stairs, a little after the rest. Her wedding ring scrapes against his cheek in greeting, an old habit, turning the stone toward the palm. Why? he once asked. To keep it safe, she'd said, and shrugged, disappearing behind the golden curtain of her hair. Lucky is the man whose greatest rival is a dog.

Today, Iris has gathered her hair into a mussed knot at her nape. Her mouth is bright. To George, she lifts her fine, crescent brows— brows so light she seems to him always to be wearing a hopeful, open expression, wakeful, unwritten—to ask, *How shit has your day been so far?* He answers, with an eye roll, *Shit*, and once again all is well. She shakes her head quickly—*Don't tell me now*. To stop his laugh, she raises her voice to the guests collecting around them.

"Any chance, George, you packed an extra pair of shoes for me? You forgot? Don't anybody ask this guy to be useful before noon, am I right? I'm taking mine off. Let's make a shoe pile. Hey, look! I've started a trend."

CeCe arranges herself in a canvas lounge chair in the middle of the boat. The weather is complying, the sun high on the horizon and a crisp early-summer breeze fluttering the sails. She doesn't understand why so many are going around with bare feet, and at *lunchtime*, but the roll of the collective voice is right. The cause will net a good number of contributions, beyond what her guests have already pledged. The ocean view is behind her and an iced plate of shrimp has been placed on the stool beside her knee. She has chosen her place carefully. With any luck they won't see she isn't standing too often, isn't moving around. Has anyone noticed? They come to her in such an orderly fashion. She wonders if they are looking at her too carefully, too long. And then they look away.

She'll never tell them, never, not a one. She's told no one beyond her household. Multiple system atrophy, a name too straightforward to say out loud. She would have preferred a more abstrusely titled affliction. Something named after the doctor who discovered it, like, say, MSA's symptomatic cousin Parkinson's. Something that might allow her to minimize her disease's exact evil. Parkinson's—her initial, incorrect diagnosis. No, she won't endure the look of horror. Or, that greater horror, sympathy. She'd appreciated it when the doctors began abbreviating it to MSA; by some aural dyslexia, MSA puts her mind to NASA and rocket launches, which allows her to feel hopeful about innovation and progress and the human endeavor. At least she doesn't have PSP, progressive supranuclear palsy, another early candidate, ruled out due to her lucidity of mind—PSP taking the inner life along with the body. With MSA, she might make it five years. With PSP she'd already be mindless as a jellyfish washed onto a rock, dead before the tide.

No, no one's staring at her. It's only the way people look at each other at parties. Here is Mr. Holbrook, to update her on his most recent work in the Assembly. The Conrads join them and the subject changes to the problem of children texting each other ungrammatical cruelties during school. Soon enough three of her favorite people are beside her: Annie Mason, the director of the Somner Fund, twenty years her junior, steady and sharp; Annie's assistant, a young man built like a mechanical pencil, from Louisville; and the foundation's head of programs, Clifton Franks. Her favorite people, not because they are her friends, but because they are, as Clifton once nonsensically said, her octopus of righteousness—it was the seventies when he said it— doing the work of which Cecilia is proud. The fund's endowment is modest compared to the likes of the Fords' or the Rockefellers'. But she's made sure over the years that her contributions are brave, offer seed money, risk supporting fledgling efforts. If Cecilia Somner gives her approval to a cause, other donors follow. It is for this reason she's worked so long to keep her name alive, to keep the table set.

"My heroes," she says, watching George circle the crowd, "what wonderful work you've done this quarter!" For the forty years she's had her foundation, she's visited each organization they fund, but this last year, after her diagnosis, they've plotted, quietly, what she will only refer to as her transition; now her transition is more or less complete. "Annie," CeCe says, "I want you to go talk to the Turners about that museum in the Bronx. Two thousand eight, remember? I think they might be of use." They leave her to find the Turners. She watches one of George's guests, Robert Barrow-Wood—or is it Woods?—follow Iris through the crowd, calling, "Iris, come look at this!" Pathetic. She watches Iris's vivid face as she turns and strides across the deck—a longer step, more graceful, than her son's, the red dog trailing behind. The guests watch Iris pass, a point of which Iris seems unaware. That she brought the dog with her today—beyond belief.

A foursome of local widows descend upon CeCe, invite her to join them on a January trip to Nice. "Old broads abroad, we're calling it," they say, slapping their white shorts. CeCe hears Iris laugh and the man Barrow-Woods shouting, "I love you, you liar!" The devil mutt comes over and jaws a shrimp off CeCe's plate and trots away. Ambassador Thompson, retired, interrupts the widows to ask if the boat is set up for skeet shooting. One of the Turners' children, Dill, not yet back to college, says, "Does that mean this boat has guns? Did that dog take your lunch?"

"I love to spoil him," she says. To change the subject she asks, "And who are we?" as she reaches out to muss the head of a passing child, who swivels in alarm. She looks into the faces of the child's parents, and into an adjacent group of guests. In this way, with her eyes and her hand, she dismisses the widows and the ambassador and brings this new group to her, mostly Bakers. Mrs. Baker leans down to kiss her, saying, "CeCe, don't you look beautiful today!"

She does *not* look beautiful. No, what she looks like now is a squirrel monkey. Her head, one day, tiny under the elegant fringe of silver and honey-colored hair. Her green eyes, muddier, shrunk into the sockets. Unchanged are her high but flattened cheekbones that, while not in fashion in her youth, were geometrical under her eyes, the eyes close together but bright and captivating. Along with her fair hair and her stark, Cleopatra eyebrows, she turned heads, the black and the blond of her, her face an assemblage of unlikely contrasts that she embellished with large, precious stones. She'd never been beautiful. But she was remarkable, and glad to not be counted in the limp category of pretty. The elegant force of her had once made her appear taller than her five feet five inches. Now she seems shorter, short. Gone is the glow of the skin but unchanged is her long, precise nose and tight nostril, as if drawn in perpetual inhalation. Her hair is blown out straight, cut expensively below the chin with a demure flip, pushed impatiently and tidily behind her ears, gold at the temples, not the high-voltage blond of some of her contemporaries—but that toy-monkey face beneath! Can it belong to her?

To mask her irritation at Mrs. Baker's flattery, she musters some of her own. "Talk about beautiful. This year I can see your honeysuckle from a mile away!" There's no denying the Baker garden is a mess. She turns to Mr. Lewis, and they laugh about the disparity in age and attractiveness between himself and his wife, whom they wave to while they speak. CeCe kisses Nan Porter, whom she's known since their sophomore year at Vassar, from the days when every afternoon they were required to attend tea wearing white gloves and pearls. She says, "Give it a rest, today, Nan," and Nan says, "Give what a rest?" and they too have a laugh.

Forty-five years before, CeCe was thirty, sitting up on the rail of a smaller boat, her silk collar fluttering in the breeze. Walter Minch—a stranger twenty years her senior—grabbed her shoulders and leaned her backward over the sea. Stranger, curio, husband, enemy, stranger once again, father to Patricia, father to George. Walter, the third and last man she ever had relations with on a beach, but who was the first? That pocket-eyed manufacturer of Italian cars, always mentioning the time after the war he drank absinthe with Picasso in Vallauris. Halfway up the cliff of a chalky Dover beach, she'd put her hand on his spine and they looked at the long shadows and no one was in sight, no one at all. How boring this party would have been to her younger self.

How the line where the ocean meets the sky—now or then, how it remains the same. The face of the man who met Picasso slips back into the black chamber of forgetting. The voice of Wickie Randall eddies in. Wickie, who always wants to know what things are made of, is asking what the boat is made of. Someone says it's teak. Yes, CeCe enjoyed getting ready for the party more than she's enjoying the party. This, the part of sliding again and again into the right tone of voice, she does as a starling reiterates a snatch of music. She could do it in her sleep.

"Well, hi, look at you," says a woman CeCe doesn't recognize, all in black, hanging over the rail in front of her. "I don't feel great either. So hot. Worst idea, martinis."

CeCe looks deeply at the side of George's head. Her guests are, as Walter would have said, getting hot under the beak—sauced, washed, squiffed. George turns and backs politely out of a conversation to join them. If nothing else, she's raised her son to weave in and out of chatter as well as she.

"Julia, hello! You know my mother? Hey, did I tell you Iris and I had this boat for our honeymoon? You won't believe its history. Oil guy used it as a floating brothel in the eighties. Port of Los Angeles. Mirror and shag, stem to stern. All restored, obviously. I'll show you the stateroom. It has the most amazing bathroom, marble and nautical gargoyles jutting out of the walls. You'll hate it, come on."

"Yuck," the woman says. "Gargoyle."

To CeCe he mouths, *You're welcome*, and hurries the woman away.

"You can't run far on a boat!" CeCe calls, but they do not hear. It *is* hot. The sun's directly overhead. The boat rocks beneath her. The guests are no longer eating, but lolling on deck chairs, drinking in a torpor. The servers work the perimeter, sweating. CeCe moves to a new seat with cautious success. She hears Mrs. Baker murmur to Mr. Turner, "I don't care about gardening," as a white, folded napkin slides from her knee. Someone asks loudly, "Is anyone getting a signal?" CeCe smiles at a man in a tight straw hat wiping his forehead, saying, "—well, clay's better for your knees and the bounce of the ball." What is his name? Iris's cool face is above her. Iris, nodding, listening to Mrs. Warren tell of her journey through Nepal, as together they pet the dog. Iris, beautiful like an actress in front of a camera, but also beautiful as the camera—blank, lodestar, animal.

"Nepal," CeCe says. "What fun."

Iris sits down beside her. "Everyone's having a great time. Nobody would've made a party like this, except you. Are you feeling okay? I get nervous at these things. I try to seventy percent listen, that's my trick. Do you want me to run around and wake everybody up? Breeze is back, feel it? That'll help."

Here is the good-hearted and clever child she never had. Here is the child she hates.

"Do what you like," she says. "Take the dog with you."

There is an unexpected grinding noise below. She turns to Iris, but Iris is gone.

"Hallo, anyone home?"

CeCe rises—it's fine, she's strong enough for now, a good time for her to stand. She takes hold of the rail and looks down. Four teenage girls in swimsuits sit in a speedboat, its motor fracturing the green mirror of the water. The radio is on, broadcasting a summer song, a man's voice calling, "All, all, all the million girls go," followed by a thumping and a scratching and a moaning sound.

"No," she says. "Nobody's home."

"Hey, hi! I'm Clover, the Rhavs' daughter? Is my mom on board?"

A few of the guests rustle themselves out of their chairs.

"Hi, Mom! Mom, can we come up? We packed this huge picnic basket and we left it on the counter. We haven't eaten for like a hundred hours."

"Girls!" Mrs. Rhav hisses, looking at CeCe. "This is an event! You can't come up in your Skivvies."

"Can you throw us down a burger or something?"

"We're starving, Mrs. Rhav!"

"There sure are a lot of you for nobody being home," the girl in a black bikini mutters. She slides from the front to the backseat, bone-bent as a snake.

"We don't have hamburgers," CeCe says.

The Becks' son joins the crowd. He sticks his arms out over the water, claps the backs of his hands together, and barks like a seal.

"Jeremy, you're retarded," Clover shouts up, on beat with the music. "Come down and swim."

"There's an idea," the ambassador says.

The guests disappear belowdecks and return in their swimsuits. One by one they teeter down the metal steps. George is by CeCe's side. An appropriately pleading chorus rises from the mouths held above water: "CeCe, it's warm!"; "Change into your suit!"

She was glad they hadn't noticed she spent the morning seated. She *is* glad. And yet how is it they had not seen? Do any of them know her? How can friends so easily fooled be called friends? Either too lively to notice or too unkind to care. And which would she prefer?

"Somners don't like water!" she calls with firm gaiety. She turns and whispers to George and, with hidden determination, cautiously sits back down.

"But you told me not to change into my suit! Fine, yes, I'll hurry back." He hurries back in swim trunks. She watches him descend the steps. He looks up at her, red-faced, and disappears under the water.

George bobs away from the boat, rejuvenated. He finds he's in the general vicinity of the girls from the speedboat, an agreeable place to drift.

"Great fucking party," one says, treading. And another: "That lady's giving us the stink eye, the one pushed up against the rail." And then Clover, explaining who CeCe is. Her parents say she's sick. Really sick, like—she grabs her nose and gurgles and sinks beneath the water, breaking back through smiling and spitting.

How do they know? No one is to know. He considers saying something. He swims away.

The girls are loud and the news skips across the water.

"She isn't well?" one of the widows asks.

"Swim's over," the ambassador says.

The guests file up the stairs, all at once. George is last to drip his way up. She asks if everyone is socializing well.

"What? I don't know. I have water in my ears. I hate swimming. I'm going to change."

There is a tapping and tugging at her calf.

"Do you know how these eggs got here?" It's the Foxes' grandniece, a plastic snorkel and goggles plastered to her wet head, water dripping from the rainbow belly of her swimsuit onto CeCe's shoes, which, now that they are wet, might as well have gone in the shoe pile. The child is pointing to the refuse of the buffet.

"How, Maggie dear?"

"First the farmer buys a lot of birds. He puts them in rows like bunk beds. He feeds them way too much so they are stuffed and he gives them medicine with a needle like our neighbor Mrs. Rose. Mrs. Rose is always allowed to come over. Then the farmer turns on a light that scares the chickens to lay more eggs—"

"No, dear, these eggs are from wild quail. That means they are quail, not chickens, and they are wild."

"My dad says they just put wild on the package because people like it."

Parties are so seldom what one wants them to be. She wishes everyone would go home. She wishes she were home. She feels betrayed by each person she'd watched wetly ascend the stair. She scoots her chair closer to the buffet and plucks two eggs from the bed of chopped ice.

"Have you ever wondered, little fox, how many eggs you could fit in your mouth at once?"

"No, but at recess when there are grapes—"

She shoves the eggs neatly into the mouth of the child. "Impressive! Two, perhaps try for three! This boat was once a whorehouse. Do you have an opinion on that? I do. Tell that to your daddy, dear!" The girl's hands fly to her mouth. Something pulls CeCe's attention—Iris, on the other side of the buffet. Iris looks away. If CeCe had known the wife and the dog were so nearby, well! She hears the child's feet slapping across the deck. She slices off the top of a fresh egg's head using a little spoon and her thumb, scoops caviar into the recesses. She watches Iris join George, now under a heap of towels, watches him reach out to Iris from inside the mound of terry cloth. CeCe calls merrily to the fleeing child, "More eggs, dear, a different kind of egg!"

Dana Barnes is looking at her oddly. CeCe smiles. "I hope it hasn't been too difficult for you, not smoking this afternoon? Was that a secret?"

"Oh, CeCe." Quite unexpectedly, CeCe finds herself crushed to the woman's swimsuit, enveloped in a wet hug. "We're so close by, you call us anytime you need. Day or night. I hope—a lovely time."

Later, CeCe stands in her wet dress and her wet shoes, locked between George's arm and the rail at the top of the metal stairs Javier has for a third time lowered into the sea. As the guests descend and board the launch, she says, "Goodbye! Goodbye, dears, goodbye!"

3

Two weeks later George and Iris are in bed, staring at the ceiling, not wanting the day to begin. George is to help his mother move to Oak Park. They've been preparing for this morning for almost a year.

"I miss you already," George says. "I don't want to be a grown-up."

"I know," Iris answers.

"Here we go." He rubs his eyes, pads to the closet. "You want this one?" He holds up a ragged sweatshirt, her favorite on cool mornings. He tosses it to her, opens his top dresser drawer, and tosses her a pair of balled socks. He takes some out for himself, for they share, have worn the same socks, his socks, since the day she moved in with him, at his old apartment in Washington Square. A mystery she hadn't arrived with socks of her own. She is beautiful by the window, the trees dense below. A surprise to them both, that their new home was in the woods and had no ocean view.

"You're inside out." He tugs the hem of the sweatshirt. She shrugs and shuffles into the bathroom to trade her glasses for contacts, then heads downstairs. He listens to her bang around the kitchen as he packs his overnight bag.

"Up or down?" she calls.

"Up. I'm slow."

She reappears in the doorway, a cup of coffee in each hand. "Why are you taking so much stuff? All you need is this. And those. Paperwork from the doctor?"

"Esme."

After toast, they walk the path, George's bag catching in the underbrush.

"Nice out this early," she says. "Good air."

He inhales the cool smell of morning leaves and nods.

"Hey," she says, "maybe it won't be so bad? No, it probably will. But you'll do it and it'll be done."

They stand a moment at the edge of CeCe's property and watch the pale ocean rolling in, buying George a few more minutes.

"Ready?" she says. They stride onto the lawn and up to the house. Soon, she's hugging George and CeCe goodbye—CeCe, looking askance at the inside-out sweatshirt, Javier standing beside the gleaming black car, Esme in the front seat, the engine running. Iris waves as the car grows smaller and turns out of her vision. She jogs home. She sits with a second cup of coffee and her laptop and looks at news and shoes and property listings and a YouTube video of a monkey playing tag with a bear and vacation packages and recipes using kelp. Because it's Monday and she doesn't have any houses to show, she'll go for a proper run, go to the grocery and the dry cleaner. She calls the real estate agency and asks them to keep her on client rotation even though she hasn't got any appointments. She's lacing up her sneakers when a truck rumbles up the drive. The father and son are back to clean the pool. She greets them in the driveway.

"Morning. It's time again," the father says. "The filters."

They climb down from the truck and make their way on the stone path past the house, the son dragging the rubber snake. The air is damp for June, overcast and still. Iris walks alongside in the grass. She offers to get them something to drink. They refuse, drop their gear. They do not like her. Still, she's glad to see them. To expect the disapproval of strangers is part of her, the bleak places she was raised: the saltbox in Great Village, Nova Scotia, where she loved the wet air and the sea and her stern aunts, her father's sisters who lived down the street. Camden, New Jersey, where her parents—Richard and Carol, devout and disappointed—were at Camden Bag and Paper. There'd been too much wind in Great Village and not enough in Camden, where Iris turned the public library inside out, the library that smelled like a diaper, even as she failed school. Failed, by bland catastrophe—nearsightedness long undiagnosed, truancy, Carol. In Lincoln, Maine, Iris finished high school but forgot about libraries—her father, still with them, working the paper plants up and down the coast. (We met at the margarine factory, her mother said, when Iris asked how they fell in love.) At least the pool cleaners' indifference is honest. The Somners' people, she can't read. How to know, when nice and good wear the same face but are not the same? She's only sure of George and Victor.

"Unusual," the father said to the son, the first time he saw the pool, its bottom and sides painted black, its edges rounded imperfectly to trick the eye into seeing a pond. "Hard to tell what's what."

On account of this opacity they claim the pool is dirty as often as they like.

"Anybody walk in by accident at night?" the son asks. "We can install lights around the perimeter. Safer. Solar charge. Right, Dad?"

No lights, she tells them. The pool's aesthetic in keeping—George's phrase, his sound, more and more replacing her own—with the philosophy of the house.

3D trails her back up the drive. She sets to pulling weeds from the flagstone at the front door. What do they buy with the money they make, cleaning a clean pool? She pictures the son jamming on a vintage Fender at the mall, the price tag hanging from the strap, pictures them at home, sunk in front of a glossy flatscreen, laughing at what a moron she is, learning the remote. In her old life, she would've been a person to them. Here, she is Wife. Silently, she justifies herself—two years ago, I was a bartender in a college town. For a decade. Sticky floor, flat tap, black mop. The college was at the top of one of the scarred granite hilltops common to northern New York. A hill like a mountain, the cluster of austere old department buildings its stone crown. Roads climbed like greedy creeper up to the college. Within the campus were sweeping colonnades of tall, bending trees. The streets outside had what the students needed: a drugstore, a taco joint, the bars, a grocery. Town below, there was her apartment and a sad-carpet guitar store—to which, her first week there, she sold her guitar—and the highway. Evenings, as she wound her car up the black roads to work, the bars strung together by their neon looked like the tilting lights of a shoreline from a ship. To the right of her bar was a bar and to the left of her bar was a bar. In the bar on the right was a woman who stood between the faded Heimlich poster and the bottles. In the bar on the left was a woman who stood between the bottles and a fresher Heimlich poster. Iris's bar did not have a poster.

One night she carded this kid. The kid still comes to mind, not because she loved him but because he was right before she met George. He is the bright rip of before and after, where her life split in two. She carded all the kids, what with the bat cameras suckered up in the corners of the wall behind her, what with not giving a shit about the kids having fun. The date on his license—a twenty-first birthday. "You're all grown up," she said, making a perfunctory flap to the stoolflies until they wet-worked their eyes off the shelves of booze and raised their glasses. The kid looked mortified. She poured a shot of tequila and topped it with Everclear and set it on fire with the apple-green plastic lighter she kept under the bar by the sink rag, put the shot in his right hand and a basket of tortilla chips in his left. "Ta-da," she said. He thanked her. Polite for a healthy-looking Ivy in a T-shirt that read LACROSSE PENNANT CHAMPIONS, NORTH EAST DIVISION II, 2008. The shirt was a film, wash-worn. They all wore their clothes that way. To say—my mother doesn't dress me and I've had this shit a million years—I'm not trying to impress anybody. That these kids were fooling no one she found endearing. Her clothes and the clothes of the men on the stools—newer and cleaner and tucked together with a distinguished necessity.

The light of the kid's shot wove under the curve of his cap. "Blow it out, dummy," she said.

Later, he slid from one empty barstool to the next until he was sitting across from her, bleary-eyed. "Doctor," he said. "Howmmm-mmidoin?"

Why not? He was pretty—sandy hair needing a cut, wide, heavy eyes, locker shoulders and a field tan, a lopsided frown she figured to be his main move, not bad. Had he connected her to her band, the one CD they'd released being titled *Doctor Edible*? No. Ancient history. He'd probably never even owned a CD. Soon she no longer drove down the hill at the end of her shift. They woke in his room and crossed the campus to the coffee kiosk. He had the rolling walk young men have, which she noticed when she walked behind him so they would not be discovered.

By the end of the semester, she'd kept him company through most of his intro classes, the big ones where she wouldn't be noticed in the darkened lecture halls with seats deeper than at the movies, with the slides and the distant professor at the podium, who in Art History 101 shouted, "Putto!" waving his red laser over each winged, chubby menace perching on a cloud. There was Art History and American Literature: Civil War–Present, and Introduction to Western Philosophy One: Aristotle–Hegel. Listening in the dark, a complicated dream. Afterward, she'd forget to be careful and they'd walk the quad side by side. (That they had to be careful she'd at first thought was a game or a joke, and later became a point of disagreement.) She'd talk about what they heard and he'd say, "That's an opinion. You're smart. If you could come to conference they'd jump all over it." She read the books he was assigned—not all of them, and not all the way through, but she read over the parts the professors discussed until she thought she might understand them. An unfamiliar kind of hunger, most satisfied when it wasn't satisfied at all. The kid stopped going to lecture. Twice she went alone, but she felt like a burglar entering the dark auditorium without him. She tried to imagine what she was missing—the paintings projected on the wall, the way one idea lit up another.

When summer came, he gave her his campus ID so she could use the library. She took a second job at a golf club, to make up for the falloff in bar tips with the students gone, and to save money for the trip they planned to go on when he returned—all over Europe, sharing a backpack. He'd show her the cathedrals. I promise, he'd said, touching his cap. At the library, they looked at the photo and would not let her in. At the Athletic Center, they didn't care. Each day, before heading to the golf club, she swam in the Olympic-size pool and walked the garden behind the School of Agriculture's Plant Science Building, her hair wet, her skin tight from the chlorine. She read the names on the markers stuck in the long neat rows of flowers and herbs, sounding out the Latin, memorizing the English. A library without a door. She didn't consider signing up for classes on her own. She called her mother, whom she was not friends with but who did have a certain way with the truth. Her mother, by then in assisted living in Oswego with her sister-in-law, four plaid rooms that faced away from Lake Ontario, but her voice still resonant as a goose, Quebecois and Jersey. "Young man's coming back, not to you." And, "You, school?" At the golf club, jackets were required in the dining room. George was the guy with the intense face who couldn't find his ticket.

"All done," the father calls.

Back in the driveway, Iris balances her blue checkbook against the trunk of a fir. She writes *TruClear Pool* in block letters, having never learned script. She writes *00/100*. And how unnatural the rip of the check off the book always sounds out of doors!

They turn away but the son turns back. "I forgot," he says, looking at the invoice in his father's hand. "Cash might be better."

"Henry," the father says.

"A processing error at the bank. Can happen," Henry suggests.

They drive away.

Iris blamed Carol for the year of the kid. All that French Catholic bullshit. Touch everything, go on, everything is delicious sex! God save you, look how your hand burns! It was comforting, blaming Carol. She'd learned to from a guidance counselor in Camden. Then it was fall, and Carol died.

Screw the pool guys. Next time, she'll tell them to wait a week. She slaps her leg so 3D will follow. On the way to the grocery in town, she drives by CeCe's wrought-iron gate. Iris's passage into the world is now always this—Cecilia's driveway winding to infinity, a glimpse of the distant side of the great white house, the sea flickering through a break in the trees, the white afternoon sunlight a magic lantern. Hard to believe CeCe isn't there.

Iris is unpacking the groceries when it occurs to her: What had Henry meant about the bank? But the house is so quiet, she turns the radio on and loses her train of thought. When George is home, opera booms from his office. Without him, nothing distracts her from the truth that she dislikes their house. Her unease grows as the sun falls lower in the sky. Maybe it's that Somner's Rest dislikes *her*. Somner's Rest, the stupid name CeCe gave the place, a name Iris and George don't use. She can't get used to all the glass—the house is low and long and split in two like a slingshot or a wishbone, sitting on a steep slope, half on exposed concrete legs. It splits around a towering white ash that rises before the front door. Windows for walls, porous concrete, flagstone—crudely, imprecisely in the style of Frank Lloyd Wright's Fallingwater. One-half of the ground floor is open, and to her eye, vast, for activities that can be shared—living, cooking, eating. Except for the support columns, this area—to call it a room is not quite right—is enclosed by plate glass and suspended vertiginously over a waterfall at the back of the house, which flows into a stone-filled grotto. The other wing is divided into standard rooms furnished with Somner heirlooms and whatever else the decorator suggested: den (TV, bar, and games), office (George, opera theme), craft room (Iris, unused), library (small-scale entertaining), Sky Guest Bedroom 1 (bird), Sea Guest Bedroom 2 (nautical), sunroom/potting. This wing hangs over the carport and the semisubterranean garage, which smells of exhaust and turpentine and holds a twice-used cream-colored Lexus CeCe gave to George with the house.

"We live in a miniature golf course," Iris said to George when they first saw the waterfall.

He'd looked crestfallen.

"That's funny," she said.

"It's funny?"

"Yes, it's a joke."

"I get it." He laughed. Later that day, they unfurled the old blueprints, left by the original owners, a pair of microbiologists, dead now, who'd included a note that Einstein, a friend from Princeton and devoted gardener, had in the spring of 1946 planted the stand of birches at the corner of the lot. George, pointing to the blueprints, said the house grew out of its site like a mushroom, designed to be a part of the woods around them. The waterfall, on a pump. One night, a few months after they moved in, she heard George say to some guests, "Somner's Rest? More like Somner's miniature golf course." In the heat that first summer the grotto collected a scrim of gnat larvae.

She makes it through the hours to nightfall. In the gloaming, the rising bank of trees presses in dark sentinel against the floor-to-ceiling glass. Because she's worked at night most of her life, night alone is strange. She feels, as in a fairy tale, that whenever she turns her back, an ogre bends through the treetops and his face fills the glass. The tattered spiral of a child's nightmare—stand too close, she risks being grabbed and pulled though the pane, right into the woods. Stupid. Still, she spends this first evening alone sitting cross-legged on the flokati in Sky Guest Bedroom 1, eating popcorn and drinking wine in front of the television, wearing the glasses she never wears in front of anyone, even George, except the five minutes in the morning and evening between contacts and bed. She's in the library, staring sideways at the spines, when the phone rings. The caller ID glows an unknown number. She wishes it were George. She lets the voice mail pick up. Someone she doesn't know, a Barker or Baker, thanks them for the boat party, invites them to tennis. The phone rings again right away. Another number. Whoever it is hangs up. The night turns windy and tree branches scrape the glass. Her phone says it's going to rain. When she finally goes upstairs to bed—their bedroom being the only upstairs room, a concrete and slat-wood crow's nest—she closes 3D in with her so he can't wander down to his mat in the kitchen, where he prefers to spend his nights. He understands her dread and flings himself up into the pillows, rolls onto his back, floats his paws into the air, and falls into a twitchy snore, running through his dream.

4

To George's surprise, CeCe had insisted on traveling by train. At the station, Esme boards with them and makes up CeCe's seat with a cashmere throw and pillows from home. Esme hugs them and kisses their cheeks. They all look away—George at his shoes, CeCe at George's shoulder, Esme beyond her employers to the exit. In the thirty-nine years Esme's worked for the Somners, seldom have the three of them stood together anywhere but inside or behind Cecilia's house.

"Go on," CeCe says. The housekeeper disembarks, lifting the gray sleeve of her uniform to the corner of her eye. She lingers on the platform in serious conference with the conductor, pointing into the car, to the wheelchair stowed in the luggage zone, making sure he's aware CeCe will need help on the other end, something it hadn't occurred to George to arrange.

"—and you would think," CeCe says from the cocoon of the throw, after they'd eaten the meal Esme had prepared for them, CeCe's voice agitated by the bounce of the train, "the best kind of sanatorium would be all-girls, wouldn't you? With a boys' home across the lake? We could have mixers—bingo, intrigue, midnight lake crossings—"

"No one uses that word anymore."

When they were first preparing for the undetermined months she would be away, George made frequent references to the lake, featured in the glossy brochures he collected from the hospital. They agreed on the Institute for Clinical Research at Oak Park because it was luxurious and optimistic—a private campus and multiple-use facility participating in drug and equipment trials, with a forward-thinking integration of holistic and alternative therapies. Its Movement Disorder Clinic, the best on the East Coast. On the brochure map of the grounds, quaintly drawn in pencil, the residence was hidden from the medical buildings by a bank of trees. No need to be depressed by the view. A game of pride, anyway, pretending she had a choice. No other facility within five hundred miles was participating in the trial. She will not be the only one there on whom they are testing Astrasyne.

"You'll make friends," George says.

"I will not."

The picture of the skinny, sun-dappled pier flattened against the lake in the brochure was what put CeCe's mind to summer camp, though she'd never gone to one herself. George offers to bring care packages full of contraband—chewing gum and a flask filled with sherry hidden in a shoebox. Since her diagnosis, they've been working feverishly on a comedy act—cutting each other off, tripping over each other's joviality. They've never joked before and aren't good at it. Jokes, she'd raised her children to understand, are like spinach between the teeth—laugh and everyone sees what's the matter, excepting you. But now CeCe's been compelled to this banter by words such as *histopathological* and *glial scar* and *unpredictable term of development*, and by the astral, plastic promise of the word Astrasyne: three syllables, fast like the train on the tracks, slow like a mouthful of hills. Astrasyne, initially and unsuccessfully developed for ADHD, might or might not—but might—still the violent shakes, restore the covenant of muscle to will, repair and light the roads rushing through the synaptic forest of her posterior parietal cortex. Her hope, and the implicit suggestion of her doctor who got her into the study, was that Astrasyne could soon be approved for home study or even market; that she might stay some months and then leave with the drug.

George asks if the sun, shearing through the dusty Plexi of the train window, is hurting her eyes. He would like to be anywhere else. Even at work, at the Hud-Stanton-Fox Foundation, where he is a program director and where they know he'll be out most of the week.

"Might as well squint through the first or last anything," she says. She means this also to be a joke, but it doesn't make sense. Oak Park runs a hospice at the farthest end of campus. Of this George and CeCe do not speak.

"Here. My sunglasses."

She takes them and turns away from him to the view. She coughs, rusty and petulant, though no part of her illness makes her cough. Her request to take the train—a rare sentimentality she's allowed herself. She spent her childhood on trains, her father's concerns taking her far and wide, until she was deposited at Miss Porter's School. She liked, she still likes, how when a train comes to a wide curl of track she can see the cars moving up ahead of her, and in an instant she is where she's just been looking. Only from the back of a train can one witness the point where (or does she mean when?) the present and the future are joined. Continuity, demonstrated with grace.

George looks out the window as well. He's fighting, quite suddenly, the urge to laugh. It's bad and getting worse—a hysterical giggle, tickling his throat like a sneeze. He counts what he sees to hold steady. Horse, horse, horse. Puddle, silo. Trees, tires, trees. Their train, on the express track, slows through a local station. River, platform, man tying shoe, woman on phone, man eating banana, man reading phone, lamppost, station sign, man with book, garbage bin, woman, woman, woman. This last woman, a teenager maybe, waves at the train as it passes. George claps his hand over his mouth, recovers. His mother is observing him from behind his sunglasses, crooked on her nose.

"Do you know her? Waving to you, you think?"

She can't help it, teasing her son. Teasing, unrelated to joking. It became her common practice after she discovered he'd met Iris—checking his *coat*—while he was still involved with someone else, someone from a family CeCe was acquainted with, a young woman with no reason to take advantage. CeCe counted the months backward on her shaking, gold-locked fingers, and, yes, George had been dating that more suitable candidate when he told her someone named Iris was moving into his apartment. That was when CeCe was still avoiding getting the shake checked. Even after her whole arm occasionally began to tremble, she wouldn't speak of it. She visited the doctor only after her own hand began petting her own cheek of its own clumsy volition. The doctor told her this forlorn symptom of self-petting was called alien limb. "Too late," she said, for by then it was a familiar, as intimate to her as the stretch of a hated sleeping lover's hand in the bed, not alien in the least. Her father had died at seventy-six, almost her present age; 1953, and she was seventeen. Her grandfather too. Seventy-six. She refuses. She will refuse.

"Sure, a little something I've got on the side. After dinner I cruise the eastern corridor. Two-hour drive. A rush home, but totally worth it." Abruptly, finally, he laughs.

"Vulgar," she says. The train hurtles past a lumberyard and through the haze of blue-gray smoke emitted by one of its buildings.

"Why," she asks, "do they put the trains through such charmless neighborhoods?" They pass row houses made from the same corrugated steel as the lumberyard's buildings. "No one needs to take a train anymore. One does it for the scenery. One wants to hear the distance accounting for itself. I would've let Javier drive us, had anyone bothered to tell me. When I'm ready to go home, we'll drive."

She takes off the sunglasses and closes her eyes. George opens *Golf America* and flips through page after page of azure sky and emerald green but cannot settle into reading. He takes out his pen and writes across the ninth hole:

EUNUCH'S DILEMMA

The Burning Papers—Act 1: y2713. Unnamed Hero escapes harem complex at top of sky tower where has been luxuriant & drugged captive of dowager queen. See office pc drft. Act II, Scene 1: Ruins of NYC. Filth. Catacombs. UH set to exit into the WORLD. Writes/sings letter of departure to Chief Eunuch. "Guard women of harem. Take special care protecting The One." Act II, Scene II: Tower, Eunuch reads letter. Eats it. V's scoring?

How much he owes to Iris. For years before he met her, he'd been scribbling bits and pieces of a libretto—on napkins, in e-mails to himself, nothing more than doodling, a secret, in a form he'd been trained to appreciate as a child. One day a few months before their wedding, Iris found a scrap under the coffee table. Red-faced, he insisted it was trash.

She paused, considering the piece of paper in her hand. "Maybe."

"What's the point? I can't write the music, only the words."

"I dunno, type-A. Fun?"

She told him to go find a partner, a composer, and about the bands she'd been in, how she didn't regret any of it even though they sucked. When he suggested that his situation was different, that he couldn't up and play an opera in a bar, she answered, "I get it. You think because it's you, people will give a shit. Get a load of the ego on Mr. Bigtime over here! You, my friend, are wrong."

Eunuchs lead women of UH's harem thru catacomb waterways. [pool/real water]

> *Eunuch 1 sings: we take your wives to the border, the queen has cast us out of sanctuary!*
>
> *E 2: we wish you were here to raise the lantern, to tell us if what we do is right. We have no papers, will we cross?(Repeat x3) It is a death sentence.*
>
> *E 3 [TRAITOR E]: how can you punish us, we who are ghosts of men, and you so far away? 'We serve your women because we serve you. But if their wish is not your wish, is this not treachery?*

Discuss with V. How make clear (visually) this is in the FUTURE?

His mother. Tugging at his sleeve. They've arrived. In a rush, they set to collecting their bags. How will they carry the blanket and the pillows without Esme? They leave the pillows. The conductor ushers them off, slapping a narrow gangplank across the gap between the steel and the concrete, just for them. I am a spectacle, George thinks pleasantly, helping his mother heave into the wheelchair to disembark, sensing the faces behind the windows of the train turn toward him, the platform under his feet a stage. His mother is acting too, smiling at the conductor, who straddles the train and the platform to help them with the brake on the wheelchair.

"I'm perfectly agile," CeCe says, which is still occasionally true. "The chair is a convenience."

In the parking lot, one car door slams after another, swallowing the passengers who exited before them, so George easily spots the man leaning against his cab, holding a piece of torn cardboard that reads SOMNER in limp scrawl. The wheelchair barely fits in the trunk. They drive silently up curving roads, crowded on either side by deep green. George sees just two houses, far from the road. He calls Iris to tell her they're on their way.

At her insistence he hands the cell to CeCe, who says, "Oof, filthy!" She listens for a moment. "Well, dear, the car smells." And: "Stiff from the journey." And: "Iris, how enlightened you are when it comes to these things!"

CeCe holds the phone out to George. "Turn this off, I don't know how to turn it off."

Iris, she explains, has recommended a type of scented oil that might make her feel better. And something deep tissue, something Swedish that involves undressing in front of a stranger. "I put your little micro-wave to my head for such rare wisdom?" She lowers and then raises the window. "Scented *oil*," she adds, after a pause.

George sees the clock on the screen is still ticking over the seconds. "Wait. Iris, are you there? Okay, bye." To his mother he says, "She probably heard you."

"She knows how fond of her I am. Though, do you see how she's changing? That it's you who's changing her? She's coming into her character, and good for her. Pretty as a picture."

Best to wait this out in silence, he decides.

"I do like her, I'm not pretending. And the world needs more sensitive men like you. She's strength itself. So charming, and that vivid face."

In truth, CeCe is thinking of her friends, more than of Iris. The women of means who never tried to make use of themselves to the world. She disdains how well they wear their languor: their polished faces, and their veins, so close to the surface, like blue brocade. By contrast, she prided herself on having better things to think about than her body, until its recent rebellion. Before her diet was restricted by the specialist, she ate buttered rolls and drank sugared tea. She ate dessert after both lunch and dinner, as most days she ate out: when dining out, the correct number of courses is three. She was voracious and remained slender. She'd offer bites of crème caramel or lemon tart to whomever she happened to be dining with, anticipating her companion's tight smile which meant, *No, no, thank you.* She considered the infinitesimal growing and shrinking width of her thighs (winter to summer and back again) and whether her eyes were too near each other on the thin hinge of her nose. But in a passing way, as she had many times passed a mirror behind a firework of flowers in a lobby. Entering a room full of her acquaintants, her hair up or down, her dress smoothed, she was content to say, *Well, there it is,* the other blade of the scissor reflected in the mirror. But the Irises of the world—the new women!—who know how much it pays to be beautiful, but not how little it matters. Their miscalculated ease to vanity! How they waste what they have gained! All time and care put to tending their bodies—what a lucky approximation of illness. She pats George's hand, clamped around the phone.

"I'm only jealous," she says, but does not believe it's true.

They pass through a set of metal gates, swung open by a remote sensor, and curve up a road thickly arbored by oak. The car turns onto a roundabout—she feels a little better seeing Oak Park. With the crunch of gravel under a clean wheel she has always associated the word *coun-*

tryside. The building she will live in is yellow limestone with blue trim at the front and pipe chimneys like an old Suffolk hotel. Yes, good, the roundabout rounds about a stone fountain. Cherubs dribble water from their mouths. Beneath them is an alternating symmetry of blue hydrangea and marigolds. The unbroken circle of the roundabout and the fountain, of the lake beyond the residence and the encircling woods, the squareness of the building—nothing institutional about it. Maybe it will be all right.

Dr. Orlow, the director of inpatient trial therapy, walks them from the car to the entrance, with George behind the chair. The doctor is boyish and tall, stooped like a teenager who's grown so swiftly he's not yet re-coordinated his posture; behind his glasses, his eyes are a vague blue. She dislikes him. But she's pleased by the urgent way he ducks over her, as if he's just hit his head on a low beam. He tells her that her room is ready, and why doesn't he take her on a tour while Mr. Somner handles the paperwork?

"Yes, go," George says. "I'll catch up."

The doctor straightens behind her chair. As her neck is inflexible and he is tall, she can no longer see his face. A sudden black wave of fear rolls her, heart to tongue. Hers is the child's dread at being led away by a stranger.

"George!" she calls, but hears no answer.

Dr. Orlow wheels her down an antiseptic but acceptable hall. He shows her a library of red grass-cloth wallpaper and dark wood; a dining room overlooking the lake, the sun shining too brightly on the filmy glassware already set upon the tables; a tearoom crowded with spider plants and overstuffed, rose-chintz couches. On to the residential wing, they pass the open door of a patient's room. She catches a flash of hospital gown, a narrow window, linoleum, a bare foot.

She twists to speak. "My room doesn't look like that, does it?"

"Let's go find out. You're on a different hall. This is the quickest way through."

"No. I want to see every type of room. I need something to compare. There is no proof without comparison. I'm not tired."

The chair turns and they seek out a few doors that are safe to open.

"Wretched! Wretched compared to mine, I hope."

George joins them and takes the doctor's place.

"Everything okay? Ready, Mother?"

"No. Tell Annie Mason I want to be briefed on all their activities. She knows, but tell her anyway!"

"Sure. Now, can we get you settled?"

Her room has a wide, white-mineral cleanliness. Her floor is not linoleum but pale wood. It's on the ground level with French doors to the back lawn. The lawn slopes to the edge of the lake. George throws open the doors with as much ceremony as he can muster.

"Round Lake, you can see why," Dr. Orlow says. It shines in the distant out-of-doors, a blot of light in the green. "Yours is the only room with a door directly onto the garden."

She thinks, then I am the only one who will escape, should there be a fire. It's a fine room; she can't disagree. It certainly contains the best furniture—hers. She had it shipped ahead. Her decorator arranged it. She'd had him shipped ahead too. She can see he did the best he could under the circumstances. Yet, what a sinking strangeness she feels, sinking into the stranger that is now herself, coming into a new room cluttered with the chairs she scrambled under as a child and sat straight-backed in as an adult. Her high, four-poster bed with the pinecones etched out of the posts. Her father's tea service, silver leaves winding up each handle. The clot of family photos in silver frames, arranged beside the tea service. The horsehair couch with the stubby claw-feet. The green marble table from her entrance hall at home now holds a welcome basket of fruit wrapped in cellophane and ribbon. A few landscapes, a few mirrors, a few more end tables than ends of couches to line them beside. The Turkish rug from a guest bedroom, a red, flattened maze on which her children used to play stones-in-the-water, leaping from one geometry to the next so as not to burn or drown.

"Jean should be here any minute to help you get oriented," Dr. Orlow says. "I think you'll like her. Amazing transformation of the room. You've raised the bar."

"Looks nice, doesn't it, Mother?"

Her eye falls on a framed photo of herself from a 1981 issue of *Town & Country*. Did she ask for that one? Likely not! Will they think she's the kind of pathological person who likes to gaze upon photos of herself? Then she remembers. Everyone is that sort of person now. In the photo, she wears a jade silk skirt suit and is smiling, leaning against a tree in a small Alphabet City park her dollars had restored. The cover text had read, "A Woman of Uncommon Energy." Nor had she asked for the photo beside that one! If the decorator's made one mistake, two, what else has been misplaced? This photo is eight, maybe nine years before the *Town & Country* shot: she's boarding a private plane, up the glinting steps on the tarmac, baby George in her arms. She's turned back in front of the open door to have the picture taken. Patricia is hiding behind her skirt, her arms wrapped around CeCe's waist, a red-yarn bow and a pigtail. Hawaii, but who took the picture? Not Walter. Walter, already inside. His leg is there in the photo, jutting out onto the carpet, as he was seated. It *is* a beautiful photo, joy in her face, her eye to the camera, but his wicked leg ruins it. The plane, on loan from a friend. Walter ignored her once they were introduced to the only other passenger in the otherwise empty private terminal—that year's Miss America, a girl from Wisconsin on a press stop with *Holiday* magazine. CeCe made sure they weren't photographed side by side. As they were escorted across the runway, Walter called CeCe Fatty Dolores. He pinched her arm in front of Miss America and the children. (He'd taken to calling her Fatty Dolores the year she had a producer's credit on a musical version of *Lolita* she'd thought was brave. Fatty because she'd been pregnant with George when the show closed. Dolores because Walter was so many years her senior. There was nothing, when she met him, to suggest what lay ahead.)

"Yes," she says to George, "the room is fine." She tries her best to look pleased. "Although I don't like how the photos have been arranged. And I don't like anything else."

"Adjustments take a while," Dr. Orlow says. "I'll leave you to it. Do you have any more questions, for the time being?"

Through the initial visits to the hospital, CeCe prided herself on accommodating each bit of bad news with ladylike discretion, even cheer. No need to make the doctors feel bad, to make things messy. Yes, she bullied the help for a bit of relief. She complained about the food, the spongy pillows, the fussy bedside manner, and the yoga pants worn by the new wife. She told George the nurses were stealing money from her purse. She told the nurses Iris was stealing money from her purse. The nurses were not seen again. What better fun, she asked George, once it was all straightened out, are nurses and children for? She would not apologize; there wasn't much else she was able to do to keep her spirits up. But entering this room, she is overcome—never until today has she noticed that all her furniture, all inherited, is decorated with a leaf or a flower or an animal. That it's all of a woodland theme. She feels her hands reaching up to her mouth, she finds her mouth is open.

"Forest," she says to George, meaning also to say *motif*, and something against the decorator, for she doesn't know what kind of chairs and tables she would have chosen for herself, had she chosen for herself, and now she will not ever. She reaches up and throws her fist into her son's lapel. The linen absorbs the impact with an unimpressive whump. She notices Dr. Orlow has halted mid-departure and that a woman is in the room, in some kind of nurse's costume; Jean, here to orient her, presumably. George's gaze unfocuses to the ceiling, as it had when she would scold him as a boy. Weakling, she thinks, unclear as to whether she means him or herself. She seizes his chin and pulls his bright green eye down to hers and tells him it is time to go home, *now, now, now,* incanted as calmly as any witch would lay a curse. She wheels her way out of the room.

"I'll get her," George says, but before he moves to follow, he is mesmerized by the look of her hands on the light gray rubber. He has never seen her touch a wheel of any kind. They find her down the corridor, inside a supply closet. The shelves are stacked with plastic bins. She has almost managed to close the door. She is sitting in the dark.

5

Iris and the dog lift their faces out of half sleep toward the sound. A door downstairs being opened, pulling her out of the well of a nightmare and back into the bedroom. It's almost eleven. 3D springs clumsily off the bed, whimpers by the closed bedroom door. She falls back. George as a boy—nine, maybe ten—this is what she is dreaming. A sunny road runs along the ruin of a stone wall, winding the loamy fields as far as she can see. She is following the squirrel from one of her band posters—peepholes for eyes, cherries for guts. They come to a column supply truck overturned in the road, abandoned so long milkweed and goldenrod climb its wheel. Medical supplies spill out the back, glinting metal. The tattered canvas, its faded red cross, flaps in the breeze. George is slumped against the wall, legs splayed in the dry dirt, head bent over his little blade of a chest. The squirrel leaps the wall and pauses behind George's ear. In the air is the slow play of dandelion. She should stay with George, but the squirrel is continuing up the road in the direction of—a church?

A church, though only the facade stands, a jagged mason tooth and a missing eye, light shot through the socket, light in the rubble of the nave behind—tongue gone, gone the interior castle. The mask of a church—not a church. Suddenly she understands. Bombed. The black of planes has already come. If the planes have come once, they will come again. She calls to little George to move, to find cover. She knows the lie! When they draw the maps, they do not include the shadows of the planes. George lifts his head. *Come, please come!* she cries. He will not stand. She sees his eye is canceled too. He points his chin at her and laughs. *I did it, Mama*, he says. *It was me.*

She's sweated through the sheet. Back in the morning light, unbidden she remembers Carol's face as it looked in the last days, skull-out, in Oswego. Her dream—what was it? A piece of her grandfather's story of the Battle for Brittany, maybe, a story Carol relayed only at the end, carried to Iris down a dark hall in the long, translucent hands of dementia.

"Lo? Hello? Iris?"

The jangling of keys, a sound so ordinary it must be real.

She cracks the bedroom door. Victor, here to walk 3D, is letting himself in through the back, the mudroom. He bangs his keys onto the marble kitchen island, stomps his sneakers. 3D barrels down the stairs.

"Mutt-friend," she hears, "devil-dog, hey!"

Victor bends on one knee by the breakfast counter. The blue leash hangs slack against his leg. From the top of the stairs, she sees he is having a serious conversation with the dog. Her work schedule is still unpredictable; she never knows when she'll be around for the mid-morning walk.

"I don't believe it. 3D, you are telling me this is happening in the park? Go on. And you went over to them and they—Lhasa apsos? Yes, it *is* a stupid name. The nerve. To be iced by the likes of them. No wonder you're feeling low. Now, don't you take it to heart. Mutts are the very best, and you are the very best of the mutts." The dog's muzzle rests in Victor's open palm.

"Who first," Victor calls up the stairs, "you or the dog?"

In the mirror she sees the disassembly of sleep.

"3D, please! I'm a mess. I need coffee. You need coffee?"

"Had mine," he calls, thumping his thermos on the counter. "Come on, dear dog, we're going for a walk."

She dresses and puts the coffee on and watches them amble down the sloped back lawn. They stop where the edge of the woods meets the grass, a crooked stick hanging from the mouth of the dog, a tennis ball in the dog walker's hand. He looks up and catches her at the glass wall and waves. She likes his face: wide-awake eyes set between round cheeks and Elvis sideburns, under short, black hair. Because of all the exercising and showering, he always appears air-fluffed and squeakily scrubbed. He's her age, but in the habit of peering all around him with a generous interest that makes him appear younger. A scar cuts a streak out of one of his eyebrows. His skin's a warm bronze, deepened with outdoor activity. What are you? she'd asked one afternoon when they were drinking beers by the pool. I'm everything, he answered, frowning at the question. India and Africa by way of Trinidad, Belarus through upstate New York, Philippines out of Los Angeles, Sicily via the Bronx. What are you? Eh, she said. Canada, France. Jersey. Acadian. A bowl of snow.

He disappears into the trees after 3D. The odd thought comes to her that the curved edge of the lawn is the rim of an eye, the dark swimming pool is its center. An eye without a reflection, without—the word for the middle of the eye. Your own name, stupid, she thinks. She isn't all awake. Idle makes idle, her mother would have said, and been right. Now that she hardly works, so many hours must glide over her to make a day. Once, when she was little, behind her mother's back her old aunties gave her an orange plastic record player and a set of twelve-inch vinyl records, the abridged audio of several of Disney's animated films. Every night she'd play one and fall asleep clutching the cardboard sleeve of the record—*Cinderella*, *Snow White*. All the same, a virtuous girl who sings a song. She never thought what happened after the end, the marriage. In the fairy tales there were two ways: off the wedding page to a blurry but total happiness, or left behind to rot into the ragged crone of the next story, her itchy heart ticktocking away in the dusty sharkbox of her chest. No, Iris doesn't miss her years alone. But her life before George felt more vital in its loneliness than this kind of day. Why George fell in love with her she doesn't know, though she doesn't doubt him. Last week, they shared a grilled-cheese-and-tomato sandwich in the grass under the ash tree. George fell asleep with a magazine on his face and her hand on his chest. The dog woke them, late in the afternoon, nudging them with his nose. Even with this—happiness—when she doesn't have any properties to show, there isn't much to keep her from staying in bed, heavy as death.

The coffeemaker wheezes full. She gets a cup and returns to the window. By now, Victor and the dog will be in the meadow dotted with blue-eyed Marys. There's the sound of the cicada and the sun tangled across her forearms resting on the table. Dragonflies skim the top of the pool—how is an hour gone already? 3D gallops out of the woods, the light on his red back and on Victor, lifting his sneakers high out of the grass. The tennis ball flies from Victor's hand. 3D bursts forward, the stick dropping from his mouth. Next time she'll go with them.

"You ready now?" Victor says, nodding toward the empty cup in the sink. 3D pants around and collapses on his mat, his legs caked in mud. He's protecting something under his paws.

"He's destroyed it. You'll see." Victor gently extracts 3D's bounty. The stick, chewed to pulp.

When Iris asked around town, Victor's was the first name given. All his services were praised: personal training, certified massage, dog walking, meal preparation, hairdressing, property maintenance. She hired him Tuesdays, Thursdays, and Fridays for the first three services, as she likes the daily ritual of cooking and has no interest in hair. There's already a gardener, a woman named Fay, who appeared the week they moved to Somner's Rest, in a blue chambray button-down and red lipstick. Sent by CeCe, who'd said of Iris, "She isn't a gardener, she's a bartender!" Fay and her fleet of assistants had spread out over the lawn like a search-and-rescue team, installing minimalist, low-maintenance clumps of shrubbery and grasses that hardly needed tending.

"Have you seen the pile of sticks 3D's made under the tree out front?"

"He's a problem hoarder," Victor says.

She laughs. 3D tips onto his back, exposing the buttercup swirl in his armpits. "He isn't much for pride." Victor nods. "Exactly what I've been discussing with him all morning."

She excuses herself and returns wrapped in a sheet. Victor sets up the massage table. She hops up and closes her eyes. She becomes aware of the starlings singing in the rustling leaves at the window, a car passing in the distance, 3D's blubbery sigh. Victor is causing pain to her shoulder she trusts is therapeutic. She tells herself quiet between friends is good. A sign they are real friends, not afraid to be peaceful together.

"Don't your hands get tired?"

"In the beginning, but not anymore." He lifts her left leg and shakes it.

"Did you hear the rain last night? You saved me from the worst dream."

"Supposed to rain all week." His thumbs jam into her spine, but he doesn't ask about her dream.

"Rain makes me miss smoking," she ventures, with a sigh.

"Smoking's the best. After-rain smoking is the best of the best. It's the humidity in the tobacco. You never heard me say that. I'm a trainer. But we have our memories. When did you quit?"

"Right before I met George. More or less."

"Convenient." He pounds the back of her thigh.

"George's mother's probably keeps me from picking it back up. The look she'd give me."

"Scared by the in-laws."

"What do you know from in-laws?"

"I had a wife," he says, surprising her, working the back of her neck. "Isabel. But I never got to know her family. New Zealand, too far. You liking the Davis? Keeping you off the streets?"

"The what?" He's changing the subject. The book he loaned her, *The Bluest Ribbon*. She turns and raises her face so it's not smashed against the table. "I like it okay. Maybe I missed something, but nothing's actually happening, right? I mean, what's her name is all—'I love this one, no I love that one.' But all she's doing is sitting on a ship and staring out to sea? Having a rough think? Both guys are basically assholes and they aren't even on the ship with her? And it's a two-year voyage? And it seems, I'm not sure, like she might already be dead? Does anything happen?"

"Yeah, something happens."

"Like, she gets out of her chair and walks over to the other side of the boat?"

"No, no, she has to choose! Dax-Fabian or Piers! What a choice! Or, she doesn't choose. I see how you almost tricked me there. I'm not telling. Maybe she can't decide. Then life will decide something for her. That usually doesn't turn out well."

Iris doesn't like *The Bluest Ribbon*. Every time she wades forward a page, it pushes her back. But is it her fault or the book's? Then it's out of her hands—upstairs when she's down, inside when she's out. The last time she looked, she hadn't been able to find it. She's hardly opened a book the last three years. When Victor pressed this one into her hands, its dreamy cover of a woman looking out over ocean waves dissolving into blue ribbons, she accepted it anxiously and hopefully, as it dared out of memory her old love, the pleasure of other people's thoughts.

"How about the part where the baby falls over the rail, into the ocean?" Victor asks. "How long does that bassinet take to sink—ten pages! Terrible, didn't you love it?"

"But that was so upsetting!"

"It's a book. The more upsetting the better."

Instantly she knows it's true, but why she can't quite grasp. The way he says it makes it sound like something everybody knows. She'd felt it in the dark lecture hall as she listened to the professor in her square of light, but she'd never had the words for how something that was upsetting doubled back and became something else, how this seemed to be what people called art. When she first got to know George, she imagined they'd have conversations about ideas the way the undergraduates did, that their kind of talk, broad and deep and open-ended, was the prize of every college degree, that the door to George's apartment in Washington Square would be another door into this kind of life. But George was happy talking of nothing beyond the chalk outline of their day. He owns and seems to have read a lot of books. But she's only seen him read the news, or about opera. When he does begin a book, she soon finds him asleep. And his music—this belongs to him alone. Maybe his apartment should have tipped her off—a cool, professionally decorated bachelor's co-op with buttoned-black-leather-and-steel-framed seating, untouched gym equipment, solar blinds, a pointy blue-glass sculpture by the door, a massive opera-churning stereo system, and a trio of black-slashed prints—Franz Kline, she learned—and the hunter-green bedding a surprising number of straight men, when shopping alone, thought was the only color they were allowed to buy. But she said to herself, some people just don't know how to make a place nice. She grew busy with early love, and later with what it meant to become a Somner, and forgot that his lack of curiosity had disappointed her; later still, when she was reminded of it, she scuffed it away again, best she could. When Victor gave her the book, she was surprised. She didn't think he was the reading type. She didn't think he thought *she* was the reading type.

"We need books," Victor says now, "because we are all, in the private kingdoms of our hearts, desperate for the company of a wise, true friend."

"That's beautiful." But how, she wants to ask, can books be good friends and good when they are upsetting? Who wants upsetting friends?

"Tell me that scene right after they get off the ship and she's all 'Where's my hat!' didn't kill you. And when—"

"Stop, I haven't read that far! Victor, I might have lost it. I'm so sorry! If I can't find it, I'll get you a new one. I want to finish it."

"You've been feeling guilty this whole time? It's only a book. Put it out of your head. Hey, I saw the Vargas place is up for sale. Great house. You doing that one?"

"Our agency, but not my listing. I'm all condos. I'm up to my elbows in condos. Or, I will be in a month or so. They're setting me up on a development. But I'm part-time. I help the other agents, mostly. Which is, whatever. You're being nice by changing the subject."

A high, whistling lamentation rises from under the table.

"Don't worry, I promise. Look, you've got 3D worried too." Together they comfort the dog.

"All I know about real estate," Victor says, "is that *sun-drenched* means 'small.' Why does *sun-drenched* mean 'small'?"

"Hmm, let's think. Maybe because the windows are so close together the sun reaches all the way in, all day long?"

A few months before the wedding, CeCe and her friend Nellie Turner—of the Turner Group, LLC, where Iris is employed—encouraged her toward this line of work after she told George she would apply for a hostess job one of the local restaurants was advertising. Over iced tea on CeCe's veranda, they suggested that if she wanted an activity, residential sales, rentals to start, might be more appropriate. A career, and only as much of a career as one liked. Nellie spoke about the historical legacy of the houses in and around town and implied the business of finding people homes was both feminist and feminine, a feminism split down to smaller and softer domestic units, atomized to the prettiness of drawer pulls and doorknobs, finials and joists, and even as Iris found this argument depressingly retrograde, she agreed to give real estate a try.

"My problem is," she says to Victor, "I imagine every house being my home. Even the sun-drenched shoeboxes. I fall in love and then they're gone."

"Doesn't that make you a good agent? When you pitch it, you mean it?"

"You'd think. But no, they said I don't have the right tone. 'Too much enthusiasm doesn't project discernment,' that's how they said it."

"Who are you getting your advice from, Nell Turner? The Duchess?"

"The Duchess? My mother-in-law?"

"You haven't heard? Whoops."

"I love it. You like not smoking?"

"I do. Even though it makes me sad."

"You don't want the old life," she says, "but you miss it anyway."

"Is that what we're talking about? Smoking? Let's cheer up. Tell me a bad joke. Make it better than last time."

"Okay. I bought a box of animal crackers. It said, 'Do not eat if seal is broken.' "

"That's awful." Victor's slim, tattooed forearm is pressed against her spine. His tattoo, a mountain lion—or is it a dog?—nobly astride the back of a giant shrimp, together riding the crest of a wave.

"Now you tell me a joke."

"I can never remember jokes. I'm thinking, I'm thinking!"

"I *am* sorry I lost your book."

"I have one! A dentist, a priest, and a hangman go to a gun show. Turn over please."

"A dentist, a priest, and a hangman."

"They get to the firing range. They have AK-47s. They stand side by side and the priest says, 'Dentist, how long has it been since you—' Shit, I can't remember. No it's—no. It goes something, something, something, alligator. Forget it."

They laugh, but an unexpected and urgent worry for her mother-in-law springs up in her chest. It has the same texture as the worry of her dream.

6

After dinner with his mother in the dining room—"The napkins are maroon," she'd said, with a quiet and sage disgust, as if their color foretold all humanity's pending griefs—George spent the night at a nearby hotel. He'd promised to return to Oak Park for breakfast and goodbyes and to make sure there was nothing more he needed to request in person on her behalf—the quality of the soundproofing between rooms, for example, she'd need the night's sleep to discover. But alone at the hotel, with the television chattering in the cabinet and the curtains pulled, as the evening wore on, a vital nervousness began to net his thoughts. So much to be done, and none of it in that gray room! Well past midnight, he called the car service and asked them to pick him up as soon as they found a man to drive out to him; yes, extra for the distance and the hour. How could he stay a moment more? She doesn't need him. He'll be back soon enough. She's already having a good time, outfoxing the staff, inventing demands.

That routine, rolling into the closet. As he'd followed her down the hall, he'd experienced an unfamiliar, mixed-up feeling. But then he entered the closet and she said, "Oh, it's only you." And so at 4:00 a.m. he stole across the dim lobby and slid into the backseat of the car. Fast to cover the miles, fast back to life. Still, five hours on the road, two in asphyxiating traffic with the city just out of view! At last, the car turns onto the George Washington Bridge and Manhattan appears in the weak early sun across the wide churn of the Hudson. Tuesday morning. He'll go straight to work, put in an appearance, ensure everything is clanking along on schedule and then attend to his libretto. From the backseat of the car, with the partition to the driver closed so the air-conditioning circulates an optimally tight flow around him, the skyline is stalagmite, elemental, each building a slice edge of steel. Looking at the city from the bridge, it's hard to believe anyone's *in* there. How nice, he thinks, the city would be if the streets were empty. To slide through gray midtown without seeing another soul, without hearing a sound but the click of the traffic lights. The car plunges into the stink and speed of summer in New York. They pass through neighborhoods where George would variously be the wrong kind of man— West Harlem, the Upper West Side. He looks away, to the yellow legal pad on the leather seat beside him. He takes it up and balances it on his knee and begins to write.

UH crossing Federation Europa in search of exiled leader of Climate Refugees, rumored hiding in principality formerly known as France. Abandoned court interior. Hall of mirrors—broken! UH sits at a table with Agent X, ambassador to the EAST. Table with skinned animals, candle. UH & X study large map.

George's vision is of a future where rain falls only in a thin, temperate band around the world; the rest is famine and fire. He's still impressed with the originality of his story, its moral clarity. But he can't quite get X and UH's duet right. UH must convince X that he is not the marauder—Murderer! Rapist!—the queen's regime has, upon his escape, broadcasted him to be. The car curves under the brownstone arches of Central Park, past a group on horseback trotting a dirt path, down the Upper East Side with its green awnings and pristine esplanades. They pass the John Stepney Somner Library, a gray, French-neoclassical hulk on the corner of Fifth and Seventy-Eighth. Incredible, always, to think his mother lived there as a girl. An only child, thirty-seven rooms. The smooth marble steps up to the columned entrance, under a sculpture-nestled pediment: her front door. Wrought-iron balconies girding the upper stories. Now it's a museum and an archive, exhibiting the history of music, open to the public. No coincidence his love of opera. It's deep in his young education, in his genes— when John Stepney Somner, George's great-grandfather, commissioned the residence in 1911, moving the family uptown from lower Fifth Avenue, half the downstairs was dedicated to music. Among the libraries and drawing rooms and gallery and dining rooms there was a music room—in honor of his wife, Fanny, an accomplished pianist— and a formal recital room with murals depicting the interior of La Fenice in the 1830s. John Stepney, too bad for him, lived only a year in his elegant fortress, killed by cirrhosis in 1913; when Fanny died fifteen years later, CeCe's father inherited the house. By the time CeCe was out of school, Edward George—Georgie—and his third wife (the marriage to CeCe's mother being his second and least discussed) had moved to less drafty accommodations nearby and dedicated John's House, as the family called it, to the public.

And how John made his fortune! CeCe told George after he'd found himself confronting his great-grandfather's name as a multiple-choice option (D, incorrect) to a question on industry barons of the nineteenth century during a middle-school history test. He was delighted when later that year his social studies class was asked to produce a paper entitled "My Family Story." As his friends complained of awkward interviews with this or that grandparent, George lifted his essay from the public record and went to the movies. From the encyclopedia and *The New York Times* obituaries, with a smattering of quotation marks and a few changes for originality and sophistication, he transcribed:

John Stepney Somner was born to prosperous farmers in 1837 in New York. At the age of twenty-five he bought out of service in the Civil War. After losing a tavern bet over the material origin of the newly invented rubber stamp, he set out on an expedition to Brazil, where he joined the Amazonian rubber boom. He invested in plantations and harvested the white sap called LATEX.

By thirty-five, Somner returned to the US of A. Somner Rubber, a manufacturing company, and Somner Chemical, a "subsidiary producer of vulcanizing agents" and solvents. Such as sulfuric acid and AMMO-NIA. He lived in Stockport, Connecticut, "having, with diplomatic finesse, enlisted as overseas managers of production and transport those expatriates of the Confederacy who fled the newly United States for Brazil in 1867." 1867 the year the Amazon opened to "international shipping." Stockport is very conveniently located between New York City and Naugatuck, where he built his plants. It's a nice drive.

"The Somners were Union folk but, as John put it, 'not opposed to hiring these our honorable cousins of a different mind.'"

The plants were on a street known as Rubber Avenue. "John persuaded New Haven Railroad to add Stockport to its station line, tripling the value of John's various real estate holdings and over the decades transformed the little hamlet to the bustling."

His plants in Naugatuck produced boots and gloves. Specialty gloves for telegraph linemen and hospital workers. Until Somner rubber gloves, hospital workers tended their patients bare. They experienced burns from antiseptic fluids, carbolic acids and bichloride of mercury. "The benefit of gloves to sterility was only later discovered." Also, CONDOMS.

John merged his company with six others to create American Rubber, a "monopolizing consortium." Right before the 1896 creation of the Dow Industrial Average of twelve stocks, a coincidence, including American Rubber.

"He became John Stepney Somner of New York, serving one term in the state senate, twice mounting failed gubernatorial runs." By the first year of the new century, he'd added to his homes in Washington Square and Stockport a gaming retreat in Virginia, just south of DC, and a

"monolithic estate on Bellevue Avenue in Newport, used only six weeks
out of the year, which, "for reasons lost to time," he named Apollo Court."

After the conference with his teacher, CeCe arranged for George to take his first private tour of the library, one evening it was closed; they ate a sandwich in the stern topiary garden at the side of the mansion, behind the ornate, black iron fence that separated them from the sidewalk. In the dim room of antique instruments, a docent unlocked the display cases. George was allowed to touch them all: the gittern and the sorna and the sitar. Sad, he thinks now, how his mother has always been immune to the pull of great music. Merely, unsentimentally, appreciative. But not George. George understands why it's the highest of all arts, the only form that can set the soul free.

The car winds into the upswing glint of midtown east. It begins to rain, a hot-anyway city rain, under a bright sun. The dank concrete pavement and the yellow warp of the walk signs through the pebbles of rain rolling down the outside of his window and the black umbrellas snapping up to obscure the faces of those caught on the crosswalk all remind him that he's tired, that it's been a week of sleepless nights. Still, he's in a good mood. The silence in the car, the muffled city sounds outside—a jackhammer, the grind of the taxi's brakes. The thought of Iris at home—he's happy to be a commuter, a man with a house in the shade of a great white ash. A man in a marriage sliding through the wet city, the city transformed into the back of a submarine just risen from the water. To be alone but not alone, what better? At a red light he taps the glass separating himself from the driver. The panel recedes and he sees which of the men who drive him is at the wheel. He knows most in the rotation assigned to him. His driver's license has been suspended twenty years—cocaine, hurricane—a status he has no pressing desire to dispute. It's the old guy. How are the granddaughters? Fifth grade, already? Easy, careless, not caring about the answer, the driver not caring either, unified in the pleasantness of not caring about each other.

At work, George ducks past the receptionist and heads down the narrow corridor toward Audrey, his assistant. She's sitting in the tight-est part of the U of her wraparound cubby, eating a pile of tuna out of wax paper and aluminum foil. The smell hangs in the hermetically vented hall. He shakes the rain from his long black umbrella and hands it to her. She'll want to talk about the Cultural Initiative Grants. He doesn't want to talk about the Cultural Initiative Grants. Just thinking about it kills his mood. He hopes she doesn't ask him how his mother is. In the last six months he's taken days off here and there, ostensibly to join CeCe at various medical appointments. At work he's had to outbright everyone, dazzle them out of pity and out of the possibility they might strike up a meaningful conversation, so he smiles and says:

"Hello—tuna! It's kind of early for tuna?"

Office jocularity affords few and simple topics, for which he is grateful. New hair. New outfit. Commuter pain. Computer pain. Sustenance. Wait—did he? He cups his chin. Yes, in his haste to leave the hotel, he forgot to shave.

"George, hi." Audrey looks startled to see him. "No carbohydrates. Pretty rugged."

"You, come on! Why would you do that? You look great. What have we got? Stacks to read, floor to ceiling?"

"I—" They pause to greet Stanton—Will, William—who's wandered silently around the corner in his usual way, relaxed a blink shy of coma: already an ambler in his fifties, with the pink of a baby out of a bath. As always, his clothes appear just-bought—today, a navy cable-knit sweater, khakis, expensive gray running shoes. The unspoken rule that only the boss gets to wear sneakers, to bring his dog. George smoothes his rough chin, his tie. The massive golden retriever glitters at Stanton's side.

"Betsy's looking handsome," George says.

"And how is—it has a strange name?"

"3D. He has *us* on a leash. Those two"—George leans down and touches Betsy with his index finger—"should have a playdate. We'd love to have you and Anita out for a visit."

"Hmm." Stanton sighs. "Glad we're all with Liz on reviewing the Program Guidelines." He must think George attended Friday's meeting. He's surprised Stanton attended. Stanton's time is usually reserved for the board and the big donors, not the day-to-day. George agrees, Liz was right on. Says he can't wait to take a look at her material. Stanton and the dog move down the hall.

As program director for the Arts and Culture Fund at the Hud-Stanton-Fox Foundation, George makes $75,000 a year. His mother supplements this income with what she calls "infrastructure" (subcategories: productive leisure, real estate tax, Iris), which is granted as a relatively modest disbursal once a year through CeCe's lawyer so they may avoid speaking of it and he may avoid his shame in taking it.

"Trust him with a trust?" she'd said. "I trust it is only through work he will not descend into moral turpitude, and I trust he will only work if I provide him with the essentials and no more." This to the lawyer— George at eighteen, sitting like a giant, disembodied pimple between them, the only time the three had met together until this year. Until her illness.

"I didn't expect you in until tomorrow. Your mom's called twice this morning. How're you holding up?"

"I'm well. I'm great."

Awkward. Audrey's concern, draining as the fluorescents. She yanks her rubber band out of her jet curls and reknots the bun with a violence that still startles George, though he's seen her do it a hundred times a day for two years. She forks a bite of the wet lump in the foil. In silence together they search and find Stress, the North Star of office camaraderie.

"Wow," she maws, "it mushed be streshfu."

"Stress can be a powerful and driving force."

"Your mom calls me Ellen. Wasn't your first assistant named Ellen?"

"No," he lies.

Lying, lying, lying. To cheer himself up he pictures lying under Audrey in her starter-kit apartment. A plastic alarm clock on top of a plastic milk crate. The Official Audrey Fantasy does not have its usual soothing effect; in its place he imagines her the damp, gunmetal gray of a Pacific tuna.

"What's first priority today? Cultural Initiative? City Hope Orchestra?"

"I got through those while you were gone." She swallows. "I had some spare time Friday. Not that—I mean, you should double-check everything, right?"

Most workdays George sits in his well-appointed office in front of the computer and clicks through glossy, photo-filled presentations sent by organizations requesting grant money. Photos of, say, a child playing a violin next to a pie chart, above an investment report. He slices open the few applications that still come by hard mail with a letter knife shaped like the wing of a gull. The knife is a corporate gift he received his first year at Hud-Stanton. All the program directors got one, but George recognized it was modeled after Brancusi's *Bird in Space*, with the addition of a serrated spine, and, having always admired the sculpture, felt it had been chosen particularly for him. Next, they batch potential grant recipients: Allocate Funds (suggested amount; timeline; rationale); No with a Note; Special Consideration; Friend of X; No. Worthy causes: endowing a symphony, or, say, last month's project—a onetime grant to restore a collection of Revolutionary-era chairs for display at the New-York Historical Society.

At first, Audrey Singer wanted to open and print and arrange these grant requests for him; otherwise she had little to do. The previous year, Hud-Stanton had absorbed—merged with, officially—the Fox Foundation, several polite years after the death of its founder, Henry Fox. Fox and Hud-Stanton shared many board members and the endowment-doubling vote to merge was near unanimous. For reasons of diplomacy, working out the balance of responsibilities allotted to various duplicate programs is slow going. George knows Hud-Stanton is taking delicate care in folding the Fox programs, one by one, into their own. He began his libretto in the bounty of extra time brought by the merger. Audrey has as little to do as he; it doesn't help that as a rule he won't let her get him coffee.

"Never!" he shouted, the first time she tried, and as she shrank back, he felt a surge of benediction, the power of radical goodness coursing through him. She hid the cup behind her cubicle's partition and cast down her eyes, no doubt moved by the luck of being assigned such a good boss. The downside is, without enough for her to do, their relationship has a vague, nervous quality as if they'd slept together a long time ago and are now forever running into each other: the only truth they share is the one they cannot speak. If they discuss work too long, they risk revealing that there isn't enough work for both of them. Then he'd have to sack her. Then he'd be the guy without an assistant.

They both feel better when Audrey remembers to look busy: an occasional test-run of the mail-merge; an update to the Contact List when the phone number of a new Influential or Charity Minded Citizen or Corporation comes their way. Mostly, she IM's with her boyfriend and reads magazines hidden in her lap while George works on his libretto. They get along best the four days out of the year Audrey has the real task of delivering the fiscal quarter's stack of closed-grant files to the lonesome archivist down the hall. Once a month, she joins him in his office for a SUM, or Status Update Meeting. Together they type up descriptions of the causes in George's Yes Pile and send these to the Board. The Board Yeses his Yes (except for one or two times a year when an MTR (Modification of Terms Request) or NCP (No on Conflicting Precedent) comes back so it looks as if everyone were paying attention. He attends a dinner and once in a while cuts a ribbon, as he had once at the New York Center for Egyptian Archaeology: cut the ribbon and sat at the linen-draped table closest to the mummy, between a curator and a former mayor, across from a donor. The donor, an airline executive, over chicken and vegetables julienned and fanned on the plate, recited to George what seemed the entirety of his new book, *Flying Strong: Ten First-Class Rules to Reenergize Your Yes*. Also verse from his self-published poetry collection, *Plumes of the Earth*.

"Right!" George says, and enters his office and closes the door. He shuffles the pile.

His phone rings. "I'm forwarding the messages," Audrey says, and hangs up. The voice-mail light clicks on. There are two recipient-foundation thank-yous followed by a Critical Mass call to a Union Square sit-in for the Sustainable Agro program officer, misdirected to George, typical, as that officer—a young guy from Fox whose rope-and-seashell bracelet irritates George—is also named George, not only George but George Stemmler, the name tripping the voice recognition on the automated switchboard and sometimes also jostling their e-mails. His mother's calls. First asking where-has-he-gone-they'd-planned-breakfast-she's-tried-his-cell-three-times; second, with a long exposition on her doubts in the doctor and her disappointment in George. Iris, from the previous Friday, trying to catch him and why is his cell off, reporting that she has an idea how to redecorate to make the house feel friendlier at night, love you, bye. He should call Iris and tell her he's back. Confess his escape. But he hasn't done anything wrong, has he? He's only gone to work! As any responsible person would.

He checks his e-mail. Junk and admin, except a sound clip from Vijay Muller, the composer he'd hired after Iris's encouragement. A two-minute update to a change he made in the libretto, a masterpiece of logarithmic atonalities. This is how they've worked for the last year, remotely. He's heard Vijay's sandpaper voice on the phone, but they've met in person only once, when George finally completed a draft and made an unwelcomed pilgrimage to Vijay's home in Montclair. Once there, he discovered Vijay's constellation of maladies and phobias—obsession-compulsion, agoraphobia, hypochondria, and that Vijay lived not in the piano-filled chalet of George's imagining, but in an efficiency apartment above a tea shop. George's initial dismay—as Vijay leaned out his window, a handkerchief over his mouth—was soon replaced by a conviction that Vijay's suffering was all the more proof of his brilliance. That the droning minors he had long been admired for in certain academic circles were the result of a bold and tragic vision and represented the future of music, just as George's libretto represented the future of humanity. Vijay works on *The Burning Papers* only through the technological divide. They have not seen each other since.

The update sounds good. George takes off the headphones and calls Aleksandar Dvorsky, the opera's freelance producer. George hired him only a week ago but feels he's known the man a decade. During his interview, Aleksandar insisted George begin looking for a small theater right away. George agreed. Finally, he is among people who believe in him! To produce his opera—what was impossible now seems fated. If he keeps his courage—his mother's being away a help in this department—soon they'll hire orchestral and voice talent, rehearsal space, and support staff. *The Burning Papers* will debut in a modest venue with a limited run, gather momentum, be picked up by—the Met or City Opera. The Met would be good. He must send the libretto to his contacts there, let them know what is in store. Perhaps they'll ask for it right away. Perhaps they'll want to see it staged. Either way, he'll be ready. Aleksandar is optimistic about returns on the limited run too, citing the finances of a few contemporary works it so happens George admires—no one winning the lottery on putting up an opera, but with the right artistic direction and publicity, no one ending up too far in the red, either.

As he listens to Aleksandar's phone ring, George reviews his calendar and is reminded of how finely appointed his soft leather appointment book is, but not of any appointments. Aleksandar does not pick up. George checks his iCalendar. Nothing there either. He opens a Word.docx and types and deletes and types and deletes, and when he looks up, he has written:

> *The QUEEN sings {suggestion for Vijay: Cavatina}*
> *Build a fence around the gypsy where you find him on your lot. / Build a fence around the gypsy, while he steals and schemes. / Look where the gypsy stakes his tent, to the moss he lays his head for he knows deep into the ground, the fruitful water-lands. / Wise nations! Listen for the gypsy / for every sound he makes—the shucking knife, the creaking wheel—sings out a murderous song: / beware the land that's common, where still the flocks may graze, for soon it will be barren, and shepherds will be beggars too*

He pauses and e-mails this progress to himself for safekeeping. With more backtracking and revision he continues:

> *and roam the green off every hill and starve we will together, not a crop be saved. / We thank the gypsy's trespass, though not his greedy heart, for he has marshaled us to caution on the warming hill. / Evict the gypsy rightly*

and when you cast him in the road / show him all your deference as if he is
a lord. / Always thank the gypsy, for though he be unclean / he is the scourge
has saved us all, and kept our pastures green.

This is fantastic. The queen: powerful first by chance access to the right natural resource at the right time. Then by cunning expansion. Then by cruel suppression. Isn't this always the way? Timeless. Genius! Is genius going too far? Does the rhythm sound, distantly—Protestant? Is it derivative? Could he be miming a hymn from childhood, long buried? It's easy to confuse *derivative* and *classic*. His excitement indicates the latter. In his vision, the narrow band of Earth where rain still falls has seen the end of democracy and the introduction of a caste system that privileges those who can trace their heritage to former countries of the cooler North; a system to which opposition is stamped out by the queen, in part through the vilification of those southwards first dubbed *climate refugees*, then, once their papers are burned and their disenfranchisement is total, *gypsies*.

He spell-checks and e-mails his addition to Audrey. Something he likes to do. *What do you think of this bit?* he writes, and after a spell opens the door to his office.

Silence. She is undoubtedly impressed and thinking of what to say.

"Wow. Only you could have written this."

She always encourages him this way. So reassuring, her straight talk. No flattery from Audrey.

"A flash of inspiration."

"Slow flash."

"You caught me. It is good, isn't it?"

"To accomplish something important is a real accomplishment."

"Audrey, don't be so shy with your opinions! You're the best assistant I've ever had, have I told you that? You're going places, you! Now if you don't mind closing the door, I'm going to have a think."

He fiddles with the mirrored box on his desk. She's right. It's brilliant. Aleksandar and Vijay have been urging him to stop messing with what is already a finished libretto and green-light development. It's time. He'll produce it, start small, and then they'll shop it around.

"Lunch!" he calls through the door to Audrey, unconcerned by the pinched hysteria he notes in the faraway sound of his own voice. It isn't even close to lunchtime. "I'm on your schedule now—look at what a bad influence you are on me! Don't move, don't do a thing. I'll call the car from the lobby, I'll get the car!" He leaps up and turns off the lights. Audrey comes in, blinking in the dim, and lifts his linen jacket from the back of his chair, holds it out for him. He thrusts one arm in and then the other. She hands him his umbrella and he bounds down the hallway and past reception, pushes the elevator button again, again, again. Next, as if he's waking from a dream, he's climbing out of the car at the foot of his own long, curving drive, clutching a bouquet of ribbon-tied balloons in his hand.

7

"Arms and abs before I go?" Victor says.

"Bleg," Iris answers. "Let me get the weights."

She pulls from the closet an eight-pound set, then George's old twenty-five pounders for Victor.

"Planks to start!" He drops to the floor.

"You're a pain," she says, grateful to have him for a friend. Once, Nellie Turner asked her to describe Stockport as she would to an out-of-town client, and now she can't stop: *Stockport, almost as fun as a wicker basket! Stockport, the top hat full of pudding time forgot! Stockport, where the women are wives and the dogs wear galoshes!*

Still, she's shy around these chicken-jawed captains of industry. Even though the men's faces, when they see her, unscramble to how they must have looked at thirteen. Vague-eyed, goofy-mouthed. At the dinners, at the parties, they command an exhausting reserve of facts and opinions: movies and wars and restaurants, mergers and congress-men and cuts of meat, health care to lawn care. She knows exactly nothing, has no position and is not positioned—positioned, this construction of the word she's only learned since her marriage. It doesn't matter. Whatever she says, they laugh. Unlike Victor, who doesn't want anything from her—never makes a flap over the Somners. Never gives her the eyes-too-long or the sneaky up-down. Never with the *ha-ha-HA!* Or the *we should.* Never with the dreadful, eager ass-kissing that George and CeCe are so used to they notice only its absence. Without it, they flail and fuss and do not know what to do. "A rude little man!" CeCe might say. Or George: "Crazy to expect the waiter to come back with the drinks before tomorrow, I guess."

Victor counts to sixty. Her torso shakes. She can feel him evaluating her plank with mild disapproval, as if she were the tangled back of a cable box. CeCe and George and their friends have traveled the world. How do they stay so narrow-minded? Like kids in a play, positioned on their marks, unaware of the scenery as it changes behind them, one painted cloth lifting away to reveal another: the looming towers and twinkling lights of Manhattan at night. The green quadrangles of the oldest universities. A ski slope in the Alps. The white and blue of an island shoreline, an umbrella stuck on a slant in the sand. A Roman aqueduct spanning the French countryside. A covered shopping arcade in Hong Kong. Round tables filling a hotel ballroom, each with a black number on a white card and a bun of flowers at its center. The polished brass and unfading topiary between the elevator and the door to an apartment on Manhattan's Upper East Side. The apse of a winged cathedral, its vaulted rib cage, the air thick and cool. The monitors on the floor of the stock exchange like the eye of a monster, glowing orange. A hundred dark dots over a hunting marsh—a flock of plover swooping low; one, two, three!—falling from the shot. A Carolina-coast golf resort, seen through the floor of a clear-bottomed helicopter, sandpits like nuclei. The swept main street of their own satellite town. Lawns a zillion miles long, zippered to the Sound, like CeCe's.

"Have you always lived in Stockport?" she asks abruptly. They have begun a round of lateral raises. "I mean, since you switched to the East Coast?"

"Me? No way. I was a trapper in Maine, for about four seconds. Believe it or not. Me and Isabel met working on a cruise. We got sick of that and joined a couple of deckhands heading back to Bar Harbor, said I'd be able to get a spot. When that blew up, I was left with a lead on an oyster-farming gig in Norwalk. Down the coast I came."

"Get out! My last two years of high school we lived in Maine. But not fish. Paper."

"Plant in Lincoln?"

"Mm-hmm. Stinkin' Lincoln. You don't just break into lobster, do you? I mean, isn't it families?"

"Yeah, nobody would let me in. Dock monopoly, even short-season crab. Best I did was net for bait. Broke even fish to fuel. It sucked."

She remembers the low, brick high school she barely attended, the flag on a pole out front, the black bark of the pines in winter. She had her first job in Bucksport, as a barback—cold nights, indoors, a place off-harbor, being embraced in the dark warm by her boss after a Seven and Seven and Seven and Seven with that hack laugh, that old-bar embrace, football on a flatscreen over the mantel and the rattling of smoke and love and the hold the old man had on her shoulder.

"Like the work?" she asks, remembering how she liked the work.

"Eh, they called me Rusty. I was the one they said, 'Had a drink with him and he's okay.'"

"I don't get it."

"Stick around ol' Rusty, we'll find ya something! Local color. Rusty Heels, that was me. Fuckers."

"No! Really?" But she could hear it: an evil thing, but said to him in friendship, a heavy arm across his shoulders, the sea stink on their clothes.

"And we did stick around, for a while."

"Why?"

"I don't know. My wife was in a book club. I was young enough I didn't know I could make a different life."

"I still don't know how to do that."

"Well, I needed a push. I got one. I fell asleep in the sun and I had a burn on the back of my neck. I went to the general store."

He tells her how he stood on the sawdusted and salt-stained plank holding two bottles of sunblock, comparing the SPFs, trying to remember which was deadlier, the UVA or the UVB.

"I had a strange feeling come to me. I think, 'Everybody's looking at me.' "

The eye of the clerk. The rounded eyes of two little girls. The eye of the girls' mother sweeping past Victor casual and regular.

"The mom's attention is all in my direction and she says, 'Stay close,' in that danger-sharp mother way. Kids grab her legs. I see this in my peripheral, as if the corner of my eye is being pulled by one of the kid's little fingers. I felt—I wasn't allowed to turn and look at them. I'm not a violent guy, but they made me imagine doing to them whatever they were imagining I'd do to them, which I don't even know what that was. They made me *want* to. Almost. Can you imagine? Me? You see what a mind fuck that is? It's like magic. Not a magic trick. That's like real magic."

They're at the kitchen counter, exercise forgotten. She remembers parking her car by the harbor before work, watching the white masts of the boats knocking against the sea. When they moved, she'd told her bandmates, back in Jersey, on the phone, "It's so pretty here!" And it wasn't a lie. But there was no passing through to the tourist's side of the postcard, and she got herself picked up by the band in the middle of the night, on their way to a gig in Montreal.

"So you moved to Norwalk?" she asks.

"Not yet. I wasn't going anywhere. I was in that way where you think there's meaning in life only when you make everything a giant pain in the ass for yourself. And Isabel loved our prefab house. Isabel was amazing. Not that she isn't now, I'm sure. I mean, she knew before I knew she knew about me, and her accent, I can't do it anymore, but, when I'd talk about how I couldn't get better work because I was nothing to them but token Mr. Rusty, she'd say, 'Year making et arll up, it's nething.' "

"That's pretty good."

They'd married for her visa, he said, but a real kind of love was also between them, and when she left him, he discovered as she was leaving that he'd loved her from the first, even in his limited way, even as they laughed through the drive-in wedding with the one witness. After she was gone, he drank in the quiet of the flimsy house and sent her a lot of bad e-mails, for a year. Driving his pickup one morning, the dry lobster traps still bouncing around the back, feeling strong and sunny with an early buzz, he almost killed an old woman carrying her tiny grandson along a half mile of dirt to the row of glinting aluminum mailboxes on the main road. He broke the slim arm that held the child and smashed her feet beyond anything a pin could fix. Her cheek, three ribbons. He was almost certain he would have killed himself after, except the baby was chucked into the bushes unharmed; he took it as a sign. He stood up beside his lawyer in court to confess as much, but his lawyer, low, had said, "Talk or walk, Victor. Keep quiet I might get you felony four." And Victor sat back down. When he got out of jail was when he headed to Norwalk. He was in AA by then. He got certified in massage and personal training because it suited his new healing way of life, because it was kindly, because the other oystermen drank in the boat and thought he was weird.

"I'm okay it happened the way it did," he says. "I might have stayed in a kind of half-life, you know? If it hadn't gotten bad. I'm not political. I'm spiritual."

"I'm not political either."

"You know it doesn't smell anymore? Lincoln?"

"I've heard. Was Isabel—"

But there's a sound and they both look up—maybe it's a branch snapping against the front door, maybe it's the dog nosing out front, a disruption she can't identify, faint, but a disruption nonetheless, and they change the subject.

8

George paces between the front door and the white ash with its strong, sagging limbs. He's taken off his shoes. The ground is cool under his feet. So much to be done. Vitality—long lost!—returning. He felt the change come over him at last in the hotel room by Oak Park. It'd been slipping toward him at a shimmering, muffled distance for months, spooling through his libretto as he typed away at Hud-Stanton, weaving its pretty thread into the dull and the gray of his office, showing him how pointless his job is and how he must no longer confine himself. At first, he thought it might be a kind of sorrow for his mother. He *is* sad to have left her at Oak Park. But his energy is bigger. The beautiful, tightening net of becoming. When the opera is fully realized—only a matter of time, no longer a matter of courage—he really will send it to the Met, to City Opera. He imagines the bidding war, the suggestions of this soprano or that, offers of a spot opening or closing the season, the glowing interviews. George, shaking his copper head, modestly accepting it all, flabbergasted by such praise.

He'd left the office to tell Iris his news, about the leap of faith he's finally ready to make. On the way home, he'd stopped at the bank to secure the last, substantial loan he needs, the bank having already made him several smaller advances. It's been his little secret, paying Vijay, paying Alexsandar. Talent not coming cheap. This last loan approved in the nick of time: his accounts are tight. He learned at the bank that one is even overdrawn, on a check to something called Tru-Clear Pool Service.

What will Iris say? She's only known the one version of him. Predictable, abiding. That pussy bore. She's never seen him at his best. Inspired, a streak of light across the ordinary field of being. As he was his first year of college before the trouble—brave and new to freedom and talking big about big to one lovely after another. She'll love him more, won't she? She loves the good man he is, how will she not love the great man he is set to be? He's found his footing because of her. Not like the other times, which turned out to be false. Iris, his rekindling of possibility. But! What if she doesn't understand, she, who's kept him steady without knowing it? Wise to save a few details for later. Better surprise her with *The Burning Papers*, with his achievement and the happy changes it will bring to their happy life. Best for now to wear the good man's face but not the great man's face, to hide anticipation away.

He'd walked into the bank and almost turned right around and left, but a free-roaming representative—not a teller—stood up and waved him over. It was so easy. All that money waiting for him all this time, waiting only for him to finally get some guts. The account his mother has put in his name for her care he can't withdraw from without the attorney—and wouldn't, of course!—but that his name is *attached* to such an account, and that account being attached to the rest of his mother's accounts, offers him eligibility for a staggering new line of credit. The bank representative, a private-wealth manager as luck would have it, seated him behind a frosted-glass partition. She asked for his information, typed a few strokes, leaned into the glow of her screen, ripped a piece of paper from a notepad with another bank's name—the name of the bank with which his had recently merged—wrote a number, and turned the piece of paper around on her green felt desktop for him to see. Her expression convinced him. It wasn't congratulatory or approving or disgusted or conspiratorial. Her face was blank. As if that great big number were nothing. Maybe it *was* nothing. All of it to his primary checking, yes, thank you. A combined loan leaned against the equity of his house, which his mother had bought outright without a mortgage. Three hundred and fifty thousand dollars.

Of course, there's something terrifying about this. But to be terrified, to be brave, to again be alive, a speck of gold on the gray wheel of average, he hasn't felt so clear in a long time. Still, he must be careful. At times like this the world has turned against him. He doesn't want anyone to worry! As a young man it was—he was at his strongest, his second year at Yale, his will set to emerge. A misunderstanding. Monster or hero, to be a man! Monster, what the girl accused him of. The girl—laid, lied, liar, lie! She'd liked him. She said so! And different problems, later in his twenties, once or twice, he was fired. Fired not even once, *really*, and now, pacing the lawn, he's saved from memory twice over: first by the stuffing hand of shame, second by the picture before him, the earth under his feet: his house, his grass, his sunlight. For so long he's been out of the sun! For so long he's been on ice! Sleep-skating a dead man's figure eight, his ears nodding low, slow-looping an infinity under gulfs of mist at the bottom of a mist-shrouded valley. The mist—each minute now!—warming and wicking away. His front door looks peculiar, as if he were seeing it in a mirror. He must be careful. Iris will understand, but not yet. Who will not understand is his mother. How little she appreciates the efforts he makes.

He stops in front of the house and catches the ghost of his reflection in the wide window set in the flagstone beside the front door. Behind him, the branches of the ash sway. He's holding the clutch of primary balloons at his back. He's smiling, openmouthed like at something funny. Funny around the mouth and surprised around the brow.

He cuts it all right, looks-wise. Broad at the shoulder, narrow at the waist. Dash enough for someone who has more important things to tend to than vanity.

He'd had the car drop him at the bottom of the driveway so he could creep up the drive. The balloons were a sudden inspiration—on the way home he'd asked the driver to turn off Route 22 into a low-slung complex with a jewelry store and a children's toy store nestled amid the take-out joints. He'd chosen the toy store and made a rubber rainbow heap on the counter that the saleswoman and his driver helped him fill from the helium tank. Silver balloons had bobbled so cheerfully at the entrance to the bank, where they'd been tied to the leg of a folding table stacked with blue brochures. Come to think of it, he *has* been fired more than once. The firm of Jerk, Jerk and Blaustein. He was a different man. Fifteen years ago, a junior analyst. They'd released him with a careful and glowing recommendation, not worth antagonizing the Somners. The security guard looked like a broom. His career subsequently reinvented by a claustrophobic but résumé-building stint at his mother's fund. And another kind of expulsion—a hotel, in a Riviera town, what was its name? A name his mind has lost. A hotel by the sea—the hotel asked that he not return. His mother's house is by the sea. His house is in the woods. He's left his mother by a lake. Fitzgerald drank summers at the Belles Rives—that was the hotel's name. Antibes. CeCe's lawyer had called the head of guest services. The hotel welcomed his return, even sending him a hefty, four-color coffee-table book—*La Bête Merveilleuse dans le Tableau: Artists of the South of France*—sent it all the way to New York, across the sea. George sent it back. Other sadnesses too. The women who'd fallen in love with him—how later, all promised to remain his friend, but not one remained his friend! Juan-les-Pins. The name of the town. Before that, worst—his break from Yale: a three-month ski trip in Jackson, Wyoming, they called it, though where he was there wasn't any skiing.

The clouds shift and his reflection vanishes. The great room becomes visible, as if he were at the beginning of an old-fashioned play, the curtain rising on an interior. The kind of play where everything inanimate has meaning, signifies—the worn armchair, the big radio on the mantel, a bundle of flowers wrapped in paper thrown across the sideboard. A table set for three, a hat on a hook. Except, the uninhabited space of this play features his own gleaming, modern kitchen. The star of the play will be his wife and then it will be him. He's memorized the rhythms of his house—this makes it his house, more than any deed. Any moment, Iris will stride the room right to left, begin making lunch. He'll enter and tell her his news, slightly modified: the financing for his opera has been secured. Backers. Iris knows he's had more trouble finding backers than expected. Now he's found them, hasn't he? A car passes on the road below. For a nonsensical moment he thinks it's his mother, come to yell at him. The balloons bump and drift in the breeze above his head. Iris crosses the room.

His mirror heart seizes. She's looking at him but she doesn't see. The sunlight's on his side. Iris, from the other side of the wide and spotless window, a stranger. Beautiful, unmade—she stretches. Lifts her arms, drops her arms. How rare to see her, to see anyone, making the no-face face of being alone, the posture of unconscious and solitary absorption. Her secret face, his secret now. He makes his thoughts loud so she might hear, a child's trick—the sublime confusion of love and telepathy—fine piece, cunty bunny. Fine and bunny, piece and cunty, words filtered from the grate-trap of his brain like sediment. She doesn't notice. She's getting something from the closet. Weights. Her hands are wide and worn, knuckles like knotted wood. He can read her age only in the knots in her hands and in the incandescent parchment under her eyes. Her eyes—marine with gold flecks out-of-doors, sky-in-the-sea. Violet in the house. He has forgotten; he can never recall the precise look of her, even when she lies beside him and he has turned away.

3D bounds in and bumps heavily against her calves. She pets him. He rolls onto his back, paws cycling. She disappears into a part of the room he can't see. George decides he will creep around the back and— Iris reappears with Victor. Victor! They sit at the kitchen counter. 3D's head jerks toward George. 3D is pivoting his gaze between the two men, Victor and the ghost at the window. Iris's mouth moves. Victor smiles. George ties the balloons to the lowest branch of the tree. He steps back, into a strange pile of sticks with his bare feet, and curses. The dog's velvet eye marks him again. 3D seems to consider what to do with George. To consider and to dismiss. With a jowly and tongue-stretching sigh, 3D pushes out from under Iris's hand, turns his back to George, and disappears from the frame of the window.

It *is* a play, and he should go in. But then she laughs. Victor—shiny black shorts, shiny jet hair—must be telling a story, gesturing as he speaks. A muscular man with a sporty buzz-flop, a white T-shirt, a clean towel folded over his shoulder. Victor, taking up the gold medallion and chain that was spiraled on the kitchen counter and lifting it back over his head. What a jerk. Jerk jewelry. Why was his chain off in the first place? Their heads are bent together. Iris touches Victor's arm. For a second she looks, what is it, sad? Sad, and George can't imagine what they could be—Iris, putting her hands in her hair. Respect is an errand run in the dark.

But isn't it rare, the opportunity for a man to be sure he is respected? Good to stay under the tree a little longer. And wasn't he going to be the first to make her laugh today?

Victor and Iris are smiling. For a second, they look in George's direction, as if they heard him. George grows bored. Now she's at the sink. She hands Victor a glass of water. George would like a glass of water. No, what George would like is a glass of orange juice and a glass of *mineral* water. Now he's really bored! Victor is folding up the massage table. They must have just had the twice-weekly massage. George pays for it. Iris disappears and reappears wearing her favorite gray sweatshirt. George is less bored but also suddenly ravenous. And then—is it? Her cheek is a bright stain. Did she put on blush when she got her sweatshirt? She doesn't wear much makeup. He loves this about her. When she'd moved into his apartment in Manhattan, she brought only clothes, a toothbrush, and a bar of alkaline soap—castile. Cleans both hair and face, she said. Holding her all-purpose soap in his hands, a few days after she'd found a scrap of his libretto, he'd told her more about *The Burning Papers*. Maybe he's imagining it, the stain on her cheek. She'd said, "Sounds crazy," but smiled, and told him all the bands she'd been in, with names so foreign he found himself too shy to ask what inspired them: the Peepholes, the Dimmer Switches, Everything Feels Great. When she moved in officially, from where, from some place low and highway, he showed her the various bathrooms she could choose from. She was quiet that day and the day after, as if she were considering something grave.

The balloons are making the sound of a children's birthday party. The air under the tree warms and gathers mosquitoes. Victor is readying himself to leave. George must go in, but something keeps him. The fear she might betray him? No. He's watching her as a stranger might. He's visiting the hypercolor world of love's beginning. His mother was wrong. Iris hasn't changed. She won't drop him or lose him or let him go, no matter what he confesses. He'll open the door and—the dog. Here is the dog, sitting in front of the front door, watching George.

"Away, away," George whispers. 3D's eyes—intent. No bark, no blink, no shucking of the head side to side. Must have gone out the back and come around the house.

"Dummy. What do you want? Use your Mandarin."

This is Iris's joke, an elaborate joke about 3D's speaking every language but English.

The dog sounds a resonant *hmmmmmmmmmm*. Not a growl, but not altogether approving. 3D looks like the dogs of Saint Martin George knew as a child, the rough mutts that ran the length of the beach in snapping packs, haloed by flies, sand packed into their paws and fur, sand spun out behind them when they lunged at each other. This makes George nervous around 3D sometimes, still. Those dogs had kept to their crews, uninterested in humans, and this disinterest disturbed young George, whose heart held that domestication was the price all creatures, boy or animal, paid for their survival. Dogs without rules could not be punished. He and Pat and his mother repeated this vacation for many years, beginning the spring his father left them. The year he was ten, wishing he remembered his father, George fell in love with one of the dogs. Tawny, gentler than the rest. He lured her away and fed her, and each day after, he and Lucy (he named her Lucy instantly and without thought) sat in the shade of a lime tree set back from the path to the beach. The birds the Dutchmen called sugar thief, small and yellow, alighted on the concrete balconies of the hotel. The mild ocean contained itself and they thought what dogs and boys may think together, until one day in a red flash he and Lucy were pulled apart, and all the plane ride home he was scolded for playing with the bandage.

"Go away," he says. "I'm busy."

"You don't look right," 3D says.

"Fuck off. I haven't shaved."

"Iris is smarter than she knows."

"Yes," George says. "Probably. I think it's going to rain. Do you?"

"You are an unfortunate person."

"What do you mean?"

"Anybody has a look at you knows what I mean."

Silent, a yellow-toothed sigh. 3D stands, stoops to lap a drainpipe at the corner of the house, turns the corner, and trots away.

Any luck, there's lead in that pipe. George opens the door to his house, his house, and steps inside.

9

Her first night at the clinic, CeCe dreams of the iced mountains of the Crimea, which she visited with her father once as a child. The nettle is carpeted in snow. Snow gusts up the trees along the high forest path. She's eighteen, nineteen, standing alone in the dark under the moon, wearing a sable over a pencil skirt. Two black horses come pounding down the path. They race into view without master or cart, bulging throat to throat. They bear past her into the thicket. They run an hour, a day, a year. She chases them over the black curve of the dark half of the world and all the way to dawn—blue between the trees, then bright between the trees. The sun's rays break over the side of the sky. She falls. Her little black shoes twist in the snow. The horses leave her behind, burst from the thicket into white open country down into the valley like a powdered bowl of moonlight, where the one with the palsy will be an easy mark. The rifleman waits on the other side, the shadow of his hat a pinhole against the snow.

She wakes and doesn't know where she is. She remembers and covers her face with her hands, waiting for courage to find her. Courage or not, she must get dressed; she's to have breakfast with George before he goes. When he doesn't come to her room, she gathers the two canes beside the door and with slow purpose locates the awful dining room with the dusty light and the spider plants. She accepts tea but refuses food. She frowns politely at the other residents as they file in and out, her back straight as a pin, in stiffness and in pride. After an hour, she returns to her room to call George's hotel, but how to dial out? *Pound 2, star 2, wait for the tone.* She can't make it work. Trading the canes for the chair, she wheels to the lobby and asks if she has any messages. "Just this once," the receptionist says. "I'm not your personal secretary, dear." No messages. The receptionist calls the hotel. George has checked out.

Back in her room, she practices her appeal to Dr. Orlow. I will stay in the trial, but at home. I will come up twice a week, four times a week, no matter the distance. I will buy whatever equipment is required. I will hire a nurse. I will hire a doctor, if you like. Hell, if you like, I'll hire *you*. No, that's not the right tone. Controls? *I can replicate the controls.* The rules of the trial have already been explained to her—to receive the Astrasyne and its army of auxiliary medications, a participating facility must supervise the data pool—nursing home, clinic—until preliminary FDA approval. "Almost unheard of," her physician, an old family friend, had said. "Requiring that trial members be in-facility. They must want to monitor the heck out of it. Multiple quality-of-life applications, maybe. I imagine they're confident in the drug's efficacy. I'd try to place in, if I were you."

She is a patron of the arts; how quickly she became a patron of the sciences. Could George really have left? No. A mix-up. When Dr. Orlow appears, he will help and she will try to seem grateful. *Am* I grateful? she wonders. Someone must have been rejected from the trial—or worse, their acceptance revoked—so she could take the vacant spot. Who was it? A woman? A blur knocking against the closed window of her conscience like a moth. A woman of her own general age and appearance, a woman losing or soon to lose autonomic function—the inevitability CeCe fears most. Inevitable, unless the Astrasyne does what they hope. This woman, a brumous silhouette, but not a ghost.

More like her own bent shadow gliding ahead of her on the pavement. It could have been a man. She hopes it was a man, and one of no redeeming quality. She will gather herself. She must stay.

"Knock-knock?" A nurse bustles into her room—the same woman from the day before, Janet or Jean. Another woman enters, puts down a tray of English muffins and eggs, and leaves. Try to seem grateful! She smiles at the nurse, who begins listing the morning cocktail of pills. Her kingdom, the shadow's, for the cocktail. Each time she hears the word, CeCe cloaks it in the same tired pun: rocks, sherry, twist, eau-de-vie? She must be pleasant, until someone of greater authority can be procured.

"You're funny, Mrs. Somner. We'll pretend we're having drinks! Just these six, a stroll in the park. Let's go big to small. Water first. Or, should I say, shooter first, and here's your lemon, and here's your salt. Bottoms up."

"Shooter?" CeCe says, remembering her dream, "What's a shooter?"

She swallows the pills. As she does, the nurse explains the rule and order dictated by each one and reminds her that the afternoon nurse will administer more. CeCe will take these separately and these together. These on an empty stomach and these with food. Why do they bother telling her when she's not allowed to administer the doses herself? Under normal circumstances she doesn't abide being managed. But she wouldn't trust herself with this alchemy. This is why I smile at the nurse, she thinks, smiling at the nurse.

"How about meeting some of the other residents today?" the nurse says. "I can take you around. They're asking after you, isn't that nice? It's a good group. Mr. Townsend and Dotty—Mrs. Burden—told me to tell you they're planning a special activity for this evening. Songs at the piano."

As she speaks, the nurse fluffs the bouquet of yellow tulips that appeared the day before, sent by Patricia. The nurse collects the fallen petals into her fists and slips them into her pocket. "I've got time to introduce you around," she continues, moving toward the closet, into which CeCe had spent the better part of twenty minutes pushing the wheelchair. "How about it?"

CeCe waits—for some serene largess to fill her spirit, but this

Dotty, whom she is already sure she should avoid, this Dotty's name has cluttered her mind. She imagines Dotty smiling from the crinkled pillow with a dreary, dearie bed wisdom, accepting each pill with a darting pink eye.

"I'm indisposed," CeCe says. "I'm expecting my son. And my daughter."

A lie. She's not expecting her daughter. Patricia—Seattle one-half the year, Rio the other, a senior Web producer for an urban-planning group specializing in the protection and modernization of favelas. With the *woman*, her wife, Lotta, Lotta the famous architect, six-foot Lotta wearing sneakers and a diver's watch. Patricia is pregnant and will come to visit on her own time, or not at all. She was surprised Pat called so early in the pregnancy—twelve weeks along now—and while their conversation was short and strenuously cheerful, it gave CeCe more hope than she's had in years. Their fight, over a decade gone, was nonsense, ostensibly about CeCe's moving out of New York after 9/11, retreating to Stockport, filling two unused spaces in the garage with pallets of Evian. Pat, stalking out the front door, calling CeCe a coward and a limousine liberal. CeCe, waving furiously in the direction of the garage, shouting, "There's no limousine in there, you simple-minded—it's water!" The true, unspoken fight being about CeCe's disparagement of Pat's then-girlfriend, particularly her lip-pierce, and CeCe's suggestion that Pat was dating women to get attention and to be special, as she hadn't yet found any other way to be special. That was the unkind phrase she'd used. Maybe even this wasn't the true quarrel, but something without incident or word. Prideful, Pat. Like herself in this respect. It spun away from them and in the end they'd said too much to forget but not enough to continue. Pat and Lotta, together five years, but Lotta, too busy for George's wedding, apparently— CeCe has only seen her in pictures.

Along with the tulips, Pat has sent a stuffed sheep wearing an old-fashioned wimple that she must have ordered from the Internet. The sheep stands on the dresser among the petals that have already fallen since the nurse tidied up, as if in its own small field. There's something indecent—she hates its fuzzy face. She doesn't want to be introduced to anyone, even a Dotty, under such circumstances. A toy, flowers—pain is felt only when pain is felt! Unlike fear, or lust, or sadness, which a person can borrow, which in health she'd borrowed from the arts—happily, without consequence. In the old days, she'd screened movies in the pool house. The projector at one end of the pool, the screen at the other, the light beaming over the water in a thick moated shaft. The lapping, upside-down reflection of the film in the turquoise deepend, the ladies clustered along the tile edge of the pool, holding their glasses at the stems—no one hosted better. No one, Nan said once, kissing her goodbye, her bark of a laugh, except Truman. CeCe couldn't argue with that.

"Nurse," CeCe says. "Could I have the bed shifted? Or could we have someone move that sheep?"

"Back hurts? That's new for you or a regular thing?"

"Not my back, the sheep."

"Isn't that cute? Look at his hat. He's here to watch after you when I'm not around. What a nice gift."

The nurse snakes her arm behind CeCe's shoulders and heaves her in an expert, cursory embrace. CeCe finds her face pressed into the woman's cleavage. It smells like spearmint and tobacco. The nurse wedges a pillow into the vexed hollow between the sheet and her spine. The pillow causes an unnatural arch in her back. The angle affords her an improved view of the sheep.

"I'd like to rest." CeCe closes her eyes, trading the room for darkness. "In the meantime, could you see that someone gets hold of my son?"

No answer, but she feels—her wrist lifted at the pulse. The audacity! She won't open her eyes until this woman's gone. She hears the nurse counting under her breath, then calling to someone in the hallway.

"Yes, she's good . . . No, can you get me a Diet Coke?"

With her eyes still closed CeCe says, "Don't call me she. It's rude. Pronouns are for the absent. I'm right here."

This is no place to be. She can't stay. She'll stay. The drug will work. She'll not fade at home, shrink the house she loves to a few rooms. Spoil it with a bed put on the first floor and guardrails along the walls and a plastic stand-up tub with a low plastic gate swinging like a pigpen's, with guest rooms turned into nurses' rooms as the private-care consultant, six months before, had diagrammed in lusty red ink over the blue floor plan of her home. Mrs. Baker had recommended the consultant, had used him at her father's place.

"That house," CeCe had said to George, "is taken over by girls dressed as nurses, trying to get their visas! I don't blame them but I don't want them." She suspected these girls handled Mr. Baker rough or kind as they chose, emboldened by their own private histories, more epic than the epic of his illness. Nor will she have her society visited upon her, peering in at how she and the house have shrunk—sutured, shuttered. She doesn't want her people to see her like this. She'll recover in private and return to resume her full life as if she'd never left.

She turns away from the nurse and opens her eyes to the curtains billowing in the open French doors, the bright morning between the curtains, a flip-book—green grass, a man cutting the hedge bordering the lake. The landscaper, wearing overalls and slick with sweat, working the shears. A bit close to the window! Tufts of vegetation fly. She hears the grind of a chain saw in the trees across the lake. There must be a crew. By the interval work of the saw, she imagines the tree's rings tell back three hundred years. A blimp hangs above the treetops. The lake is smooth and bright—a fine view, no one lied about that. But how can it be that pain has brought her here?

The nurse is petting her arm. "Hey, now. Let's get you dressed."

"I am dressed." She gestures with exasperation to her outfit, one she'd carefully planned—a silk pantsuit, taupe with a green stripe, unstructured but chic, with a tie at the collarbone. In this context, however, expensive as it is, she sees how it might be mistaken for pajamas. "If you thought I wasn't dressed, why on earth did you open the curtains? Pull them shut!"

The man in overalls stops his work and glances up, incurious. To him she is a neck corkscrewed into a pillow. He nods, maybe to her, maybe to himself, and turns back to his work. "Pull the curtain," she says again. "And go!"

The nurse draws in her breath. CeCe remembers herself and adds, "Aren't you a dear. I should have said please. I should have said thank you. Thank you for coming. A pleasure. Do come again. Now I'd like to change clothes alone. Fetch me anything, no—the green one; there, and the jewelry from the top drawer. Allow an old lady a point of pride. Yes, that's a good girl."

"Make sure to eat," the nurse says, nodding toward the tray, and leaves.

Cece turns her attention to the tray. Has she ever before laid eyes on such a terrible breakfast? Muffins made a million at a time, probably by pistons! Eggs, scrambled to jelly. George will call. She would like one of the breakfasts of her youth, brought up to her as it was each morning on a tray, through the cavernous, clicking lobby of this or that hotel when she accompanied her father on business, those summers before school and before he remarried. After John Stepney's death, her father took over the company, and by the time she was born he'd bought and sold scores of rubber plantations, by then in South Asia—over port, under ivory, in the backseats of embassy cars. Before her enrollment at Miss Porter's, he'd dragged her all across the map, though most winters she remained in New York City with the staff. The traveling months provided few objects of comfort or permanence, a reason, perhaps, she grew into an adult with convictions about routine. Such as: breakfast should consist of runny eggs poached with vinegar, butter pastry, chocolate in a silver pot. Where else but on a tray arranged by invisible hands does one find and acquire a taste for the tasteless kiwi? All her life, until today, she's begun her mornings more or less thus.

Her father. She misses and hardly remembers her father. Georgie had taken the helm as John Stepney became ill. At least John's death, the family maintained, spared him the pain of witnessing his business erode as his son adjusted haltingly to responsibility, and as the economy buckled: the Amazonian rubber market began its collapse in 1912. Georgie and his brothers neglected the plantations—empty jungle, ghost shelters, overgrown tracks. The tens and the twenties of the new century, they enjoyed a gentleman's business, content with the diminished Amazon-based company and the Connecticut processing factories. Georgie was a playboy, a buyer of fantastical properties, a commissioner of musical reviews, a collector of actresses at the Barrow Street Playhouse, famous for his charm, his bootlegged parties, his brokering of unusual alliances, his generosity to politicians on all sides, the ruined women in his wake. But saner than his brothers. The Somners had mostly left the game by the rubber-market spike of the First World War. Oldsmobile and Ford contracted to other manufacturers. Georgie did eventually get into the manufacture of sneakers, a new kind of footwear that wasn't catching on. He never told her what focused his ambition, but in the decade preceding the Second War, Georgie shifted from South America to South Asia—importing rubber from Malaysia and Sri Lanka for processing in Naugatuck. (Rubber, natural rubber, had long before left South America in the coat of a man named Wickham, who smuggled the seeds of the tree to England. Soon the tree grew in Malaysia, in Africa, and every other tropical destination England controlled or could broker with.)

Then, the Second War. The war needed rubber wheels to roll on. Rubber for the bandage companies, rubber for the hospitals, rubber for the boot makers, and rubber for the planes. When the Japanese threatened the Pacific theater, along with all its rubber trees, the Somners' dormant Brazilian plantations became vital to the effort. Georgie remanned them. At the same time, in Naugatuck, Somner Chemical collaborated in the government's initiatives for the better development of synthetic rubber, so that issues of territory might never again jeopardize U.S. production.

This is why there must be some mistake, her, stuck in this room. Another mistake—the nurse neglected to pull the curtain before she made her escape, and the man's still working outside. She can hear the snip of his shears. She won't change out of her suit after all.

The chain saw cuts off. Maybe she really will try to rest, now that the racket's stopped, now that the dresser is clear of petals, now that she's decided she won't touch the tray, will never eat from such a tray. She'll see what they do for lunch.

10

At the sight of the door swinging open, Iris's heart leaps. She's missed George! She didn't know how much, until this instant. She throws her arms around him. She gives him a multitude of indiscriminate kisses—side of mouth, eyelid, underside of chin, side of the head, each trailing an exclamation as if he's returned from some distant expedition. "It's you! What the hell! You handsome dummy! Why are you here?"

"Oh, my, God," he says, dropping his bag and shrugging his crumpled linen jacket to the floor. "My poor mother. I've never felt so tested, been asked— Victor, how are you? Didn't see you there. Sorry to interrupt. Good to see you. Don't you look well."

How kind George is, even when he's exhausted and probably wanted to come home to her alone. Helping his mother, asking after Victor. Always putting other people's cares above his own. Abruptly and formally, she steps back and shakes his hand. They all laugh. Away only a few days and he's new to her again—how well made he always looks, his easy, strong-shouldered grace, the color in his cheeks, his features firm and lively. She loves how his sharp green squint suggests something rude or reckless meant only for her. How he runs his hands through his flop of hair, how she should remind him to get a haircut, but not to let them cut it short. She even likes the slack way he tossed his jacket down, the way he takes over the room. He picks the jacket up and folds it over the back of the chair. It is the same one he'd handed her to check at the golf club. These things—the chair, the jacket—belonging to her more as time goes on. She loves how he shifts his weight, his gaze dashing from her to Victor with a look like guilt, like the anxious kid he says he was: so respectful of rules he spent his childhood certain he'd just broken one. She can see he had a hard time at Oak Park. Only as good a person as George. Once he told her that if suffering is the precondition for sympathy, and sympathy is the precondition for love, then love required the continued suffering of the loved one. She wasn't sure she understood. She'd poked him in the ribs and said, "Smart garbage, Dr. Professor," but thought about it for days. It *was* smart, but too smart to be true, and neither of them could possibly believe it. He told her it was only with her that he's been able to cast off the world. Honest to a fault. She loves that he always looks the same, always like himself.

"But, George," she says, "where are your shoes?"

"Ah," says Victor, "they were so in love, the sky stuck to them. Now what's that from?" He's rolling up the blue leash, hooking his travel mug to his belt, tucking the gold chain under his shirt. "I'm well, thank you, George."

"I hope you are! If a man of the country like you isn't well, we're all in trouble!" George cries, crossing the room to slap Victor on the back. Something about this is unlike George, she thinks. CeCe must have put him through the ringer.

"I hope we are *all* well," George continues. "The kind of trial I just endured reminds a person—"

" 'A man of the country'?" Victor asks.

"You know, so skilled with the dog, and the hiking and exercising and being so handy and capable and, for example, this arm"—George thumps Victor's arm—"rugged as barbed wire, not babysitting a desk like me, not babysitting, what?—*ideas*. No, you've a certain rusticity I wouldn't even aspire to."

"A what? What did you say?" Iris asks, looking not at George but to Victor, who turns sharply at the word.

A look passes between them. What are they saying? They are conferring without any need for language, like twins, or house cats. George suspects her—not of adultery, no, certainly not, probably not, but of having a bond with this man that he can't guess. "Believe me, it's a compliment. I'm jealous of guys like you. Keeping it simple. Balance and all."

Victor presses his lips together, but George is certain he is saying something important, getting to a truth overlooked. "Needing so little, none of this plastic feel-better we allow to pile up around us." He waves in the general direction of the large, chrome espresso maker he recently put on the AmEx, a delightful machine that reminds him of a Victorian train. "When the earth is nothing but fire and garbage and drought, it will be people like me relying on people like you for our survival! And I bet no one had to teach you the things you know. I bet you just know them. I bet you could survive out of doors for a week without help. I bet you were born with all the wisdom and courage you ever needed. And good on you."

"Thank you. I'm sure that isn't true."

"Incapable of lying too! Convincingly, anyway. I wish my office had guys like you. But you don't find 'em like this on the elevator going up." He stops, for Iris has put her arms around him again.

Victor disappears into the mudroom.

"Hon," she says, "I didn't think you were coming until tonight. Sit, sit down, how are you back so early?"

"I missed you too much."

"How was it—wait, let's see if Victor needs anything. Victor?"

"It was," George says, not waiting for a reply from the other room, "the worst thing in the world! But I got through it. I had to be strong for my mother. And for you and for us! I looked it straight in the eye. Hospitals make a person sick. Hospitals convince you by their smell that you are dying! I'm especially sensitive to that. You look extra beautiful today. I got you a present. It's outside. It's weird. It's a joke. I'll give it to you later."

"You helped your mother," she says, putting her hand on his cheek.

"Anyone would do the same."

"Speaking of, Pat called. She wants to know how it went."

Victor returns, wearing his backpack. 3D clicks in behind him on long black nails, and after several turns, arranges himself in a doughnut on top of the folded massage table. "That's all for today?"

"Yes," Iris replies. "Victor, we need to pay you."

"Not excited to see me, is he?" George says, nodding at the dog.

"I tired him out this morning. Lots of running," Victor says. "In the woods. Where we primitive folk track lunch."

"Pardon?" George says.

"3D's made a pile of sticks by the tree out front. We've been monitoring its progress. We think 3D is very advanced. Did you see it?" Iris asks quickly.

"He's a smart dog," Victor says.

"No, I didn't."

"It's way too late for this." Iris gestures to her sweatshirt and gym clothes and heads for the stairs. "I'm getting dressed."

George opens the front door. Victor scoots the dog off the massage table.

"Nice balloons," Victor says, nodding at the tree.

Iris calls down, "See you Thursday!"

"I almost forgot." George opens and closes his wallet. "Let me get my checkbook, I'm out of cash, been on the road—be right back."

He heads down the hall to his study, which he is looking forward to seeing—the vintage poster in its gilt frame of Verdi's *Aida* at the Teatro La Fenice, a watercolor rendering of Wagner's debut of *Parsifal*. To have caught his wife in the attitude she strikes when he is not around is not a bad way to spend a morning. Every window a mirror, every mirror a window: as a boy, he was sure that when he turned away from his image, that other George remained, the opposite-facing-he was still *in there*, the broken twin, receding out the door of that room, down the street into that world, and that one day his two halves might suddenly reunite and merge, like one drop of water absorbing another. Or like the Rorschach butterflies the psychiatrists held up to him from time to time.

He enters his study and sits behind the desk. Cool and dark. He opens the drawer, looks at the blue checkbook, closes the drawer. He sits a minute longer, gently bouncing the back of his chair, humming the overture to *The Burning Papers*, picturing the standing ovation, the lights finally coming up in the theater, and still the crowd remains. He plots a last addition to the libretto. After he vanquishes the queen, UH will avenge himself against the eunuch to whom, in error, he'd entrusted his purest harem wife. George leaves the office and walks quietly back down the hall. Outside the window by the door, the same window he'd stood at looking in, Victor waits under the tree. The branch to which George tied the balloons almost brushes Victor's neck, lest George forget Victor is the taller man. The folded massage table rests against his leg, the mug at his hip.

"Hang on another minute," George says softly through the glass. Victor holds his hand up and nods.

There are decisions a man may make, if he's got the nerve. George goes upstairs.

"All taken care of," he says, and begins to undress Iris. "You are the best person ever."

"Oh," she says, and she's everywhere, all around him—legs at his back, arm around his neck. She covers his mouth and covers his eyes, one hand timid, the other brave, and in his mind's eye, in the dark behind his wife's hand, in front of the front door, Victor waits beside 3D's twigs, the mosquitoes rising in the muggy heat, the mosquitoes in full float and menace. Victor looks at his watch, for he probably has another client all the way in the east end and the hour approaches— soon the bell of the town church will ring and the question is, will Victor leave without his money? Iris, George is holding Iris. She exhales, her languid hand at the base of his spine, and the heat outside must by now be getting to Victor, knitting a fine beaded net of moisture across his forehead. George has the sudden bright idea of going clamorous and audible, here beside the open bedroom window, and now she is using him, delightful! He hears a shy knock at the front door. Maybe, he can't be sure. Again she covers his eyes and all he can see is her foot as it pushes off the floorboards, the weight transferring from him to her foot and down and he flings the clothes still bunched around her hips over her head and her hands lift to the wall, to the bedside lamp, which topples but does not fall, though the sound brings the dog, the dog circles them and she cries, "Go!" And the dog does go, down the stairs, bank, plunk, bank, plunk, pink, pink, pink, and, oh, how he sees Victor's hands are twisting, twisting with what to do. Surrender his fee or interrupt them and appear the peeping Victor, a lurker of the hedge—*Something's wrong with him*, George will say, and—ah, here is a bright pain, a stinging purple nova ricocheting off the anterior wall of his eye socket, for his wife has managed to kick him and they are laughing and then he is obliterated and forgets Victor and everything else and finds himself leaning on her warm back, her ribs, her heart, and she looks at him over her shoulder and her teeth are white and she says his face is rough and he apologizes, and he says, *I am, I am, I am*, and she says, *I want you to* or *I want you too*. He's holding his pounding eye against the damp hair at the nape of her neck and she says, *Do what I say and I say do it* so he yanks her back by the hair and she hears a car firing up and pulling out of the drive, but Victor's already left, hasn't he? It must be a trick of sound, a car at the neighbors' down the road.

Looking vaguely at her husband's ankle as they lie next to each other in the bed, Iris realizes what Victor was about to tell her. Victor wants to buy a house. He's always asking about the market. His wife loved their house in Maine. He still loves his wife. How pained he looked, when he said Isabel left him. How he smiled when he tried to imitate her accent.

Yes, he'd been warming up to asking her advice all morning. *How's the Vargas place?* he'd asked. A house to win back his wife. George came home at just the wrong moment. Now Victor won't need to tell her outright—she'll offer her help. They are friends. She imagines Victor's wife, this woman from New Zealand, getting out of a taxi, an antarctic eye and a red mouth turned up to Victor. She climbs the steps from the sidewalk, Victor at the door to their new home, opening his arms. She forgives Victor for all that came between them in the dark days. Iris even knows the house. *I have a couple of ideas,* she imagines herself saying. *But there's this one place I want you to see.*

11

In the dark, her arm and leg sprawl heavily across his torso. Her breath is loud in sleep. She *is* the best person, not simply the one he happens to love. He trusts her even with the stories in which he is not the hero. He tries not to shift and wake her. Earlier that day, after they'd left the bed, eaten cold spaghetti, swum and watched television and swum again and drunk screwdrivers and cooked a chicken and watched a movie and returned to bed but couldn't sleep, he found himself describing his life at thirteen to her, and he finds himself waking her now, to tell her the rest of his story, for only Iris understands how awkward and unappealing he felt as a young man, how miserable they were in the house on the Sound, how he came to music. Not George, remember? Edward George. Called Edward. He hated the name—the way his mother would stretch it out into a bossy song of ownership. No one at school would shorten it. To be anything but a boy with the name of an old lord! His grandfather, his namesake, dead sixty years. Edward George knew his grandfather only from the darkly caked oil portrait he avoided as if the man in the black coat might lean out and steal his breath. In the portrait, Edward George senior—Georgie— held a newspaper, his thumb angled toward the date. He looked like a snapping tortoise—yellow, imperious, weary. Razor-eyed, clever but not wise. Like a man who, without ever a sudden motion, got what he wanted by force. A replica of the painting hung at Town Hall in Newport.

Edward George II dreaded Saturday mornings at Booth Hill, the hour of his weekly piano lesson, for the portrait waited opposite the Steinway grand, in a formal parlor of black and white marble, green velvet curtains, and views of the sea. (Until he left for boarding school, George spent weeks in New York City and weekends and summers in Stockport.) His teacher, bony Mr. Foley, kind, and frail as parchment. They spent much of each lesson protecting the piano from themselves: Foley combating fits of allergy and George, a sufferer of anxious nose- bleed, widening his eyes at the first drop of blood on the keys. In all, six ancestral portraits watched him play. Edward George's brother Junius. Junius's wife, Constance, whose eyes were crossed. John Stepney and Fanny hung in the center: John Stepney with a green squint like George's, so handsome it couldn't be a lie. Fanny, warm and solid, with a crinkled bow for a mouth suggesting she thought portrait-sitting funny. CeCe liked to point out the National Women's Suffrage Asso- ciation sash in Fanny's hands. Next to Edward was CeCe herself, in a later, lighter style, as a girl of seven, in a pale blue tunic and a puff- sleeved blouse, sitting at a three-quarter turn, looking out a window.

He didn't practice much. Disobedience was unlike him; he blamed it on the piano's location. Usually, he made a great effort in the com- pany of adults, his most common company—obliging a simple ar- rangement of Mozart's Sonata in F Major at parties, tooling through the crowd with an ice bucket and tongs. It followed that he was also a child of lonesome vice—a tearer of butterfly wings, an exploder of gar- den snails, a fearless explorer of the inside of his nose, a bully of cats and babies momentarily unattended, a pounder of fish tanks, a leaver of cultish rock piles and relocated goose shit on driveways, a nighttime weeper, a sufferer of crippling neurasthenic stomachache, a child en- gaged in regular, silent, pleading prayer. He'd learned to pray at school, his mother being of the conviction that religion was for people willing to trade reason for comfort, who couldn't handle their affairs in private. He prayed in case his mother erred. He suspected God's absence might be a deficiency not of the cosmic order but rather of his own little spirit. For fear of being overheard and made fun of, he would bury his face in the damask of the bed and, tasting its dry thread, begin thus: "Hello, God, I don't think you exist, but if you're listening right now, I guess you do and I'm sorry for doubting you. Pat called me a phony today. Can you lightning her? Please, please, let me wake up as somebody else. Anybody. I leave it up to you."

He didn't dare hope God's big ear was bent toward him, but he did have the uncanny sensation he was being listened to—through the wall or the door by someone in the house. By Esme, or a ghost—Fanny, maybe, or even Constance, peering out of her picture with gritted mirth. There was something derelict in letting so much desire escape into the world. God or no God, it was hopeless either way. Either his skepticism and his shame had offended everybody in heaven and they'd voted he did not merit reward. Or if he were correct in doubting the possibility of anything so stupid and awesome as guardians with feathered wings and bright light and sitting down to munch on golden cakes with your favorite Heroes from History in chairs built of cloud and a benevolent father who knew all about you, then too his wish would not be granted.

Once he asked CeCe why there wasn't a picture of her mother on the wall.

"There isn't one I know of," she said. Evelyn, nineteen when Cecilia was born and her father fifty-seven: a middle marriage, hasty and brief.

And what about her father's first wife, Edith, or Gloria, his third?

"In storage," she answered.

And why wasn't there a picture of his dad?

"Portraits were out of style by then. Imagine, asking an abstractionist to sit for a portrait! What a suggestion, dear! Walter would've hated it. I wish I had. But those are his." She'd pointed to two tiny indecipherable ink drawings tucked behind a fat wucai vase, low on a display shelf on the opposite wall, and reminded him that if he was lucky, and so far he was lucky indeed, he would grow into a bearing like his grandfather's, steady as steel.

He did indeed grow into a certain steadiness. He didn't swear or horse around. Didn't laugh much. By boarding school, at Choate, forty minutes from weekends at Booth Hill, he stopped laughing altogether. He did not understand that when girls referred to him as "brooding," it might be to his advantage. For many years they left him to his imagination; weekends home he'd sit on the same damask edge of the mahogany four-poster bed where he used to pray. He kept on the night-light. For practical purposes—in no way did he still believe monsters hung in his shirts behind his closed closet door. In his diary he wrote, *I keep the light on only to write this and also because it is an antique of some historical importance.* The light, a French globe issued during the Crimean War, had been retrofitted with a bulb through a hole in Antarctica. It cast an amber glow in the darkness. From the bed he saw Africa—saw-toothed, divvied by an earlier time, with a misleading proximity to the sideways scrawl of the beautiful word *Persia.* He was hopeful. He was ready. They were ready—a Susan or a Catharine or a Penelope, the choicest girls from school. One would fall into the grass. Once, in Persia-Africa, but usually at the corner of the field-hockey field. He would slay her, excellently. Unless he became distracted, worrying that Esme or another might enter his room, and the reaching hand of Susan or Catharine or Penelope, reaching out of the darkness, the dark grass, a simple thing he wanted, would mangle with the scrubbing hand of Esme. "Wrong!" he would say to the bedpost, and Susan or Catharine or Penelope would dissolve behind the clattering interference like snow-static on the television when a storm hit the wire.

"Edward!" they would cry into the abandoned field-hockey field. "Edward, where are you? Where did you go? I'm all alone! Are you alone too?"

"Yes!" he would call, his hand on the post, his wet eye falling on the globe. "I am!" But he could only picture the dark trees and the grass, not the girl. Staring at the ceiling, unable to sleep, he couldn't help noting that his thoughts of Susan had led to Esme, and Esme had lead to his mother, and he was doomed.

One Friday evening, he looked across the dinner table at his sister's sad-horse face. Patricia and his mother weren't speaking again, typical in Patricia's fourteenth year, his twelfth. George was used to filling the silence, turning to one and then the other, summarizing notable items from the newspaper or inflated anecdotes of his adventures at school, but that day, after PE, a bruiser named Shelia had grabbed his jaw and jammed a Chinese jack almost down his throat, chanting, *Deadward, Deadward, Deadward!* At dinner, looking into his glass of bluish milk, he decided he did want to die, in the uninformed but certain way twelve-year-olds do. Pat and his mother were fighting about Patricia's barnyard—in a far corner of the back garden so that no visitor could see or hear, Pat kept potbellied pigs, ducks, two lambs, a snake. Earlier that week, six ducks of a special breed had arrived from North Carolina. CeCe told Patricia they would be the last of any live import. Patricia was soon to transfer to a new high school, farther away, for girls inclined toward misadventure. On their plates that night was duck. Not a back-garden duck, but his mother was making a point. He looked at Patricia's long horse face, the sparkling-blue eye powder she'd grudgingly been permitted, her crimped hair hanging over the uneaten duck, felt the rough scratch at the back of his throat, and said:

"The sick thing is flying a duck to us inside a plane when a plane is an imitation of a duck."

"Edward," his mother said, "have you entered your dark period? No one appreciates sarcasm over food. Could you two coordinate? Patricia, please finish up with your dark period before Edward enters his. I can't handle both."

"Mother," Patricia said. She turned to Edward. "Edward, are you feeling okay? Was school better this week?"

In his diary: *Patricia is my hero. Except when she is a giantshitmonkey.*

"School was fine. School was great. I climbed the rope in gym. I aced my finals. I have a million friends. May I be excused?"

"You had finals?" CeCe asked.

"Liar. They're not for another month. And he needs a math tutor."

"It wasn't a lie. It was a joke."

"If you knew how to tell a joke, you'd know that wasn't one," his sister said.

"Yes," CeCe said, "you may be excused."

Edward trudged into the dark garden. He decided to look at the new ducks; maybe there were babies. It would be helpful to have a father at this sort of time. He thought this so often it was like a wheel groove running though the middle of his head, deep and worn and hardened, dividing every other thought he had, making everything more difficult than it needed to be. His mother said Walter was a kind and decent man, but not to be contacted. She said his early work occasionally auctioned at Sotheby's, which was something to be proud of. He was probably still in Antibes; while the distance between them was sad, it was not an occasion to be sad. Theirs was a lack but not a blight, she concluded. Most children suffered some greater hardship. She shook her head in a way that meant if Walter were to live with them, it would be worse, which George did not understand if the man were so kind and decent and talented.

The ducks honked, butted his shins, begged noisily for grub. There were no babies. His sister's animals only interested him when he was missing his father, because Patricia, who had a watercolor memory of the man Edward had been too young to know, said it was Walter who'd assembled the petting zoo. He'd taught her to care for the animals and love them and how caring and loving were not the same. She told Edward this one night they were still young enough to be friends. He crept into her room and sat on the edge of the bed and shook her big knuckly feet until she woke and asked her what their dad had been like. In her half sleep she said, "He sang to me and got the animals, other stuff like that."

"You're so lucky. Was he great?"

"I think he was. It's her fault. I don't remember."

"Why did he go?"

"I dunno."

"But you were there. She did it?"

"I heard her say 'fucking fucks.' "

"No! Mother?"

"Shhh! Yes." He crawled to the top of the bed and lay his head below her mouth, to hear better. "I was behind the couch. She thought I was outside playing with Nanny. She was at the rolltop. Her face was practically stuck in the cubbies. She was writing something. Then she went to her bedroom for like a week. After that she was in the city, but we stayed here. I missed a month of school. When she got back, she said it would just be us."

"We missed school? We've never missed school!"

"No, I did. You were too little. We went to Esme's house."

"Esme's house? Why did we go there?"

"Mother took me to school in the morning instead of Dad. Esme was with me in the back. But I didn't stay at school. Mother said something to the teacher and we got back in the car, but Mother got into another car and Esme drove our car home. Mother called us the next day, but then she had to go, because 'here come the suits.' I didn't get it, but they were keeping us out of the news. Big gossip divorce. And I'm not sure, but I think right before he left, Dad switched all my ducks. I know that's crazy. But we were in the city, and when we came back, they weren't the same ones. They looked the same, but Maudie, my favorite, didn't act like Maudie. She snubbed me every time I tried to feed her. And Princess Cassiopeia was tiny and spotty and had been in love with Peter Pan, but then she wasn't any of those things anymore. For a long time I thought he took the old ducks with him to remember me. Shut up, I was little."

Edward lay down in the grass. The ducks had given up on a feeding and waddled idly; one bent to groom Edward's hair but soon realized her mistake and rushed away. He heard Esme call him to dessert several times. Finally she tromped out into the garden, smoothing her apron. Though his eyes were closed, he could hear her shape in her step: solid as a doorstop, one leg dragging a little, the scarred knee hidden under her gray skirt.

"*Pequeño* Edward, your mother wants to know why you are not back at the table. It's table time." Her hair, back tight, stretched her brow above her pocketed eyes.

"You tell her," he said without opening his eyes, "she has to come get me. Not you. You tell her I ate breakfast and I ate lunch and I ate dinner and Javier lets me buy candy on the drive home because I'll tell lies about him if he doesn't, so he lets me. Look! I broke my tooth on a Gobstopper last week and nobody noticed. I am full. You tell her."

Esme shook her head. "You want to get me in trouble too? I made macaroni special for you and your sister, as extra, a secret, for later in the kitchen. Come."

"I will not."

"Okay, we'll stay one minute and you can answer a grammar question for me like you do."

He hated her for comforting him. It would never be enough.

She brought out the small notebook she carried in her pocket and flipped to a page. "You are very helpful. When somebody says, 'This will have been' in English, what time do they mean?"

He didn't know the answer. He suspected, even worse, that she did. He sat up, and in an ugly knockoff of her accent he said, "I think that is an e-specially advanced question, Esme. More e-special than your macaroni. I think you should be focusing on the basics. You think you're doing me a favor? You're always in my room. You're paid to be here. I can't stand anybody, and that includes you."

He loved her as much as circumstance allowed; she had been kinder to him than anyone else.

"Edward, I've known you since you are small. Small enough, I forgive you for being a *pendejo.*" She turned back to the house.

(*Dear nobody,* he wrote that night, *I spit on purpose and it went on her leg!*)

"Shelia said I am an asshole. But I am not an asshole," he cried after her, and trembled at using the word out loud. But it didn't count to use it on some old no-person. "I am not the asshole, I am the monster!" he shouted, and closed his eyes. When he opened them, his mother was squinting over him in the dark.

"Edward, what do you think you are up to?"

"I am thinking where my father is."

"You are wondering where your father is, or you are thinking,

Where is Father? Clarity is half the battle. To the point, you treated Esme wickedly. I could see it in her step."

"Stupid." He hid his face from her. "George is an asshole name like Edward is an asshole name, but I like it better. Don't you, Cecilia? I am George!" The sting of her hand spread across his cheek, but he didn't flinch.

"Don't be smart," she said, trying to yank him up by the wrists. When this did not work—if he knew how to play anything, it was dead—she dropped them. Through his slit eye he watched her put her face in her hands and laugh.

"Who cares, anyway," he said.

"Look where I am. I am in this pen with you. At dinnertime. You know how this muck depresses me. We'll call you George for a month and see if we like it. But only if you come in, because Patricia will not eat without you. Will you come have dessert?"

"Yes."

"Whatever you did to Esme, you will apologize."

Now, so many years later, he hardly thinks of this time. When he's asked why he goes by his middle name, he tells the story that he came upon Esme sitting under a tree, sad about some news from home. She misses her home still, after all the years. He comforts her as only he can. He gets her to laugh, and laughing, she calls him George Edward instead of Edward George. It surprises them both and they laugh some more. Once they compose themselves, they go back inside and everyone sits down to cake and the new name sticks. George did apologize to Esme, but her face was closed to him ever after. That year, CeCe allowed him to give up the piano.

He tells Iris every old detail that springs to mind, maybe because he hasn't told her about the bank. She nods and makes noises and smiles at his youthful despair and frowns when he describes how his mother treated him and Patricia, and when he is through, she murmurs, half-asleep, "You freaks. I have my stories, but not like that," and pulls him close.

12

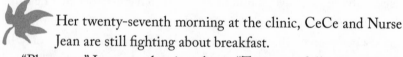Her twenty-seventh morning at the clinic, CeCe and Nurse
Jean are still fighting about breakfast.

"Please try," Jean says, leaning closer. "Too many full trays go back
and they recommend appetite stimulants. I've never had a patient
enjoy those. Make your heart knock around and your hands sweat.
And what a thirst! Much worse than a few bites of muffin and egg.
Muffin? Here."

Their morning routine. The nurse takes her vitals, doses out the
pills, checks the cleanliness of CeCe's station, pulls her limbs various
directions, tells her all the nice things she can do outdoors as long as
the weather holds. The possibilities indoors too. This evening, some
soul-annihilating jamboree in honor of Bastille Day. "Songs in French,"
the nurse explains. "I didn't know what Bastille Day was. Happy Bastille Day!"

CeCe takes the spoon from the nurse's outstretched hand and helps
herself to three bites of the gray scramble. The nurse squeezes CeCe's

feet through the light blanket. It is odd and unpleasant to be made so aware of one's feet while eating.

"This should be a fork," she says, and sets the spoon down. She'd awoken inside the well of a wild thrash, soaked in sweat. The nurse prattles away, ticking along the wide, dusty road of the daily schedule: what time the doctor will stop in, when the physical therapist arrives, when the afternoon nurse takes over the hall, what's good for television. She recommends a reality show about a rodeo, ranch hands competing for prizes under the high sky. Birdpoison, brainrot. Limited, doltish girl. CeCe nods and smiles.

George called and apologized the day after he left, though he made no comprehensible excuse. She was brave, complained only a little, asked him to bring a few items up, forgave him. He complimented her adaptability and said he had a phone conference coming on the other line. He'd call right back. They've spoken four times since. Each time, he's quicker to sign off. He says he's coming to visit, but doesn't say when. His voice, an armor of impatient cheer. This week, he hasn't returned any of her calls. Hardly anyone's called. Nan, last week, but CeCe forbade her to come. "I'll be home sooner than you could get here," she said to Nan. She's spoken with Esme to ask about the house. And about George, if he seems off—Esme, the only person who knows enough to understand this question. Esme said George seemed fine. Pat called once and complained about morning sickness and brain fog, delayed a visit. CeCe answered she didn't remember being impaired by pregnancy in the slightest. Pat sends flowers every week, but they haven't spoken again. Just enough and not enough. Just like Pat. Good Annie Mason's kept her up on the fund's doings every Friday as planned, but CeCe has not allowed those conversations to stray beyond business. She will never let the invalid and the philanthropist coexist. The business of charity becoming, so suddenly, her only remote gratification. Whole days have gone by when she hasn't spoken to a soul beyond the doctors and this tobacco-smelling nurse. Today's the day. I'll call George and demand he come. Right away, and that he bring proper drapes.

The nurse lays out a quilted, blue kimono, pulls the curtain, admonishes her to eat a few more bites from the breakfast tray, and is gone. Twenty-seven days. Though, what is the date? Where's the newspaper, did they take it away before she read it? Look how again the nurse hasn't properly pulled the curtains. What will she do until lunch, now that she's swallowed the requisite boli of egg and pill, and the paper's missing?

She watches the landscaper through the gap between the curtains. Her hands knit and unknit independent of her will. She can't track what sets them off. She suspects it's her mood. Once at dinner, to Iris, George had actually said, "Don't excite Mother." CeCe had been chewing and bit her tongue instead of her food and put her hands in front of her face to hide the blood inside her mouth. How bitter the pith of aging is, and yet, when the tremors cease and when the pain subsides, how peaceful and vigorous she feels for a time. The pain's break like that other breaking, the marshaled adrenaline. In the hours after an episode she feels happy—lithe as a ten-ton seal, mean as a girl of twenty.

The storm fades into a dull zing up and down her arms. It's almost over. Her hands bird up in front of her. One brushes the tray. She adds a breath of her own strength to the alien motion and knocks the tray to the floor. The twitch and she can work together, now and again. Her hands drop and root through the sun-cut blankets. How satisfying! The orange tray is upside down. The egg glops across the floor. She considers the emergency buzzer, a red aureole set in a cube of gray plastic at the end of a cord placed on her bedside table. Is such a mess an emergency? What would she like for breakfast instead? Should she press the button? When she was a child, her father would allow her a sip of his coffee across the linen table of a hotel dining room. His face, severe and regular as a clock's. She misses him, she wishes she'd known him, she misses knowing what time it is. He was so tall, she only re-members him from below, the underside of his bearded chin like a rusty trowel, clearer in her memory than the shape of his nose. *My lone eaglet*, he called her once, as they sat facing each other on a rattling train. Her mother, dead by the time CeCe was old enough to look for her. Perhaps her father has come back into her mind so much of late because he too was ill, all the time he carted her around the continent.

As darkness stitched the windowpane, he would button his coat and leave her with one of a thousand foreign hotel maids to point to what she wanted. He told her to think of this as a game of charades. Whether the woman was French or Dutch or German, Cecilia became accustomed to taking care of herself by way of pantomime: to hold up her brush and cross her fingers meant *plait my hair*, to fold down the air above the unfamiliar pattern of the bedclothes meant for the maid to carry out this motion in the real. Weekends, her father was hers. She'd gather the wickets from the lawn, fertile and clipped, and behind her was a white umbrella, his white poplin pant leg. The skin of his large hand when it held hers was red and blistered and smelled oddly sweet. He hid his sickness well until the end. He comes back to her now with such clarity that the intervening years—her marriages, her children, her dabbling in—oh, what?—are like the drag of a slippered foot in someone else's room far down the well-lit hall.

Now only her pointer finger wiggles. Where it began a year ago. She'd been sitting alone at her writing desk, writing to the mayor about the noisy drift off the water, those noisy little boys from the sailing camp sailing into her cove. She was writing as she did almost every day, but soon her index finger felt thick around the pen, and her writing, the clerically dull phrase *noise pollution*, fell onto the page in a haphazard scuttle, as a spider drops off a table. She put down the pen and found the finger gesturing, an insistent come-here curl. She watched with incredulous detachment—the hand so far from her eye, independent of her will. The gesture didn't belong to her. It didn't immediately upset her. It reminded her of the stories Toto had read to her and she had read to George and Patricia: the cottage in the woods, the witch's coax to enter. Dear Toto, her nurse. Now, again she has a nurse.

She tries best to challenge fear with boredom. How much the twitching pain forces her to think about her body, she has long decided, is not a worthy use of time. *How boring*, she says, whenever she feels afraid. Her skin is ashen and dreary, and yet how much more sensitive it has become, the sheets as hard and variegated as braille. Lately, she can feel her lower lid rough against her eye. Tongue to roof of mouth, the strange metal of the blood pumping through the tongue. Iron, she guesses. And food! The passage of food down the throat. At least her speech hasn't slowed or become halting. Not yet.

Her body stills itself. She presses the buzzer. Why not? The phone rings. She explains about the tray. Soon a man knocks and sets to silently mopping the mess off the floor. He draws the curtains open before he leaves. She doesn't protest. She won't speak to a strange man while wearing pajamas. Next, a woman in candy stripes drops lunch beside her. Next again, the sun is lower in the sky, but the grass still shines. The time passes over her.

Her attending doctor, a young man with sharp cheekbones and shaggy hair, enters without knocking. This indecency jars her limbs, but not, thankfully, into an electrical storm. He's only surprised her. Which is more vexing, the arrogance of doctors or the ineptitude of nurses? He pats her hand and says, in a voice meant for Shakespeare's, or Eakins's, theater:

"How goes it? I hear we've had a rough day. Have we had a rough day? You're familiar with how we take the holistic view here. The emotional life—" He paces and poses as he speaks. He stops with abrupt drama and lowers his voice. He is young. "In anger, there is sadness. We have someone on staff you can talk to."

For a moment she feels she might—but then he smiles lavishly, in the way young men think they are doing old women a favor by flirting with them. He's enjoying himself. She doesn't care he's noticed her untouched lunch, a sandwich cut from cardboard.

"You are misquoting," she says, "a facile axiom about death, about a person's response to the news they are terminal. It's denial, anger, depression, bargaining, and then I don't remember. Besides, I am getting better."

"So, you're feeling better?" He picks up her chart, holding it between them. "A good response, Mrs. Somner. So far so good. Any new feelings you want to tell me about? More tremor, less? Change in strength, motor function, pain—more, less, different? Side effects? Headache? Nausea? Registering any side effects?"

"None. You are a resident?"

"And your energy?"

"Are you—" She sits up and takes the sandwich in her hands and lifts it as if she might take a bite. "Are you *learning* on me?"

She's had her effect. She sees him trying to hold his face, his authority, steady.

"Dr. Adams and I are working in tandem. You can rest assured."

"Schoolboy, dearest, I've been resting here *in*sured all week long." She's meant to shame him with wit, but he doesn't understand. Her embarrassment at this—even she could hear how her sentence wobbled to a halt—cretinous man! "Is it true that doctors no longer pay attention to the flesh-and-blood patient? That all your generation of medical people cares about is the bottom line? Now, Dr. Adams, would he be someone more senior? Would he perhaps provide me better treatment?"

"That's not how it works."

"I'm sure it isn't. But, what if you run along and find him anyway? The answer to all your questions is no. All's the same. If you are done with me for today, let's see if you and he can't make a switch."

"We don't really do consultations within—"

"What a good suggestion, dear. I would like to consult Dr. Adams. Don't forget to tell him my name. You need a reason that doesn't put you at fault. I know! Tell him I'm not eating." She smiles and takes a bite from the sandwich, chews it thoughtfully, and drops the remainder in the plastic trash pail beside the bed. She turns her head away from him to signal his dismissal. In the mirror of the open closet door she sees her scowling, patchy face. She thought she'd been smiling. In the mirror, the resident takes three steps backward and turns out the door.

The woman who says, "Sorry, no English," brings and then clears dinner. Then no one comes. The last light outside the windows fades. CeCe is full of the dread of night. *Boring*, she says, to no improvement. She can't sleep. The floating curtains slip and suck in and out of the French doors in the black breeze. Again, Nurse Jean has forgotten and left them ajar. The lake is bleak and blurs into the black trees of the woods behind. Every so often the doors bang and startle her. The wind pushes them open, revealing a wedge of damp, black lawn. The lake murmurs and the hedge looms. She turns her head the other way, but this puts in her sight the open closet—her clothing dangling from the hangers, the monster outline of the wheelchair, lurking in the dark.

She needs to be patient. It's hard to sleep in a place that isn't home. Tomorrow she'll set George straight.

Has she slept? She sits up in the bed, feeling as if a great hand is pushing her. She doesn't remember falling asleep, but it must be close to four in the morning. She is restless and feels strong enough to walk, stronger than she has in weeks. Is she imagining it? They said it would take time to accumulate in her blood. Even then, no guarantee. She is almost steady on her feet. She takes the phone in her hands and pulls it over to the chair. Iris answers. CeCe says, why no, she hadn't realized the time. She reminds Iris that absolutely no one has come to see her since George dropped her off; what has it been, a year? She flexes her free left hand and arm and watches it move by her will and feels its blood and matter. She uses her feeblest voice, but also her buried-treasure voice, and holds the phone away from her lips to make the guilty distance seem greater and guiltier still.

"It was so kind of George to take me by train when he preferred to go by car. I want to tell him he can pick me up by car—whichever car he likes. I'm all better, I'm better than ever! I've changed my mind. I just needed a rest. George will explain that I'll take the medicine at home, being so strong and well. I do hope he hasn't dumped me here for good, dear, don't you?"

In an eyes-shut voice Iris says, "How's the place? Same?"

"How has the place been, you mean? I'll tell you a story. You remember a lot of stories when you're lying around with nothing to do. My beloved father was once given by some corporate friends a wastebasket. For his birthday, for his office. Made entirely of gold. The wire lattice around the sides, the base that sat on the rug. Weighed a ton. I think it was part of some private joke those men had; they had a lot of private jokes. It sat in his office until he died. He used it too. I could see a naughty pleasure on his face each time he tossed a crumpled sheet of paper into the thing. A golden wastebasket still holds trash, doesn't it, dear!"

"Mmm, gold, sure, golden bag," Iris says, then claims George isn't waking up and she'll have him call first thing in the morning. But Iris is not to be trusted.

CeCe stands again and walks the perimeter of the room, grazing the wall with her hand. She makes an X from corner to corner to corner to corner. She slaps each piece of furniture as she goes. Could it be? The drug restoring herself to herself? She walks to the closet and closes its door. She sits in the chair, tired. When she wakes next, she is sunk back in the tangled bed, trapped inside the swirling cotton like a mite in a cottonseed pod. An odd, three-point pain radiates along the small of her back. She pushes herself up and the pain disappears, but it's so hard to push herself up! She cries out upon discovering she's as weak as she's ever been. Her jewelry, lost in the sheets—the two rings and the bracelet the nurse laid out—was what caused her pain. She gathers them in her hands and puts them on and lies back down. She is exhausted and wide-awake. There's nothing to do but wait.

At the first light of dawn, the landscaper reappears. She's become accustomed to watching him. Today he pushes a wheelbarrow across the wet grass. He parks it by the hedge, for the first time close enough for her to notice the lettering on his T-shirt. It reads DE ROSA'S LAND-SCAPE AND TREE REMOVAL and features a drawing of a riding mower. He looks Greek to her, Egyptian, maybe. He sets a mug carefully down in the uneven grass—from its cheerful color she suspects he has a family. He sits against the hedge, opens a newspaper. He pulls a loose cigarette from his pocket, lights it, contemplates the evenness of the topiary, returns to his reading. The smell of the smoke mingles with the smell of dewy grass and the dawn mist rising off the lake. It steals into her room. Not a cigarette but a joint. Does everyone smoke a joint at dawn? She should introduce him to Dana Barnes. Its stale pungency—first husband, Raymond Fitts, who made his job at MGM seem far more than it was, who charmed her out of sense. She'd had no parent alive to tell her charm was not enough. She can still feel their ancient life, though they were married only three years: Raymond, sitting on the floor beside her chair, everything an electric confession, the ice cubes melting in the heat. A party in a railroad apartment in the West Village, her hand on a battered cello case, lugged from so far uptown. The year they tried it his way, a rented bungalow in California, and CeCe wore an apron; Raymond, leaping up and padding off to find a record. Raymond, pushing her against the hot stove for dancing with Art Blakey. Maybe it was only they were young.

They divorced discreetly. She was twenty-one. She flew to Mexico on the Juárez Special. He agreed to be out by her return. A three-day package: a round-trip flight from New York, an appearance alone in Juárez family court on the day between planes. She stood and said her name before the judge. She kept her hat on. It was new and expensive and American and made her feel protected, with netting hanging over the eyes between her and the judge. She handed him her passport and the divorce papers the New York lawyer had drawn up. The judge stamped them and warned her not to drink the hepatital water. She slept a fitful night at the fleabag no-tell that was part of the deal.

Boarding the small plane back, the passengers nodded hello, recognizing each other from the flight over and the lobby of the courthouse where they'd stood in wait, each holding a ticket with a number. Twenty- and thirtysomething women, white, wealthy enough to divorce on the quiet so far from home, dressed right. The plane got through the clouds and turned toward New York. The divorcées leaned their sleek heads together to commiserate and asked the stewardesses for stingers and mai tais, pregnant or not, drinkers or not, secret safe with the Mexicans. They kept it together until somewhere over Texas one began to cry and the rest began to smoke. They pulled tissues and photos of children out of their purses and stood to smooth their skirts. They bumped their heads against the coat shelves, clutching the crumpled tissues, holding their heads as they pitched up the aisle to the ladies' room and back. They ordered whiskey and fanned themselves with their gloves and the emergency-discharge cards, and half were laughing and half were crying but they were all gat-gun drunk loud:

locksmith, vacuum, dog, baby, loan, alone, telephone, darling, carpet, washup, cheer up—and by the time the farm fields of Ohio were under the wings a special kind of exhaustion, a special melancholy, had set in and together the women drew the blinds of the slight, white plane to listen to the stuttering whir of the prop, having decided in unspoken communion that they would not look at the line of the earth meeting the sky or the jagged silver welcome of midtown in the distance. They asked for coffee, coffee please on descent, because their mothers were picking them up, because no one was picking them up, because they were clown-faced with relief and grief and CeCe decided, alone and sober in row one, having talked to no, no thank you, no one, that she was not interested in landing and hallelujah if the maiden 707 kept gliding north right into the granite of the Appalachians because what life after this could be called life?

But then, she met Walter. Patricia was born, and George. She discovered her good work, the work of converting her inheritance (of which an almost unnoticeable portion was awarded to Raymond) to the good.

The man out the window stubs his joint. He hasn't seen her. Her divorce from Walter, though, she hadn't been able to keep private. It was her public embarrassment, and her last. She aims to keep it that way. She won't allow her illness, the spider, to have witness. Spider—what the shaking has done to her handwriting, and how the black spots between the white branches of her dying nerves look on the scan. After that divorce, she'd restored her and the children's surname to Somner. Walter's consent cost her a pretty penny, but why go on as Minches? She'd applied Nan's rule for clutter: an item must be beautiful or useful to retain its place. Minch. A name without beauty, a name without use.

The man out the window deserves as much privacy as she. She will not report his misconduct. She looks into his face, thinking, Look at me, I am here! He balances the dead joint on the lid of his mug and picks up the metal wings of his shears. Left unnoticed, to notice herself alone, she finds she's cold and hungry. What an insult it is to wait. To wait like an addict for a handful of pills, to await the return of one's son.

13

After an unbearable morning of grant evaluation, George escapes the office and walks east and north, clacking his umbrella on the splattered pavement. Thunderclouds rag behind Grand Central Station's pediment clock. Eleven-thirty. He's in a foul, acid, debilitating spirit. The weather conforming to his mood. Warm, pounding rain. Rain, again! Though at the moment there's a break in the clouds. At least the temperature isn't ninety-nine, like yesterday and the day before. The last few years, the end of July in New York City has become as bad as the end of August: rotten and ratty and fetid. He turns onto Lexington Avenue, hurrying to keep pace with the crowd so the crowd will not bump him—the lunch deliverymen in baseball caps and aprons, the couriers, the polyblend administrators, the slouching media kids, the sallow men in suits, jackets off in the heat. All, in their various capacities, no doubt more successful than he. All with somewhere to go. So many women who look like Audrey—an army of Audreys on Lexington! New York, the city of assistants with long, dark hair. The bike messengers, tubes on their backs and chains around their waists, tattooed and bloodshot and pop-veined, rocketing the narrow passages between the moving cars. Midtown makes everyone ugly.

"Cranked," Audrey had said to him once after they shared an elevator with a bike messenger who spent the ride arguing a private injustice to the lit panel of buttons, jutting his chin side to side. "Those guys are cranked."

"No doubt," George agreed as they exited onto the thirty-eighth floor, wondering how much he didn't know about life, about her life. Cranked, which one was that? How could she know particulars about the world he didn't and still remain the nonentity sitting outside his office day after day? Considering these two Audreys' simultaneous existence unnerved his sense of superiority, and so in time he came to misremember Audrey's observation as his own. It was *he* who divined this vice of bike messengers, detective of the human condition that he is. Now, whenever a bike man with a chain and a tube hurtles past, George thinks, *Cranked,* and the breeze the bike makes is the very incarnation of George's world wisdom. Today, however, he's reminded only that the world is dingy and mysterious and hasn't any use for him.

He walks without a destination until he remembers the racket club—there might be an early squash single for a pickup. Maybe he'll find a novice to kill on the court, maybe a sweat will help—wait, he does have some place to go. To the watch repairman, only a few blocks back. He retraces his steps. He finds the awning that reads KEEPING TIME, WATCH AND CLOCK. The generation of business that's all but extinct in Manhattan—a shop instead of a store. One day, he'll turn the corner and see a mobile-phone kiosk or a juice bar in its place. No, even the jingle of the bell on the door and the hunch of the man on the stool behind the counter do not cheer George. He takes off his cracked watch, hands it over, fills out the ticket. Upon exiting, he discovers the sun's come out. The racket club forgotten, he turns toward Le Petit Daudet. A light lunch, why not, though it won't dent his misery. The maître d' claps him on the back and sweeps him down the *allée* to a table in the main dining room.

"—And never accept a table along the *allée*, where everyone will pass you by," his mother had taught him. "Some ladies prefer it as it's where they're most likely to be photographed. Pushed up along the wall as if they're waiting to audition. For whom? For *Women's Wear Daily*? For the waiter?"

He is seated at the best table. His mother's table for twenty years, until a decade ago when her trips to the city decreased. At first, George thought he'd inherited the table, as for a long time the maître d' ushered him to it, expecting CeCe's return; he doesn't often get it anymore. He feels lucky to have it without a reservation today. Without his watch, he's forgotten it's not yet noon. He's not in the habit of looking to his phone for the time.

"But do you remember *why* ours is the best table?" she'd asked, the second time she brought him.

He was small, holding her hand. "You walk in the middle of the room. Everyone sees you and says hello."

"And because it's in a corner. We can see everything from here. Look, dear, not by staring, but through the mirror, yes? Madame Daudet hadn't gotten the relation of the table to the mirror right, but I corrected that. Go, stand over there. Over there. Look how you can't see my face in the mirror, but I can see yours."

She'd required such a table. Her social network, webbed and twined, her finger in so many pots. She'd take her Wednesday lunch alone before going to the theater and have ten different visitors by the time she was drinking tea. To young George, on the rare and dismal occasions she brought him, her ringed hand remained stretched over an iced plate of cucumber and roe or celery rémoulade to be kissed or shaken, palm down, through the entirety of the afternoon. Rarely does anyone approach him, though he likes the place and comes all the time. Such is the thinning of the blood, the dwindling market of inheritance.

This morning he'd learned that neither the Metropolitan Opera nor the New York City Opera will consider *The Burning Papers*. He can't believe it. He'd sent an e-mail to Mr. Fielding, general director at the Met, and another to Mr. Peterson, the artistic director at New York. In the last five years, he's administered project-specific grants to both institutions through Hud-Stanton; they know George attends each season's productions. They know of his continued, if unsuccessful, efforts to increase the Somner Fund's modest annual contribution. He'd attached his just-finished libretto and Vijay's score with real confidence, noting his team's search for rehearsal space and talent and how he'll open in a small venue, as a showcase, for a limited run, early as January and no later than spring; that when the time comes, he trusts they will attend his humble production any night they like. It will give them an idea of why *Papers* should be developed for one of their great stages.

Inexplicably, there was no reply. He'd checked and checked and checked his in-box, until on the pretext of discussing their Hud-Stanton funding he lured them separately to lunch. They were both complimentary. How they admired the work! They couldn't believe (both men shook their heads, one over a salad of nasturtium and sheep's cheese, the other over a strip steak) he'd been writing all these years. They had no idea. *Give me a few more weeks,* they each said.

They both called this morning. As if they'd consulted each other. Wished *Papers* the best of fates. If only they didn't have obligations to their budgets and schedules and boards and subscription holders. If only public acclamation to innovative work weren't so slow, so arduous, especially within the opera community. "Remember how hard it was for Mozart to find a stage in Salzburg," Fielding said. "Remember how the Academy chided Debussy for courting the uncommon interval," Peterson said.

George hands his umbrella to a busboy, orders from the waiter, asks for a newspaper to be brought to his table, receives it. He breaks his roll and brushes the crumbs to the floor. He starts when the phone in his pocket rings. Aleksandar.

"Yes, I called. Seven times? Listen, they're not considering it. Too *radical*, basically. I'm at lunch. Come meet me . . . A revised budget? I'm not surprised. Well, I'm a little surprised. I don't care! We're not quitting and we're not cutting corners. We'll show them. Why don't you come down here and . . . Brooklyn? Yes, that's far."

He nods without looking as the waiter transfers a Dover sole from a sizzling copper pan to his plate, fillets it in two strokes, and wheels the cart away. The meunière is left in a silver boat above his knife.

The waiter—ancient, in a white coat, a napkin over his wrist—returns and presents a bottle of wine. "For the fish."

"For the fish." George hadn't ordered any wine. It is not embarrassment he feels, exactly.

He eats and drinks and rustles through the *Times*. He puts his pen to the newspaper's margin:

UH posture hunch despair whn learns falsely accused of crimes

There is so much about Aleksandar George likes. He likes that Aleksandar wears a wide, bright paisley silk headscarf folded low across his forehead, above a pair of black glasses. To George, this looks ridiculous and thus artistic. He likes that Aleksandar's fee is so high. He likes that Aleksandar's family fled Dubrovnik during the Croatian War of Independence and ended up on Coney Island; he likes how Aleksandar reconciled himself to his new city and to his brutal unwelcome at PS 225 through American musical theater—starting with *Oklahoma!*—and that musical theater lead him to opera, a journey backward, to sounds invented back across time and the Atlantic, back to the grandfather of the musical. Aleksandar agreeing wholeheartedly with George that musicals are light and foolish by comparison. He likes the flat hint of rudeness in Aleksandar's tone when he answers George, followed by a swerve to the friendliest of commiseration, a pattern George thinks might be Croatian, might be theater, might just be Aleksandar. Last time they conferred, Aleksandar said, "But this with the sexy ladies is not meant to be comic? What I am hearing from you is that it isn't—not even satire?" Tipping his paisley head from side to side. "Okay, not for making funny, you. The desert in the set mockups is yellow. You like that? No, me neither. So obvious. You're right. We hate it. I'm going to get rid of it for George. You have the good eye." He likes that Aleksandar is young—very young to have such expertise. Early on, once they settled on a retainer, Aleksandar said,

"George, at first I thought you were a terrible person. Then I reread the libretto and I cried. You lift the veil of power! You show us the one percent future! From four to seven in the a.m. I could not get up off the floor of my apartment. The floor of my apartment is vile, vilest in the middle of the night. I'll never get so close to it again. Can you believe me?"

George writes, *harem costume—massproduction logo/tattered spandex/primarycolors/logologo*, nodding as the waiter refills his glass. He draws a costume on the editorials page but it comes out as two blobs and a line, and he runs out of space before he can get to the legs. The wine is gone. He waves away dessert. He doesn't want to go back to work. Not today. He calls Iris and leaves her a message:

"Bunny, let's spend the afternoon together. Have the car service bring you. Or hop on the train, it might be quicker. Call me when you're close."

He hangs up, pays, and fast as that he's pushing his way across the street. He enters the purple and silver spaceship of a boutique hotel, reserves a room, slides the key card into the disapproving slash below the knob, plunks down on the white bed, turns on the television, orders more wine and something called lobster three ways. His phone rings.

"You're on your way! When you get into town tell the driver—"

"I'm hosting an open house, dummy."

"Today?"

"The Weils's weekend place. Uptick in people selling their weekend places, you know that."

"You can't reschedule?"

"Are you kidding? I'm here already."

"What time are you done?"

"After this I've got a block of apartments we're doing rent-to-own. Nellie rolled it out last month. Remember? The one we got five signatures in an hour? I told you all about it."

"You sound like Audrey. That thing they called her in the beginning. What was that?"

"Temp-to-perm."

"Which apartments?"

"Condos in town behind the supermarket. And a few units at Kingsgate."

"Didn't I read a local-crime something happened there?"

"Evergreen Terrace? I'm in the middle of town. The condos start at two-fifty. You're thinking of when those kids stole the shopping carts from the parking lot and threw them in the woods." She sighs. "I have to go or I won't get this place straightened up."

"But, no one's having lunch with me. My second lunch."

"Are you for real?"

"Come on, we'll have fun."

"George, this is my job. A job means you have things to do that affect other people, so you show up and do those things the best you can. And you assume your partner will understand that."

"All I mean is—this is fun," he says with a weird force. "Fun, fun, fun!"

"You're being a jerk." She hangs up.

He falls back into the bed. It feels good. He pulls the sheet over himself without taking off his shoes. His shoes are wet from stepping in the gush of rainwater and runoff, sandwich wrappers and cigarette butts streaming into a grate in the curb in front of the hotel. He watches two sloppy ellipses appear, gray ghosts of his feet. This slight rebellion, he decides, is the point of hotel rooms.

She *has* changed, in the last year, he thinks, with a rolling, blacking self-pity. Bolder every day, because of him. Good! Fine! But shouldn't he get a little credit? The happier he makes her, the freer she seems of him. Doesn't seem fair. Used to be he could do no wrong. She'd sounded—impatient.

There is a knock at the door.

"Yes!" he calls out. A bellman wheels a sumptuously arranged table to the center of the room. "Three! Someone's made a mistake. I ordered lobster *five* ways. Don't bother, it's too late."

The bellman thanks him and leaves. George drinks and picks at the chilled pink jelly he assumes is the premiero of the trio and watches the news on mute over the wet lump of his feet. The headline—a singer's helicopter missing in the Grand Canyon, the camera panning the banded crater, rain streaking the lens. An international story next— what country, he doesn't catch—fire, the black and wicked skeleton of a car, ash in the air. Next, Manhattan, a camera following a plump, silk-suited man and his lawyers through the press and up the court-house steps, their jaws set.

If his helicopter went missing in the Grand Canyon, it would not be on the news. He considers the hotel porn but declines. It would force him to admit to himself that his plan—vital, spontaneous—has slipped into failure like a coat loosened from its peg.

He wants dessert, maybe a stiffer drink, something with lime. He puts his jacket back on and heads down to the cavernous dining room, lit by a series of crystal chandeliers like drooping onyx earrings. The carpet hushes the room. He sinks into a plush chair. In Manhattan it's only in a hotel, a place for people from other places, that you sit among so much fabric while you eat. The room is mostly empty: one table with what can only be a mother and daughter, waiting for lunch in si-lence, another with two men he guesses are finance, women, maybe escorts, on either side of them. A group of tourists, pointing at each other's menu.

He orders a Scotch and regrets it. He doesn't want Scotch, he wants company. He pulls out his phone and asks to be put through to Bob Barrow-Woods. It was Bob who looped his arm over George's shoul-der and took him out for drinks when he got engaged, and it was George who took Bob out when after all that time he and Martha an-nounced they were having twins.

"Bob, hey, I'm in town and I've—I'm supposed to be meeting with some guy from the Preservation Society . . . Yeah, no. I've been wait-ing for an hour. Guess they don't want that grant so much after all. Unbelievable. At a hotel. I'm jammed in by tourists . . . No, the one across from the church, on Fifth. Come and have a round. What are you on today, pharma?"

Bob's voice is so loud George holds the phone away from his ear. "Today? Fucking forevery. I'm looking at that IPO you said you didn't want to bite on. Guess what? None for you. That's what you get for pretending to know shit. Next time, listen to Bob! Hey, whatever. Watch it tank tomorrow. Then all these shits I work with—that's you, Big Frank, you heard me—will be out on the ledge, jackets flapping in the wind, counting the little people on the street below through the void between their shiny shoes. I mean, what the fuck, right? Hey, weren't you going somewhere? A little vacation? Shit, I remember. The old mama—not vacation. Sorry. I'm a jerk."

"My wife just called me a jerk."

"I love your wife. I mean it. No, I'm trying to tell you, man, I really love your wife. Hold on a second. Gretchen, shut it down out there. Pretty don't give you the green light to talk over my call, does it? . . . Seriously? We're out of—not even a Tylenol? George, as my friend, it hurts me that you don't consider how hard I'm working, like I can drop it all to drink the day away with you."

A woman's laughter, and the line disconnects.

14

After staring at the periwinkle ultrasuede wall beside his table for an hour, George is ready to settle his check when Bob appears, slicking his wet hair off his big forehead, waving for a drink.

"Earnest George," Bob says, "you thought I wasn't coming? Don't know when a man's joking. Fucking pouring out there too. Asshole."

And before he's removed his coat he's on some art he wants to buy—a Warhol lithograph nobody knows about—shit, a shit-fucking, genuine, one-run Black Marilyn that's been languishing in a demented old lady's Brighton Beach rent-a-cube—and another piece at a gallery in Chinatown that took eight years to make and is thick as barbecue sauce, the artist painted thousands of coats, some real OCD shit, built up three dimensions, built up a house out of house paint for the love of God, it makes him cry, and why isn't George getting it, he can tell George is not getting the breathtaking poignancy, whatever, you're the music guy, I guess, and they know how to make a martini here, you should see the face you're making, like the goat that ate the poison toad and what, are you loaded? Oh, no, what are you, *sad*? No, no, no, we're going to fix you right up, you'll see.

When they were reintroduced a decade back, George recognized Bob with a vivid and tongue-tying flash of hero worship. At boarding school, Bob was two classes ahead, a hard shoulder and an unlaced rugby cleat, a poet and a captain, and at the parties where George dourly slinked the perimeter, there would be Robert, bending over the table with this girl, that girl, making nice tight lines, expertly helping a tremulous young one get the stuff up her nose, tipping her chin with his hand. A house abandoned by someone's parents for the weekend— there was a polar-bear rug, its fierce head thrust under a glass table and Robert saying to the girl whose face he held, a math-mouth George had thought he might have a chance with, "Nobody owns you but *you*, Barbara." And while there was no crisis anyone got wind of—no flashing red lights, no flashing blue lights—one day he was gone, and George heard nothing of him for years.

"I tell this woman with the Warhol," Bob says, wiping the rain from his face, "I'm her cousin. I'm like, I don't want to take your painting away. We're family. I just want to bring my friend the appraiser over. Then I want to give you money. And the old girl, she's practically holding a horn to her ear, she says, 'Cousin Bobby, mow my lawn.' Bitch of it is, she doesn't have a lawn. She has a folding chair on the sidewalk. We're at a stalemate. How's Iris? She go up with you to the, what was it, PT?"

"Nope." George reaches for his glass. He finds it is empty. He finds he is reciting Iris's work schedule, for reasons that elude him, and concludes, "Sometimes I am the doer when there is a thing." Adding, "You miss my point."

"Hey, why the long face? This is a great hotel. I always forget about this place. It's so close to the office. You've ever been up in one of the rooms?"

"Never."

"They throw some unusually classy bric-a-brac up, the prints on the wall are half-decent—not watercolor sailboats, anyway. And the concierge." Bob drops his voice and leans farther in. "Great concierge.

Want to rent a tiger? Want a toothbrush, and a tiger to brush your teeth? Done. Look at those assholes over there, that one knows the concierge, for sure. Ten bucks. Hey, *you* all! You know the concierge?"

The suits with the two women look up.

"Bob," George says, "what the hell."

"You can't turn a tanker around with a speedboat." Bob leans low over a fresh drink, eyeing it with ardor and suspicion as if it might be the unfaithful love of his life.

The women frown and look away. George becomes aware of their plastic sheen and how hard they've worked to look that way—shining, straight hair, gleaming sandals, fingernails tipped white. Their eyes, cups and saucers, banded gold and green. One looks to have begun the day olive-skinned and the other palest white, but they've met in the middle courtesy of spray tan. Something about this disturbs George. Their essence, despite the bronze, is not out-of-doors but rather of those public indoor spaces that aim to be eternally sufficient—the airport, the mall. They *are* escorts, looking right only under something electric. The grounds of Oak Park come suddenly to mind—the bordered gardens, the small lake with its precise edge, the cool promise of the surrounding woods.

"The concierge you're thinking of is Demetri," the older, stockier man says.

"Right, Demetri! Did he introduce you all?"

"Oh, no," George says.

"Ah." The man frowns. "That's hilarious."

Ten years back, George and Bob were briefly employed at the same D-list securities firm, George's last job in the for-profit sector after several humiliatingly unsuccessful placements procured for him by his mother's friends. By then, Bob was drained and slack jawed and lubberly, telling sad jokes about how the girls at business school liked holding on to his love handles during all the oddly positioned fucking he'd been busy with while blowing off Domestic Markets 202. On weekends, he wore a leather jacket that was wrong-decade tight. His glory was behind him. George and Bob became friends, playing wheezing games of squash or retiring to the Penn Club after work or to the Oyster Bar at Grand Central, and over the years they saw each other's lot improve—Bob was doing well at a hedge, Tryphon Capital, and well by his what-is-she-doing-with-him wife, Martha. Their twin boys, Robert Jr. and Thierry, six this year, his pride and joy. White-blond, pie-faced future captains of industry, their wisping hair parted a deep right, their navy blazers with gold buttons matching, the school insignia on the breast pocket. Bob's favorite thing about Martha, he said, was that she didn't give a shit except she did, God bless her.

"I know you," the second man says, looking at Bob. "Delaware? Media incorporation. Laurus? Friar? No. Corn Refiners Association, Lunch-n-Learn."

"Shit, yes, those assholes! Lunch-n-Learn!"

"Jim Frame."

Then they are shaking hands and pushing the tables together. George leaps to his feet and begins shaking everyone's hand as well. Bob is telling the first man, from Munich it turns out, a Carsten with a *C*, that they'd bet one hundred bones that Carsten with a *C* knew the name of the concierge, and now George is in the red.

Something is expected. George takes out his wallet.

"Give it," Bob says. And to the men: "You guys do a next-level drill down with those corn pricks?"

"Menus," Carsten says.

"Do the trick," pale-to-dark says to Carsten, looking at George's money, with a low, practiced kind of baby-brightness in her voice. She has an accent too, but too faint to identify. George raises his empty glass, a salute and a plea; he's both dejected by whatever is coming next and beginning to enjoy himself. Good old Bob.

"Corn refiners, not easy," Jim Frame says. "We were almost on the wrong side of that demographic. Dropped out right before the FDA sent a corpse down the sales-and-delivery pipeline, yeah?"

"Christmas bonus," Bob says, by way of praise.

"Cash," Carsten says, "is what we need for the trick. Funny Face here doesn't trust me with hers."

"We don't have any cash, I told you."

They all laugh at this. George is still looking at his wallet when he sees Bob handing a bill to Carsten. He's missed a cue. He finds the glass in front of him is full again, this time of cold vodka. He swallows and shudders. The woman who is dark-to-pale claps her hands tightly over her mouth. She is laughing, but isn't making any sound. Is she deaf? He decides he *is* enjoying himself.

Carsten gets serious. He folds and unfolds the bill; he holds it up to the light as if to inspect it; he shows it to the bronze women and the tourists, now watching over their menus. He holds it up to George and Bob, who says, "Another round," to a passing waiter.

"Love the city!" one of the tourists says.

"No," Carsten rejoins, "I learned this trick in a village. From a villager." His hands clasped midair.

"A round of drinks for that table too," calls Bob.

Carsten clasps his palms together. He whisks them around his ears. He separates them and the bill is gone. "I stole your money."

"Lame!" George shouts.

The tourists clap. "Great job!" one says, but they look a little nervous. George claps too. He takes a sip—was it always vodka? He's lost track of what they're saying. Food arrives. At some point they turn back to the topic of Bob's pending art acquisition. George forgets to listen, until he hears one of the women say, "We'll miss you." The man named Carsten is shaking George's hand. Next he looks, Carsten is gone and the women are eating in silence. Bob and Jim are talking stocks. Dull gibberish. Something—"That's your sector now? Interim clinical? Phase three? Suicide. What are you going to try to turn me on to next, fucking commercial printing?"

George drinks and picks at a shrimp cocktail he's discovered on the table. He has no idea what Bob is going on about. George looks down and finds the silent woman's hand is resting on his forearm. Why, it isn't Bob who's speaking. It's he himself! He's complaining about Peterson and Fielding. He's saying something that must be clever, because everyone's laughing, and now Bob is shouting, directly at him—something about a piano, or someone named Pianot, maybe Bob is back on art, Pianot could be an artist, or a town, sounds like a town, or maybe Bob is saying *IPO*, and George feels he's responding well, but then Bob says, "Why so silent, Georgie boy? You look like a moose. My man started early, I think."

George would like to share that he hasn't been sleeping much. Instead, he answers, "Goor tired."

"Want this?" Bob asks, and with a *plink!* a pill lands on George's plate.

"Dernt take that shut since college."

"Suit yourself."

"What's it?" George asks, recovering a little. "Do I get cranked?"

"No, what? Where have you been hanging out? It's that shit all the kids use to stay focused in school. A little-kid dose. Jesus."

"Over here," Jim Frame says.

"Eh." George shrugs and takes it. "I'm why so quiet because I have nothing to talk about."

"Want my dad's advice on that?" Bob says. "If you have nothing to add, ask a question. It's flattering. Everyone's a narcissist. Everyone's an expert. How about asking these gals to explain something of the world to you? How about opening your mind, Georgie? It doesn't even matter what you ask. Right?"

"That's the way it's done," the woman with the accent agrees. "Timeless advice."

"Okay. Are you religious? Because in *The Burning Papers*—"

"No, no, no," Bob says. "Not that."

The quiet woman grabs her friend's hand and squeezes it. They look at each other and nod.

"I love secrets, don't you?" Bob says, smiling at this exchange.

George *is* feeling better. The little-kid pill isn't half-bad. The room is sharpening up. The women's plates are cleared. Soon, their glasses are empty. Jim is on his cell. The people entering the lobby are drenched. The waiter asks if the women want anything more. They shake their heads no, but sadly, and look at Bob.

"Waiter!" Bob calls. "Where have you been? What is your name?"

"That's rude," George says, opening his eyes, feeling passionate about the matter. "It's rude to ask them their names. Their names are their private business. Unless they offer."

"I'm Travis," the waiter says.

"Travis, thank you. A bottle of champagne, have the bartender pick."

"Shampoo!" says the talking woman, whose name George now somehow knows is Gita. "Our favorite!"

The other woman, who he's now decided is mysterious and beautiful, pulls a notebook from the leather satchel beside her on the banquette. "Carrying a big bag—gauche, don't you think?" Gita says to George. "But she likes her little books, to communicate. I'm trying to learn—" She waves her hands in mock sign language. "But it's a lot of work. And"—Gita cups her mouth out of sight—"you know how it is, best friends this month, and next month she'll be all 'Gita who?' "

Her friend writes a moment without letting him see, shows it to Gita, and—she really *is* something—plunges the notebook back into her bag, which is red with a black fringe. She reaches over and rustles around in George's pocket. She smells like sugar and the thick aisle-air of the CVS he occasionally frequents in Stockport. She pulls out his phone. She taps and puts it on the table. Floating on the contacts screen he reads the name PENNY.

"You're kidding me," he says. "Is this for real?"

Jim Frame looks up and does not smile.

"Look who's the favorite man today," Bob says. He shakes his head.

"I've got to go," George says, handing his credit card to a passing waiter.

"You sure do," Bob says.

"No, home." George stands, steadily enough. Who cares if the Met or City won't consider his opera? All it proves is he's ahead of his time. He's more confident now than ever. Confident as a knife! Confident as a clock! Confidence itself meaning secret, something to wait for, to be confided. When the time comes, everyone will see what a fine work he's made.

"Home, right. Jim, we're staying, yes? Jim's got some ideas to loop. Then maybe I'll get to go home too."

Bob grabs and pumps George's hand, giving him a mean, tight sort of pull toward the table. "Comes down to it," Bob whispers, "you don't fuck the face."

"No," George says, "huh."

The waiter returns. "Is there another card?"

"Forget it, we're not finished. Take mine, keep it open," Bob says, waving the waiter away. "George, I'll call you on those numbers. We don't want the grass to grow too long on this one."

George does not remember talking numbers.

"Good meeting you," says Jim Frame. "That was a lot of insight."

Gita holds out her glass. "Champagne's turned."

"This I will fix," Bob says. "Don't you touch."

"Sorry," George says, looking into the spoiled amber of the flute, one hand still caught in Bob's and the other around his credit card, his voice embarrassingly flooded with sorrow. "Opening week, you're all going to have seats in the first row. You'll come to the theater and see it and hear it and, I promise, it will be the most beautiful you ever did."

"What's he talking about?" Bob asks.

"He's a big shot up in here maybe," Gita answers, tapping the side of her head.

"You don't believe me? You don't even know me!"

"Americans," she continues, ignoring George. "Ask them what they want to be, they say *famous*. But it's usually the ones younger than him."

"I've done my very, very best," he tries.

Gita's laugh is sharp. "God has a glass eye. A bullshit country saying, but I like it." She turns her back to George, back to the men at the table.

15

They take Iris's car. They have the narrow, sunlit highway to themselves. 3D is in the backseat, one ear flapping out the window, one eye scrunched against the warm air whipping around the interior, the bright trees spinning past. The smell of new tar rises from the road.

"A perfect day," she says.

"I still don't think I can afford a house."

"Did I show you the brochure?" She reaches over Victor's legs into the glove compartment and tosses the glossy foldout onto his lap. "Don't bother with the text, it's all pitch. Look at the pictures."

"I can't help it. The words are so big."

TOP 5 REASONS TO LIVE AT
KINGSGATE ESTATES

1. Award Winning Master Planned Community
2. 20-Year Real Estate Tax Abatement—Low Taxes—less than $800 a year!
3. Special Financing as Low as 3.5% Down***
4. Location, Location, Location, Breathtaking Natural Views
5. Convenient to Train & Express Bus—40 Minutes to Midtown Manhattan

Buy a Home with Peace of Mind Included
*Mortgage Payment Protection Program****√*
See page 2 for details

"Moving to Kingsgate has been a wonderful opportunity as a homeowner. It's like a vacation every time we come home! It's great to be part of this budding community."

—Jeff & Melinda

"Kingsgate is a hidden treasure. Beautiful homes, great people! Words can't describe how happy we are in our new home."

—Ramon Carreras

DID YOU KNOW?

Our sales center is open Monday evenings 6pm to 8pm to accommodate your busy schedule. Come take a tour of our new independent models or the luxury renovation of the historic Baxter Tower Apartments. Enjoy the spectacular sunset from the West Tower's rooftop terrace. Meet with homeowners and hear why they love living at Kingsgate Estates.

"The developer updated the units in the towers and built the clusters on the adjacent lot. But your house is nicer than those." She gestures to the row of semidetached colonials in the photo.

"My house?"

"I'm showing you the good one."

"But they're all the same."

"Except the property manager's house, built with the towers in the forties. They weren't allowed to bulldoze it. State-landmarked with the towers. They sure wanted to. Its footprint is twice the new units."

"I can't be looking at landmarks. Not to live in."

"No, landmarked. It's a regular bungalow. Real bones. Modest. Tree line separates it from the newer units. A little stained-glass window. Not in the shadow of the apartments. Anyway, you see if you like it."

"A stained-glass window?"

"Top of the stairs."

"Stairs?"

"I like showing at Kingsgate. Appraisals go up four to six percent every year. I don't have to feel like I'm pushing."

"3D, she's taking me for a ride."

"I *am* taking you for a ride."

Victor laughs. 3D sits up and barks twice.

"We're so close to the city, you don't see big market fluctuations. Wall Street buys shoreline no matter what. Why the schools aren't bad. Important when you're looking for room to grow," she says, smiling at him.

"How do you know about that?"

"Seminar for the licensing course, I guess? And they brief us at the office about how the market's doing. Downside is stiff taxes. And nobody qualifies for the abatement. The abatement is bullshit. But even the worst-case scenario—if something happened and you needed to sell right away—it's break-even or profit."

"No, what you said about room to grow."

"Aha! I guessed the other week. Tell me how you first met Isabel."

"Isabel?" He looks puzzled. They head down into a dense, tree-puffed valley, the blacktop unspooling behind them. He's quiet so long she wonders if it was wrong of her to ask. The asphalt turns pale gray, zigzagged with tire tread, writ with pits and fissures. A front tire bangs over a pothole. "Okay. It *is* a phenomenal story. We met on a cruise."

"Romantic!"

"No, we both worked housekeeping. A thousand passengers. Ugly as the Pentagon. I was in the kitchen, talking my way into a plate of french fries, and bam!"

3D nudges his paws between them, his head up onto the dash.

"Sit," she says.

"Cruises hit rough water more than you'd think. Every few passenger cycles. Nothing to you if you work the boat. But the captain fucked up and got us sucked into the tail of a monsoon between Sydney and Madagascar. Half the rescue boats blow off the sides of the ship. Crew coming down from the deck say the passengers are grabbing up on anyone in a uniform. I get under one of the steel prep tables. A raw shrimp falls into my hair right as the captain gets on the loudspeaker. To read last rites. I swear to God. *Last rites.* This tinny voice through the speaker in the ceiling."

"Why are you laughing? That's terrifying."

"Well, he's doing 'Happy are those who are called to His supper,' the part with the Lamb, and Isabel comes lurching by. I grab her and pull her under the table. Another ten minutes and the storm's over. Everyone's fine. Captain was plastered. Went to jail."

"Your tattoo! The shrimp?"

"Good eye. I was raised with a lot of God, so I thought, This woman is the one who will save me, like I saved her."

"But you didn't save her. Everything was fine."

"I know."

"A wife and a weird tattoo. Some takeaway."

"Izzy and I quit right after—holy shit! Is that you?"

The billboard grows larger as they approach. Under the word KINGSGATE is an image of a winding sidewalk under a burst of pink cherry blossoms leading to one of the same semidetached colonials from the brochure. Iris stands in front of the house, her arms crossed high over her boxy, mauve jacket at a friendly tilt, her thumb pointing to a TOWER UNITS & SINGLE-FAMILY HOUSES AVAILABLE! shingle hanging from the mailbox. She smiles down upon them, her violet eyes a six-inch diameter. The car slides under the billboard. Even though the back is nothing but wood scaffolding, Victor turns in his seat, watches it recede. 3D licks his face.

"I was hoping you wouldn't see that," Iris says.

"You're famous!"

"No. I happened to be free the same day as the photographer. We have a bunch of agents at Kingsgate."

"Or because you are the prettiest one, *obviously*. Let's go back. No, let's drive by very slowly on the way home. I brought my camera. I want a picture of the picture of the picture."

"I thought they were taking it for something small, like the brochure. I'm so embarrassed. They've got eleven more in a three-hour radius. The jacket is so churchy! We give up the ad space as soon as we close on the last units. I'm counting the days."

"Which is worse—they paper over you or they don't paper over you? What if no one buys the spots? This is a low-traffic road."

"The rains will fade me? The birds will crap on me?"

"The snows will drift and cover you? I'll call the toll-free number and it will be disconnected?"

"Maybe when I'm long in the tooth, I'll drive out here and look up at my big young mug. I accept my fate. Back to your plans. Tell me."

"Well, we're not sharing it much yet, but we're trying to adopt. Keep it to yourself please, for now? If it doesn't work out, we'll be sad and we won't want people asking us how it's going, or, like, *not* asking, in that awkward way. I think it'll take forever, but Bill's optimistic. And more patient. I said to him last night, maybe owning property would strengthen our application." Victor peers down at the brochure. "I see kids here. That's nice. I also see a lot of bullshit. I don't get why the prices are this low. Is there a terrible smell, or something?"

"Bill?"

"You met him. The time he picked me up."

"Of course." Bill. Of course. Her cell phone rings. "Can you look?"

"O-Park," he says, pulling her phone from the cupholder.

"No, no, no, don't touch it! When George doesn't answer his phone she calls and accuses me of his not answering. She's figured out if the rings stop short, I'm killing the call. Let it ring!"

"Yikes."

"Selling houses is about knowing right away what people want. Seeing who they are. I thought you wanted a house for you and Isabel. It's a mystery I sell anything."

"Isabel!" He bursts out laughing.

"You *were* married to her."

"I'm not laughing at you. I shouldn't have assumed, except—"

A helicopter churns a diagonal descent across their vision.

"No, I'm an idiot. Anyway, the helicopters—you can hear those from the house. They don't go over too often though—one helipad, one runway. Fifteen miles away. Private planes only. Small. You think about if it bothers you while we walk around."

She slows the car. They turn and pass between two stone gateposts scarred with long, black iron hinge marks. "Kingsgate, no gate. I keep singing that one to the developers. They say next month."

She drives slowly. He takes out his phone and leans his forearm on the window, taking video. Spiraling maple pods fill the air and litter the colonnade. The sound of the helicopter fades.

"What the developer has done here, see"—she gestures to the nearing towers—"is refresh the facade and modernize all the interiors—upgraded appliances, countertops—and created more traffic-friendly landscaping. See how the sidewalks aren't straight? See the flower beds and the benches? It's community-minded. There's the parking lot over there on your right. Every unit gets a spot. You can buy a second spot, for not too much. Your house is a ways, but let's get out and take a look. Come, 3D, come."

They stand in the bleak glint of the two buildings, rising before them like giant cheese graters.

"There's a gym in the West Tower you'd have access to. Garbage, snow shoveling, that's taken care of."

Victor raises the phone eye level, lowers it, raises it again, but does not take a picture. "These are housing projects."

"They were housing projects. Now they're homes. But, yeah."

They get back in the car and drive slowly beyond the gray monoliths. Iris waves out the window to a woman pushing a stroller. The woman is leaning over and does not see.

"Basketball and handball," Iris says, pointing. On the handball court are three teenage boys, leaning their noodle bodies in unconvincing menace against the wall, watching the car.

"I'm proud of how many of the original renters we were able to convert to owners. First-time homeowners. Didn't have to move. Didn't have their lives turned upside down. I used to think before I met George that homeownership was for other people. I didn't understand all you need is access to the right financial information. Our team structures the shit out of a loan. A responsible loan. Anyone can buy a house. It's a secret they don't tell people like, well, people like me." She gestures out the window. "The developer wanted to first jack the rent before conversion, squeeze them out. Our firm said, 'No, let us try to sell to the occupants. Save a lot of time and legal if you avoid eviction. Built-in buyers.' And the developer said okay, and I thought, *I* can help. *I* can do this. They need someone like me, who understands both sides. Have we talked about transportation? I don't know how much time you or Bill spend in the city, but we're only twenty minutes from the train station. Parking at the train is wait-listed but not impossible. There's a bus that stops a half mile up from the gate, or the no-gate too."

She parks the car at the last cluster of houses. From this distance the towers are not as fierce. The ground is thick with leaves, more beds of green maple pods. They walk the narrow concrete path. Squirrels scrabble up and down the trees. The blue leash goes taut in Iris's hand. In front of one of the houses across the street, a woman with a plastic cane sits on a bench.

"Hello, Mrs. Baldwin," Iris calls. "How are you?"

"Eh," the woman says.

They come to a medium-size house behind a low hedge. As she promised, it's different from the rest. A sturdy bungalow with dark green shutters, a front porch, and a gabled roof.

"On a private lot," Iris says, "a house like this would cost double."

That day, Iris takes Victor to four other houses. They see six the day after. But she knows this is the one, a good house at that price. The next week they return with Bill. Bill is older than Victor, with a mantis frame in brown, age-smoothed corduroys. He folds his legs in and out of the car like an accordion ruler. He wears large, unfashionable rectangular glasses, a gray-and-tan beard like a peel of birch. He is a jewelry maker, he tells her. She imagines him bent over a tiny green gem. He has a shop in town—Stone Soup—has she seen it? A pretty decent Internet business too. Roman coins on leather strings, and brooches of owls and flamingos pounded out of copper with jade or turquoise for the eyes. A series of pins sold as mother-of-the-bride gifts, filigreed silver starbursts with a tiny uncut diamond nestled here and there.

"After the chandeliers at Lincoln Center," he says.

"I know those! At the opera."

"I like poking into the shop and catching him bent over the table with that silly thing in his eye," Victor says.

"It's called a loupe," Bill says.

"Look at this, Bill." Victor leads him to the stained-glass window at the top of the stairs. "If you were a giant, this is the rainbow you'd see with your loupe."

"Oh my, my," says Bill quietly, touching it with his whole hand.

They make the tour—the kitchen with its cheery yellow backsplash, the terrible tan downstairs bathroom. The two bedrooms upstairs, with pitched gypsum ceilings and skewed electrical sockets set in the stark Realtor-white walls. Still, full of light and promise. They return downstairs and Bill sits in a rocking chair, his legs extended across an oval rag rug, into the room. 3D, who's followed the group silently from room to room, curls up in the spot of light at Bill's feet.

"Bill, I love it." Victor says.

"It's a big decision."

"Listen," Iris says. "We have a mortgage group our agency's worked with for years. You see what they say, and if it isn't realistic, we'll keep looking. I'll put you in touch with some recent buyers here, if you want. See how they feel."

"Every car my dad bought was with a cashier's check," Bill says. "He was that kind of guy."

"Bill is like a dog in only two respects," Victor says, putting his hand on Bill's shoulder. "Strong sense of past routine, zero ability to envision the future."

Bill laughs. "I like the known knowns."

"The rate Bill and I make decisions," Victor says, smiling at Iris, "the first property we buy will be at the cemetery."

"If this isn't the time, it isn't the time," Iris says. "You have to feel right."

"It's true, Victor does keep me jumping into life." She hears the pleasure in Bill's voice. With his long arm he reaches down and scratches 3D under the ear. "And what about this dog? He's a strange-looking fellow, isn't he? I've heard a lot about you, yes, I have."

"I'm going to step out and make a call," Iris says. "Give you a minute. No, 3D. Stay with Bill, stay with Victor. Good dog."

She ambles out to the mailbox and rests her hand on the curve of the aluminum. Mrs. Baldwin has vacated the bench. Iris looks up into the trees. She looks at her nails and listens for helicopters. She counts to one hundred and back down. She winds her way back to the house and opens the door.

"Here she is." Bill rises out of the rocking chair. In three strides he crosses the room. He reaches out and wraps his cool hands around hers. "Okay. Okay, we'll do it."

16

To his own surprise, George sticks to his promise—a promise to a prostitute who had dismissed his most serious utterance, who turned her back on him, whom he'd never see again. How these last weeks Gita's face has risen above him night after night in witchy derision, Iris sleeping soundly beside! "God has a glass eye," Gita would say again, her glossy lips pursed. What did that even mean? It meant she thought little of him. The flick of her shoulder was what spurred him to secure the final loan he needs to keep up with the minimums on his other loans. A less reputable lender with a complicated and punishing interest rate, but all to the good. Most nights now he doesn't sleep more than one hour, two. He hasn't slept in weeks. He never sleeps! Though he feels fine, better than fine. That secret, stolen time when the world in darkness belongs only to him—he uses it well, expanding, perfecting his vision. When he gets tired at rehearsal or at Hud-Stanton he has several remedies on hand, the kinds prescribed to the attention-deficient and hyperactive. The pill Bob had given him was harmless, doctor-sanctioned, and beneficial to keeping focus, though George lied the tiniest bit to get a prescription. He failed to mention his youthful enthusiasms, his previous psychiatric history, his pitch into insomnia. No, he didn't lie. He wasn't asked. He's also procured, for when his bouts of sleepless productivity become too much, an excellent sleep aid.

They will make their investment back once the reviews come in and *The Burning Papers* is picked up for a longer run. (Aleksandar, over a long evening of Stolichnaya, had agreed.) And even if they lose money, won't it have been worth it? Maybe after a season in New York, *The Burning Papers* will tour. Nationally. Internationally! A commission for his next opera to follow. In that case, breaking even is only a matter of time. With George's approval, Aleksandar has booked a small theater on Water Street called the Abbott, for rehearsals and the opening run. George has sent Vijay the finishing additions to the libretto, and the composer—at last!—has finalized the score. Four, five times a day Aleksandar calls George to sign off on various decisions, calls George takes with adulterous thrill at Hud-Stanton.

"There are visionaries and there are administrators and there are visionary-administrators," Aleksandar says into the phone. "And you're the first and I'm the last, and Lord knows this month we're hiring out the middle."

At the office, George keeps his door shut.

He approves—more than approves—the score. When he heard its rough incarnation a year prior, he knew that Vijay was worth his fee. But this is beyond what he hoped. The Met, City—of course those conservative marionettes turned him down. Good. This way he'll be in charge, start to finish. They'll be sorry, all right. Maybe he'll let the Sydney Opera have it first. Or the Royal. His phone rings.

"Directors, the short list," Aleksandar says, and within a week they narrow the choice to two—a competent veteran from the Buffalo opera circuit, Bernard Lieber, whose strawberry wisp-over and anxious shoulders bob in time with the music, or Anatole Stratolin, a brilliant philosopher-tyrant, bizarre and unpleasant, just out of jail for tax fraud. George wants Stratolin but heeds Aleksandar's point that above all else a director must be a stabilizing and unifying presence. They hire Bernard.

"I am honored," Bernard says.

"*I* am honored," George says.

"I'm thrilled and bored and hungry and nauseous all at the same time," Aleksandar says.

Within three weeks, Bernard and Aleksandar find a conductor and assemble an orchestra on retainer. Not first tier, George admits, but a solid group—a few retirees, a string section pulled from noteworthy private quartets. When George is introduced, the retirees blink at him impassively, and the string players' ponytails make thin snakes over the black linen humps of their backs. They do not make small talk. He suspects they don't yet understand the work. He is glad that early orchestral rehearsals will be off-site. Aleksandar recruits the rest—young regional talents yet to gain wide notice. Bernard brings in a choreographer and a rehearsal pianist, defectors from the New Orleans Opera he'd met online.

George, Aleksandar, Bernard, and the conductor—with counsel from the newly hired stage manager and dramaturge—cast the voice talent. An exciting process! In the dim theater, George sits at a card table, beside a fire extinguisher clamped to the wall. He says, "Thank you," at the conclusion of each audition, blandly and clearly, just like in the movies. With a shiver of pleasure he watches each vocalist walk off-stage. Aleksandar settles on a scenic designer, orders costume sketches, retains the best wigmaker in the business. When the cast and crew are assembled and a date for opening night is set, George dips into the budget's miscellany fund to take everyone out for food and drink— everyone except Vijay, who suspects a sand fly of biting him and giving him Toscana virus—and seats them at a long wooden table under a dim chandelier on Mercer Street. The table grows loud and jovial. The voice coach and the lighting director are serenaded upon their late arrival. After four hours of Chianti and antipasti George stands heavily and asks, "Do we get a fight choreographer?" The vocalists featured in the battle scene vote "Yes!" and the vocalists not in the battle scene vote "No!" Until they are thumping their fists on the table to no particular end except their own merriment and on Aleksandar's whispered suggestion George orders everyone ouzo. After this, George calls Iris. She says she's proud of him and he sounds pretty shithoused and she won't wait up, he should have fun and it's fine if he gets a hotel instead of the train.

Today, Bernard is leaning on the wall of the empty orchestra pit, looking up at the stage, his hands on his pink head.

"Katya," he says, "how can I impress upon you the importance of coming in on cue? It's a little late in the game for you to miss an entrance. Sorry, everyone, go again. Katya, start at the top. Jill, please, right now you are a rehearsal pianist, no more poker on the phone."

George is in his usual spot, second to last row center aisle, wearing his new uniform: jeans and sneakers and a sweater, muted and luxurious as Stanton's; his hair shaggier, his belt buckled a notch tighter, feeling good as he did at twenty. Yes, the venue is not exactly regal. One hundred and fifty seats. The air-conditioning could be quieter and more effective. When they turn the lights all the way up, the floor is scuffed, the velvet on the seats worn. The stage is tighter than he'd envisioned and gummy with tape from the blocking of other performances. The pit's cramped, the curtains slow and stuttering in their draw. But it has what Aleksandar calls "historical, historical, historical charm"—reputedly once a dance hall where Melville drank beer and felt the oyster shells crush under his boot. George doesn't mind the theater's shabbiness. It will vanish with the beauty of his production. Here he is, in a theater, his theater for a time!

The phone on Bernard's hip blinks. He frowns, breaks rehearsal to take the call. He motions—*Ten minutes*—up to the tenor who's replaced Katya onstage, then shambles up the aisle to the exit. George, engaged in his usual observation—clucking with pleasure, shaking his head as he takes notes, trying to control his new-old tic of bouncing his leg in a tight and constant spasm—knows he is not to interfere. Still, he waves to Aleksandar, eating pepitas and texting the publicist, in the sound booth. Aleksandar does not look up.

"Brian," George calls to the tenor. "How about we speed up the tempo? With a more staccato clip of the consonants? Consonants are what separate us from the animals, Brian. Jill, would you take it from the last measure?"

Aleksandar appears by his side. "Fantastic suggestion. Edgy. So very."

"Thank you!" George says.

Bernard sweeps briskly back up the aisle.

"But now I think—Bernard?"

"Yes, let's move on and block scene three. We have the harem here in its entirety today, but only until four p.m. Thank you, George, we'll remember that for next time. Harem, please."

At Hud-Stanton, with increasing frequency, George claims his absences and half days are in the service of his mother's care. After all, the Arts and Culture Fund practically files itself. At home, he's suggested that Hud-Stanton is allowing him flexible hours, in full support of his endeavor. Often enough, he finds he is agreeably convinced of this himself. There are administrators and there are visionaries, he reminds himself. He dreams of quitting, but he needs the income, even if his income is a pebble in the shadow of a mountain. He won't ask his mother, trade his freedom for the face she'd make, and if he quit Hud-Stanton—he doesn't want anyone to know how much he's devoting to *The Burning Papers*. Not until it's opened, until its art has been revealed. He can't bear how they'd look at him if he gave his notice and told them why, how they wouldn't understand. And Stanton (Hud unavailable in Palm Springs) *had* conveyed that George should take all the time he needed, tending to an illness in the family.

"All right," Bernard says to the harem, scattered in jeans and sweats along the edge of the stage. "This is a complex scene. Our Unnamed Hero is outside the gates of the city formerly known as Paris. The gates will be far stage left. The gates have been bombed. As you know, Unnamed Hero is about halfway through his quest to find his exiled father . . . Yes, Judith, in the strictest sense it would be unlikely for a Paris of the future to have city gates. But this is, this is—George?"

"I suspect I can be of help here. Judith, everyone. This isn't just

Paris. This is the Paris of our collective understanding. This is every Paris at the same time simultaneously. It's the *idea* of Paris, if the *idea* of Paris were bombed."

"Thank you," Bernard says. "Powerful stuff. There you go. The city gates will be over there, and around the gates will be rubble and debris. We don't know if we're getting the turned-over tank yet, but keep in mind you may need to block around a tank. Unnamed Hero and Agent X—Brian, Eric, come on over—will stand in front of the gates. You are under the great dismantled crucifix and are conferring as to the dangers ahead. Sotto voce, as far downstage as possible."

"I hate to interrupt," George calls from the back, where he has resumed his regular post.

"Please."

"Don't forget we need a good amount of dust floating in the air around the gates, catching the light. To indicate the bombing is recent."

"I think we discussed that with the voice coach? A few days ago? If we fill the air with dust, it will harm the voices. For singing."

"But visually, it's important."

"George, it can't be done," Aleksandar shouts from the sound booth. "You'll have to let it go. We'll get a smoke machine. You're taxing Bernard."

"Oh, all right," George sighs.

"Wonderful." Bernard continues, "Yes, Eric, stand right there. Have we talked about the scrim splitting upstage from down? Upstage, behind the scrim, the Compound. Enslaved ladies of the harem, please recline in a half circle on your marks. You'll be in semidark. Eunuchs on either side of wives. Unnamed Hero and Agent X and the Paris gates downstage in spotlight. With dust, if we can. Harem, you will be the chorus here. Chief eunuch and second eunuch, let's try pacing inside the circle of wives. Ensemble's not here today, but there will be, ah, Gypsies peering through the windows. Wives, you are unaware of them. But, eunuchs, how do *we* feel? We feel paranoid! . . . What's this? . . . Thank you, Aleksandar. We have a note from George. Shall I read it, George? Yes? . . . 'Should be brushing each other's hair. More beautiful. Should be more like mermaids.' Ah, okay, let's try that.

Tighten up so you can reach each other's hair. Thank you. Let's try the chorus please, starting at line 214. Jill, when you're ready."

In the confines of the harem, the women begin to sing, in a soft, murmuring round, of the faraway places they imagine the hero to be.

"They are all *brilliant*," George whispers to Aleksandar. Aleksandar nods.

We love him so, sì, sì, sì, the women sing. *Sì* is the only Italian in the opera—a linguistic compromise George and Vijay devised together. George feels his phone go off. His mother's number at Oak Park. He sits on the phone to muffle it.

The principal wife steps out of the chorus to begin her duet with the hero, stage left, in Paris. They will sing together, unawares. She begins alone, with her dilemma: He may never return. How long can she remain faithful? She sings of the kindness and beauty of the eunuchs and wonders if, as harem rumor has it, one eunuch among them is an impostor. She recalls the hero's extreme masculine vigor with longing, but as he joins her, singing of her beauty, she laments how her memory of him fades.

"Magnificent," George whispers.

"I still think it would be a hell of a lot easier if you gave them names," Aleksandar whispers back, leaning in from the row behind. "Look at this. Press, already." He hands George his phone.

"Hmmm." George says, squinting. He reads:

As talent even now continues to defect from the once robust New Orleans Opera . . . soprano Judith Havemeyer . . . taking contract roles in independents such as this year's mysterious vanity project *The Burning Papers* . . . In an unusual choice of venue, opera newcomer George Somner is staging his original production in New York's South Street Seaport area . . .

" 'Vanity project'? I can't believe this. This is *hateful*."

"It's not great," Aleksandar says. "But that's how it works."

Panic twists through George from gut to ear. "Fire Judith," he says, his voice unexpectedly breaking.

"Listen, it's just a gossipy side-item in a trade rag. Our content isn't public yet."

"So?"

"So all they have to talk about is the casting and the lease."

"But it's spiteful!"

"You prefer they start with a positive angle we have to live up to? Let them start negative."

"Judith draws unnecessary attention. She called them, I know it."

"*We* called them. Our PR called them. Don't pretend to be naive. Take a breath. Stop sulking. Unsquinch your face. That's bad energy. You're like an angry little raisin! You know all press is good press. You know we start low and little. You're the business guy. This is 101."

"*I'm* the business guy? I hate that!"

"Taking criticism is one of your roles as producer. You're our captain, George."

"Then as your captain I order you to lower your voice. Rehearsal is *in progress*!" he cries, folding his arms over his chest.

"We're a small potato. In our case, all press really is good press. With my heart, I believe that. But I will lock down the publicity if you only want sunshine. Do you only want sunshine?"

"No, I understand. It's good to be written about."

"Hey, look. Your name. Those are real pixels, my friend! Zoom in. Blow it up. Yum. Hello, Mr. Somner."

"There it is, huh?"

"There it is."

George has to get back to the office. He nods to Judith, sitting in the first row, drinking her ginger tea with honey. He waves, and as they do sometimes, the group erupts into scattered applause. He raises his hands in the air. "Not me, you. You, you, you!" He exits the dim theater and strides out into the bright day, scanning the street for a taxi back to midtown, the warm cobblestones of old New York under his heel.

17

"Well, hello! You surprised me." Iris is killing the evening in the supermarket, inspecting a fan of kale.

"Did I?" Bob replies. "Good thing that was my plan."

"I haven't seen you since the boat, have I? How are the twins?"

"Taller and louder. Back to school, thank God."

"Of course. I forgot. September still feels like summer to me. County Day?"

"No, we moved back to the city. George didn't tell you? Sixty-Third and Second, right between the boys' school and work."

"Convenient."

"Sure is."

"How's Martha?"

"Fine. What the hell's happened to George? Haven't heard a bark from him in a month. More than a month. I miss my drinking buddy."

"He's so busy. He's consumed. The opera's in rehearsal. It's all he talks about."

"Lucky Iris." Bob laughs, reaching his big hand idly into her shopping cart, lifting out a yogurt. "You must be short on company. You a fan of opera? Between you and me."

"We went a few times last year. It's not my thing, but I get having the bug. I was in bands as a kid. I've never seen him so—driven, I guess is the word."

"Look at you! Slick. Nice and evasive. You're learning, kid. Sounds like George doesn't know you ain't froufrou enough, am I right?"

She can't help smiling. "Bob! I *am* learning. About opera. Maybe you're a little right. He's excited. I'm excited for him. Really."

"And I'm excited three. Now, how about I could use your help? If you don't mind."

"My help?"

"Let's say George was in the doghouse. What would he buy you here to cheer you up?"

"Here? At the supermarket? I don't know about here."

"All the other shops are closed. So early, these small towns. It isn't even dark. I've been visiting a client, but by the time I get back to the city, all *those* shops will be closed, see?"

"They have flowers up front. But they're tired. You could go across the lot to the wine shop."

"Could we take a look?"

"At the flowers?"

"Wine gives Martha a headache."

They move to the front of the store. A few plastic buckets of roses and daisies sit among mixed bouquets already rolled in tissue paper and tinted plastic.

"I don't know what to do," he says, looking at the daisies.

"Let's try to fix something together." She pulls two clumps of browning pink roses from the water and then four bunches of lilies. "Hold these." She pulls the baby's breath from the roses and plunks it back in the display bucket. She removes the browned outer petals from the roses and puts the little pile in her cart. She gestures for Bob to unwrap and loosen the lilies.

"I'm going to hand you a few roses at a time. Mix them all up and make them fall together," she says.

"You can't be doing that," a cashier calls from the register.

"It's okay," Iris says. "We have two bunches of roses and four lilies. We'll be right over."

"What do I do next?"

"You hold it and I'll wrap it up. The plain white paper from the roll. See? Not so bad. The twine, not the ribbon. Fancier the girl, plainer the string. I only learned that recently."

She pulls the six neon price stickers from where she's saved them on the back of her hand and holds them out to the cashier.

"My hero, Iris. Why don't we all have dinner? Guilt George into it. Next week."

"You think Martha will have forgiven you by then?"

"Hope so." He raises the fat bouquet and they say goodbye. When she turns at the far end of the aisle, she sees he's right where she left him, still under the surveillance of the checkout woman. Iris wonders what keeps him from stepping forward to pay, what it is he forgot.

18

Something isn't right. It's hard to breathe. She sees a rolling hill of daffodils. It is in her eye. She is aware—there's a flickering, a bird flying close to her over the field, a red hawk torquing low, too close to her face—oh, it's not the wing of a hawk but her own eye coming open. A flat field of dandelions—dandelion, daffodil, dandelion, daffodil, but which is the yellow word? Over there—is it? The black button lost off her sweater, shining in the field. She will sift the field and catch the button up. But now everywhere is white. Is it snow? No, she's so hot it can't be snow. White with blue. Not lines. Dots. Dot-dot-dot-dot-dot-dot-dot—dots make a line. Cloth. A gown. A hospital gown for sleeping. Yellow again, rolling past, skipping under the side of her eye. The floor. Oh, no. The floor is sick! Poor sick floor! I are lying in a bed and I are moving. There are people by her side and they are moving too. Now they're in a metal—she—a freight elevator? It clangs! Gurney. *Gurney* is a word that must be related to whatever is going on. Out of the hot refrigerator and down a hallway. Small windows at the top and gray pipes in the ceiling. Basement. Underground! Bags of trash, passing a pile of black bags of trash. She cannot hear! Air, a swinging door—a different hall, brighter. Woosh, another hall, brighter still. A room. Stopped. Something beside her breathing like an animal, wheezing like a dog, but made of plastic. The dog is bright red plastic! A man giving an order. In the fluorescent she sees two silver spears, one under each of her hands. Now, why are they so silver? Someone puts a mask over her mouth and nose. It's blue and hard and attached to a tube. It hisses and makes mist into her nose and throat and tastes bitter and is frightening and what, she tries to say, why? The silver spears must be for her to save herself. They are beautiful. But why can't she gather them up? She must pull, like Arthur. She pulls but they do not come free. A man—a doctor?—directs her: "Get up! Borrow the arms and legs of your children for that is why you made them!" No, she pleads, that's not why I made them. I don't know why I made them. I didn't have a reason! Guardrails. So stupid! Stupid, stupid. Guardrails in the sides of the bed.

Someone puts a clipboard on her chest for a long, a very long, time. She forgets. There is a nurse whose head is a balloon tied to the silver rail of her bed. Through the mask she tells the nurse, where there are rules, there are secrets, nurse, where there are rules, there are secrets! But the nurse does not notice and the effort exhausts her and—here's the hawk again, the awful ripping sound of a hawk and her arm has been caught up in its talons and—it's not a hawk but another nurse, holding a knife or a pen or a spoon to her arm and she knows: this woman is communicating something to me. This is a secret way of giving me a message. But what does this nurse try to say? Ah, the nurse tells her, through the spoon pressing the inside of CeCe's elbow— You're not white, didn't you know? You're black. And you are very young and plump and you are here to make some babies! She looks down at herself and sees, yes, indeed, she is young and plump and black—why, she's Patricia's friend from school, that dear fat friend, and she is there to have some babies. How lucky for them to be having babies the same time! And it's not just Pat who loves her, there is a man who loves her too, and he will come and sleep with her and then they will have the babies, which is why she is at the hospital, for there is no glad reason to be in a hospital but the coming of babies, and why didn't they tell her this right away? Happiness and peace envelop her— she's hot and it's hard to breathe but it's all for babies. And! She's free to be anything she likes, young and black as she is, and what will she become—a singer, like that woman in Paris with the beguiling name? But in peace there is danger, for—she almost forgot them, they are so slippery—now have arrived the men in the suits. There are three of them and they are trying to kill her. Their suits are dark gray. They come when no one else is in the room. Ah, they are lawyers! They talk to her like she is a little baby. They push a pen against her hand and want her to sign a paper. She wishes one were her son, but none is her son. There's something she is thinking she must tell Patricia. Dear Pat, where have you been? But it's not Pat, it's the woman with the spoon. The woman says, There, there. But where does she mean? She looks there and there, and the dog, the wheezing red dog is still beside her. He is very unnatural. And! He's found her button in the field of daffodils. He's going to the clapboard shed at the edge of her property to meet her and to give it back. The shed is very low. She crouches in-side. She is naked and there are a pair of oars and a wooden box of heavy iron hinges and gate hooks and door knockers and lock tumblers and the window is broken and the dog is there and he stands atop the pile of rusted license plates and he has the black button from her sweater for his left eye. Here is your button! He shakes his head and out it comes. Why aren't you at home? he says. Go home. You are safer at home. If you stay here, the man who stands outside the window and watches will come to the bed and eat you. Oh, Dog, she tries to say, I am so thirsty! But when she looks around the shed and tries to read the license plates, not anywhere can she find the word *thirsty* and her button has rolled away. Esme, help me, Esme. Now she is so mad at Esme! Why didn't you clean upstairs like I asked? It's dirty upstairs and because of you I have to live down here in the basement. What am I paying you for? Bring me water, and bring my husband a Scotch and flat ginger ale, his stomach is bothering him. Esme, please-oh-please. Esme—no, it is the woman with the spoon. Thirst is the most terrible madness! She must make the idea of thirst come through her eye because her eye is all that's left of her mouth. Other people are in the room too, but none of them listen.

Night, it is night. Bed, she is in a bed. Something beside the bed. A bag. A red plastic bag that is big and has words on it she can't read. Stupid as always. Her legs are locked but they want to be unlocked. It is always shameful in the dark. The men in the suits are under her bed. One of the men has left his violin case on the chair. It is filled with birdseed. She will kick it away. A violin case filled with birdseed is an evil thing. Red, red, she must be inside her own eyes. Open. Maybe it is Son who is across the room. Son is sitting in the dark, watching her, far away. George! George, look at me, I am here! George is not looking at her. Inside her racking tremor there is no tremor. Inside where there is no tremor, there is a child. She is in the hospital, and she will have a batch of babies, and after she has them her hair will turn white. Come here, Son, come to me. I am having a nightmare. Son's face is a stone that waits for water. Hands at her throat. Not the lawyers, but her own hands, the sides of her hands are beating up against her throat. Hands, do please take this mask off me, hands, oh, please. Son in the chair so far away. My son, what has happened to your legs that you sit and do not come to me? Son must be hurt! Son would come flying if he still had his legs. Oh, so sad. She is so sad for her son. How did this happen to her George, did they never tell her he was in the war? Now it is day. So bright her eyes will not open. Back in her room upstairs! She was this close to firing Esme. A man at the window. Green in the glass rectangle. Green at the bottom and blue at the top and the man in the middle. A lawn. Green and sounds like *hrrr hrrr hrrr hrrr hrrr.* There is a helicopter. Walter is in it. Walter says, evil is made of all the things you forget. Walter says, the more you forget a thing, the more beautiful it can make itself in the dark. A hand in her mouth. Cleaning. Fingers inside her mouth. Water. Water on her forehead. She's on the beach. She has slid down the sandy dune. Here is her tremor. Racking every limb. She looks into the sky. Walter's helicopter is gone. She stands where the surf has made a white line of sputum. They will never let her get out of bed. She will lie and shake until she is a paper husk, and rising on her own, she will tear like the shell of a dried chrysalis.

Then it is many years of dreaming.

Then there is waking.

"You." She says to the landscaper passing her window. She has gotten her mouth back.

"Good morning," he says.

It's nothing to him, that she has made the words and he has heard them. The blue mask is gone. Hedge. Lawn. Lake. Man. Green. Window. Bed. Sky. Door. Herself, where she had been.

"Help me," she says.

He disappears from the window. Soon a doctor and a nurse are by her side.

The nurse takes her hand and pats it. "You had pneumonia."

"Of course I did," CeCe replies. "You think I don't know?" And as quick as she is able, she turns her face so they will not see her cry.

II

THE BURNING PAPERS

(Fall)

19

"But those types of loans are unstable," Martha says with a cold, little laugh, like ice cracking in water. "The language is intentionally obscure."

George is sitting beside her, the smooth brass balcony rail under his hands. He leans out, surveying the empty seats below. He can barely contain his pride. Bob and Martha are the first friends he's brought to the theater. Iris's idea, to bring them and go to dinner. Four weeks of rehearsals already come and gone, and here they are, arrived at a preliminary run, with orchestra. No costumes yet, but part of the set is assembled. I can barely contain my pride, he thinks. I can hardly sit still.

"My wife," Bob sighs, "is fond of reframing the incompetence of individuals as ethical violations of entire industries. No credit, no these United States. Truth. Boom."

"George," Martha says, "have you lost weight?"

"A little."

"Culture of academia's finally got Martha. Grousing about the powers that be using words nobody knows in undecipherable combinations."

George had insisted they sit in the balcony—"I need the artistic distance," he said, as they entered the theater. He'd leaped the curving stairs two at a time and felt Martha's gray gaze on his back. He also doesn't want to distract the soprano by sitting too close. He suspects in the last weeks she's become overwhelmed by the relentlessness of his creativity and has developed a crush on him. What else explains her sudden aloofness, her disinclination to respond to his suggestions?

"What word did I use that was too hard for you, monkey?" Martha says. "*Obscure?* But I agree with you. Something the academics and the businesspeople have in common. Language against clarity. Against its purpose."

"I probably have the name of the loan mixed up," George says. "Iris's agency knows what it's doing. It's not like the subprimes. A program, affordable something. Fiscal Future Brighter something."

"Where is she, anyway?" Bob asks.

"Running late. A closing."

George looks at his phone, on silent. No update from Iris. A missed call from RESTRICTED. Likely a payment he's fallen behind on. Doesn't matter. It actually encourages him when the creditors call, which they do with increasing regularity. It's a jolt, that word, *restricted*. Reminds him he's got something on the line. The stakes are high. He's finally in the soup of life. Pursuing something big, he is in turn pursued. It's practically natural law, this hero's chase to opening night. How the droning voices of the agents delight him! Unaware of what they're up against, ignorant of all that's in store for the man to whom they speak. If only you knew who you're trying to hook, he thinks, when they call.

"A housing program," Martha says. "Is it public?"

Her eyes remain fixed on the empty stage. George observes the tight stroke of ash-blond hair behind the pearl screwed into her ear; the blue convexity of her nose; her flimsy, sallow neck jutting from the taupe collar of her suit jacket like the stem of a parched fawn lily. Before he can answer that he doesn't know, George hears Bernard call, "We're ready," from the back of the theater. The lights dim.

"Martha's practically a socialist in her middle years," Bob whispers loudly. "Welfare for everyone! Anything makes a profit can't be trusted! Excepting me, of course. A long way from Delta Gamma, huh?"

George scans the rows below. He doesn't remember Bob and Martha being so irritable with each other in the past. Where is Iris? He strains to keep the entire room in his vision. Aleksandar and his paisley headscarf appear under the red glow of an exit sign. She'd texted earlier, a mode of communication she employs with enthusiasm even as he disapproves of its putrefaction of language: SELLER'S LAWYER JKASS. ½ HR DLAY SORRY SORRY SORRY.

"You're confused about what socialism is," Martha whispers.

Iris's following text had been: BILL=BEUTIFL SUIT. VICTOR=SOCCER SHORTS. HAHAHA. BIG DAY SORRY.

Nothing since. The curtain stirs. George hears—backstage, stage left?—a thud like a piece of furniture being dropped.

"Aren't you a twitchy, fucking mess," Bob says, reaching over his wife and slapping George's bouncing thigh.

"He really is," Martha agrees.

"Don't jump, like what's his name."

"He fell," Martha corrects.

Earlier that year at Lincoln Center, a man had plunged from the fifth ring to the orchestra and died where he landed, during the final act of *Coppélia*.

"My people say he jumped," Bob whispers loudly.

"You don't have ballet people," Martha replies, leaning over George, folding her hands tightly in her lap. "I know because I have ballet people and they've never heard of you."

"Martha," Bob says, still in a hoarse stage whisper, "had a sex dream about the guy."

"Shhh," George says.

"*After* he fell. The dream was about *after*."

Bob sticks his fat hands out over the theater like a diver.

"Go for it," whispers Martha, without parting her blue incisors. "Send us a postcard."

The conductor strides to the podium and bows to the empty room. The spotlight shafts through his hair and sets it ablaze, the dust around his head lit like a galaxy. For a moment, George is jealous. The conductor turns his back to them, lifts his arms. The violinists begin to play. PLEASE LET ME KNOW WHERE YOU ARE, he texts Iris, frowning, soldiering clumsily through the keystrokes. The overture ebbs and crests. The curtain lifts into the rafters. No reply. The spotlight sun of the New Desert races across the first few rows as if eight to noon is but a second's passage. Here's the exterior of the harem—the simulacrum of a glass and steel skyscraper, fronted by two sphinxes, which he insisted on because the first opera he'd seen had been *Aida*. At that opera's intermission, twenty years ago, he'd stood under the lamplight outside the theater where everyone was smoking—when everyone still smoked, except George. He leaned toward his date, an equestrian copy editor for the *Hampton Classic Newsletter*, to kiss her. But she recoiled and, wiping the back of her hand against her mouth, admitted their mothers had conspired to bring them together but she'd heard stories about George her mother hadn't. And that it was weird how all through the first act he'd burst into laughter each time a high note was achieved. He tried to explain how it embarrassed him, so much feeling let into the world. More important, what stories had she heard? The school had cleared him of any wrongdoing. But she turned her bare shoulders and bummed a cigarette from the man standing next to them. So alive, leaning over the glowing match. She hadn't said goodbye, but instead looked at him with a deep smoke-spilling frown and took off, almost at a run, down the street. For years, this humiliation would rise before him each time he entered a theater, but moving to his seat, he'd recast the moment in his favor: pity her as she fell in love with him, dismiss her advances, comfort her as she wept and begged and stomped out her filthy cigarette, put her in a cab, and return to the jostling lobby, where another woman, a less judgmental and more pornographically endowed woman, would be waiting for him at the bar. He came to feel a righteous, galvanic pride as he crossed the threshold of a theater, an impassioned swell of fellow feeling for the fellow that was himself. After that night, he never missed a season. He doesn't even remember her name.

How late is Iris? Iris understands. Iris understands he listens critically because he believes simply, because he believes in music's potential for perfection. Isn't this the optimism of high standards, and not pretension, as the horse woman had implied and yet another girlfriend had claimed? To have aesthetic disappointment mistaken for arrogance! Now she's missed the entire overture. I am queasy with dread, he thinks, patting his stomach. Two years ago, nothing could have caused him such fear. His thoughts rise on the first aria. All day he'd planned what to whisper to her tonight, about the music, about their future. How much there is for them to do together. If they can get away the coming winter, to celebrate the opera's reception, he'll take her to the bluest sea. Santorini, or Sicily. Could she have e-mailed instead of texted? He opens his in-box, holding his hand over the screen.

Patricia Somner <psomner@gmail.com>   Sept 18 (4 hours
                                                            ago)
                                                to bcc: me

dear loved ones,
    i'm SO happy to share that Lotta's been commissioned
to design the annex across the street from the Sao
Paulo Museum of Art! it's official, so i can let the
cat out of the bag! 218,000 square feet dedicated to
three-dimensional work from around the world. babies
and buildings, what a year!
    w/love and pride,
    pat

More good news from Pat. Well, isn't that loathsome! Isn't she obnoxious! Isn't Lotta the best! What an achievement! Everyone on Pat's bcc must be so impressed! He thrusts his phone into his pocket. He must focus on what's important, what's happening onstage—the soprano's kneeling in the waters of the catacomb, where she's been caught attempting to escape by the chief eunuch. An hour gone, and no Iris! The soprano is lamenting harem life, and lo! She is beheaded. Martha's making a clucking sound beside him. She loves it. He's thrilled. And yet, he's distracted, listening and not listening, worried about Iris, angry with Iris. Iris in Santorini—with him in a bleached rowboat, floating among the black volcanic stone that rises in mountainous clusters out of the water. They're drawing the shoreline with bits of the stone they've broken into their hands as they float by. She's leaning back, the sun on her collarbones. In happy silence they admire the whitewashed houses terraced up into the old hill. For a moment he forgets she's not beside him. A crash of the cymbals and he remembers. Looking at the dull velvet of the empty seat, his vision mingles with a nightmare of why she is late: a car accident! She falls out of the boat. He dives in to rescue her, her hair ghosting around her sinking blue forehead, her hands twining above her. Back in the car, terrible vision, do not look. Now, out of the water, dead and streaming wet. Back in the car, the car no longer wrecked, but she's fucking someone who isn't him, hiking her dress up in the garage, leaning her dripping hair over the hood of the Lexus and singing his libretto, her mouth twisted with malicious joy.

Despite the small size of the theater, Bob has produced a pair of binoculars, alternating which end he presses to his eye.

George touches Martha's shoulder. "I'm so worried about Iris," he whispers into her ear. "I'm imagining all kinds of terrible things."

"I know," she whispers back, leaning toward the stage to signal her concentration. "You've been jabbering away over there for the last ten minutes."

"What should I do?" he asks, louder, for now there's the insistent call of trumpets as the Unnamed Hero sings of how the queen has slandered him, sent out the alarm, border to border. Sings of how he will prove her wrong and gain his honor back. How he will tear apart her house, how he will break her rule.

20

"I'm so bummed I missed it," Iris says, a little out of breath.

They'd watched her dash diagonally across the busy street, the concrete wet with rain, Iris ignoring the white lines of the pedestrian crossing and the DON'T WALK sign ticking zero, to catch them as they entered the restaurant, a new brasserie designed to appear as richly worn as an interior by Manet. Through the crowd at the bar, past the red banquettes and smoked mirrors, they pick a round table over square.

George takes her hand under the table. "I had this horrible idea you were in an accident."

"George, I was! I was already late and—"

"Are you hurt?"

"I'm fine."

"What happened?" Bob asks, sounding serious for the first time that evening.

She explains they closed on the house at the lawyer's office and drove out of the generic office park, she in her car, Victor and Bill behind. They had a ways to go in the same direction and the cars stayed together. Victor got Iris on his cell and put her on speaker. They were all happily discussing how ugly the tiles in the downstairs bathroom were when a deep, low fog covered the road, unexpected for the middle of a warm September. She saw the flock of wild turkeys too late—fifteen of them maybe, but it seemed like fifty—lumbering across the road. She caught one under her front left tire.

"I screamed, *'Putain!'*—the only French I have from my mom comes out when I'm in trouble. She never spoke it with me. Anyway, I panicked and I turned the wheel. I heard Victor brake."

All she could see, another and another russet fringe of wing bursting in and out of the mist.

"Drove right into a ditch. One tire sunk, the other plastered with blood and feathers. Horrible."

Victor and Bill pushed while she steered the car—a silver Range Rover she'd chosen because it seemed to be what she was supposed to choose, a popular model in town, both showy and restrained—backward out of the ditch. She began to cry only when Bill set about making sure the tire wasn't damaged or off the axle. The way he was kicking the tires—this, inexplicably, was what did it. "What'd you think you're looking at?" she said to Victor, in her best wiseguy voice, to stop him from consoling her. "Wild turkeys, dumb as rocks!"

He nodded and left her alone to stare angrily into the trees. That morning, as she'd dressed for the closing, rain dripped through a crack in the skylight and rolled down the mirror, onto her glasses, where they sat beside the bed.

"I was so embarrassed."

"You should never be embarrassed," Bob says, his hand a thick crescent around his glass, "to have a feeling."

"Why didn't you call? Why didn't you text?" George asks.

"You forget to turn off the sound. I didn't want to interrupt. I was fine."

"Dumb as rocks. They are, indeed." Martha says.

"I can see you on the road, you poor girl," Bob says, "with all those birds."

George can see it too. Not too, *better.* There she is, dabbing at her lashes with the knuckle of her index finger, the birds lumbering past her into the misty shroud of the woods. It was a premonition he had had in the theater. He *knew.* Nothing separates them. Not even the usual impossibilities of time and space.

Iris looks at Martha's prim outfit. "Oh, God, I'm super overdone," she says, in the same affable, self-deprecating voice with which she's been telling her story, gesturing to the short, sequin-dotted meringue she changed into after the closing. "It made sense at home."

"It's lovely," Martha says.

"Bill drove my car and Victor drove me home. I called the car service and, George, it was that nice man, the nice older man, who keeps his hat on?"

"I knew something was wrong!" George cries.

"We were worried about you," Bob says.

"No, no, the salad's for me, over here." Martha waves. "And I'll have a look at the wine list now, please."

"Doesn't wine give you a headache?" Iris asks.

"No, you?"

"Maybe?" Iris answers, confused. "If I drink too much of it."

"Now, George," Martha says. "Your opera. It's about—is it about the end of civilization?"

"That's right." Happily, modestly, he studies the glistening mound of steak tartare that's appeared before him.

"And what were those blinking things on wires?" asks Martha. "Towards the end? During the battle?"

"Nano-drones. Weren't those neat? Operation Tinkerbell, in the annotated version."

"No whiplash?" Bob asks, looking at Iris. "Nothing like that? You're sure?"

"I'm fine. I want to hear about rehearsal. I bet the music was"—Iris tries out a word she wouldn't have used a year before—"glorious." She regrets it immediately.

"You mean, you haven't heard it?"

"He's very secretive."

"I didn't want her to hear bits and pieces of it until I was satisfied. I want her to experience the full effect. Tonight was to be, but . . . There are as many chances as we like from here on out."

"That's why I couldn't stand I was missing it!"

"There was some Spanish or Italian?" Martha asks.

"*Cazzo*, Monkey. My money's on George doesn't speak either," Bob says.

Iris laughs. It seems to be what's expected.

"You know what that word means?" Bob asks, surprised. "Where'd you pick that up?"

"Oh," she says. "Oh, no, I don't know what it means."

Bob and Martha smile at her in the warm light. They look alike, Iris thinks, though Martha is thin and Bob is not. Mineral-blue eyes, turtled and almost lashless; translucent skin; chinless as pilgrims. Expensive teeth. Hairlines high up their foreheads, alien, royal. Though Bob has the scrambled nose of a gin man and Martha's is as long as the fingers tapering around her fork. Odd that Bob's fingers are delicate too, considering his thick, square palms and the plump, womanish ferocity of his big frame.

George clears his throat noisily and leans back in his chair.

"Please, go on, George."

"Well, it began with the harem—I thought, Wouldn't a harem make a good chorus. Fooling around, but Iris urged me to take myself seriously. So I found a composer. Sometimes I set the text to the music Vijay sent me, sometimes I wrote the text before I got the music. The point is, it's not a story laid over a sound, you see? Our bid, Vijay's and mine, was to make the union in-di-visible."

"They were e-mailing each other for months before George told me," Iris says.

"She wasn't even jealous when she found out."

"Why would she be?" Martha asks.

"I suppose—well, what Vijay and I came to understand was, how to put it, in a foreign country you hear the language all around you *like* music. Right now, you understand what I mean, so you don't hear the sounds. But when you can't use a language, its color, its chroma, appears—my partner's phrasing is a bit romantic—he says that the 'language undresses for you,' it reveals its sounds and rhythms, its form. Its innate musicality. To write, at least parts, anyway, in a language I don't know for a score I haven't heard—the mystery may be returned. We are writing about a fractured world, after all. The process reinforces that. We tried to keep the meaning from each other as we went, so we might have a shot at—how can we return the sound, how can we put sentiment, real sentiment—by divesting the creator of the ability to create! So he—I should say, I, would have to be smart enough to know—an expert, but not in what he is doing—so he stumbles in the dark, so he may experience the revelation—if the right hand does not know what the left hand is doing, it is only in the dark that we may—" He circles his hands in the air.

"What a load of shit," Bob says, pointing his fork at George. "High concept, why not? One day Martha and I will be at a party and your name will come up and we'll say, That edgy fuck? That guy? That guy used to be our friend."

"Thank you," George says, genuinely moved.

"Bob, language!" Martha cries. "George, that portion when the harem women were attacked by the gypsies was striking. Is that how you meant it, for the treatment of the women to be so degrading?"

"You are thinking of the chorus in Italian where the women sing *yes*? Because they're enslaved, so that's all they can say, sure. And when they go up and down the octaves, *sí, sí, sí*—"

"Is that your mother's name?" Martha asks.

"Where?" He glances around at the adjoining tables.

"And that," Bob says, "is what you get when you're married to an analyst."

"I'm not an analyst. I'm a professor of clinical psychiatry."

"How clever," George says.

"But that's not why," Iris prompts. "Tell them like you told me."

"Okay, as we see it, after so many iterations, the word becomes a pure color wash of sound. In this way, the women are freed. Metaphorically.

By accepting their yes. That's Vijay's. I can't take credit. Try it: *sí, sí, sí.* Say it again."

The three sit silently looking into each other's face, mouthing the words.

"Still, I wonder—" says Martha.

"God, yes," Bob says. "Another bottle, the same."

There's a long pause, punctuated by the rigorous motion of silverware.

Iris laughs, suddenly and without precedent. "What does *cazzo* mean?"

"Cock," Bob says.

"Tell us something about yourself, Iris," Martha says.

"Oh, hum. I've got nothing. I like hearing about George's opera."

"Iris also has a musical background," Bob says.

"You do? What kind?"

"Not any real thing. A couple of bands. Punk. Glam, for a second. Ridiculous. The glam wasn't—it was mostly about the makeup for us, so it didn't work out. Turns out glam on women is just women."

"You were the singer?"

"No way. Too shy, no pipes. I played bass. Shitty bass."

"Wait." Bob puts down his glass. "Tell me you were into the Pist."

"Yes! I worshipped the Pist. I wrote this extremely bad song that was a total rip-off of 'Threat.' Remember 'Threat'?"

"What's Pist?" George asks.

"Best band," Bob says, "ever."

"We played CBGB's once."

"You're breaking my heart," Bob says. "What were you called?"

"That was when we were the Peepholes. But we were booked to play so early, like five people were there."

"How'd you trick it up? Eye makeup and a serious belt? Everything else shit? Shit jeans, shit T-shirt?"

"Yes, yes, yes."

"Record deal?"

"Not really."

"I bet you signed your rights away to some slug. If I go buy your album on Amazon or whatever, you wouldn't see a dime, right?"

"Not a dime. But we never had a real album. I don't think the slug made much off us."

"CBGB's," Bob says, shaking his head.

"Was that the coffeehouse?" George suggests.

"I don't miss it," Iris says. "Stage fright."

"When does the opera open?" Martha asks.

"Three months. Christmastime."

"Get the tourists. Smart."

"Will CeCe be hosting something?" Martha asks. "To celebrate?"

"I didn't tell her," Bob says, staring at Iris.

George explains. When he's finished, Martha shakes her head and offers her condolences.

"We hope she'll be coming home soon. But you understand, she doesn't want the word out. Not until she has a sense of how she's doing, one way or the other."

"On the upside," Martha says, "it's good to hear her trial's phase two. And that it's open label."

"I'm not clear what that means," George admits.

"It means they've got a lot of money under it," Bob offers. He lifts the lemon peel from his espresso saucer and chews it noisily.

"True." Martha continues, "At this point, sometimes a drug's already on the market for something else and they're working on a different application. Label expansion. Viagra was like that. Sometimes regulatory submission is pending and they're looking to see if benefit exceeds risk. These tend to run over longer periods of time, like your mother's. But a fair shot at FDA approval. Phase three, the number of trial participants expands. Phase four is postmarket surveillance. Open label means you know what she's getting. She's not getting a sugar pill."

"Pull a few strings, George?" Bob says. "Who'd you sleep with, business or medical?"

"That's not how it works, Monkey."

"Who's developing?" Bob continues. "It's called Astrasyne? Bad name. Come on, I'm curious."

Iris notices a blotch flowering on Martha's pale neck. "No," Martha says. She flips her napkin onto the table. She stands abruptly, heads for the bathroom.

"Well, that was dramatic," Bob says dourly. "Hey, how are those?" He points at the half-eaten profiteroles on Iris's plate. "Good?"

"Do you want me to go check on Martha?" Iris asks, to get out from under Bob's attention.

"Whatever."

She finds Martha at the sink in the large, dim restroom, wiping her cheeks with her hands.

"I'm sorry to pry," Martha says quickly, straightening up, "but is George doing all right?"

"George?" Iris dislikes both of them. She'll make an excuse, next time.

"He seems like he's under stress."

"Yeah, he's a wreck. The opera's a big deal for him. Hey, are *you* okay?"

"Bob pushes my buttons."

"More flowers, right?"

"Flowers?"

Iris has made a mistake. What mistake, she isn't sure. "Isn't that what they do, these jerks of ours, when they piss us off?"

The door swings open. A woman rustles past them into a stall.

"Are you suggesting Bob and I end fights with flowers? Is that how grown-ups resolve conflict where you're from?" Martha looks at Iris through the mirror.

"Wow. Okay."

They return to the table. Martha suggests that she has to get up early the next day.

"Hate to let the drinks go to waste," Bob says, reaching past the coffee cups to swallow the warm remainder of Martha's wine. He pays the check, waving George away. This pleases George. Yes, he treated them to his opera. Only right they pay for dinner. They'd loved *The*

Burning Papers. They'd asked him hard questions and he answered impressively. They stride through the mirrored room. How sharp he looks with Iris by his side in her hot, crazy dress. People glance up as they pass.

In the car home, she holds his hands in her lap. "Martha seems unhappy. I'm glad we're not like that. I'm glad *I'm* not like that. Bob is so gross."

"He's my friend."

"He has his charm. But he's a fucking pig to Martha. I mean, didn't you notice how he was staring at me? Martha did."

"Not pig. *Monkey*," George snarls, lifting his hands to scratch his head like a cartoon primate. "And as far as I'm concerned, everybody's hitting on you." His naked wrist. When will he remember to pick his watch up from the shop? Tomorrow, tomorrow on the way home from work. He pushes up his nose with his index finger and makes his best snouting-pig sound.

She gasps and fixes her eyes on his. "No, Mr. Pig. Mr. Pig, no!" she cries, and as he leans toward her, she recoils down into the trough between the seats, disappearing into the glittering foam of her dress, laughing as she sinks.

21

The next morning, exiting the 8:42 into the rush of Grand Central, George pauses in surprise. The canvas tarps that hung like great dingy sails against the station's east windows are gone. The terminal is filled with light. Gone too are the workmen in city coveralls, rigged to the ceiling. All summer they hung from the painted-blue sky, cleaning decades of grime. Sunlight beams through the scaffolding, still erected against the glass. He strides through the crowd, swarming its concentric circles under the ceiling's constellations.

Caffeine, he decides. A cappuccino. He's paying for the venti at the kiosk when his phone buzzes in his pocket. His mother. How free and consequential he feels in the noble station, that should not technically be called station but terminal. He can't answer now! He resolves to call her later. He's struggling with how to arrange the hot paper cup and his newspaper while returning the jangling phone to his pocket when he sees the woman ten feet away, standing in the pool of sunlight by the information booth under the terminal's central clock. She's leaning over a child, a boy of seven or so, placid and reedy in khakis and short-sleeved plaid. She licks her thumb and rubs something sticky from his cheek.

George raises his hand with the coffee in a tentative salute. Where does he know her from? She looks in his direction but her gaze remains unfocused, or focused only on the totality of the thronging crowd; he squints his most arresting, brooding squint, puts his free hand in his hair, to no result. Who is she? A neighbor from Stockport? An employee at one of the organizations he's evaluated for the Arts and Culture Fund? She's small, pretty, with close features and a serene air, maybe thirty, maybe twenty-eight, a lavender mouth, a lavender shirt, her black hair in a low puff. "Hallo!" he begins, but then she's past him, tugging the boy. Penny. No wonder he had trouble recognizing her, in this different costume. But how is it she doesn't recognize him? He, looking the same? Penny's hand, tight on the strap of the boy's backpack. He watches them hurry away. She could at least have smiled.

That afternoon drinking with Bob, George had exited the hotel meaning to go home, but after several blocks he turned around. His umbrella! With the single-minded commitment of the inebriate, he'd retraced his steps. He paused at the threshold of the bar. Across the room, Bob and Jim Frame were laughing at something Gita was saying. The umbrella, likely under her feet. The prospect of again looking into her clever eyes under their sticky black lashes—"he's famous in here maybe"—sent George into a quiver of fresh resentment. *Ravens*-something, he heard Jim Frame say. Football? At the gloom of the word *raven* he retreated. They had not noticed him. "May I be of assistance?" The concierge. George blinked. Then he asked how he might find Penny. The concierge gave him a puzzled look. George remembered Penny had put her number in his phone. He texted ARE YOU STILL HERE? and ten minutes later watched her walk past him and get on the elevator, watched himself get on the next elevator and make his way to the room. She pulled the curtains against the glow of the street-lights and clicked off the lamp. He could hardly see her and could hardly remember her face from their woozy time in the dining room. His being there, he decided, was Iris's fault, a little. It had put him in a mood, her not joining him in the city. Iris and Victor—the smallest tear along the seam of their marriage. Not often, but lately George catches Iris looking at him with a kind of alarm, as if he were a stranger. Was there really even an open house? And, and, and. Penny. What of it? Iris's betrayal, greater than his. Oh, maybe it hasn't happened yet, maybe it's still ripping along toward them in the distance, but here it comes.

Penny, being deaf and in the dark, didn't ask him what he wanted, but set about undressing them in a way that made it clear he'd get whatever it was she chose and be grateful. It was, he decided, *interesting*, what with her silence and her precision, which, while effective, reminded him of the lifting and lowering of the metal arms used in the assembly of cars. Strange too how in this brief time with Penny he was some other man, a free, lonely man, lonely because he was free and free because he was lonely. But then, all at once, even before she climbed off him, how gloomy he felt! How wrong he'd been to doubt Iris! That night at home he hid in his office listening to Bartók and staring at the vintage poster of *Aida*. All the following week, he waited for the black storm of guilt to roll his chest, for the fear of discovery to consume him, for his wife's eyes to gutter doubt against his soul. It never came. His transgression served only to remind George how much he loves Iris. Did this not justify what he'd done? Justified too as a remembrance of freedom. Remembering freedom—an extension of love, not love's rival. He never wants Iris to suffer. He'd almost forgotten that wish of early romance, to keep his Iris from suffering. His life's very reason is to protect her from harm. How can being reminded of this be anything but good? He will never cheat again. Until now, he'd almost forgotten he had.

He hurries out of the station to walk the few blocks to work. He waves away the taxi that pulls up beside him. The walk through midtown will steady his nerves. Its predictable, numeric transparency—the streets, on a grid, demanding a series of rights and lefts; the jobs all for the accrual and dispensation of measurable units of output or gain; the windows flashing up the tower facades and the white stripes of the crosswalks flashing underneath the wheels of the cars; the orderly panels of buttons inside the elevators lighting up and going dim—the rule of the grid extending skyward, all around him, floor 40, floor 60, into the blue, but also down, through the steel bars of the gutters packed with grime—even the sewers built by math. A new-world city as numerical in its desires as a metronome, first and always designed for trade. Not like Paris, not like Rome: a city without curves. One, two, three.

At the office he's halfway down the hall when he notices something new and strange. Like a dream, to pass a second unexpected something in one morning. Fish. He doubles back. Behind the receptionist's head, enveloping her station, is a softly glowing crescent—a long, curved aquarium, six feet maybe, sleek and expensive-looking, filled with corals and the dashing iridescence of fins. The receptionist's coffee and a pen rest on the gleaming mahogany ledge at the base of the tank. She smiles at George and points to her headset: *On a call.* He turns back down the corridor to his office.

Audrey has nothing for him to review.

"Nothing?"

She shakes her head. "I took care of everything. I didn't expect you'd be in."

"How long has that tank been there?"

"Since, like two weeks."

"It doesn't look right."

"Reception said the new guy wanted it. The life aquatic, it's his thing." She ducks her head back toward her computer screen. "From Atlanta," she adds, as if this explains the tank.

"I didn't know there was a new guy."

"That's the big challenge of being new, I guess." She locks her eyes to the monitor.

Ah! He understands. "Listen." He leans over the wall of her cubicle, spilling a glop of his cappuccino down its gray, fuzzy side. "Listen. Audrey, I owe you an apology. I owe you serious proper gratitude for picking up the slack these last months. I know I haven't been around as much as usual. It's been a difficult time. My mother—the visits, her situation up and down, so far away, you understand. I really appreciate it. I've been meaning to see if we can't up things for you in some way—keep you on in your current capacity but improve your salary, maybe your title. What about *associate* instead of *assistant*? I don't know if they'll be amenable, it's not my call, but I'd like to take it up with Stanton one of these days. Or Hud, if he ever comes back from Palm Springs. That guy. He's got it all figured out, right?"

She looks quickly into his face and back down into her paper-clip drawer. Perhaps she is overcome. She clutches her cardiganed elbows. The place is always over-air-conditioned.

"But only if you want me to, Audrey. I don't want to presume I know your plans."

"Okay, thank you."

He enters his office but leaves the door open. As it seems he has no pressing grant evaluations or donor follow-ups, he opens the file on his desktop that says "Program Guidelines: New." He's been meaning to revise their language for elegance. He reads:

"Supporting the Arts in New York City: dynamic creative capital for one of the world's most dynamic creative capitals." Fine. He moves on and reverses the order of the words *innovative* and *team-based* in a sentence. He changes "fostering partnerships and institutional leader-ship" to "cultivating partnerships and strategic institutional initiatives."

"Audrey," he calls, waving her through the door and lowering his voice. "If you ever want to talk about anything—career, long-term goals? Fire away. Anytime. I wish someone had been available to me for strategizing when I was your age."

"That's really nice of you." Her hand is on the door. "Maybe that would be so helpful sometime."

His e-mail in-box is empty. He'd go to the theater but today they're in costume and wig fittings. It's happening so soon! He sticks his head out into the hall. "Hey, I have an idea. Why don't I go talk to Stanton about you right now?"

She blinks at him over the top of her cubicle. Oh, he remembers being twenty-five, everything a torment.

"Waiting would be okay. No rush."

"Nonsense, don't be shy! Call him up, find out when he can work me in. I won't commit you to anything. I understand how it is. Even if I can sweeten the deal, you'll have the last say."

She nods and after a few moments on the phone enters his office. "His assistant says give them five minutes to assemble. That's all they need."

"Assemble! That's a very good sign. You must already be on their radar."

"I just said you wanted to come by."

"Any requests? A bit more money, a better title? Sound good?"

"Okay, sure. Thanks, George."

Stanton's assistant ushers him in. Stanton sits heavily behind his desk in a cabled pullover. His pink face, as always, appears babyish and ancient at once. Betsy, the majestic retriever, makes a pile of gold straw on the blue carpet at his feet. George is surprised to see an unfamiliar presence in the room, a trim man of about his own age sitting in a chair beside Stanton's desk. Tight, salt-and-pepper sideburns, a purple tie. A slim, purple-and-emerald-argyle ankle sticking out toward George. As George sits, the man sets his Android on the desk. Stanton blinks at George in his slow, scrubbed way.

"You must be the new fellow," George says, half-rising from his chair.

"No, I'm Daniels."

"Daniels," George says.

"One of the consultants. But in a way, yes. The new man came via us."

"Of course," George says. "I'm looking forward to meeting him."

"Ah," Stanton says, resting a heavy, yellow knuckle on Betsy's head.

"He doesn't need to be at this meeting," Daniels says.

"Who?" George asks.

"Young," Daniels says.

"From Atlanta," George says.

"Can we get you a water," Stanton says.

"No," George agrees, "Young doesn't need to be here. This is pretty routine stuff. But happy to have you join us, Daniels. Why not. I'd like to talk about how much my assistant, Audrey Singer, does for this company. I'd like to begin the process of recognizing her contribution more than we have so far. It's been a few years. I'm wondering if there's any room in the budget for a raise, any wiggle on her title. She does a lot. A ton. And the question at hand—is she getting her fair share of the credit? I don't think so."

"The thing is," Daniels says, adjusting amiably forward in his seat, "I'm still trying to understand what you all do."

"The Arts and Culture Fund."

"Yes, but what do you do?"

"Well, we take it from beginning to end. Over a million dollars a year. Cultural institutions. That's what we do."

"But with your day? What's the day to day?"

"Day to day," George repeats. "Look, Audrey's fantastic. Is there an issue here I'm unaware of? Our process runs like a well-oiled machine. All our grants are up-to-date. Is there some question about her performance I can speak to?"

Stanton's eyes widen a fraction and slide in his direction, before settling back on Betsy.

"Not regarding Audrey. Or the fund, no. It rolls out fine. Very organized. But what do you do?"

"I just said—isn't that the same question?"

"Not really. It isn't the same at all."

"Okay." George opens his hands, stifling an impatient sigh. "I find and liaison with potential donors and grantees. I determine and enforce our program guidelines. I oversee the grant process from application to execution. I maintain grantor-grantee relations. I make site visits. I make sure our support staff, like Audrey, is keeping the records and accounting up-to-date. Among other things."

Stanton clears his throat. "You've submitted your revised program guidelines, like everyone else?"

"Not yet."

"What was your last site visit?" Daniels asks, in an encouraging tone.

"The Met. I went to the Met."

"Museum or Opera?"

"Museum."

"Winged Victory," Stanton says. "They stole it from the Greeks."

"It's striking," George says. "At the top of the stairs like that."

"The Met's is a replica."

"Then they didn't steal it," George offers.

"The French did!" Stanton says, raising a thick finger in the air.

"Now"—Daniels nods—"I understand from Will here that you've been under some personal stress. An illness in the family. Understandable. Totally sympathetic. But. You've been absent from the office for almost the entirety of our review process. Look at it from our perspective. An external firm is hired to review efficiency and we can't even find you to talk about your program. For nearly two months—"

"I've been here," George cries. "My hours have been unpredictable, it's true. There's a most lamentable—yes, a family situation. An illness in the family, as you say. Have I put it above my regular presence here?"

"You have," Stanton says.

"Indeed," George agrees, feeling the heat rise from his neck to his brow, knowing he must be eloquent, that something, unexpectedly, is at stake, "I have. And I wouldn't go back and do it any other way. Family first. Maybe it's still unfashionable in the corporate world for a man to say he loves his family! Well, I don't care. And I don't forget that Mr. Stanton, Will, you told me. You told me to take the time I needed. Here I've been juggling and struggling and still the program runs beautifully. Shouldn't this be testimony to, to—and this is the response I am hearing, this beat off?"

He'd meant to say *down*. Beat down. Maybe it's the fault of seeing Penny that he said that. The fault of a temporary madness! He squares his shoulders and works hard not to blink, to keep his mortification at bay.

"But, George," Stanton says, "George, we know this is not where you are. We know this is not what you're doing. For Christ's sake, you're doing press."

Daniels holds up a copy of *Opera News* with a periwinkle Post-it stuck between two pages. George knows it marks a small but exciting piece on Vijay, mentioning George as producer and librettist. How hadn't he seen the magazine right away on Stanton's desk? He has a dozen copies on his own desk at home. Now Daniels is handing George a stack of printouts from various opera websites that surely mention *The Burning Papers*. He recognizes the page on top, Operamania.com, as Aleksandar has bought ad space like rows of teeth up and down the virtual ribbon of the site's periphery, every day for the last month.

"You have been cheating on us." Stanton shakes his head. "If only you'd been honest. Then we would have understood better this problem with George Stemmler."

George wracks his brain. What could he have to do with anything? Stemmler, a kid, but already a program officer. Two floors down, Sustainable Agriculture. With that hippie seashell bracelet peeking out from underneath his suit jacket, rendering the lifestyle signification of both the jacket and the bracelet ridiculous. He hardly knows the guy.

"Audrey deserves—" George begins, and hears how her name hangs in the air like a mourner's cry, how his sentence will not finish.

"Did you send this e-mail to George?" Daniels asks, leaning over his purple sock to hand George another piece of paper, dated several months back.

From: George Somner <georgesomner@hudstanton.org>
Date: Mon, June 18 at 11:09 AM
Subject: asdfasfdkjdkldj
To: georgestemmler@hudstanton.org

The QUEEN sings {suggestion for Vijay: Cavatina}
   Build a fence around the gypsy where you find him on
your lot. Build a fence around the gypsy, while he
steals and schemes. / Look where the gypsy stakes his
tent, to the moss he lays his head for he knows deep
into the ground, the fruitful water-lands. / Wise
nations! Listen for the gypsy / for every sound he

makes—the shucking knife, the creaking wheel—sing out a murderous song: / beware the land that's common, where still the flocks may graze, for soon it will be barren, and shepherds will be beggars too

"I sent it to myself. I think it's very good."

"But you sent it to George."

"I sent it to George instead of myself?"

"To Stemmler."

"The address line, see?"

"So I did."

"George brought it to HR right away," Stanton says, speaking more slowly than Daniels.

"Why did he bring it to HR?"

Daniels holds his hand up, toward Stanton, to indicate *Let me.*

"He felt the content was unsavory. But, he was uncomfortable knowing it wasn't meant for him. He was torn. He didn't want to cause you embarrassment over something private. He says he won't mention it to anyone or speak against you in any way."

"Good man," Stanton says, petting the dog.

"So, George and HR agreed. As he refused to file a complaint, and as it was your first strike, it went in the file and would only be brought to bear if other issues arose. But in light of the rest—"

"What rest?" George asks. "Maybe you don't know how to read composition, maybe you don't know what you're holding, but there is nothing wrong with that. It's part of a greater work. I've heard that text sung in rehearsal fifty times this month alone and it is beautiful and it's right, and it's none of your concern!"

"So you concur you've missed more than a few days here and there," Daniels says mildly.

"George," Stanton says, "this material isn't fitting for our officer in charge of culture grants."

"You can see that, from where you are," Daniels adds pleasantly, as if he's pointing out a butterfly nestled in a flower.

"But the villain sings it!" George cries. "The villain!"

"Sometimes the villain and the hero are one and the same," Daniels says.

"This is where we part ways," Stanton says. "I'm sorry, George."

"Sometimes the villain and the hero are the same? They are *not* the same. There is no same! Any third grader will tell you they're *opposites*. This is a vision of the world gone *wrong*! Not an endorsement, a warning! I want to talk to the new guy. I want to tell him a thing or two about loyalty and how not to waste it here. I guess you're giving him my office. I guess that's the big surprise. The new guy is me."

"No. He's more senior," Daniels says, the Android back between his thumbs. "We're reevaluating on a macro level. We haven't decided if your funding will remain or be assimilated into other programs."

"Assimilated? Oh, consultants! You viruses of nothing, you—"

"Enough," Stanton says. "Thank you for your service, George, I mean that. Thank you. Ma-*rie*," he calls to the outer office, "Mr. Somner is ready to go. Get him a water."

Marie pops her silver head around the door and gives George a tight, heard-everything smile. She stretches out her hand, clutched around a bottle of water and a limp paper napkin. Betsy raises her head.

"I'll walk you," Daniels says. "We'll go over severance in your office."

George stands, nods his assent. The fight's gone out of him. He feels exhausted and forlorn and sure he shouldn't touch anything, like a child left in a store. He will not cry, he will not cry. He will not take the water.

Audrey's desk is more tidily arranged than usual. Her light and monitor are off.

"Sent her home," Daniels says, following his gaze.

"She knew? Will she get to keep her job?"

"She'll be fine."

An hour later Daniels and the corporate counsel that joined them have left with his signature in triplicate, with instruction not to contact anyone—grantee or affiliate—under penalty of suit and potential loss of compensation still due. George could see that Daniels could see that George was properly defeated and wouldn't make any troublesome phone calls. They agreed to leave him alone to pack up. He sits at his desk. He doesn't call Iris. He sits beyond the lights being dimmed in the hall. For the last time, out his window he watches the gold reflection of the sunset in the fins of the Chrysler Building. A woman pushing a cart enters to empty his trash bin. She wears blaring headphones and appears surprised but not interested to see him.

"You want I empty?" She gestures to the trash basket under the desk. Before he answers, she wrests the bin from between his feet and tips out its only item, the to-go cappuccino cup. She returns the basket and turns her cart around. The music leaking from her headphones is a hard, generic, danceable Eastern Europop. He hunts around in his pockets. Empty. No pill to cheer him up in his bag, either. He pats his hands deep into the back of each of his empty desk drawers. He stretches his arms in an awkward embrace around the pile in front of him—his copy of the severance contract and his heavy leather appointment book and his grandfather's box of snuff and the beautiful letter opener shaped like Brancusi's *Bird in Space*. He turns away from the glow of the adulterous computer. He rests his cheek on the cool shellac of the desk.

22

Walk, stay—these words came into her mind that first day at Oak Park, when she put herself in the supply closet. How embarrassing that was. She thought it was a room and that she'd find a telephone and call for the car. *Stay*—when she heard George squeeze in behind her wheelchair. She didn't have time to reverse. "You don't want to live in here, do you?" he'd said, almost gently. She'd clamped her mouth and looked at her hands on the rubber handles. Nothing to be said to nothing.

Every few weeks she takes a phone call from Pat, from Nan, from Esme and Annie. She tells them all is well. She'll be home soon. Brief and cheerful and nothing about the pneumonia. They must not suspect how reduced her circumstances are, how she is afraid. The less they know, the less it can be true.

Toto used to say, "Please walk me to the corner, Cecilia," her Irish accent buoyant and stern. Or "Walk your old Toto into the park." Halfway along shouting, "Stay!" Startling and hilarious. In the beginning, to teach CeCe to mind the curb. Later, to make them laugh. CeCe was nine when the United States declared victory over Japan, and Toto (properly, Miss Moira Quinn) deemed CeCe old enough to join the crowds. For an hour they walked south, to Times Square, the scraps of cloth and ticker tape thicker and thicker under their feet. They jostled in among the revelers. Toto laughed with a stranger, something CeCe had never seen her do. Adults so happy it was frightening. A man lifted CeCe up and Toto said, "Stay," in a different voice. When she was done scolding the man, CeCe screwed up the courage to ask if her mother could finally come home.

"What's this now?" Toto asked, leaning the starched wall of her torso to Cecilia, the crowd flowing around them.

"Mata Hari" was all CeCe could say, staring at her patent shoes. She'd learned the story of the female spy from a joke her father told. She didn't understand the joke, but she divined the truth: her mother was a spy. Evelyn had gone away just after the invasion of Poland. She returned to visit only twice, and with many other people always in the room. So beautiful! Never saying anything, but with the feeling of something important to say. What else but great sacrifice could explain why Evelyn left, and left again? Each mission more daring than the last. CeCe had kept her mother's secret. This made CeCe a hero of the war too.

"Dear little lady," Toto said. "Poor little-little, no. Your mother loves you as I do. She's no sinful woman like that Mata Hari. Who's been telling you stories?" Toto yanked CeCe back uptown. No *walk*, no *stay*.

The Astrasyne had been working. Sorrow, to have her progress smacked away by pneumonia! Now, when walking is difficult, her mind taps and drags with her feet, *walk-me-stay-walk-me-stay*, as she moves from bed to chair, from chair to hall, from hall to garden, from garden to lake. "A beautiful garden, a beautiful lake," someone is always saying—a nurse, a physical therapist. Yes, she nods, but she doesn't care to reply. *Walk me*—at the oddest times, the plaint loops and insists upon her sanity (binding her to sanity, or rasping sanity from her, hard to say), and its sound is odd too: the hush of Toto, faint for all the years.

By her fourth week on the drug, her limbs shook less. The pins and needles still rushed up her legs, but not as often and not as hot. The muscles in her legs connected one to the next. By the seventh week on the drug, her neck had uncoiled. Like magic, one morning in the mirror her head and neck rose out of her body like a new flower in a vase. Was it later that day or the next came the fever? Fever, and falling out of time and place, tumbling down the dark where no one could follow. She's recovering well. The doctors remind her. But she's weak. Breathless over nothing. George doesn't even know. Not because she's pretended to be fine, but because he doesn't call.

Dr. Adams, who is now her primary physician—the dismal young resident dispatched—says her treatment is back on course. But, to have gathered this second illness to herself, to be moved by any passing current like a frail curtain, is dispiriting. She wouldn't have contracted pneumonia outside Oak Park. It's the hospital bed and the doctors that are responsible for her needing the hospital bed and the doctors! When they visit her room, it takes a rousing of deceitful gusto to hide how much she hates them, and as she listens and smiles, she can feel her bitterness shrinking and tightening her features into her head like bright screws. To be so agreeable fatigues the soul. Yet as soon as they leave, she wishes them back. Out the window, an undecided sky, the color of weak tea. It's still morning. The nurse has come and gone. It's hot, not even close to lunchtime. CeCe is at the round table where she eats her meals. An outdated *Time* magazine is in front of her, its pages fluttered. She's read it all. First only the parts she was interested in, then the rest. She wishes she had the newspaper. "Always so late bringing the paper," she says, and her voice in the empty room chills her. No, self-pity is for the younger generation. For the younger generation, there's self-regard and self-interest and self-reflection and self-promotion, in a sea of handheld devices.

She will not feel sorry for herself. Instead, she will write Patricia a letter, tell her to come. It will take courage. She will forgive Patricia. It's time. Forgive her for moving so far away without making it right between them. Forgive Pat for living on the West Coast and for sending flowers, flowers, flowers—this week, a fuchsia orchid with moss in the pot, like a business gift. Forgive Pat for not allowing more time for

CeCe to get used to Lotta before they moved away. Anyone would need a moment to adjust to that Brazilian giant with the sneakers and the men's crew cut and the men's thin, gold-wire glasses and the custom dress shirts from London and the pretentiously outmoded black-and-white camera slung like a gun against her crushed and prodigious bosom! She will force herself to love Lotta. She'll say to people, *I love Lotta. Did you know our dear Lotta is a prominent architect? Did you know our family's been tied to Brazil for over a hundred years, first by business, and now by love?* She had at first wondered if Pat's attraction to Lotta wasn't an unthinking rehearsal, or did she mean reversal, of the Somners' dark presence in that country. She will no longer allow herself such unkind thoughts about her daughter.

Patricia must be showing. Nearly six months along? So old to be having a child. But! The birth of a grandchild may restore a family. She'll avoid the phone, write her thoughts so her anger does not get ahead of her. (Her first call to Oak Park, the voice said, "Hey, it's Pat," and CeCe replied, "Pat who?") She'll forgive Patricia. Patricia will forgive her. The Astrasyne will cure her. She'll leave Oak Park. Once she is settled back home, they'll bring their new baby boy. She hopes it's a boy, because isn't it livelier when lesbians have boys? Pat and Lotta and the boy will visit her all the time. When they're not visiting? There are so many books she hasn't read. She's never read *Anna Karenina*. She's never read *The Magic Mountain* or Churchill's letters to Clementine. Once, before they stopped speaking, Patricia told her to read Coetzee's *Disgrace*. She hasn't forgotten. She hasn't read it, but she hasn't forgotten. She'll read *Disgrace* in her garden by the ocean. She'll do some of the gardening herself. She'll give Esme a little raise. She'll buy Esme a little house. Maybe she'll give Esme George's house, to teach him a lesson. She'll take trips into New York to see her old friends and go to the theater. Rejoin a board or two. She'll take trips to the places she hasn't been since she was a girl and trips to places she's never seen. She's never been to Egypt. The corrections she will make! She'll take the *Queen Mary 2* across the ocean, though she expects it's not like the *Queen Mary* of her youth but rather a synthetically carpeted shitcan inhabited by the kind of tourist who wabbles about the deck clinging to his baseball cap and a sandwich, its stuffed lettuces flapping in the headwind. Yes, she'll be open-minded. She *is* open-minded! When winter comes, she'll stay at home and have fires built in the living room. She'll huddle the chairs around the fire. The chairs, as she currently has them arranged, are too far away from each other. She'll lean over spiced hot chocolate to listen with great appreciation to whoever is to be her company. She will, she will—she will stand by a tree in a snow-covered field. She'll set off across the field making footprints, her hands thrust deep in the pockets of her coat. She's not had the balance to walk with her hands in the pockets of her coat in a long time. She wants to let winter into her lungs and she wants to hear winter under her shoe and she wants to stand inside the bright made by the snow and not be dying and not be dead.

No. She can't bear to write Patricia this morning. What she needs is exercise. Her eye falls on her new walking stick. It leans beside the door. The landscaper made it for her, cut a branch not far from her window and made it smooth and level. Those first days she was recovering from the pneumonia—"We haven't connected with your son. Is there anyone else you'd like us to try?"—the landscaper made it a part of his day to check on her, by passing her window and glancing in. She suspects that since she called to him for help, he's felt a minor responsibility for her welfare, as if by doing her one favor he owes her another. She began raising her hand hello whenever he appeared. Even when she was tired, each morning she took the ghastly walker to the garden's closest bench, hoping he'd be by. The other day, surprising herself, she called to him from the bench, "Where are you from?" From Yemen. He told her his name, Yasser, and that he has a son and a daughter, "this high, and this high." He flies back twice a year to see them.

"I also have a son and a daughter, this high, and this high." She raised her twitchy hand as high as it would go. He looked down at her—right into her eyes—and said, "I'll make you a stick," and the way her heart knocked it was as if she'd fallen in love.

She looks out the window but doesn't see him. For a few days, she's listened to them again pruning the trees with the chain saw across the lake, too far for her to walk. Nothing left but to go find Dotty. She gropes her way past the wheelchair, folded against the wall—bedeviling, relentlessly leaning there, like a person waiting for her to make conversation. Today is a good day—she rejects the walker too, with the ironic horror that is the addition of bright green tennis balls to its feet. She takes the stick. She ejects herself into the hall. For some time there's nothing but air vents and the bar to steady her hand. She peers into the open rooms as she staggers past—the patients lumped under the sheets like gray octopuses—that can't be good. Farther down, she passes a room from which she hears an unusual commotion, a large man with a sparse white beard flung on the wave of seizure. Someone inside closes the door. She's never seen that before. More closed doors—145, 147, 149, the numbers shuttling away until she reaches the stark little gym with the wall of glass. She waves to the two women who walk a steep incline on the treadmills, who she's seen walking behind the glass all the days before. She reaches the bulletin board. Activities sheets and smiling photos of the physical therapists, with one or two salient details—"Did you know Inez plays the ukulele?"—pinned beside. Down, down, down. A purple-faced man shuffles toward her, gingerly escorting a mobile IV, eyeing the rod and bag as if it's a spirit companion he can't believe has chosen to walk the earth beside him. She is obliged to step out of his way. *Water for the ghosts*, another unlikely phrase that loops her thoughts. She wonders how her mind's underground stream— when the bucket is lowered, she is no longer sure what will be pulled back up. Like—*shitcan*—where had that come from, so obscene, so unlike her? The man with the IV turns through a door that someone's opened from within. A visitor's pocketbook hangs on a chair.

Down to Dotty's room. Knock, knock, knock.

"Come for a walk?" she asks.

"I'm tired," Dotty says. "Let's play cards."

23

But how to account for the hours? For it's another day and they are still or again playing cards. As if no time has passed, as if no other experience has intervened. The humidity's climbed. In the distance, the shabby racket of thunder. They are playing gin with the air-conditioning on and the window closed. In CeCe's opinion, Dotty, being from Arizona, is excessively interested in temperature control. Dotty in the recliner. As they play, black-winged clouds roll high above the lake, churn inward, bring sideways sheets of rain.

"—no other way you and me would have become friends," Dotty's saying, moving on from an elaborate oral diagram of the politics and allegiances of her church. "You hiding in your room. Good thing I don't have a dime's respect for the wrong side of a closed door. Otto and I got lost in Mexico one time, in San Cristóbal, and I marched right up to—"

"Your discard."

"Oh, yes. Have you been to Mexico?"

"Once."

"Then you know what I'm talking about. Breathtaking!"

They *have* become friends, CeCe realizes, with a disagreeable twining of mortification and gratitude. It's as if she's known the scrap of Dotty's brow and the puddle of Dotty's mouth opening and closing forever. How many times already have they double-caned it down the lawn to the water, CeCe scanning the landscape for her friend from Yemen, this woman like a bundle of white rags, ruffling at her side?

Dotty uses her good hand to pull a card from the fan she's arranged in the waxwork of her stroke arm and drops a two of spades.

"We have much in common," CeCe says. Better than talking to the wheelchair or the wall. Onward and upward.

"Back home they call us Dotto because his name is Otto and my name is Dotty, from when there was Deano and Dingo and names like that going around in the popular—"

"A dingo is a dog." CeCe says, not paying attention. The landscapers are not in sight. Dotty is telling her for what might be the fifteenth time that Otto is in charge of the Spanish-language division of Greetmark Greeting Cards, and would you believe, it's bigger than the English-language division, and she can get CeCe as many cards as she wants for free, and Otto is bringing his famous chef salad tomorrow, he's doing such a good job being on his own, flying out to visit every other weekend and never complaining about the trip.

No Yasser. They don't work when it rains. But the blimp that harasses her sanity is there, floating above the horizon in a bath of light, far beyond the storm. Floating as it does every weekend, moseying a circle. It's silver with a red bull's-eye logo she can't make out. She's been told it's the name of a brewing company.

"Isn't that pretty. Over the football stadium. Watch your cards!"

CeCe's fingers have slackened without her noticing. Her hands tremble. Now that Dotty's brought the situation to her attention, she can feel the jerking sting that connects the tip of her index finger to the inside of her shoulder socket. The jack and queen and king of diamonds she'd organized at the left corner of the fan loosen and slide over her shuddering thumb onto the table. She scoops them back up and switches hands. It's awkward, like playing from inside a mirror.

"I don't think there's a football stadium around here," she says.

"No? Let's keep going, I'll pretend I didn't see. Anyway, knock on a strange door in a strange land, that's how we met our Fernanda—my honorary Mexican granddaughter—now we do a house stay every year. To keep familiar with the culture. Even the oldest traditions change here and there! Fernanda was in the Christmas pageant, two feet tall and wearing a beard and a sheet and carrying the urn for the myrrh. Nearly toppled each step she took to baby Jesus. They have a special day for the Three Kings? The sweet little children leave their shoes out at night and find presents tucked into the toe in the morning. Otto's done a whole line of cards called 'What's in your shoe, pequeña?' Wouldn't it be nice if we woke up one day here and had presents in our shoes?"

How is it that even in front of this prattling and vacuous woman she's ashamed to have lost control of her hands? How can she endure another moment of this chattering—from her only companion, of her nervous system? Her head's shaking too, agreeing, despite the disagreement of the mind within.

"If I woke up here and found a present in my shoe," CeCe says, trying, mostly successfully, to keep the anger from her voice, "I'd consider myself terrorized, and I'd look for a way to escape before the arrival of breakfast." The trembling ebbs. "Gin."

"Will you look at that. Can you shuffle, do you think?"

"Yes, I'll try."

"When I get the shakes, Otto calls me his hummingbird. Every moment he isn't here I miss him. Passionately. Know what I mean?"

Maybe Dotty will die instead of me, CeCe thinks. "Do you think," she ventures cautiously, for they've never discussed it, "the Astrasyne is having any effect on us?"

"How would I know?" To CeCe's surprise, Dotty's voice rises. "Oh, I can't tell!" She chucks her cards onto the table.

"I ask only because you look much stronger lately," CeCe says quickly and untruthfully. "Pinker." She pats Dotty's hand.

"Really?"

"Really." If Dotty dies, it will be simple because Dotty believes in God and Dotty has a husband. God will hold her spirit and Otto will hold her body and that will be that. "I myself feel much better."

"That's great. Come to the pool with me today? Don't say no!"

"I swam when I was young. But I don't want to swim here." As a girl, CeCe had an instructor who wore a floral bathing cap and treaded water with a cigarette puffing out her mouth, while clutching an umbrella to keep the wrinkling effects of the sun off her skin—an elegant and rakish feat of synchronization CeCe admired. Many Saturdays, CeCe dangled over the lip of the pool, under the glass ceiling on the top floor of her childhood home, now repurposed as a recital space for the John Stepney Somner Library. When the instructor wasn't present, Toto or a maid would sit on the edge of a lounge chair. Toto's hem was starched and the mica-speckled concrete glinted and the lines on the bottom of the pool shifted blue. "I was a strong swimmer. Or was I? Maybe I was a poor swimmer and it's only they told me I was strong. I don't know."

"I forget lots of stuff. Facts. But nothing physical like that. Not memories you can feel."

CeCe returns to her room and lies down. She wants to be awake when they bring lunch. She'll close her eyes a few minutes—and. In her dream, she's Fernanda of Mexico. She's also a nurse. She's in a hurry to get dressed for work. With a gathering desperation she searches for her puffy white nurse shoes—she'll be fired by Dr. Orlow if she's late one more time. But she can't make rounds barefoot, and how will her feet survive the pilgrimage to Jesus over the hot sand? The shoes must go under her robes, her costume for the pageant. She's the king that carries the myrrh. She's sure she remembers setting the shoes neatly beside the bed. They must be under the bed! Carefully she bends and ducks her stiff head through the hanging blankets, but the shoes are gone. They *were* there, she's sure of it. Instead, here are the red sands of the desert, stretching for miles. She sets out across it, the myrrh in her hands, scouring the shimmering landscape for her shoes. The myrrh releases a reddish-brown sap that makes her hands sticky and drips onto her legs and her frying feet. For a flash, her father's hog-gum trees are in the dream and she's *his* nurse, whispering a filthy deal to him in the dark, ushering unsuspecting little Fernanda into his room. The shoes must be in the closet! She rushes to the closet. Gone. God, why, it's God. He's playing a mean game with her. God keeps moving her shoes. Just as she discovers their location—now on the windowsill, now buried in the red sand, now on a shelf too high for Fernanda to reach, he puts them somewhere else.

George. The wife, by his side. They are leaning over her, calling her from sleep. Why, she isn't put together! And she hasn't yet decided how to be! She will—she pretends she can't be woken. She watches through her eyelashes as they bend upright and confer.

"Go get someone," Iris whispers.

"She looks okay to me," George says. "How about lunch and we come back later?"

From the side of her eye she sees George turn away, his fine, firm profile, handsome, though still a copy, less the rangy verve, the beautiful glint of his father. George could almost be a stranger to her in his middle age, except for the nervous way he's raking his hair, his oldest habit despite all her corrections. She'll forgive him. Not right away, but forgive him she will. Her son. And Iris, wearing something ugly.

"Wait! Stay. I'm awake."

24

He's been mulling how to ask her for days: "You appreciate opera almost as much as I . . ." or "I've been working on the libretto to this new . . ." or "As a patron of the arts, I know you will . . ." and "In an age of diminished public funding for innovative, independent . . ." or "When an increasingly conglomeratized media control the very institutions that might serve to question . . ." (this from one of Vijay's early e-mails, and probably the wrong tack). And "If you ever doubted me, I want to thank you, because it's only pushed me to test my courage, and tested it I have . . ." His skull jangles like a bell. He's not slept. He has no reason for sleep, in his now-usual state of wired exhaustion, with his increasing appetite for everything and nothing. He watches his mother wave away Iris's help, prop herself in a chair at the table, tidy a pile of blue-backed playing cards into a stack beside some magazines. He tries to hide his restlessness, to keep his foot from tapping, his leg from bouncing. Her mobility is confusing him. He ducks over the table to kiss her cheek. She receives him without comment.

Her hair, usually so neatly flipped, is fluffed in the pale halo of the aged and napped behind the ears. She's perfumed, though, her same perfume that smells of orange rind and violets and that he's always vaguely thought of as Soviet. In the old days, her habit had been to spray it in the air and step through the sinking mist, wearing one of the bouclé suits she favored for meetings in the city, but now she's stuck squirting it right on. In the last year, he smelled her illness underneath the perfume—a different kind of sweetness, like molasses crossed with the odor pennies leave on the fingers. Today this is gone. Maybe she really is improving.

"Seriously, you look fantastic!" Iris says. "How do you feel? Tell us everything."

"Strong as an ox. I'm walking every day."

"I'm so happy for you. I can hardly believe it."

He should say something too. He forces himself to sit on the stool beside the bed, to pin his shaking hands. The midday light branches across the sheets. It had rained most of the trip but cleared as the car wound up the drive, the sun breaking through as they parked. He doesn't feel well. Queasy. Why doesn't anyone ever show an interest in how *he's* feeling? His mother won't look in his direction.

"There was a woman sitting in the lobby who guessed right away who we were," Iris says, looking at George. "Tiny and round? She seemed nice."

"Probably Dotty. Isn't she, though."

"Mother," George bursts forth, "so great! You look great."

She does not turn her attention from Iris. Not even a sidelong flicker. She seems, however, to gather some almost imperceptible light and strength to herself upon the sound of his voice. She smiles at Iris. "My word, look at this blouse you've worn! How is it not the first thing I saw? Isn't it festive. You're like a glass of sangria. Did you leave your paper umbrella in the car?"

"My what? Oh, I just got it. The top. The top and the joke, I guess. It's new. Can we take you out to lunch? Are you hungry?"

"Of course it's new. So many new things! Naturally it's due to your athletics you can wear any unpredictable item and look so lovely. When I was your age, we didn't have gyms. Or, there were a few. But they were for—boxers, taxidrivers. Men, anyway. A pity!"

"Huh, thanks, I guess. We're just so glad you're finally letting us visit."

"Did George tell you—did George suggest I didn't want you visiting?"

This is trouble. How had he not anticipated this? Iris, under the impression he's called his mother every day. CeCe is finally looking at him, but out of the side of her head, like a bird at a button. She seems to be uncoiling, the silk of her emerald housecoat gleaming in the sun. They're both looking at him.

"Getting away from work's been difficult." Against his will, his eyes remain lowered and dashing; he's committed himself to the alternate study of the tip of his shoe and a table leg. "I'm sorry we didn't come sooner."

"They promoted George," Iris says. "Did he tell you?"

"Not really a promotion. More time off. More flexibility to work from home. It's very trendy now, Mother, to do everything remotely."

"And he's been keeping me updated on how you're feeling. Is the treatment what you expected?"

"Has he," CeCe says. "I'm glad. Did you bring your dog? Shouldn't you go check on him?"

"3D's with Victor. Our friend Victor? He has a key. I think you've met him."

"Ah. The man who gives massages and walks the animals and prepares your lunches. The hybrid butler."

"He doesn't cook for us," Iris says. "I cook. I mean, if you can call it cooking. How's Pat? Coming along?"

"I imagine so. Haven't talked to her lately."

"We haven't either, I guess. Have we, George?"

"You," CeCe says, turning to him. "Hiding in plain view. I haven't talked to *you* lately."

"What?" he cries, attempting his most extreme *thunderstruck*, his mouth agape, his hands in tight fists. Soon enough he finds himself genuinely so, as sometimes a true feeling may be awakened by its false expression.

"I'm going to have a look outside, I guess." Iris gestures toward CeCe's French doors, the sparkling view beyond. Only now has it dawned on her that she's been told to excuse herself.

"Yasser's planted an abundance of late perennials. Have a look at his garden. It's still quite impressive. Go ahead. We'll miss you."

"Okay," Iris says. George will not meet her gaze.

As the door closes, George whispers, "You don't have to be rude to her because you're mad at me."

He's right. It's only—Iris has everything and doesn't care. Doesn't care or doesn't know. Hard to tell which. "You're right."

"I am?"

"Yes. I was unkind. I'm sorry."

"You are?"

"I am."

She stretches her arms out to him.

"I need some money," he says, looking at the ceiling.

"And so, you've come." She folds her hands in her lap.

"No, unrelated! Just now, on the drive up, I was thinking I should share more of my progress with you. I thought, Maybe I'm not forthcoming enough. Maybe that's something I should apologize for. Maybe she'd—you'd—like to be a part of the exciting things that are happening in my life."

"What an odd kind of promotion to receive, that you have more time and need more money."

"It wouldn't be for me! It's for—listen."

Nervously, he removes the huge padded headphones and the iPod from his bag. He fits the headphones heavily and loosely over her ears. Her cranium looks reduced by the headphones, both walnutlike and fragile. He's afraid to touch her and neglects to tighten the band before stepping away. It slides forward onto her brow. By reflex, she reaches up and grasps at the air to catch the band and push it back. Now that it's on her head and she's helped put it there, it seems she's agreed to listen. She feels ridiculous and will endure.

"Antinoise. These headphones are almost completely sound canceling. Because of the ear cup."

"What?" She makes a face like sour lemon, pulling one ear cup back.

"Don't take it personally," he says, gathering confidence, "that I've never shared this with you before. It wasn't ready. Even Iris hasn't heard it yet." Though not for lack of trying, he thinks. Since she missed the rehearsal, why has she not asked to come to another? Or to listen to a recording? "Anyway, my team, we've been working away, and it's only this month I've let anyone come to rehearsal. It wasn't time. Now it is."

As he says the word *time*, she looks at the fluttered cover of the *Time* magazine on the table. The red letters *T-I-M-E*. George summarizes the plot of *The Burning Papers* for her. She nods. It sounds like nonsense. He is speaking all in a rush, more ragged than she remembers. He puts the iPod into her hand, shows her how to change the volume, and presses play. She listens. He paces back and forth, looking out at the lake, until abruptly exiting into the hall. He's gone for the good part of an hour. He returns, just as abruptly, carrying a plastic cup of water. He sets this on the table in front of her. While he's gone, for a brief spell, she turns the volume down and puts her face in her hands, but this he does not see.

When it's done, she takes off the headphones and puts them on the table. She sits looking at them with her hands folded in front of her.

"You wrote this?"

"Yes."

"The words? And that's your, the story?"

What can she say? The music is that of a train hitting a merry-go-round. It sounds like the very incarnation of atrocity. The instrumental is both gastric and inorganic. The discordant principals' duet is like the nocturnal emission of a cancerous horse tethered in its dolorous slumber to a barbed aluminum fence during an electrical storm. All she can picture as she listens is a windup toy from her childhood, a tin monkey on a unicycle with a painted red coat and bellman's cap and cymbals that clap together, herky-jerky. The noise is not what surprises her. That the opera will surely be an embarrassment is also not entirely a surprise. What surprises her is that the story's dream is—of all things!—evil. Lusty for the ranking of and ordering of peoples. For the supremacy of the one over the other to be not by accident of birth but by nature's design.

She's about to tell him what she thinks when something stops her. It is—he hangs his head, waiting. His hair is damp. His forehead shines like an ostrich egg. His brow twitches. He's ready for her to insult him. The slump of his body, his quivering lip, his flinched emerald eye—already he wears the mark. He's long made an effort to hide his troubles, her son. How had she convinced herself that stowing away his troubles was as good as curing them? But who wants to believe her child is sick? Who wants to admit she's traded her child's ease for her own? She sees how much he needs her to love his music, to love him. Someone must tell him not to stage this opera. But how desperate he is, how unsteady, what an incapable individual he's become. Someone must believe in him. It's his mother who must. Her poor boy. His bowed head. How is it possible he does not know what he's made? This atonal, eugenic braying. How is it possible for the generations to evolve *backward*? The natural order should be that each generation becomes more enlightened. Her trouble with Lotta, for example—at least, in her better moments, she knows it to be a limitation. She fails, but sometimes she can admit it. She was taught wrong, for that is how they were taught. But that was long ago. By now, she can't blame anyone but herself. She will never forget her father telling her of a punishment he heard as a young adviser to one of Theodore Roosevelt's delegates in Haiti: slaves, a century before, rolled downhill in sugar barrels, the barrels' interiors fitted round with spikes. Her father raised her to a better world than that. She in turn raised George in a world more generous than hers. But is it? Maybe it is not. Maybe it is as terrible as it always was. Had she taught her son anything? He's meant to pass her, to become more than she—more valiant, kinder, to see more, to invite more of the truth of the world unto himself. To be left behind by one's child, this is the way it should be. But here, in his libretto, is foolishness, mostly, but evil too. The bit about the black and the white eunuchs, good God. Who are these Gypsies of the future meant to be? And the women! Each scene worse than the last. Her son, reversing the order of progress—a bad seed, a rotten egg, a man of shadow-clung fantasies and hungry, scrabbling fears. She's failed. Parents fail all the time—she'd be the first to say that most people are mediocre and most people have mediocre children. She's not romantic about the world. It's a common failure, and to be forgiven. But this is different. George's opera, dragging to mind—the year after the war in Naugatuck. Her father decided she might lend her charm to a promotional film. The major manufacturers were all making them, in the style of the U.S. Army reels boosting the war effort. Georgie was considering a step into politics; the film would make good cross-promotion. She'd forgotten it until Annie Mason's assistant found "Taking a Look at Rubber" on YouTube a few years ago. Annie wanted to post it to the history page of the foundation's website. CeCe refused. Uncanny, to watch the folksy actor playing a Naugatuck foreman take his grandson through the plant, explaining each stage of production and rubber's miraculous everyday applications. At the end of their tour, they step out onto Rubber Avenue.

"What do we have here?" the foreman says, squinting into the sunlight. A crowd of workers and reporters is gathered in front of the plant, actors all.

"Whatever it is," his grandson answers, "it looks exciting. Let's go and see."

Here, watching, CeCe had glimpsed herself. Ten years old, sallow and bolt-eyed, on a podium in front of a banner that read THE SOLE OF AMERICA, beside Georgie and his pretty wife of three months, Gloria. CeCe, in a checkered dress with a white collar, her pale hair tidied off her face. She remembers the dress was blue, but she will never be sure.

"That's Mr. Somner himself," the foreman says. "Let's have a listen."

The camera shifts to Georgie. "—this industry, so vital to our noblest endeavors overseas, to the protection of the freedoms and rights of all peoples in all nations. With the fine product we now make here at home on Rubber Avenue, the next generation"—here he gestures with a droll smile to CeCe—"will invent greater than we can dream, for we Americans are as strong as we are flexible—why, just like rubber."

She could hardly bear to watch. To recognize his speech's banality and its lie, a YouTube banner ad for a fitness system beneath. He was promoting synthetic rubber—during the war, Japan was poised to take the pan-Asian fields that supplied the United States with 97 percent of its rubber. The Somner company, along with a dozen others, restored production at their plantations in the Amazon; back in Naugatuck, Somner Industries, as part of a consortium, was commissioned by the government to improve synthetic-rubber production so the United States might never again find itself reliant for an essential commodity on foreign, tropical climates. By 1945, synthetics were so improved that Somner Industries again deserted the Amazonian fields. Deserted too, CeCe knows, were the workers who'd been force-migrated, without their families, and deposited in the jungle to man the trees. Left behind in the dense Amazon after the plantations' second closings, they died—from malaria and hepatitis and scorpion. Died by panther, died by thirst. The number, unofficially admitted by Brazil and officially denied by Somner Industries, seven thousand.

"Last," her father continues, "let's not forget it's our young people who know a good thing when they see one. They do badger and needle mother and father for the best, am I right, Cecilia?"

"Right," she says. This is her cue. Gloria lets go of her hand. CeCe lifts one foot and the other, showing off the rubber soles on a pair of sneakers—a thick, thumpy kind of shoe until that day she'd only seen other children wear. (The film's great challenge was avoiding reference to the automobile. Ford would not work with Georgie, and Somner Industries had never broken into private-sector tires. CeCe's bit had been the answer. At any mention of Ford, her father would quote *Henry the Fifth—How he comes o'er us with our wilder days, not measuring what use we made of them.*)

With the camera whirring and the fake reporters' flashbulbs popping, an actor-reporter calls out, "Now, missy, how would you like to be in charge here someday?" She looks back at her father. They hadn't gone over this part in the car.

"How about that," her father says, smiling at the camera. Gloria smiles too. But CeCe didn't know the answer. She didn't know! Then she did.

"Sir," she said, her voice high. "No thank you. I'd prefer to have a family."

"That'll be all, boys. We promised a visit to the ice-cream man."

They step into the crowd, Georgie shaking hands, working his way to the foreman and his grandson, who, in a final shot, declares that one day he wants to be a rubber man too. At this moment CeCe trips and falls, clumsy in the unfamiliar shoes, shaken by the pop of the flash-bulbs and the attention of the crowd, even if it is pretend. Gloria reaches down—not her mother!—and pulls CeCe up, saying, "You all right? We'll try it again?"

On the drive back to Booth Hill (not in a Ford, never in a Ford) her father said, "How'd you like that question? I pulled a fast one. Spontaneity. Good answer, Cecilia. You can think on your feet." Adding, with a burst of laughter: "Even if you can't stand on 'em!"

"What about the ice cream," CeCe answered.

In her wispy voice, Gloria said, "Dear, let's do really stop for some. It's been a long day."

And now, here is George's bent head! She can't shake the certain, if nonsensical, conviction that if she doesn't praise him, he'll fall down dead at her feet like a little bird from a tree. She can't speak against his work. But his opera mustn't be staged. He'll be humiliated. *She'll* be humiliated! Her name—his humiliation will make it into the paper. Nasty gossip. He'll lose his job, if he hasn't already. She won't have as easy a time finding him a new one as in the past. Easier when he was young, without so many terminations to his record, without his increasing age and her waning influence. Who on earth are these people working with him to produce this opera? Can they all be so sinister? No. He's paying them astronomically. That must be it. It's why he's here. He must be desperate. He's never managed money properly. Not for long. No one will back this monstrosity. Without her help, *The Burning Papers*—what a stupid name!—won't see a stage.

"It's a masterpiece," she says.

"Yes?" The light, breaking over his face. His body, settling. "Yes."

"Am I relieved! That is good to hear, good to hear!"

"It is exceptional. But—"

"And that's only a recording from rehearsal. Not even proper audio. And Judith was hoarse that day. She—I'm somewhat disappointed in her. But. Can you believe I made that? Can you believe I've done all that myself? And! It's a safe investment. *I* think, anyway. The arts are doing better than you'd expect. People are still going to the theater. People do take risks! We'll break even on ticket sales. I'll pay you back, of course. And that's only the beginning. After box office, we—"

"George, I'm very proud of you, but I will not help you. You're on your own."

"What?" He leaps up, his hands in his hair. He doesn't appear to understand. He sinks back down onto the stool, leaps up again. "But you said it was good."

"It is. However, you are a grown man, and if you've ruined your affairs, which I suspect you have"—she can barely bring herself to say it. She sets her jaw and hears her own voice, slow and steely, such an effort it takes to keep the pity out!—"you'll have to find a way to unruin them by yourself."

"You won't—you mean to say this is because I didn't visit?"

"Do you know I had pneumonia? I almost died?"

For the first time she understands it's true, she *had* almost died, and quick as lightning what began as a plan to protect her child catches up to her as wrath.

"Telling your wife you've been calling me, that I refuse visitors?"

"We are from this, from all of this!" George cries, pointing at the table of photos, to a black-and-white photo of John Stepney, the year before he died, standing stiffly on the lawn in front of the immense fortress that was Apollo Court. "And you won't help me! What's it good for, then? What's it for? You're happy to give it away as long as it isn't to me! You don't know anything, you—"

She has the same feeling as when—Walter, how much money he asked her for, over the years, after their divorce. By letter and long-distance call. She'd wire it to him, two, three times a year. One day, she opened an envelope from Italy. He'd forwarded the bill for a suit. After that she stopped helping him and he disappeared.

"But, but you have to."

"I do not."

"You ruin my life," George cries, "because you like to."

"Now when you tell Iris I don't want visits, it needn't be a lie."

It is the only way she has left to look after him. She's done what had to be done.

"I provide for my wife," he says, a defiant choke in his voice.

"No, I provide for your wife. I provide for you by letting you forget it."

25

Shitty shirt, shit stuffed animals from the claw arcade, shit white compact cars, old issues of supermarket tabloids (alien babies, diet disasters), fringed purses, crusted bottles of bright nail polish, bright manufactured anything, plastic anything, glass figurines, Disney merch, ballerina music boxes, stadium-concert ticket stubs, mugs with quotables, tracksuits, aluminum cans, cherry pop, cherry anything, scratch-n-win, chips with a neon-orange dust, carnations for special, antifreeze blue, antifreeze green, daisy petals with brown seams bruised into the white, white leather clothes, black leather furniture, limited-edition sports memorabilia, mesh hats, dirt bikes, rabbit's foot, shamrock, cartoon pop, kitten heels, martini-glass stems shaped like legs, novelty dice, dogs in the yard, dogs tied to the fence in the yard, turds in the yard, no yard, money-grams, cinnamon candles, musk oils, French braids, false idols, bubble gum, boozy booze, Tic Tacs, hair spray, death-by-machine accident, death by sugar, death in the bathtub, acne scars, crooked teeth, bloody noses, cardboard boxes, blood outside the body, garbage on fire, cutting down trees. As far as her mother-in-law is concerned, it is from this catalog of crap Iris was procured, along with her shirt. This, or whatever CeCe's idea of white trash happens to be. Not that she's given it much thought. Not that she's right.

Iris hurries across the damp lawn. She looks back once, but there's only the yellow limestone and the sun glinting off CeCe's closed glass doors. *Did you leave your paper umbrella in the car?* Blam! The old gal's in fine form! A sneaky way of calling her cheap. Hey, what'll it be? Is she cheap, or is she a gold digger? How can she spend too little and cost too much? She continues past the lake, its surface ruffled by the breeze. She climbs the shallow hill around the side of the facility and steps through a strict topiary colonnade, into the garden. She's on a path of loose, white gravel. The garden is big enough to wander an after- noon. She just might, rather than go back. To calm, she leans in to smell the even tufts of sea lavender, tall as her elbow, filled with bees. As she stomps along the rows, the names come back to her from the learning garden behind the School of Agriculture's Plant Science Building. Maybe it's because she's angry, maybe because she's escaped, but the flowers teem, unnaturally vivid to her eye, too high and radiant for the beginning of fall. Here are butterscotch dahlias and purple ver- bena. Pitcher sage, with its fan of sky-blue flowers. She crosses a foot- bridge over a dry streambed and follows a low stone wall bordered with mottled leopard flower and silver curry plant. Crimson butterfly weed, coral zinnias. Here is clematis, a name she remembers for its ugliness, like a welting disease. Hoping to get lost, feeling a little better, she touches the tops of the flowers, humming with insects. Rain from that morning scatters off their tufted heads. She finds her anger's been re- placed by the strange sense that she's being followed—not by any per- son, but by her own gathering dread, a dread she can neither see nor shake. George, lately. The way he moves, the way he speaks.

She's come to the end of the garden. A stand of fruit trees, already half-wrapped in plastic for winter. What looks like woods are just be- hind the fruit trees, though she can faintly hear the highway beyond. She tries to put George out of her mind. Peaceful, to head back down the hill through the woods, though she still isn't peaceful. She enters a soft grove, pulls some pine needles into her hands. Deutschland astilbe—there's another name she remembers for its ugliness, though there isn't any of the ivory firework here. Fear drilled that one into her memory her first day at Booth Hill. She and CeCe were leaned up against the flagstone balustrade of the veranda. CeCe, thin as a latch, pointing a ringed finger at the distant curve of the lawn's terraced perennial border, cataloging her garden, jabbing left to right as if her gold-laden knuckle were a brush and she were painting the flowers into existence as she went. George had escaped into the cool kitchen for what seemed to be a long time, to relay to Esme his mother's instructions for sandwiches and a pitcher of tea. Iris, knowing the names, but so stunned by Booth Hill she was only able to offer that her own name was a flower. Like a six-year-old, or a half-wit. And that, she thinks, is pretty much how it's gone with CeCe ever since.

Halfway down the slope, she enters a clearing. Three men in tan jumpsuits sit on the ground, their backs against an oak. More like a man and two boys—the boys look sixteen, eighteen, but are taller than their boss, whose stout torso reminds her of an old-fashioned wine jug. Maybe this is Yasser. He snores lightly. His legs are splayed and a pole saw is balanced over his knees. His jumpsuit is dark with sweat at the collar, unbuttoned to the waist. What she can see of the T-shirt underneath reads OSA'S ANDSCAPE AND EE. The boys sit up and stare at her. The younger boy has a runtish, narrow look, his flame-red hair swept over his forehead in a soft bowl. He's sucking on a silver chain that hangs around his neck. The older one tosses sticks and clumps of dirt, a pale chicken arm swinging from the rolled-up sleeve of his jumpsuit. His wide-set eyes are on her, but lazily, oddly uncoordinated. The boys sit up and look at each other, momentarily surprised to see her. The younger one lets the chain fall from his mouth, smiles, sticks his tongue between his index and middle fingers and makes several slurping passes in her direction. His friend laughs, but silently, looking to make sure their boss is still asleep.

Twerpy little shits. What a terrific day! She knows this type of kid. Pea-brained, all defensive posture and slide-eye, their life's work to make sure everyone knows it's women, and only women, they like to fuck. Her disapproval—this is how CeCe must feel, all the time.

The older boy stops laughing. "Hey, where do I know you from?"

"Great opener," Iris says. "You've done this before."

"No seriously. You're standing like—" He crosses his arms over his chest and leans back. "Wait, I know! You're on those ads. I'm going south on Route 22, it's you, right?"

The younger boy pulls the chain back into his cheek. "Now I think on it, we do see her like six times a day, do we not? Tasty old thing. Selling houses?"

"You got me." Sometimes she misses the straightforward rudeness of the bars, of real life. "Have a good one." She continues down the hill, thinking suddenly of the day she met George. She'd spent part of it wandering the School of Agriculture's garden. After a swim at the athletic facility, she'd gone out of her way to drive past the kid's university housing at the edge of campus, a cluster of low houses with aluminum siding, mostly empty for summer, thinking, That's where we sat on the stoop at night, that's the tree we studied under. She parked and strolled over to the house, pretending to no one that she was a touring parent or a touring alumna, out to see the pretty trees. His housemate came to the door and waved. She thought they were all gone and could think of nothing to do but walk on over.

"3D, stay," she said to the big red dog she'd just adopted, against all reason, no life to keep a dog. The housemate was one of those kids left on campus who didn't have anyplace to go and had stayed to work off his loan. He had spiked black hair, heaped shoulders, a worn black Slayer T, a studded belt to which his pocketed wallet was attached by a chain, no ass, bare yellow feet, giant headphones around his neck, stubble and acne competing for real estate on his chin. A style that made more sense in cooler weather. He leaned in the doorway. She with her wet hair, in her mint-green golf-club uniform.

"Glad I cleaned," he said, and opened the door wider for her to enter. A baseball game was on TV. He lifted a bowl of rainbow cereal and a heaping ashtray from the couch and pushed aside a paper plate. She'd missed the house, the house she'd slept in many times.

"Hang on." He disappeared into a bedroom. "You should say hi to the girls." Iris muted the game and listened. No one else was home. She smelled weed and incense. The roommate returned with a mangy ferret wiggling under each arm.

"Pretty as ever, aren't they? You want some?"

She shrugged, sure. He handed her the slinking ferrets and rustled his pocket for the joint. She let them squirm off her lap and ooze under the couch. It was strong weed. She and the roommate forgot each other awhile, he watching the game on mute, she watching the poster on the wall behind the TV, its title and artist's name in large fascinating letters across the bottom: WATER LILIES CLAUDE MONET.

"I can tell you miss him," the roommate said abruptly. "But he's not an interesting guy. I'm not being a dick. It's just true. Just because the pool's got a diving board don't mean it's got a deep end. You want a beer?" He pulled two tall cans from the minifridge at the side of the couch. "Nice, right?" He patted the fridge, thoughtfully draped with a faded Tibetan flag, topped with a stuffed gorilla and a tray of sand containing a tiny rake.

"Can you tell me, have you talked to him?"

"I haven't—Iris! Shitting outside the cage." He laughed and pulled the smaller ferret into his hands. "He named her after you, kind of. I couldn't think of a name, and he was talking about you, and I said, that's fucking fantastic, it's totally an unpet name. Like Paul is an unpet name. Like com'eer, Paul, what? It doesn't make any sense on a pet. Missing the C-factor. You been swimming? You look all swimmy. You into this baseball? You like movies? I could change it to a movie."

He knelt and fiddled with the pile of DVDs. She had ten, twelve years on him. Like a knife at her neck, remembering that, though it could have been the claws of a ferret, out from under the couch to thrust its sock length into her hair. She was thirty-one.

The housemate held out his finger, covered in peanut butter. A ferret leaped to it.

"Not that you don't have the C-factor."

She put down her beer. "Sure, what's the C-factor?"

"Cuteness."

"Get this one off me." She, stood to go, swiping at the animal still clinging to her neck.

"Don't worry. That's not Iris. That would be one phenomenological mind fuck, am I right? That one's Earl. Earl's a girl!" This killed him. He bent over, laughing.

"Ah." She shook Earl to the couch. The roommate followed her to the door and scrounged around for paper and a pen and handed her his phone number, which was only four digits, his campus extension, he knew she knew the system, the prefix. He wrote Norefills, which she guessed was his instant-message name. He snatched it back and added his cell.

"In case you want to call me. Hot costume," he added, looking at her uniform. "Like out of an old movie. You're very statuesque."

She whistled to 3D, who at the smell of the ferrets had abandoned his post in front of the house and was pacing under the open living-room window. She got in her car, and for a minute she looked out at the house. She wiped her face and made it on time to her shift at the golf club.

Now she heads away from the landscapers, toward the bright garden. Everything, and also not much, has changed. Still being put out to wander, like a big gangly cat. Her thoughts are interrupted by—a rock, hitting the soft dirt between her feet. Another bounces hard off her ankle.

"Hey!" she shouts. The boys have followed her to the tree line.

Behind them, a ways away, the sleeping man shifts.

"We'll be seeing you around." The older boy laughs. "Literally."

"What's going on?" their boss says, stirring awake, the pole saw falling to the ground.

"Nice afternoon," she calls to him. Rotten as they are, she'd rather let the kids be. "Nice and cool." She heads quickly out into the sunlight. To rejoin her husband and her mother-in-law, to see if she can't convince them to drive somewhere for lunch.

26

He can't get it right. He can't understand—everything's ruined. He paces the tasteful and unremarkable lobby, waiting
for Iris to return from wherever she's got off to. No, he'll figure it out.
If only he could think. Or, think one thought at a time. His heart,
thumping. Fine. He doesn't need a thing from his mother. He never
has! He was doing her a *courtesy*. Risking his well-being by sharing
his life, trying to be the good son. By giving her the first opportunity,
moreover, at a worthy investment. How many two-bit theater programs has the Somner Fund supported over the years? How many
stages has his mother already lit? This is exactly why he made it a rule
never to count on her for anything. How had he forgotten? As soon as
he asks—she thinks of no one but herself! It pleases her to watch him
fail. As if he were his father, as if he were to blame for who his father
was and to be kept under thumb as his father was, how callow, how
obvious, for her to be exercising her bitterness on him, all these years!
She doesn't want to see him succeed. She's the only one allowed any

kind of reputation, any attention. He'll leave her, like Walter, is what she thinks. Has he left her yet? Is there no reward for a lifetime of loyalty and sacrifice? Where trust? Where faith? If he has a child, he will never be so mean. He'd never put his wishes and his disappointments on a child. A poor little child! He doesn't have it in him. He'd let it be its own wondrous creature. He would—he realizes with a pleasant thrill, the first bright thought in the polluted roil of the last hour—*his* child would be extraordinary. A young master at the piano, maybe, a composer maybe, and one day they'd write something together and the world would hold its breath. Or maybe the child would become something he can't envision, something all his or her own, and that would be okay too. He's no tyrant. He'd let the child be!

After his mother had ejected him from her room—"Tell Esme to send the ormolu" were her parting words—he stood desolately in the hall outside the closed door, calling Iris's cell. No answer. He called it again as he thrust himself through the automatic glass front doors of the lobby. He stormed past the lake into the garden as it rang, threw himself against a tall and well-clipped shrub in deepest agony, called again, forcibly parted a clot of sunflowers to scan the other end of the garden, saw no one but a happy old fucker photographing a butterfly, twisted his ankle on a low, obscured stone border, caught his balance on an expired rosebush, emitted a shriek, the sound of which flooded him with embarrassment even though he was alone, and returned to the lobby of the residence no less angry but sweatier, with red palms and ruined bucks.

He's at a loss for what to do when he hears—women's voices. Around the corner in the hall. Not his mother, not his wife. He can only reel a word or two out of the murmur. No, he will not go back to his mother's room and beg. He'll wait. He bends and touches his toes. Calisthenics. Not a moment wasted! He has to fix this. His entire crew—the orchestra, the singers, tech, production—their salaries will again come due. Such a drag, how he has to keep paying them! He can probably make it to November. He has a little time. December, if he delays the rent on the theater. Where *is* Iris? He pushes one hand against the other, his elbows out, until he feels a slight, satisfying tingle in his armpits. He turns to face the lobby's only wall decor, an enormous oil painting of, according to the plaque, the founder of Oak Park, then called the College of Physicians of Greater Connecticut, one corpulent and puritanically beaked Dr. Forum, wearing the black, high-collared coat of his era. George begins a series of squats, keeping balance by spotting the doctor's eye; the doctor might have benefited from some calisthenics himself. First thing he gets home he'll order a treadmill, or one of those bullshit elliptical trainers that's easier on the knees. Maybe he'll hire Victor for some personal training. No, he knows what he's doing. And he hates Victor! He'll take up running. Running with the sunrise on the road.

"Are you okay?"

A nurse has padded up to him. She looks alarmed.

"Super!" he cries. "Just biding my time."

"Are you Mr. Somner?"

"I am."

"Your mother asked me to give you this. She forgot. I'm her afternoon nurse, most days."

With her slender hands she puts forward a blank, unsealed envelope. Has his mother reconsidered? Is it a check? He shakes out the folded paper. A list. Clearly made before the visit, written in a moment her hand was steady, in the beautiful, precise, and softly slanted script she'd perfected at the ladies' junior college she attended before Vassar, a script he's always grudgingly admired. A list he understands is no longer for him but for Esme to dispatch.

To bring or send
  photo of George and Patricia on beach in St. Martin—
    halfway up the wall 2nd floor kitchen stair
  walking boots & winter coat—the red
  fox gloves
  ormolu from bedroom mantel
  Walter's portrait of me—in storage
  the Rathbone
  Dragon brooch—at bank

Talbot
the two bergères, if possible to ship
writing desk, ditto
As Soon As Possible.

E-mail. How about e-mail? More convenient, less dramatic! But maybe Esme doesn't like e-mail, either. Maybe this is a handicap his mother and Esme share, for different reasons. The Talbot—a carved wood dog that stands on the piano. A white, English hunting dog. Ridiculous. The ormolu clock transfixed him as a child: nestled in front of an ancient ladies' fan from China, the clockface sat in a lump of marble meant to be a rock rising out of the sea, with two marble figures wearing intricate accessories of gold. The myth of Perseus saving Andromeda: marble Andromeda, naked, draped backward over the rock, her head resting above twelve o'clock, her feet and hands bound. Perseus, on the other side of the clock, his sword raised to break Andromeda's chains. Medusa's severed head beside his gold-clad foot. George crumples the note, jams it into his pocket, and resumes his calisthenics, palms together. None of these items are necessary.

"I interrupted your prayer. I didn't realize. Sorry," the nurse says. She smacks her forehead and crosses herself, so fluidly he wonders if she doesn't often combine these gestures. He looks down at his hands and suppresses a laugh.

"You have," he says, giving her a grave look. Why not? He probably should be praying, given the circumstances. "You could pray with me. Nurses and nuns used to be the same, right?"

The nurse glances over at the receptionist.

"This is the first time I've prayed," he whispers, leaning toward her, "since I was a boy."

She nods and folds her hands together.

He takes his squat down into a kneel and bows his head. *I am I am I am,* he prays silently. The nurse lowers herself next to him. In a high, timid whisper she says, "We nurse and son pray for the peace and comfort of Cecilia Somner. In your great wisdom may you bless her and allow her swift passage to a bright future that is healed whole. Amen."

He's startled by the quick splendor of her speech. "That was beautiful," he says, looking into the eye of the painted doctor, ashamed to look into hers.

"Thank you. They'll think we're praying to the painting." She smiles, nodding her cashew ponytail toward a security camera he had not noticed, tucked into the corner molding. "I'll hear about it later, I'm sure!"

"Blame it on me. Tell them I insisted."

"I'm only kidding," she says, standing.

"I bet you have a lovely singing voice." He gazes up at her imploringly. His knees are killing him. His twisted ankle hurts too. He's not sure why he's still on the floor. "Can you sing? I'm in the music business, did anyone tell you? I have a pretty good instinct for these things."

"Back to work for me."

"Don't go, I want to"—she looks away as he ungracefully rises to his feet—"to apologize. My mother can be difficult. I appreciate everything the staff is doing here. I want you to know that."

"Mrs. Somner? She's easy as pie. Well, after she got adjusted. And now that she's back from the pneumonia. A hard few weeks, those were."

"But, it wasn't serious."

She is looking at him more carefully than he likes. "It was. She went to ICU and Telemetry. But now she's doing well. That's what matters."

His mother had smelled different, not like fishy coins. Like normal. Like health. He feels the back of his hand at his mouth. The word *bankruptcy* flies past his vision. The nurse seems far away, at the other end of the shining-resin lobby.

"Her numbers are right back where they were. And her mobility's improved, *I* think, and— Are you feeling all right?"

He's seized by a ferocious desire to touch her nameplate, which says TANIA. He points at it, as if its letters prove him right, though he doesn't know what he's right about. "I'm fine." Mercifully, here is Iris. He throws his arms around her. "You disappeared!"

Iris starts to cry against his shoulder. Dear Iris, crying quietly for him! But how could she know? She doesn't know anything. The nurse's eyes widen. She nods and backs around the corner and is gone.

"What's bringing this on?" he asks.

"Nothing."

"Why didn't you answer your phone?"

"It's in the car," Iris snaps, straightening up and wiping her eyes. "I didn't think we'd be separated."

"What happened?"

"Some kid threw a rock at me. Never mind."

"Where? Are you hurt?"

"No. It's no big deal. Let's forget it. Are we taking your mother to lunch?"

27

But they were *not* taking George's mother to lunch, and George—tugging her down the hall by the hand, his brow furrowed, the receptionist calling after them—didn't seem to hear Iris's questions. Had the nurse been telling him bad news? The receptionist's eye had been on George even as she wiped the dry-erase board on the easel by her station. This caused Iris to succumb to her tears, more than those rinky-dinks outside. George, so spiraled away from himself. Still, it was a relief to cry on his shoulder under the musty and menacing portrait. She'd studied it earlier, while they waited for permission to visit CeCe's room.

But now they're sitting in Dr. Orlow's office, on the interview side of his solid mahogany desk. She hardly knows how they got there. George had pulled her down the hall at such a speed. He's holding her hand under the desk.

"A rock," he's saying. "Thrown at my wife."

Dr. Orlow is her age, maybe younger. He's just referred to her as

Mrs. Somner. He's apologizing, leaning his tall frame forward, explaining that he doesn't know who does the landscaping. He'll speak to Buildings and Grounds. He takes off his glasses and rubs his eyes.

"Endangered," George says. "On Oak Park property. Awful! How do you think this makes me feel?"

"We'll get to the bottom of it as soon as we can."

"Do you know I twisted my ankle? While I was out searching? For my missing wife? It's a mess out there. Uneven ground. How about oversight? Well-run places of business are known to keep track of their employees. Check references, even. Believe it or not, periodically observe and assess the functionality of their staff. I want to speak to the supervising grounds person right away."

She hears Dr. Orlow say that the landscapers are not employees but contracted; she hears him apologize again and suggest it might not be the best idea, at present, to have the individuals in question join them. He asks her if she might walk through what happened again. She finds herself nodding. She looks down at the corner of the desk as George insists again that the supervisor be brought in. She can't bear to have George in her sight—how his flinty eyes are widening and narrowing as he leans forward, his free hand balled in the air. She's surprised when Dr. Orlow relents, makes the phone call, speaks to one person, waits, speaks to another. The receptionist from the lobby enters holding a notebook and a pencil, closes the door quietly behind her, and takes a seat in a corner.

"It was nothing," Iris says firmly.

"She's too kind. Tell him how it happened, Iris."

"We'll straighten it out," Dr. Orlow says. "Again, I do hope—"

"You will fire them." George is squeezing her hand, over and over, hard.

"Hey, what? Don't." She is—it's only because he loves her so much, isn't it? "Let's all please hold up a second."

"My wife." George stops. He lets go of her hand. "My wife," he says again, with a slow, gathering calm that's rare for him of late, that she realizes she's been missing, but that also reminds her of CeCe, maybe an attitude he's picked up from being near his mother again. "My wife,

Dr. Orlow, is pregnant. Can you imagine what could have happened here? Throwing rocks at a woman. A woman alone. On facility property. I'm amazed this isn't enough to merit your genuine interest. Here I am forced to share our private business with you, just to make an impression."

"George?" She can hear the receptionist's pencil moving across the paper. For an insane moment she wonders if he's discovered or decided her to be pregnant, if her crying earlier was hormone-induced and she *is* pregnant. That he's been waiting to surprise her with the news. And those kids were shitmouths, but they hadn't really done anything. Or is he right, and they had? If you don't decide, the decision gets made for you. Who said that? Victor. They'd been talking about *The Bluest Ribbon*, the book she still hasn't found. She will concentrate, count to a hundred to keep from exposing her anger, exposing George. Here's the dark mahogany edge of the desk, a triangle of carpet, her knee.

"I am sorry," Dr. Orlow says. "And congratulations."

"I mean," George continues, "is there even security here? My mother's room is on the ground floor—my God, I'm starting to rethink this whole thing. I have half a mind to pull her right out! A shame, with her record of generous investment."

"This is a safe environment." Dr. Orlow's soft voice is all the more remarkable for George's pitch. "We have an active staff presence inside and out."

"Investment?" Iris asks.

"Oh, of time and faith," George replies impatiently. "But if rapists and murderers are skulking the brambles, well."

Out of the corner of her eye she sees the receptionist half stand, look to Dr. Orlow, and sit again.

"I understand you're upset, Mr. Somner, but, let's make sure we keep perspective." Dr. Orlow turns from George to Iris. "You were walking in the treed area at the north end of the property. Two young men in uniforms made unwelcome comments, made you feel unsafe, and twice threw a rock. You're shaken but physically unharmed. Do I have it right? Is there anything else I should know?"

"No," she says.

There is a knock at the door. The man who'd been sleeping against the tree enters, worry and irritation on his face. She can tell he's never had a reason to be in this office before. The boys mope in behind him, discover there's not enough space for all seven of them, and duck along the wall to stand with their backs against the windows. They bring the smell of earth and sweat into the room. Their handiwork is evident behind them, a burst of color at the other end of the lawn.

George springs from his chair, smooths his hand over the buttons of his pink dress shirt, glares at everyone, including Iris, and sits back down.

"I didn't mean them too," Dr. Orlow says to the receptionist.

"Are these the ones!" George shouts, at Iris, at the boys.

Yasser sighs. "I asked Russ and Kyle if they knew why we were coming up here."

"And?" George says. "And?"

"Tell him what you told me," Yasser prompts.

"It isn't a big deal," Iris says. "Nobody should be in trouble."

"I said hello to the lady is all," the younger, runtish one—Russ— murmurs, to the floor. She sees how small he is in the jumpsuit, rolled up around his ankles and wrists.

"Mr. Al-Saleh, am I saying that right? Where were you during this exchange?" Dr. Orlow asks.

"Yasser," Yasser says.

"Working nearby," Iris says quickly. "But I'm sure he couldn't see."

"And you, Kyle?" Yasser says, for a moment looking at Iris.

"We said hi, but that's it. Swear."

"Yes, yes," Iris says, impatient now. She doesn't like anything about them. But they're young. They need their jobs.

"Why are you treating this scum so considerately?" George says.

"Hey," Kyle says.

Yasser turns to the boys, appears to be thinking about George's question. "I can get focused on a task. I am sorry this happened."

"You've done a great job out there," Iris agrees.

"More important is, Russell and Kyle are very, very sorry, right?" Yasser says.

They nod.

"There we have it," Dr. Orlow says.

"So you agree, you stopped paying attention to your employees. You weren't doing your job."

"George, let it go," Iris says. "It's fine. Everyone, it's really fine."

"You don't deserve to be on the same *planet* as my wife. We will be waiting for a satisfactory outcome."

"For Christ's sake," Iris says.

"Thank you," Yasser says.

"There's no problem," she says. "Please forget it."

"You're lucky I'm a reasonable man," George whispers, scowling at the boys. Something put on about it. The loud whispering, the squinching up of his eyes, like an actor in a soap opera.

"I'm leaving." Iris takes the room in three steps, angles around Yasser, who squeezes closer to the boys so she may open the door, and presses on down the hall.

"It's a bad world, Iris," George calls after her, his footsteps rushing up behind. "You may be too good a person to see the truth, but I'm not."

28

The lobby doors whoosh closed behind them before she speaks.

"What a great visit!" she shouts over her shoulder as she plows past the gravel roundabout, the fountain with its water-spilling cherubs. "Look at how pretty it is, just the kind of tasteful bullshit your mother appreciates!"

She'd parked in the middle of the lot. The silver door is warm under her hand. She slams it shut and yanks on her seat belt and puts the key in the ignition and powers down the windows. The car's atmosphere is a synthetic boil. He climbs in beside her.

"The windshield is kind of dirty," he offers.

"Why did you say that?"

"I mean, look." He gestures, and as she turns the car onto the road, the sun catches the glass. It's true. Still splattered with mud from hitting the turkey.

"No, why did you say I'm pregnant? Who does that?"

He narrows his eyes on the road as he considers his answer. "Maybe I don't want to live the kind of life where we get kicked around, Iris, maybe that's why. Maybe you think it's acceptable to be harassed, maybe you expect to be objectified, maybe you have some internalized thing about that because you're attractive. Do you?"

"What? Whatever."

"I think you do. And it isn't healthy. How is it *I'm* the one who knows to be outraged? We all have our hang-ups, and if this is one of yours and you can't see it, if you can't stand up for yourself, then I choose to stand up for you. That's what we're meant to *do* for each other, Iris. I'm strong where you're weak, and you're strong where I'm weak. And I for one am tired of being ignored."

"I don't know what you're talking about. I don't think you do, either."

"You know what I was doing back there? I was setting the terms of the negotiation. I have more experience managing people than you."

"Is that right?"

"People don't listen unless you nail it home, you understand? Unless you get them to sit up and pay attention. Nobody understands what's worth throwing support behind anymore! That's the only reason I said it. Maybe you think I'm cynical. But I think you're too pure to see the ugly truth. I love you for that."

She's not even seeing the road, is she? Sort of. Yes. It's bright and there aren't too many other cars and they're going the right way and the trees are luscious and deep and they've got fifteen more minutes until the highway. In all their days together he's never asked her if she wanted to have a kid, and because he never asked, she avoided it too, being ambivalent about the prospect and having long assumed her ambivalence to be unnatural and best kept to herself. But for the subject to come up like this! And for her to be unsure, at her age, to dodge away from thinking of it! What the hell is wrong with her? Wrong with her, wrong with him.

"You can't say someone's pregnant when they're not, George. What happens next visit? Announce I've had a miscarriage? Maybe there's a doctor available for a pretend abortion!"

"I don't want a next visit. So. No problem there."

She merges onto the highway. They drive in silence. From the hot corner of her eye she becomes aware he's turning in his seat, watching the traffic out the rear window.

"That van behind us," he says. "Do you think it's them?"

"What?"

"The white one. The van."

In the rearview mirror, a few cars back, a van is sloppily weaving lane to lane, dropping behind, revving forward. "Who?"

"Those kids. Their boss. He was a quiet one, wasn't he."

"That's how jerks drive when they're in a hurry, George. It's called tailgating."

He runs his hands through his hair, his shoulders hunched. After twenty miles of silence, he says, "I hope Victor won't be at the house. He's always at our house."

After fifteen more miles of silence, he says, "Why don't I get to drive?"

"You don't have your license."

"I do have my license. I just haven't had it renewed. I'm going to drive, starting now. I'm going to drive us home."

"Great, great idea. I don't care!" She pulls over to the shoulder and they switch.

"That's better." He pulls back onto the road. "Van's past us now."

"You're fucking insane." She adjusts the seat to accommodate her longer frame. "You know what those landscapers are doing right now? They're *working*, George. They have to work. Doesn't that make more sense?"

"Once more, you defend them."

"Use your mirrors. You're going to get us killed."

"I was joking about the van."

She turns away. Watching him navigate is nerve-racking. She feels as if her life has spun ahead of her, too fast to see. A bright, tangling panic. Also: it's as if some other person is wearing George. He is again going over what was done to her in the garden, explaining to her the various ways society encourages the hypersexualization of the female body, something *commodification*, something *signifies*, something *product*. She thrusts her hand into the wind and watches the gas stations and the exit ramps and the sad malls go by. In three perilous hours, George manages to get them off the highway and onto their local route. It occurs to her—it's coming, here it is—they slide under the sign bearing her giant head and mauve torso, her arms crossed over her chest, just as Kyle described. She is reminded of those other teenage boys, the ones on the handball courts when she first showed Victor around Kingsgate. How they stopped their game to watch her pass. Stone-eyed, their fingers hooked through the chain. The old-timers too, not so welcoming. Not so happy to see her. She, who represents the company that is increasing the value of their properties. She, who is aiding in the renewal of their community. "No good deed goes unpunished," Carol had liked to say.

"The turn off to Kingsgate's up ahead." She looks dully out the window. She's pretty sure he hadn't noticed the sign. She doesn't dare distract him from the road—the car moves forward in erratic bursts of acceleration and drift, either well above or below the speed limit, correlating roughly to where he is in a sentence, jerking back into the middle of the lane just in time, the tire under her thumping the white warning line, George unaware. Other drivers lean on their horns as they speed ahead of him, take the other lane.

"God, this road rage is a real thing, isn't it?" he says. "People are maniacs. Kingsgate? Did we miss it? Do you want to show it to me?"

"Maybe another time. Do you ever see any of my ads? When the car takes you to work?"

"Yeah. I like them. Makes me laugh."

"How was your mother?"

"Great. Loving life," he says, so bitterly she doesn't respond. They don't speak again until he's parked sideways to the garage, beside the pool cleaner's truck. She waves hello to Henry, skimming the deep end. She opens the front door, takes a knee, and 3D slaps his paws onto her shoulders, flings his head happily from side to side. George, after what appears to be some deliberating as to the proper spot, drops the car keys on the line where two seat cushions of the couch meet, pours himself a glass of juice, flings his shoes off into the middle of the kitchen, and pads down the hall to his office. She hears his computer power on. Why does he have any right to be angry? Her right, not his.

She hits play on the home answering machine, taps the kitchen counter, staring at one of George's yuppie shoes as she listens to three long messages of dead air. In the second message beats a faint sound—*thwap, thwap, thwap*. In the third she hears a voice in the background. She plays this message again. It's muffled, but might be—*Papa? Papa?* Small and high, right before the click. Great. The only person who's called her today is a kid playing with a phone.

George returns to the living room. She doesn't know why, but she's relieved he hadn't heard the messages. He sets 3D barking by opening and closing the front door. He makes a tour of the foyer, peers behind the couch, and, staring through the glass wall and down into their little waterfall, cries, "I left my umbrella. Again! God, this is the worst!"

"We'll get another one," she says, shooing the dog toward his mat.

"But it's a nice one! Come and look at this."

She follows him down the hall to his office. He sits in his leather chair in front of the laptop. She kneels on the rug beside him and reads:

<psomner@gmail.com>   Sept 25 (1 day ago)

dear george
    i can't come see mother yet. it's unfair, but you know how it goes with us. why should i pretend? she wouldn't want pretend affection anyway. isn't honesty better? i was just at the doctor myself, all's well. i want to lie and say i can't travel because of morning sickness or something, but i'm trying hard to be honest even if i do end up looking like a BAD daughter or a BAD sister. i'm sorry, g. maybe someday you will need me to do something big and sad for you. in a heartbeat, brother. hey you guys should come visit us

already! it's been a hundred years. did I tell you for
a few of babys early years we might go live in SP,
while L's overseeing construction? then we come back
stateside for the American Education whatever that's
worth these days so first come visit us in Seattle
then come visit SP.

XXX

Pat

PS Lotta and the little guy inside (it's a boy! boy
oh boy!) send their love to you and Iris.

"What a joke!" George says. "Who cares if she is honest if she's
never here?"

"She's right, it isn't fair to you. But I get it. I mean, your mom with
Lotta."

"Why bother writing *now*? Too little too late. I'm always leaving
my umbrella places!" He covers his face with his hands. "I'm so sorry
for saying what I said this morning."

"It was weird, George."

"Why don't people change? People never change."

"Of course they do. We change all the time, you and me."

"I don't mean us." She sees his face is wet. "Do you forgive me?"

"What are we talking about here? Are you okay? Lately you
seem—I guess your heart was in the right place?"

"I feel"—he frowns again, a fresh tear running down his cheek—
"like I make this great effort to be better, but no one else does. Everyone thinks they are the exception. But I *am* the exception," he sniffs.
"We should sue."

"George, it's done."

"Okay. I'm sorry. I'll do whatever you say. It never goes away, no
matter what."

"You wish life were so simple." He sniffles again and looks up at her
hopefully, for he's slumped all the way down to the carpet and lies
curled beneath his chair. She hugs him awkwardly.

"You know why I really said it, Iris? I do want to have a baby! I'm so bad at saying how I feel the right way. Let's, do you want to? Do you?" He buries his face in her shirt.

"Come now." She pets his head, hoping to trade her contempt for gentleness. *Uncaring girl,* her mother called her, and maybe she was right. There should be no room in her marriage for scorn. She's no fair-weather wife.

From the muffle of his face pressed into her chest, George adds something that sounds like "—can't stay mad if we do."

"I'll get over being mad."

He lifts his glistening face. "I never thought I was allowed."

"What do you mean? Everybody's allowed. Look at all the goons who have kids."

"Not me."

"Life keeps happening," she begins, gathering conviction as she speaks. "Whether we want it to or not. We can choose, George. You already have. Look how you found me. Look how we found each other. Remember what our lives were like before we found each other?"

"Yes. Iris, do you really want to have a baby?"

"I do." She says it because of his tears, but is caught by an unexpected happiness. A certainty that they will, one day soon, be people they wouldn't now recognize in the mirror.

"We will!" he says, sitting up, and they are holding each other properly, and he is laughing, and she laughs too.

"Can't you see how great our life is?" she says. "We have each other, and we have everything we need. Your opera is opening soon and I'll be so proud of you. And we'll have a baby! How could we be any better?"

"*The Burning Papers is* opening soon," he repeats, brightening. "And"—he looks up into her eyes—"most important of all, you are so beautiful, and we will be a family!"

III

THE LAND OF SORROW

(Winter)

29

Snow on snow on snow, and drifts at the corners. Beyond the indigo slick of the lake out her window, behind the trees' brittle tangle of branches iced to black, the bald hills wait under an iron sky. Some days, the sky is so clear and still it seems to CeCe emptied of air. Other days a thin cloud appears like a puff from an old man's cigar, like the puff from her father's friends' cigars, her father never having touched them. Clouds that feather to nothing before they chance cross the sky.

Dotty died so suddenly.

Stupid, delighted Dotty.

That Dotty died unexpectedly on Valentine's Day might in another person be remembered as the last flash of a brave and wicked humor, an ultimate defiance of the sentimental mush of the day. Except, Dotty was not that person. Dotty was the opposite, earnest sort. Not a person like CeCe.

Her sorrow over Dotty. This too came unexpected, an ache of

mysterious origin. Her grief—greater even than the news that Pat had her baby, a healthy boy named Douglas at the beginning of February, a little early but to no harm. Pat called from the hospital, described the sudden labor, the baby's rumpled brow, said, "I can't wait for you to see him," and CeCe felt sure it wasn't the ragged euphoria that followed birth. Pat meant it. But even this proves hard to hold on to as the days at Oak Park beat on, and her old life slips further away.

The truth is, nothing has caused her such an abiding sorrow as Dotty's death. How can this be? It catches her at the moment of its choosing and whatever she is doing is lost. Such grief! Sometimes a physical grief, snapping over her chest like a vise. Sometimes, a kind of vacancy, black as the waters of a subterranean pool, sensed instead of seen in the pitch. Grief, not like this at her father's death, not Walter's leaving, not Pat's leaving, not the first time she heard them say multiple system atrophy, not at what kind of a man her son has become, not even for the child she had before Patricia, who so quickly died. Maybe that. But that was so long ago, before they'd known to tell pregnant women to eat bananas. Grief, in its empty way, reminding her of the summer she was sixteen, the year before her father's death, back from Miss Porter's to New York to visit, at the lavish, modern apartment he and the wife had bought in her absence. After sitting the morning by his side, she escaped into the sunshine and walked the six blocks south to the house she'd grown up in, now a museum and library. She hadn't been since they'd moved. She climbed the steps and paid the entrance fee—a dollar, it being 1952—and received a tin visitor's button to pin to her collar, with the scrolled letters *JSS*. Inside, the lead-crystal chandelier and the gilded mirror still hung over the marble mantel. She'd invented characters for herself in that mirror, standing on a striped silk chair. The chair was gone along with the rest of the furniture. Without furniture, the wood floor's zagging, French herringbone inlay overwhelmed her eye. No one recognized her. New were the display cases with rare and ancient musical instruments, placed at regular intervals around the room. There were only a handful of other visitors, and she chose a handsome, young couple to follow as they passed quietly from room to room—through the double doors into the library, which she found more or less the same, though velvet cords pressed across the rows of leatherbound books and across the old couches. Her father's elephant tusks made their broken arch on either side of the pocket doors at the other end of the room. Gone were the stuffed birds from the Brazilian rain forests for which there'd been a special glass cabinet with a heavy iron key, always waiting in the lock. Many afternoons, she'd turned the key and placed the birds in a jumble of color on the rug. These had been moved to the Natural History Museum across town. She left the couple and passed into the drawing room, found a piano on a stage facing a fleet of empty chairs. A performance space, of little interest to the other visitors. A few ducked in, gazed up at the painted ceiling, and left. Back in what was now the lobby, she noted the passages to the dining rooms and kitchens were locked behind a new, plain set of doors, white with a metal bar. She could not climb the roped-off marble stair or ride in the mirrored elevator that had brass doors engraved with dancing jaguars and a velvet seat. She asked the docent what was upstairs. Administrative offices, a recital space, practice rooms, an archive open to the public by appointment. Did she want to make an appointment? She shook her head no. Five years went by before she had the will to return, for a tour from the museum's director of the renovations upstairs—a floor over the pool, under the curved glass ceiling! She refused to see Toto's room and refused to see her own. She was twenty-one and the board's newest trustee.

Otto hadn't made it in time. She mourns for Otto too. What is *wrong* with her? Shouldn't these last months have hardened, not softened, her? She'd prefer that. It's only, Otto loved his wife. A tall man with beautiful white hair and wide blue eyes and nostrils like an iguana's, who had all these months rented a condo a mile from Oak Park and shuttled from his and Dotty's home in Phoenix. The morning of Valentine's Day he was only that mile away, sleeping.

It can't be for silly Dotty that CeCe has lost her appetite. Dotty had become a little dear to her, she'll admit, but mostly, Dotty annoyed her. Her prattling, provincial, short-time friend. But for Otto— running up the hall where only days before she and Dotty had taken one of their inching winter constitutionals. Dotty had leaned against her, but no more than usual. Otto had disappeared around the corner without seeing CeCe, frozen with her hand on the wall. Watching his coat flap around the corner, she shut her eyes. Dotty and Otto, heart-landers who believed in the sentiment of holidays, who had built their life in a seasonless state on seasonal greetings, not only as his business, but—that story of little Fernanda in Mexico, had they not had children of their own? Had she never asked? He's probably good at his job, she'd thought, as she made her way slowly after him. She had a vision of Otto's future. Back at work with one of his subordinates, a designer with a red wax pencil stub behind his ear. She'd chastised herself: they don't use pencils anymore! A young person, without a pencil, then, bringing Otto a folder of new designs for the following year's Valentine's cards, hearts spilling onto his desk. Poor Otto would probably never know when a valentine might be delivered, reminding him of the morning Dotty died alone, the morning no tie of their spirits tugged him from his dream. He'd probably bought her a Valentine's present. When he returned to the rented condo in the dark, would he put it out of sight? As unbearable to keep as to throw away.

By early afternoon, Otto was waiting in the lobby, for the bereavement coordinator to assemble Dotty's paperwork. CeCe sat beside him, across from the portrait of Dr. Forum. "It's an imitation of a Copley," she said, pointing until Otto looked up. "And a poor one. Notice the strange proportions? Dr. Forum's eye is the same size as his ear. The artist painted the backgrounds and the bodies at his shop and brought his faceless portraits from town to town by wagon to be sold. He filled in his buyer's face last. I tell you this—I don't know why."

Had Dotty looked worse than usual the last time they played cards? Not that CeCe had noticed. But maybe she hadn't looked closely enough. As CeCe understood it from Nurse Jean, early in the morning Dotty had the stroke and managed to grope the red emergency button by the bed. The heart attack, shortly after. After, but enough time between for Dotty to be moved from one room to another, the wall going by. Time enough to know that as the windows of her own eyes failed no one who cared would be there. Time enough to cry *husband* and time in the dark to hold his name against the end of seeing. Time to hear the slamming of the trap, to hear the end of hearing.

In the lobby, Otto bent his big, white head low (so silky, like a bird's) and put his hand over his eyes and became a statue. He was so still CeCe didn't dare move, which was how she came to spend many minutes studying Dr. Forum. She was glad that as she put her hand over Otto's, it was free of any tremor that might disturb him. His long wool coat hung open. Underneath he wore evergreen-plaid pajamas and running shoes without socks, his naked ankles jutting out.

If Dotty hadn't looked worse, had she *been* worse? These last months, CeCe has grown stronger. Fluidity, sometimes, restored to her movements. She dares, some days, to think the word *cured*. The shakes don't visit for days at a time. She experiences the side effects they warned her about: the racing, steroidal energy, the hot flashes, cramps in her extremities, a red, dashing kind of heat-mania she feels even in the sockets of her eyes. But these she can live with. They can be concealed. When she walks, the joints of her fingers and toes are stiff, but this might be the cold. Dotty complained of the same. Every day, CeCe asks if she's allowed to return home with the Astrasyne. The answer is the same: she must be on-site, under the auspices of a participating care facility, like everyone else, for the observation of her motor reflexes and the habitual measure of her blood pressure, her liver enzymes, the biweekly EKG.

Still, since Otto took Dotty home (out the back, in a lights-off ambulance to the airport), CeCe can hardly bear the days. Though everything is as before—the nurses' bright greetings, the sun crossing the February sky, the pills, the sleeping and waking. "How's your mood?" Jean asks, and this only serves to remind her that Jean asks this exact question up and down the corridor, to other patients, in other rooms. That life is the same for every other patient as for her: the bright Velcro rip of the blood-pressure cuff, the iced lake, the same tiny stamp of the manufacturer on the back of each spoon, the same weekly appearance of the blimp in all their skies, twisting above the empty trees, cruising the frame of each window. Each day, a ghost of the day before. Where is there proof that any given moment belongs to her, and not to a stranger down the hall? No one comes to see her. She reminds herself she's kept her whereabouts a secret and forbidden the few who know from visiting. But how graciously they comply! Only Esme and Annie Mason and Pat phone her. Each day, strange visions of George creep upon her. Always he is out in the world, enjoying a fictive jumble of pleasures from her past and his: George at Le Petit Daudet, a dripping filet mignon in his hand; George, passing through the rooms at the Gallerie dell'Accademia in Venice, licking an ice-cream cone, stopping to consider *The Feast in the House of Levi*; George, drenched in sweat but gray as a corpse, returning his squash racket to its case with a terminal *zip*.

"You've lost someone. You're depressed," Jean says, the first week of March. "That's called depression."

This is untenable. "You have an obvious mind," CeCe answers.

Standing on the narrow, black point-ends of the hands of the clock, trying not to fall. Where would she go if she did? Out of dimension. Out of favor. Out of range. The clock's minute hand, owned once by pain and now by side effects, moves on its own unpredictable schedule, too slow or too fast, whereas the hour hand moves steadily toward meals. (Is it possible she misses the pain? Does she not remember how to organize her soul without its interruption?) Her father, who at his end could not breathe, said it felt like a lung full of storm.

"Thank you," Jean says, and laughs.

"No, by *obvious*, obviously you don't understand me. What I mean is, you might be a bit of a disappointment to—I don't know to whom. Your parents? A boyfriend? Do you have a child? . . . Oh, dear, do you not yet have a child? But how old are you? What are you feeling now, dear? Is it depression?"

That was the last she saw of Jean. For a week or three, she's not sure how long, she doesn't answer the phone and doesn't call anyone back.

When she finally dials Esme, her husband answers. "She'll be so glad you're calling. We've been worrying and worrying. Wait one second." There is the sound of the phone's being dropped into something soft, then Esme: "Cecilia!"

Two days later Esme arrives, holding her duck boots in a plastic grocery bag so as not to drip snow, having changed into dry sneakers in the hall. They embrace, and how good and familiar Esme smells! Lemons and bread.

Esme will hear nothing from CeCe until she's straightened the bed, straightened the pile of newspapers on the table. She bustles around CeCe's room as much as a person with a limp can bustle. She shakes the curtains—to evaluate their cleanliness rather than to clean— makes a sound of disapproval, and takes a seat at the table across from CeCe, putting her thickly ringed hands on the knees of her ample jeans.

"Why didn't you call for so long?" Esme says. "I am not happy."

"I'm sorry." CeCe cannot, bathed in such kindness, remember why she kept Esme away. "I didn't think I'd still be here."

"No one comes, what's happening to you is no big deal. That's what explains it."

"Did I tell you Pat had her baby?"

"The grandson. About time! But we're talking about you today. I come every week from now on. Mondays."

"Too far. I forbid you."

How has she hardly thought of Esme and missed her all along?

"The decision is not yours anymore. I go where I like. You haven't got a say."

And after this she doesn't, for Esme embarks on an update on the doings of her husband and son and niece and on the state of CeCe's house—in January, a snowstorm knocked a branch from the willow tree into the window of one of the upstairs guest bedrooms, but Esme oversaw the window's replacement and the tree is fine. Esme interviews her at length about the food she eats and the company she keeps. CeCe tells her about Dotty, and even though she doesn't cry, her fists are clasped tight under Esme's patting hands. She feels better.

"I don't see jazz hands," Esme says, for Esme is the only nonmedical professional to directly address her tremors, which she calls a variety of comical dance terms and, when it had been bad, *going to the big dance.*

"I'm doing well. I think it works. I'm only waiting."

She gets up from the table and walks a steady circle around the room, turns her neck side to side, raises her arms over her head and behind her back, and sits back down again.

"Wonderful!" Esme says.

The following visit, Monday as promised, after less amiable chatter than usual, Esme says, "Now we have to talk about you not answering George's calls."

"You've seen George?" She'd watched Esme and George grow apart when he was in his teens. She never knew why.

"No, Iris. Iris is worried. Now I'm worried too. You know about his play? That it came and went?"

"What do you mean?"

"I saw it. Iris's third time, my first. Front row. We had our night of it. I don't get to the city much. It was a special night for me, very nice. But the show closed. Quick-fast. Two weeks."

"How is it possible? Where?"

"Manhattan."

"But where?"

"Not where the action is. Near where the tourists go. The—what is it called—South Street Seaport."

"I wouldn't help him. I was sure no one would. What did you think?" she asks, hoping it might not be what she heard. Transformed, maybe, by outside direction.

"I think it's impressive to make the people come together and sing with the costumes and the music and the sets."

"I'm sorry to ask, but do you know how he did it?"

"Speak to Iris."

"Just tell me."

"Iris says the bank likes you so the bank liked George. Now she's having trouble with the payments. Credit cards too. I believe her that she didn't know. She's very worried and very surprised."

"But you say the opera's closed. That's good. I'm sorry, Esme."

"Why sorry?"

"Well, it's rude. The opera. Offensive. You know that."

"It's okay." Esme nods and shrugs at once.

"And—is George all right?" Every call, she'd almost picked up, almost called back. But then she would remember the feeling of how he put the headphones over her ears. His calls stopped. Iris tried twice after that, asking how CeCe was, asking for her to please be in touch. These CeCe also ignored. For reasons beyond her, Dotty's death cemented her resolve.

"I don't see him. He's in their house. Iris comes out, he stays in."

"He'll need time. At least it's finished."

"Not yet. I don't like to give you these, but you should know. My son helped me with the Google."

Esme unzips the nylon bag and hands CeCe some tidily paper-clipped printouts. The first is from the website of the *New York Post*. She reads:

> There's not much to write home about *The Burning Papers*, a new opera at the Abbott, written and produced by son of New York royalty George Somner.

She skims over the opera's god-awful plot summary and resumes:

> If you're looking for some silver spoon schadenfreude, this production doesn't disappoint. Somner has responded to accusations of racism and sexism by claiming *The Burning Papers* is misunderstood. According to a tweet from his hastily opened and closed Twitter account, it is an "engaged response to the alls [*sic*] of contemporary society." Prior to opening, this nutso project's press material stated *The Burning Papers* is "confidently anticipating" a national tour. Only hours after speaking with us, however, the production's publicist, Simon Padgett, released a statement of his own: "The nature of this material and its presentation were not accurately represented to our firm. We do not condone or promote projects that traffic in negative stereotypes of any kind." This reviewer agrees: eventually, the unpleasantness of the music and its message is so over-the-top you can't help but giggle—or leave.

"How is this the first I'm hearing of this? No one called me for my comment? Not that I'd have given one."

"You're not taking calls for three weeks, remember? That's how. They called your house. They called and called. They even called me."

The next review is from what must be a blog, because Esme's son has thoughtfully written *BLOG* across the top.

Highnotes.com
The Burning Papers
The Abbott: 425 Water Street
In Previews show times TBA
tickets at www.ticketwicket.com

As I endured this mad dream conceived and produced—or perhaps committed—by George Somner, I could not but ask, why? This opera is described by its composer, Vijay Muller, as an "experiment in dislocating boundaries and borders," and the night I attended, *The Burning Papers* tested the boundaries of a palpably uncomfortable audience. A variety of conceits, including a group of feuding eunuchs whose status, in this dystopian future, is determined by their skin tone, as well as ugly portraits of enslaved women and homeless "gypsies," are so jaw-droppingly weird, obscure, and offensive it was difficult for me to focus on the musical composition itself, but I can report that the original score is both jarringly scattered and numbingly dull. Particularly misguided was the use of chains and shackles as frequent costume elements for the women: it was unclear to this viewer if their clanking was an intentional or unintentional addition to the score. Rumor has it the show's director, Bernard Lieber, quit the production several weeks before previews began in what may have been a career-saving move, citing that old standby, "creative differences."

Not Recommended.

And the next, from the *New York Observer*:

PRODIGAL DONE

Amid fresh claims of chauvinistic misadventure, the terror-and-apocalypse-themed *Burning Papers*, a new opera at the Abbott—a venue just blocks from the Freedom Tower—has closed. *Papers* launched its creator, George Somner, onto New York's classical music scene with a bang, though probably not in the way he hoped. Although the production was only seen by a few lucky—or unlucky—audiences in previews, it remains a hot topic in New York's social circles, prompting many to wonder what his mother, Cecilia Somner, thinks of the opera's Queen. Those in the know imagine that Lady Somner—who in all her years of high-profile philanthropy has famously granted only one interview, to a seventh grader at a school her foundation built, must not be enjoying the publicity.

Somner junior, a scion of the American Rubber fortune, describes himself as a contemporary librettist who is "not afraid of challenging material." A neighbor to the Abbott Theater, Helen Gomez, said she had not heard of the opera, and while she "supports freedom of expression," *The Burning Papers* "does not sound like something [she] personally would go out of [her] way to see." When told the show was closing, she added, "Tough town."

She can't read any more.

"There aren't any legitimate reviews? Nothing in the *Times?*"

"My son said Google has a lot. But mostly other people making copies of the first thing, the *Post.*"

"Nothing more measured in tone? A profile? A process piece?"

"This too shall pass," Esme says, putting her bag on her lap to signal her departure. From the door she says, "I see you next week. Call George. Get out of this room. Cold outside is no excuse. Now your friend's dead, you go make another."

"I hardly knew her and she wasn't interesting!"

But Esme is already down the hall.

The next day CeCe screws her courage and calls Nan to ask how much people are talking.

"It's pretty bad," Nan says.

Tonight, the moon is full and catches in the ice hanging off the trees. It glows so brightly on the iced lake it's as if the lake were another moon. There's a drifting fog. The weather is turning. Remembering Esme's admonition, CeCe forces herself to have dinner in the dining room with the rest of the waxworks.

She chooses a seat by the window, next to Mr. Townsend. He would prefer for her to call him Carl. She does not honor his request, Carl being a name she finds deflating. His skin is thin and mottled on his high, hairless forehead, and he has the bright, energized eyes of advanced sickness. His feet swing under his chair. He and a woman she does not recognize are in the middle of a conversation.

He turns to CeCe. "You enjoy the movie?"

"The movie last night," the woman says.

"Yes, very funny," CeCe lies. She hadn't left her room, but she remembers from the schedule it was *The Seven Year Itch.*

Esme wants her to forgive George. Esme is looking out, worrying ahead to who will take care of CeCe. But he'd come only for the money. And there is the matter of her own shame. Her son's ugliness, in the papers. All this time, she's let no one visit. Look how he's gone and humiliated her, ten times what any hospital room or wheelchair might! What are they saying about her, right now? Who is always blamed? The mother is who. The mother, right or wrong. They've probably dusted off her divorces. Probably gossiping for the first time in thirty-five years about her unfortunate choices. They'll assume he learned his odious prejudices at her knee. That her good work was only made to increase her influence and is no reflection of her spirit. They'll decide either he learned his intolerance from her, or that she neglected him so thoroughly she warped him out of all compassion. Too much or not enough, one or the other! How dare they? Maybe she doesn't want to return after all. She certainly won't be calling on anyone in the musical philanthropic circles. She'll need to call the John Stepney Somner Library, hear their concerns. The institutions she supports that combat discrimination too. How unpleasant those conversations will be. Will they still be able to use her name? Her name, which attracts the other donors, the name she's established so carefully for just that reason? Maybe she'll stay in this terrible facility forever. She will increase her donations to the various causes of music and art and justice she already supports. Quietly. She'll call Annie in the morning.

Carl turns again to CeCe. "Did you enjoy the movie?"

Poor man. "Yes. It was funny. Did you?"

"Funny? Funny to think a movie like that is funny. It was sad as all get out!"

"Which movie are you thinking of?" the woman asks. "Not last night's. Are you thinking of a different night?"

A hazy cloud has settled over the moon, turning the lake yellow. The light from the dining-room windows stretches away from the building, yellow too, long bars over the snow.

"Whom do you ask, him or me?" CeCe says.

"Well, either," the woman replies.

"If there's one thing I know, it's movies," Carl says. "Please pass the branches."

CeCe looks around the table. She slides over the tray of asparagus and rises to retire to her room.

IV

THE WOLF AND THE SPIDER

(Spring)

30

It is Bob Iris decides to call. She is confused when he tells her that his offices are on the thirty-fourth floor of the Lipstick Building. He adds, "Fifty-Third and Third, you'll see."

She exits the subway on Lexington and walks east. Manhattan, a constellation of ATM machines and chucked chewing gum. She makes her way past the slick black piles of garbage bags and the snow heaped at the curb like dirty rags, dense and unmelting despite the coming of spring. From the jaundice glow of a parking garage, its sloping cement throat, an attendant calls to her softly, "Good morning, beautiful." When she doesn't respond, he says, "Eh! Now that's fine," in what seems to be both a rebuke of her silence and a further appreciation of her figure.

She marches along until the gray river appears. She's gone too far. She turns back and endures the parking attendant once more. This time, now leaning against the door of his booth, he tries a *sss–sss–sss*-ing sound, compelling her to flip him the bird. Finally, Bob's building. A looming cylinder of red granite and steel. Why is she supposed to be impressed when something ugly as a skyscraper resembles some other ugly thing, such as a tube of lipstick?

She turns through the brass revolving doors into the airy, modern vacuum of the lobby. At the bank of elevators, a security guard sends her back to the concierge desk, a giant marble egg under a fan of international flags. She presents her license. A phone call is made. She receives a laminated badge. She proceeds to the thirty-fourth floor, her ears popping, checking her image in the mirrored ceiling of the empty, speeding elevator. She'd left George in the bedroom. He wouldn't let her raise the shades.

She passes through a set of glass doors with an electronic click. Here is her reflection again—a sliver of her face, one of her violet eyes, a collarbone—in the large mirrored letters set in a luminous resin panel behind the head of the receptionist. T-R-Y-P-H-O-N C-A-P-I-T-A-L, and the raised resin outline of a lion with wings.

"Hello," the receptionist says. "Have a seat. I'll let him know you're here. Water?"

"No thanks."

Iris is craning to see behind the partition—a wedge of the open office, rustling with employees on computers and phones, the ovoid panoramic view beyond—when Bob finally enters reception.

"Wondering why it's Tryphon instead of Gryphon, right?"

"You mind reader, you." She laughs. She hadn't been. She's not sure what either means.

"Well, the idiots who turned this canteen—follow me," he says, and they walk through the corridor of unwalled cubicles, through the rows of men and the occasional woman at their desks, "—into, you see, what we are"—he waves at the skyline—"they wanted it to be Gryphon. But someone already had that. So they went with Tryphon. Sounds strong. *T*s are strong. And they kept the visual, like no one would give a shit. And no one does. Except me. You know what a Tryphon was?"

"No?" As they pass, the people at their desks look up at her, briefly, without shifting their expressions.

"Jackass goose herder in ancient Syria. Got himself martyred. Became the saint of keeping bugs out of gardens. Apparently, I'm the only senior partner here who bothers with *Wikipedia*."

She laughs her brightest, most encouraging laugh, wondering if George has by now at least slumped downstairs, if he's in the same pair of sweatpants—her sweatpants—he's been wearing the last four days. She hopes Bob hasn't noticed the change to her appearance, slight as it is; in the mirror she sees a woman whose face has gone thin with worry, a harried expression that surprises her, that will not go away. This morning, she made an effort with the blow-dryer. She chose her outfit carefully. Not too much, not too little.

"*You* get it. Of course the great Iris Louise Somner gets it. Here, come on through."

They pass into his office through an antechamber where a young woman sits behind a glossy white desk stacked with manila folders.

"You know my middle name."

"How about that. Come, sit."

She takes a seat in one of the two chairs facing his desk, the same white model as the assistant's, but twice as large and messier.

"Water?" he asks.

"I'm okay, thanks."

"Whiskey?"

"Oh, no."

"You are transfixed, I see. It's something, isn't it? They literally installed it two hours ago! I said to myself, 'I'm so glad Iris is coming today, I'll get to show her my new painting.'"

Behind Bob's desk is a canvas of many colors, a chaotic crowd of bodies on a beach. The canvas is as large as the wall. In one corner, two men carry a gigantic umber-and-polka-dotted torso of a woman, feet-first, into the surf; an oil rig floats in the sea. A tangled clot of figures riot at the front of the painting, fists skyward, one looking right at her with wild eyes as if he needs something she's failed to bring. There's a man whose head is a triangle like an African mask, and a naked woman with a gun, and two men in army uniforms embracing a giant red tulip that is without question a vagina, except the vagina *is* with a question, as beside it is a cartoon bubble that reads *I o u?* The paint is thick.

"An early Monez. You know his work?" Bob peers for a moment at the side of the canvas, sliding his fat hand behind it, pushing the painting an inch outward and releasing it.

She tilts her head, trying to reconcile the painting with her memory of the artist's name. It sounds familiar.

"It can't be the same painter," she ventures, remembering the housemate with the ferrets, the poster behind the TV, "who did *Water Lilies*?"

"Water Lilies!" Bob cries. "We would be drinking whiskey if this were *Water Lilies*. You're hilarious."

She's said something stupid, clear enough.

"Mon-*ez*. Contemporary guy. Really has it, don't you think? A bit *Guernica*, a bit Guston. I got a deal."

"It's very good."

"Come, look at the view."

Because of the strange shape of the building, Bob's office is a glass bowl. The East River, the meaner of the two rivers, spans beneath them. From so high up, the view divides into patterns: the dirty lace of the whitecaps; the wake of a slow-moving barge; the tight rush of cars on the FDR, hugging the curve of the waterway.

"See there." Bob stands close beside her. "North is the Queensboro Bridge. And all the way down is the Williamsburg."

"Oh? Yes?" The Queensboro looks to her like a great discarded leg brace, all silver screws and pins. A helicopter heaves sideways over the river. The landline on Bob's desk rings. He ignores it.

"See the neon Pepsi-Cola sign?"

"Cool. Is that Queens?"

"Roosevelt Island. Between us and Queens. Okay. Look down and right. South, right there, you see that building? See how only the exterior is left, the light coming through the windows from behind?"

"The one that looks like a castle?"

"It totally does. That's the old smallpox hospital. Abandoned."

"Makes the back of my knees feel weird. The height."

There's an infinitesimal pause, a moment between them, where she knows it's up to her. Instead, she says, "That's great," referring to nothing in particular, and quickly goes around his desk and sits back down in her chair.

"How's real estate?" He returns to his spot in front of the painting. "Still fucking brutal?"

"I'm not selling anything these days, to tell the truth. I'm trying, but nothing's moving. I'm kind of getting the freeze. Being the newest hire, I'm the lowest on the pecking order, so I don't get the good listings. I guess they thought I'd bring in my own clients, I'd know a lot of people because of the Somners. As it turns out, I don't know anybody. I don't know if it's the right kind of work for me, anyway. I go in every day, in case, and help out whoever."

"How's George? I've tried to get him on the phone."

"Not so good."

"All my fault, in a way."

"What is?"

"How you met George. Because of me."

"I did? I don't know about that."

"You don't? There's not much to it. I'm the one dragged George on that golf trip. So, that's the first thing."

"Deep down, he doesn't like golf."

"Right? He thinks he does, but he never wants to go. And, he's no good."

She's seized by a new worry. Is George paying dues at clubs? If so, why hasn't she found contracts or receipts? She'll need to cancel them. In all their marriage he's never even suggested they go to a country club.

"What a stink he made that day, like a little girl. *It's too hot, I forgot my clubs, I'm wearing the wrong pants.*"

"I didn't know you were on that trip! I don't remember seeing you. I only remember George."

"Well, I didn't have anything to check."

"Right."

"I saw you first. With that dog. I told George to go talk to you. I said, come on, man, ask her about her dog. It's easy."

"No!"

For a moment, his jowls tighten. He sticks out his lower lip and leans back in his chair. "Yes," he continues. "I saw you, and then I stayed out of the way. I mean, I'm so fucking *charming*." He leans forward and laughs a genuine laugh, his mood apparently passed. "Your husband, no offense, never would have said boo to you if I hadn't shamed him right up into it."

"I can't believe it! That was one of the only days I had 3D with me in coat check. I mean, that's a fancy old place. Didn't you think it was weird I had a dog in there?"

"I assumed you were blind."

"You didn't."

"No, I didn't. You sneak him in there?"

"I did. I had him with me less than a week before they spotted him under the counter. Fired me on the spot. Whatever. 3D showed up the month before, getting in the Dumpsters, wandering around the sandpits. They'd pinpoint him on the security cameras and rush out to catch him, but he'd be gone. For the staff it got to be like tracking Bigfoot. One day I'm at security check-in saying hi to this old guy Marvin, and he's playing me footage on the monitor from the night before. 3D, making a bed on the lunch terrace. With a tablecloth. Circling and circling. Awesome. Then 3D, the real 3D I mean, leaps through the open door of the security booth. Right into my arms. Scared the living shit out of us. That's how I named him. He went from 2-D to 3-D, get it?"

Why is she gabbling on and on? A relief to be asked a question she can answer without feeling out of her depth, a relief to stall asking the favor she's come for.

"Holy shit, that's delightful," Bob says, ignoring another phone call.

"If it wasn't for 3D, I guess I wouldn't be here."

"No, I think it goes, if it wasn't for *me* you wouldn't be here."

"Yes."

"As much as you enjoy my company, I'm curious. To what do I owe the honor of your visit?"

"It's hard to talk about." She takes a deep breath. "George is not doing great. I mean, he's fine, we're fine, but he's having what he calls"—this is not how she meant to start—"an existential crisis."

Bob's guffaw is so loud it startles her. "Well, fuck, sure he is. Existential is the only kind of crisis available to a person as loaded as that guy. Between us, boy, oh, boy, that show was a mess."

Was she right to come? He cares about George, doesn't he? She hasn't got anywhere else to go! At least he isn't like the other people George had counted as friends, pretending not to see her in town.

"It's not the embarrassment. We're not doing so well with—" She takes a breath. "There's a lot of debt."

"What? Is it bad?" he asks, looking genuinely worried.

She must say as little as possible. She must protect—she doesn't need to tell him how she ransacks the house for the unpaid bills George has hidden from himself. How she's taken over his cell phone, screening the calls he receives from creditors day and night, has been receiving for many months, as it turns out, as she's learned from the various creditors' agents—Steve and James, Yolanda and Kate, Kevin and Anthony and Velda and Maria and Frank and—infuriating, how they give phony first names, as if they are friends. She won't tell Bob how George scowls and mutters his way from one end of the house to the other, hours at a time. How he didn't seem to notice when she took over negotiations with the banks and the credit-card companies. How with what savings Iris and George retained in their joint account—what a short leash, it turns out, CeCe kept him on—Iris paid the most pressing debt outright, the balance on the orchestra's contracts, as well as the stagehands and performers and staff. She won't mention how they'd gone to the warehouse in Queens where George was storing the larger set pieces, saving them in the hopes the show might still tour, and he sat on the dingy floor and cried while she negotiated a payment plan, organized the staggeringly expensive pickup and demolition of the sets. How she's sold almost everything she thought he wouldn't notice go missing: her wedding dress on eBay; the espresso machine; the crystal and china from the wedding they never used anyway; a pair of austere leather-and-wood chairs from Sea Guest Bedroom 2, which the dealer bought for $6,000 after declaring them authentic Stickleys; the living-room

TV and the second plasma screen from Sky Guest Bedroom 1, explaining to George she was making home improvements and wanted to upgrade their entertainment system. One day, she remembered he used to wear an old, valuable-looking watch. He'd worn it at the wedding and the first year of their marriage, but she hadn't seen it in a long time. She took a stealth look in his dresser and found the brown velvet case, empty. She decided she shouldn't look any further, that his personal treasures should remain off-limits, but that she might sell the jewelry he'd given her, her old aunt's voice—*Foolish, the women who think stones are for beauty. Stones are for disaster.* After the jewelry was gone, it struck her there might be value in the mostly forgotten library, with its collection of books assembled from the Somner holdings by the decorator. To the slight bespectacled man who drove up from the city, first she sold a book from 1790, from Scotland, called *Travels to Discover the Source of the Nile*, then, a first-edition double volume of Dickens's *Our Mutual Friend* and an illustrated folio *King James Bible* from 1711. Next, a water-damaged seven-volume set of Audubon's *Birds of America* and a first authorized edition of the piano-vocal score of Giuseppe Verdi's *Il Trovatore*, and a signed copy of a novel by Evelyn (a man, the dealer corrected) Waugh titled *Handful of Dust*. She'd fired the part-time groundskeeper and the pool maintenance and Erika, the housecleaner who came once a week, a niece of Esme's, and canceled the car service— George has stopped leaving the house anyway—and halted their various institutional and recreational memberships, and cashed out what was left of their wedding registry, and she was still barely holding the creditors at bay; she means to trade her car in, but week after week puts it off. She would like to sell the cream-colored Lexus that waits exclusively for George in the garage, though she's never seen him drive it, but she can't find the title anywhere in his papers and can't think of a way to ask. She won't mention how, for a man who is depressed, George has developed an increased, insatiable appetite for sex and at all hours presses himself upon her like a glum, murderous rabbit; that his desire to have a child has grown more fervid by the day, certainly more fervid than hers; that they have, to her mixed relief, been unsuccessful in this endeavor. She can't mention how he'd quit Hud-Stanton so he could attend rehearsals and never told her—she'd discovered the truth only when she called his office and gotten Audrey's assistant. Audrey, program officer of the renamed fund, mortifyingly compassionate and graceful, George's fund having been dismantled. How George, stamping around the house or burrowed in his office, found the absence of the people who tended to their home, and the increasing mess (though she does try her best) unaccountable: Where have they gone? Why does Iris insist they drink brewed coffee, when he prefers espresso?

Firing Victor was the worst.

"As you can see, we're making lots of changes," she said, opening her palms to the sparse great room, avoiding his eyes. "It doesn't have anything to do with you."

He was kind. To avoid her sadness, they discussed unimportant things: he had a key and would bring it by next he remembered; they'd see each other at the gym maybe; he and Bill loved their house and had painted the upstairs bedroom an olive green that you'd think would look terrible, but in the morning sun was the warmest color. That the vibe at Kingsgate was still weird, transition pains maybe, not exactly neighborly, but okay. Abruptly, he hugged her goodbye.

"Wait! I found your book!" She ran upstairs, returned, and handed him *The Bluest Ribbon*.

"Did you finish it?"

"No, it's yours." As if this were an explanation. She'd discovered it wedged behind the bed, cleaning for the first time after firing Erika. It hadn't occurred to her to read the rest, as if by losing it she'd given up her right to the end of the story.

They hugged again and he closed the front door gently to avoid 3D's nose, as 3D followed him, expecting a walk, Victor saying, "No buddy, not today," finally pushing the dog back in by the rump. As the door shut, 3D gave her such a pitiable look that Iris put her head down on the kitchen counter and cried. George emerged from his office saying, "Who was that? Victor?" Quickly, she wiped her tears, because there wasn't room for two people in one house to be unhappy, two unhappy people in one house would be the end of them. She'd called CeCe a few times, but heard nothing back.

"I paid the cast and the crew—I wanted to pay all the real-live people before the collection agencies. But, yes, it's bad."

"How much?"

"Hard to know, exactly. George isn't much help. Not right now. I mean, I never had money. I know how to be. I don't mind. But George won't be any good at being poor."

"You mean to tell me you married our boy because you *liked* him?" Bob says in a voice meant to lighten the mood.

"Of course I did." Too forceful. She is insulted. "It's just, he doesn't have sense—to keep records. I have to go by what the creditors are telling me, and the best I can figure is it's eight hundred thousand, maybe nine. He got it from so many different places! There are a lot of cards."

"What was he thinking? When did this happen?"

"I don't know. I only noticed the money was gone when there wasn't any left."

"You paid the crew from your personal assets?"

"We had the retirement accounts and Treasury bonds I cashed. And some joint savings."

"Equity in the house?"

She shakes her head. "The house belongs to CeCe and to George."

Bob whistles. "Shit's creek. What does George say?"

"I asked him, if it's a flop, you don't owe the backers, right? Isn't that the deal? It's their risk? And it's not like the type of people who back opera hurt if they lose the money. He kind of goes 'Yeah, yeah.' So at first I think maybe he's disorganized, because he's devastated. Then I take over and . . . he didn't have any backers. He paid for all of it. I'm fielding these calls, and they're saying every kind of thing to scare me, about us going to jail and sending people by and finding our relatives and asking them to pay and lawsuits and—"

"Well, what about that?"

"What about what?"

"Your mother-in-law's not exactly lacking."

"That's the problem. They've stopped speaking. He won't tell me what happened. She won't return his calls. Or mine. I don't think it's true, what they're saying about him."

"A very lot's happened in a very little amount of time here, hasn't it? What a perfect fuckstorm. Isn't there a sister? I remember from school. Nice hair. Could she help?"

Iris shakes her head. "That wouldn't work. Bob, please don't, I don't want you to think less of George."

"Listen. There was a time I took Martha's money—it was Martha's money then, eh—and in four years I spent it all on coke. She'd just married me, and that's what she got. I foreclosed on a building taller than this one. Although, it was in Florida. I mean, fuck Florida, right?"

"It's nice of you to share that," she says, suddenly holding back tears.

"Her parents still do not adore me." He laughs.

"I've been so worried," she whispers.

"Poor Iris is handling all this by herself?"

"Yes."

"And how the hell are *you* holding up?" He reaches across the desk to take her hand. She looks at the corner of the Monez behind him, at the tiny oil rig in the ocean.

"I'm fine. I'm a strong person."

"One in a million," he says, releasing her.

"I still have the cars. A tiny inheritance from my mother. And I made a little commission on Kingsgate. That's the last of it. Not nearly enough, and if I use it, it will all be gone forever. Then I had the idea"—she forces herself to look steadily, directly at him and smile brightly—"I thought, Our very best friend is the most talented broker in town. Why didn't I call you right away?"

"Investment adviser."

"Oh, right?" She doesn't know the difference. "The best, whatever you call it!"

"You must already have financial management."

"They don't want to work with us anymore."

"Okay, let's think out loud together for a minute here. How much do you have left to invest?"

"Thirty thousand."

He looks at her and shakes his head, puts his fat palms flat on his desk. "Tryphon starts investors at a five hundred thousand minimum.

And I don't take on anyone. Half the guys that come in here begging to work with me I turn down."

"Sure. I understand." How had she convinced herself she could fix this? Stupid idea. All she's managed to do is humiliate herself. And George. Stupid to think she's the kind of person who is clever and brave and well-connected enough to vault over all that debt without having to—five hundred thousand. Waltzing in here, acting like she knows something. Her last good idea.

"Now, don't cry! What kind of asshole do you think I am? Look, but you're not just anybody, are you?"

"I *am*. That's exactly what I am. It's okay. I totally understand. This is your job. Your office is so big!"

"Where are the—I don't have any tissues? Listen, how about this. I've got something coming up I'd bet the house on. Big and stable and already halfway home. Your timing couldn't be better, actually. How about I front you part of the principal, fat up your thirty-K nest egg. Anything we make over the initial investment, you keep. I'll only take back what I loaned you."

"Why would you do that?"

"I like you. I like you a lot, Iris. We're friends. You and me."

"I can't take your money. It doesn't seem right."

"I won't notice it's gone. That's the truth. What, now you're making me beg to do you a favor? That is fairly fucking unbelievable. I'm onto you, lady. Just like a woman. You're quite the ace."

"No! I don't mean to be—"

"It'll take a little time. But if you hang in there, we'll catch a nice big one for you. Probably not as big as you need. No one makes that kind of return on a short. I'm not Superman. But big enough to stop the bleeding."

His phone rings again, again he ignores it. She hears his assistant pick up in the outer office, her murmured response. In her mind's eye she sees the door of a bank vault being opened by a guard and behind it a silver heap of fish.

"This would be me advising you personally, privately, you understand. Not as a client here. I can't justify thirty grand."

"You really won't notice it's gone?"

"Nope."

"Can you please take your—is it a fee? A percentage? However you do it. I don't believe in something for nothing. I couldn't live with myself."

"However you and George want. Talk it over."

"That's the other—the thing I need to say. George isn't himself. He can't tolerate much, right now. He doesn't know everything I'm doing. To help us. He's not able—it's stressful, when I try to involve him. It would be hard. He never would've asked you. I'll tell him, but maybe after I've taken care of more of the debt. He doesn't know I'm here today. I mean, obviously." She's exhausted by this attempt at discretion. At conveying why George can't know, without exposing how fragile George is, how bad it is at home.

"A man's pride is the castle of his soul. Say no more."

A cell—one of three arrayed between them—begins to skitter and hum on the white desk. She recognizes the ringtone. The theme to *Star Wars*.

"Listen, I have to take this." He grasps and squeezes her hand. "But we'll fix it up. Don't you worry. I'll call when I have a sense of the timeline. Gretchen! Show Mrs. Somner out."

The woman steps into the room and Iris stands. She hasn't properly thanked Bob, but he's swiveled his chair around and is already on the phone, studying his Monez, saying, "Well, he's a prick, that's why. Get a new cellie then . . . Because, I have to tell you because?"

Just like that, she's past the glowing gryphon at the reception station and back out on the street.

31

<psomner@gmail.com>   Mar 7 (12 minutes ago)

hey you not answering your phone? are you ok? i
read about your opera. ooooooooof. i don't get it but
i'm feeling for you brother. remember that trick of
waiting i taught you when we were kids? wait long
enough, things get okay again? i want to run
something by you. after we had douglas, mother sent me
the most incredible letter. a real letter very serious
on that stationery that must date to the eisenhower
administration about how grandchildren are new
beginnings and how she wants us to bring douglas to
booth h. blah. she apologized for being rude all
these years to lotta. i mean she REALLY apologized.
super-paraphrase: my life's mission, the foundation,
has always been against inequality and here you are

GAYS right in my own family and i wasn't accepting of
your lifestyle choice. she used the phrase lifestyle
choice, which would be very forward of her if it was
still 1990. which for our mother, very forward. it's
hilarious and so CeCe how her letter mixes us in with
her causes like you could substitute lupus or landmine
for lesbian. it still made me super emotional. we've
had some phone calls. not bad. to be honest i always
suspected it was less of a gay thing and more that I
dared have my own life. that and she probs can't stand
another woman mattering more than her, right?

point is, i'd like to visit but i get the idea you
guys aren't speaking? i had this thought maybe she
wrote to me only because you're fighting. i'm afraid of
coming all the way out east just to get my heart
broken again. tell me what you think. and tell me
you're okay, okay?

love & abracos to esme and iris,

pat

<psomner@gmail.com>   Mar 7 (2 minutes ago)

ps!
pls thank Iris for Runaway Bunny and the jammies.
i'll send her a proper note as soon as i come up for
air. having a 6 week old is nuts.

Lately his life, George recognizes, has come to resemble an endless
chamber of revolving doors through which he passes and passes and
passes and passes and passes and passes, as one might in a nightmare,
for when he isn't, what—sleeping or staring into nothing or crashing
around the house with chemically induced purpose that so fast disinte-
grates, leaves him all alone again, either too heavy and raw to move or
too suspicious of the world to sit still—he's aimlessly on the Internet,
seven, ten hours at a time. How many screens can a person pay atten-

tion to at once? Is it unwell of him to have read Pat's self-congratulatory, sparkling flatulence of an e-mail with the page beside it open to a paused video of a woman being rigorously and impersonally fucked over a leather recliner shaped like a giant baseball glove?

He's hardly left the house since the opera closed. All his days are of this nightmare pattern. Today, no different. He woke once when he heard Iris drive away, and again at noon. (Like most nights, he'd lain awake until dawn, his eyelids twitching.) Finally up, though not dressed, he slumped into the club chair in his office to read the newspaper; dissatisfied with the doom of the world, he shifted to the computer so he might for several hours monitor and rebut the slanderous comments made against himself and *The Burning Papers*. The collective interest has moved on, though. The commentary's dwindled, almost to nothing. To have an enemy that doesn't care—a different problem. Still, there are repostings and lesser weeds to root.

He closes his e-mail and trolls around some music sites. In the comments section of a minor classical blog, he writes anonymously, *But the Magic Flute has the wicked Moor, and you don't see Mozart being stoned to death!*

Moving on, he rereads some windbag's comment at opera-ra.com who calls the score *pretentious, phony Dada.* Into the empty office he cries, "It's not Dada. It's the opposite of Dada!"

After the article in the *Post* came out, alerts had alerted him to his presence not only on music-related sites but also on a website called angrywaitress.com, where an anonymous server asserted George to be a crap tipper and a belligerent back-sender of a totally decent lamb shank. It hadn't seemed important, a few weeks ago, when there were worse accusations to address. Now he begins, *To the contrary, I am*—No. It's beneath him, and the woman being fucked over the baseball glove is still being fucked over the baseball glove, only waiting to be unpaused. Next he looks, it's three o'clock. How is it he's *hours* into an anxiety-reducing porn bender? Fleeing the ugly reflection of himself in the mirror of the Internet, then finding he must flee again, that he is on the run, one site to another. But even porn—dirge delight, inexhaustible undead, tireless companion to all and none—has come to exhaust him, though his exhaustion has not decreased the amount of time he devotes to it, nor to the amount of dextroamphetamine and amphetamine-based concentration-boosters he consumes between clicks—new interventions, so easily procured—to keep the exhaustion at bay. Against logic, in fact, the exhaustion has increased his commitment, intensified his quest for some eye-smacking shock of video that will bring him back to life, that will, if not bring him pleasure, at least remind him of what happy future was once possible, like smelling the clothes of the dead.

Four o'clock. He hasn't dressed. Here arrives his second, daily, panic—when did this numbing time-suck suck him almost all the way to evening? What can he recall having viewed or written or read? Shame, shame, shame, the scouring of self-wanking and the scouring of self-googling melting into one raw-eyeballed morosity, and maybe he'll have a little pick-me-up, and that's a little better. Who isn't taking a pill for something or other these days, except his perfect wife, who should not be blamed for her perfection? A little help from science, if one is capable, if one is disciplined, if one takes science by the horns and uses wisely what the market has to offer, instead of being told. Why not admit unto the body those few pleasures the modern terror of technological advancement has to offer?

He leaps from the chair and marches upstairs to dress. "Enough!" Time to take charge of his affairs. He returns to the great room in a powder-blue pullover and khakis. "Hello, jerkface," he says to the recumbent 3D, his red, spindly legs hanging off the couch, a rubber grenade Iris sometimes fills with peanut butter on the cushion beside his ear. "Care to join me?" He slaps the dog's flank as he heads back to his office. No. The dog never wants to join him. He and the dog have now been alone in the house over sixty days in a row. Not once has 3D shown interest in George's company.

Now! Where best to start the noble task of Taming Life but with a cleansing dispatch of the e-mails he's been avoiding? Here he is back with Pat. Pat, pretending to be on his side. Gloating. Aren't they doing well. Aren't they full of exciting news. He didn't know Iris sent Pat and Lotta a gift. He doesn't know *what* Iris does these days. For example: Why the hell has she fired everybody? The house is a goddamn mess.

He has a hunch, though. The black pebble of an explanation. He doesn't dare ask her, but maybe, just maybe, she fired them because they can't be trusted. Because Iris loves him and is protecting him. They were spying, maybe. Rifling through his effects, looking for a story to sell. Things have gone missing from the house. More than the chairs and the televisions, Iris on this decorative cleanse. Were they stealing? Or talking to who knows? Collectors, reporters. Good riddance. Especially to Victor. Yesterday, for example, a man called and asked for Iris and refused to leave a message. It hadn't sounded like Victor, but the voice was familiar. And all the week before someone calling and hanging up. His unease is like a whisper at the back of his ear, like the faint beating of papery wings coming at him from behind, far away, not so far away. Three days before, a car he didn't recognize came up the drive and turned around. And yesterday, Audrey called from Hud-Stanton, apologized for calling, her voice distant and, it seemed, tense (Was someone standing behind her?), with a question about where some grant files might be stored in his old office computer. A likely excuse! What's left for Hud-Stanton to accuse him of? Could it be someone is checking to see if he's home? It isn't inconceivable that he's being watched. Today he suspects he hasn't been entirely alone, that somehow, somewhere, someone's watching. He stays mostly in his office, away from the great room's wall of glass. He keeps the curtain drawn. "Are you hiding in your room?" his mother used to say to him when he was a boy, when she was having a party and he didn't come out in a timely fashion to greet her guests. He mustn't hide! This is his house. His house. He must be brave. He'll check the road. If anyone's there, once they see him, they'll go.

Outside, he fills his lungs with cold air. The snow's melting in smeared patches on the lawn. Cautiously, he makes his way down the long, steep, curved drive, sweating in the cool. In the stillness, he's listening—what's he listening for? He stands quietly in the middle of the drive, for a long time. He hears only the rustling of the bare trees and returns to the cave of his office. He texts Penny, *SPRING-TIME!!!!!!!!* He's texted and called Penny, a few times, more than a few times, this past month, for no real reason beyond general self-loathing. He doesn't even want to see her. She never responds. This makes him sour, and sometimes he asks the air, asks the dog, "Do you feel sorry for me? Do you feel sorry for me now?"—until ruminating about Penny slides into worrying that Iris and Victor are having an affair. For if George transgressed without notice, how can he be certain that Iris too has not transgressed? And why wouldn't she, being married to such a smear, such a seedy humiliation? No, he's being paranoid—*paranoid,* a word they'd used against him when he was young and in trouble, called paranoid what he called truth. He's aware of his mother's secret intervention at Yale: paid off the security guard he punched in the mouth on the dark path behind the library. The security guard, who turned and maybe did, maybe did not, see the girl scrambleupandrun, eyes like an animal. The guard, and a sizable donation. Toward a cause his mother would surely not otherwise have supported, a Puppet Laboratory for the Drama Department, facilitating his return to school from his ski break with a clean record. To the disciplinary committee, to his mother, to the psychiatrists, he agreed he'd been wrong when it came to the guard. The girl, though. Who knows why she was telling such a destructive lie. And, whatever: she dropped out the following semester.

He returns to his chair and tries again to read a section of the newspaper, but the words have gone impenetrable. It's like when he was a boy, playing the piano for his teacher, kind Mr. Foley, who told George he had talent, natural grace, if only he'd apply himself. But to try to be good at the only thing anyone had ever told him he was good at was too consequential a charge. If he failed, it would mean he wasn't good at anything. At the keyboard, in his mounting distress, he'd find the notes closing off to him like little iron gates, slammed and locked. The harder he looked, the more it felt he was trying to see behind them, but of course he was trying to see *into* them, to read them. Impossible, once they were gates that closed. Soon enough, he came to dread the dull yellow paper of the music sheets, their crackle as the teacher turned the page. How he envied Pat her sinewy, untouched violin, the amber cube of resin neglected in the case.

Now Pat has a son. He wants to have a son. Badly! These days, it is the only happy longing left to him. A month back, when everything was at its worst, he googled his father and found nothing new. He'll try again, he decides, closing his e-mail and the window with the woman over the recliner. When will Iris be home? He needs Iris. *They went broke overnight*, he imagines people saying, a whisper in his ear, a whisper and a lie. *The mother with all that money.*

The search of his father's name pulls up, as always, little more than the half-page profile *Life* magazine ran as part of a series in 1964: "New York Artists: Breaking the Landscape." Here's the black-and-white photo of the wiry man in the white undershirt leaning against a ladder in his studio, a cigarette between his knuckles, his pants belted high. Someone would tell him if Walter was dead, wouldn't they? And the search would turn up an obituary, wouldn't it? Walter's work had been a little famous in the sixties. Walter had fought at Okinawa. He presumes his father still lives in Mougins, in the hills above Cannes. If he isn't dead, he's ninety-five. The last time George saw his father was in 1989, when George was eighteen and his father was seventy-three. Maybe Walter's tan has faded and he has a tacky nurse, a nurse like a hooker. Maybe he does not.

Not that the previous visit had gone so well. George had flown to Nice, CeCe having relented and arranged it by phone with Walter. At the last moment, by a message left at the front desk of the hotel, his father changed the date and would not see George until the following night. George strolled the marina and the streets under the palm trees in Cannes. He took a taxi a half hour west and spent the day on the beach, marveling at the bronze, topless women on the white, imported sand. He returned and had dinner outdoors, by himself. *Lapin à la moutarde* in the warm, dark breeze on the balcony café of his hotel, overlooking the sea. A fine night's rest in the plush and tasseled room CeCe's travel agent had booked for him. From the wheels of the plane bumping down on the tarmac to waking in a sumptuous and sunny hotel room— only twenty-four hours it took him to be certain he was no longer a child, but a man of the world. To walk and walk and walk, a stranger in a strange place, the happiest he'd been. The next day he awaited his father at the appointed place and time: the bar at the grand entrance to

Casino Croisette. He could hear the dull roar and clang of the game floor. The venue too had been changed from the one CeCe agreed to, a sitting room at George's hotel.

He took a stool at the end of the bar under a potted palm and ordered a martini but received a syrupy cup of sweet vermouth without ice and drank it down with mortified haste, trying not to breathe. He then ordered a whiskey, having read Hemingway that year in school. After the better part of an hour, George spotted Walter crossing the room. He looked worse than in the photos. Shorter, brown as bacon, oiled and papery, like a discarded lunch bag twisted around a soda straw. A spectacular, rickety wreck. He appeared no more interested in George than anything else in the room. His expression was set in a fierce but diffuse neutrality, like a politician's under fire. He sat down on the stool next to George. In good French he ordered a beer, pushing up the sleeves of his linen jacket and putting his elbows on the bar. He looked a decade older than he should, his hair grizzled and white, but to George his sinew contained a mesomorphic power. He was, George decided, a Great Man, in the way only men of his generation could be. Walter received his beer in a delicate glass.

"Hi," George said. "Thank you for meeting with me."

"Yes."

There was a silence, in which George became aware he was not breathing. But then they spoke about George's flight and his hotel and of the beauty of Cannes and of Mougins, though Walter did not invite him to Mougins, saying only, "That bastard Haitian's moved next door, but I don't think he's got any real money and I don't think France will let him stay."

"Oh," George said.

And after another silence: "Your mother every few years tries to sell what she's got left of my work. All at once. Know what that does to my market value? This is not its decade. Tell her to cut it out. She's pissing out my legacy."

George tried to meet his father's gaze, but Walter spoke looking at the bottles lined up behind the bar. Even in profile, above the livery pouches, Walter's eyes were ice, smeared with pink. George couldn't think of anything else to say. Walter didn't seem to want him to say anything. Later that night, in the final entry to his youthful diary, the last time he would write anything for a long time, George wrote, *The milky veins across the cool watery blue were like the drag strokes of the wet remains of animal prey freshly pulled across the warming surface of a slowly melting glacier.*

"I didn't know she was doing that," George said.

"No."

"Do you ever come to New York?"

"Sometimes. New York is over. New York ate itself."

"I think so too."

"Well"—Walter took a sip of beer—"a bridge only ceases to be a bridge by falling."

"Uh-huh, yes."

"I'm glad we understand each other." Walter put a ten- and a five-franc note into the wet circle his beer had left on the brass rim of the bar and lifted and shook George's hand.

"Wait. What is your life like? What do you do? Where do you live?"

"I told you all that."

Before George could protest, his father had crossed the room and disappeared into the casino.

The bartender came to collect the franc notes.

"But I'm not done, I'm not done yet!" George cried. The bartender lifted his hands away from the money with a little twist of a smile and went away.

George spent forty-five minutes wandering the casino, through the drifts of smoke and talk in many languages and the ringing bells and the whir of the roulette wheels. He jostled between the tables and worked his way up and down the rows until he found Walter playing roulette at a full table, holding a fresh beer. A man at the table with a glistening beard and merry eyes looked up at George, smiled warmly.

"Ça c'est votre nouvelle Coccinelle?" the man asked, turning to Walter.

"Why can't I see where you live?" George asked. "Why don't you want to know anything about me?"

"Something wrong with you, boy," Walter said, his glance flitting only briefly over George before returning to the red-and-black-checkered felt.

"A pity the table is full," the bearded man continued, as the croupier pulled the chips in with his silly miniature rake. The man pointed to Walter and said, smiling, "Last night I beat him like a borrowed mule! Oh, là!"

"Come on," Walter said. He stood and began moving through the crowd. George found himself hustling to catch up. Then they were in the men's room, standing at the sinks. George looked at his father's face in the mirror, and at his own. There was a resemblance. The strong jaw, the high set of the cheekbones, the shape of the skull.

"Here." Walter took George's hand. He pried George's fist open and pressed five one-hundred-franc notes into his palm. "Do it up the rest of your stay. Have a good time. If you don't think that makes a dent in my pocket, well, it does." Walter washed his hands and left.

He hadn't any paint on his hands, the phony. Not that that meant anything. Not that anything meant anything. By the time George collected himself and returned to the casino, pocketing the money as the men's room door swung closed behind him, he didn't see Walter. But he didn't really look.

Something wrong with you, boy. The awful thing about this was that when he'd heard it, George's soul had leaped up, waved its hands high in attendance, and shouted, "Here!" Known at long last. Walter was right. But who says such a thing to another person? Exiting the casino with an eyeful of the bright evening sea, for a moment he sided with his mother. Her attendance to formality, her calcified politeness, her evasions—not the bitter bird's way of keeping the world ordered, but rather a kindness, displeasure used to hold the obvious-terrible at bay with all its bland strength, to spare and protect the soul.

Enough with the glowing, cluttered screen. He slams the laptop closed. He shall tend to his house, if he's the only one left in it! Iris, going every day to that stupid job. Why aren't he and Iris on a boat someplace dipping their hands in the water, squinting into the sun, sails whipping against the mast? That's what a man in his circumstances should be doing. They should be making a baby on a boat off the island of Mykonos. He should be recovering in dignity, in warm, luxurious isolation.

"Come on," he says to the dog, back in the great room. "Come!" 3D raises his head, lifts his black nose, exhales once, forcefully, and puts his head back down. What dog, alone in a house, doesn't want a master to follow from room to room, to curl up under the desk of, to join on a walk? Fine. He will without the mutt survey what the house needs for the coming of spring.

First of all, there's the murky grotto under the glass wall. Its waterfall is full of iced leaves. He goes though the mudroom, puts on Iris's rubber gardening boots, rolls up his khakis, and descends into the shallow pool. He pulls the brown tangle from the pump and throws it up the embankment onto the lawn. He wades around, collects a raft of more brown leaves and scum, and tosses this too onto the mini-embankment. Done! Are you interested? You, who may or may not be watching? Is *this* of any interest? He goes to the garage to find the switch that will activate the burbling fountain. He succeeds in switching off the power to the house, room by room. He likes it better that way, he decides. Dim and quiet, disconnected. *Silence*, spectral data! *Away*, invisible hum!

The front of the house could also use an assessment. He drips across the living room and exits the front door, slamming it shut. He sets to untangling the balloon strings still twisted around the low branch of the ash, now tatty and faded. 3D comes around the house, the rubber grenade in his mouth. How did he get out? 3D drops the grenade at George's feet.

"You want the ball?" he hears himself say. "Yes?" He throws it once, twice, again, again, until they have, by way of toss and retrieval, shifted across the lawn to the swimming pool, still wearing its cover. Had Iris said something the other day about not opening the pool this summer? About how they hardly use it?

He tosses the grenade onto the pool's cover. He watches 3D dash out onto the vinyl, the vinyl, meant to hold a blanket of snow but bowing and bouncing under the dog, who looks back, uncertain, but fetches the grenade and leaps out after it onto the sagging cover, again and again, until they hear a car and pause. Ah, it's Iris! George is so relieved it's Iris. He's so relieved she's home. He watches her car curve up the drive and out of his vision again, hears her park in front of the garage and slam the door. He and dog united in this leaping relief. He resumes their game of fetch.

"Come join us!" he shouts, as she crosses the lawn.

"My God, my God, what are you doing? Don't do that!" she cries, but he's caught her in his arms and 3D is circling with the grenade in his mouth and George is kissing her feverishly and she looks at him, appalled, and at first she twists away. She smells like fatigue. But it's okay, because finally she gives in.

32

CeCe walks a half-moon around the lake, a determined expression on her face. The cherry blossoms and one of the dogwoods have begun to bloom, white and pink. The grass under her feet has turned from straw to green. The morning sun is pale as a wafer. As she's trained herself these last months, for ballast her arms are lifted high away from her sides, bent in the attitude of a marionette pulling its own strings. This and the crooked yank of her legs under her black coat—what she must look like from afar. A broken spider; a vigorously expiring crow. She's left the walking stick against the bench. She walks around the lake every day, sometimes twice. She is, relatively speaking, swift. Last evening, wearing instead the bright red jacket Esme brought, she watched the sun set in the water, the molten color of a monarch's wing. The lake has melted, save the twiggy ice slushing the far reeds. She'd like to feel the bracing green-black water, to smell the brine on her hands. She can't bend far enough, but soon she may be able. She reaches the farthest cherry tree and rests lightly against its trunk, the closed petals dipping above her head like balloons. Across the water, she sees her French doors. *I was never there.* Yesterday they told her: the study is expanding. She is going home.

She has learned to distinguish Astrasyne's side effects—that spike of murder-energy, once or twice a day; the gnashing insomnia, once or twice a week; the snapping, neural fervor that's not mania, but like it— from the feelings that are her own. Her excitement upon learning she is free is hers alone, though she feels a minor bout of murder-energy coming over her now, as she circles back around the lake. One of its features is a blazing impatience that makes her unpleasant company. For example! The blimp with the red bull's-eye. She'd like to sail a dart over the treetops to pierce its side, watch it sag to the earth in flames. It's better to be alone when she's like this, to carve her erratic groove around the lake. To keep the burden of her moods. In her room, she risks tormenting a nurse. Once, scrambled with irritation, she kicked Esme under the table. She pretended it was a spasm.

"I'm sorry!" she said, and sorry she felt.

This side effect's most seductive feature is how it imitates the wicked pleasure she used to take in discovering the weakest edge of a person, the pleasure of saying something truthful and unkind. A part of herself she'd meant to protect her children from. Only, had she? She'd pretended the pleasure of her invective didn't have its price. She'd come to understand this after Dotty's death. From Dotty, who never guessed when she was being insulted. Walter would have called CeCe's feeling for Dotty fool-pity and been right. She makes her way up the grass. Walter, if you could see me here, what would you say? Walter, in the good early days, inviting this or that group to Booth Hill for a weekend, a week, whomever, anyone he met in the city, then disappearing to the barn to put a line on canvas, just the one line, often enough. They were all for it, the brilliant friends, following him to the barn to name it: *Reindeer No. 17, Blue No. 12.* She, sitting in his lap sideways, her legs crossed over the arm of the chair. How powerfully he made her laugh. The only man she'd known who was not afraid to scandalize her. He'd understand about the blimp.

When she returns to the bench, a man holding a folder with Oak Park's logo is sitting in her place, staring at the lake.

"Yours?" He tips his head toward her stick. "I'm in your spot. I should be getting back, anyway." He heads in the direction of the parking lot. She sits. The cherry tree she'd leaned against is now on the other side of the lake, pocket-size. Distance, restored with the muscles of her legs. The tree's reflection oscillates in the water. Poor Iris! What does Iris think of George, now that she's seen what kind of person he can be?

And what, will CeCe block him forever? The last day at Oak Park is fast approaching. A piece of paper with a date. She doesn't know if she can forgive George, but she will see him. Astrasyne has not yet been approved by the FDA, but it has passed some safety or efficacy marker and the trial is entering its third phase. Their eighty-three-person treatment group will expand to become two thousand people dispersed across the states. They will receive the drug, at home, and she will be one of them.

"You're doing well these days," the doctor said. This doctor, using *these days, as of now, so far,* or some other temporal qualifier. "So far, your rate of degeneration has slowed. If you keep to it, you'll live long enough to die of something else."

"Like old age?"

"Like old age."

"Have you got a trial for that?"

She's kind, this doctor. She knew to laugh. She smiled at CeCe, a miraculous, charming doctor's smile, her skin wrinkling at the eyes. Two days after, Pat called and they talked the longest they had since Pat was a girl. They planned a visit with Lotta and Douglas for the beginning of summer. Before she hung up, Pat put the phone to Douglas, and there was the wondrous gurgling of baby.

From the bench, she watches Yasser and two new landscapers head toward the woods behind the lake, one with a ladder balanced on his shoulder, the other with a set of pruning shears hanging from his hands like talons. Gone is the little one with the flame-red hair and the lummox by his side. Last summer, looking so often as she had for Yasser, she'd come to recognize his help, even from far away—the set of their shoulders, the way they dragged their feet.

"Hello!" she calls. "Hello!"

Yasser nods to the boys to continue without him. He comes to stand beside the bench. Winter, she missed him. A few days after the first thaw, she looked out the window and saw the wheelbarrow by the lake.

"You're looking well," he says.

"Thank you! Have you seen me out walking?"

They hear the saw rev and branches clatter through the canopy.

"Walking and walking." He draws a circle in the air around the lake with his finger. "Very nice. Very good. You're so strong, you could get a job cutting trees."

"You've got new help."

"I had to." Something in the way he looks at her she doesn't understand. "My nephew is the young one." He gestures toward the trees. "From Maryland."

"How's the rest of the family? Your children?"

"Everyone's good. We're having another."

"Well, congratulations! But—with you here, and them there?"

"I visit winters."

"I'm happy for you. I have a grandson. Born this winter. Not—" She's about to say *conceived* but becomes embarrassed. "Isn't it nice when friends have good news. Yasser, thank you." She's scowls with fresh discomfort. "For making this beautiful walking stick. It means more than you know."

There is another crackling of branches falling through the trees. It's followed by a harder sound. Yasser is already up and striding the lawn when they hear the shout, the older boy running to meet him. They dash into the trees, out of her vision. She rises, her hand on the bench, but before she's thought what to do—stupid, she's in front of a hospital, stupid, go get someone!—Yasser and the boys reappear, walking slowly along the curve of the lake and past her toward Oak Park. She hasn't moved. The nephew from Maryland has one arm draped over the other boy. Yasser's arm loops his nephew's waist.

"He's okay," Yasser calls over his shoulder. "Cut himself out of the tree."

The boy turns and stares at her. He's tucked his left arm against his ribs. From the crooked angle of his elbow she sees the arm is broken. His eyes go wide. He had not realized his injury until he read it in her face. She'll follow them inside and be useful and meddlesome, make sure they know Cecilia Somner is invested in his care. She lurches after with the wide step of her disorder. She hopes the boy is not in too much pain. But even as she worries for him, her worry excites in her the certainty that she won't be at Oak Park to see him come out of his cast or to see the lake turn blue, to see the lake's ring of trees bloom, unbroken in the fullness of their prime.

33

The real estate agency has given Iris some freelance administrative work at the decent rate of $23 an hour while she waits
to land or be granted a new client. No one mentions George or *The
Burning Papers*, but they know. She can tell. Those two times she found
him muttering his way along the main street in town, looking right
enough from far away but not quite right up close—she can't be the
only one who saw. Her coworkers are kinder to her than before, with a
careful reserve—stopping to make small talk, including her in lunch
runs. It takes her a while to realize that no one in Stockport who's
aware of George's mistake—the mistake is mostly what she thinks of it
as—will want her as an agent. Giving her the administrative work is
an act of charity. Maybe this will change once time wears some of the
gossip away. She's grateful for the income and for how dull and soothing the work is. One morning, she organizes the mailing of five hundred glossy cards advertising the agency's services; the next, after
claiming to know Excel, she teaches herself Excel and reorganizes a

list of past clients by buyer and seller and sale price, confirming who still lives at the houses that had been sold to them, or, if they'd moved and used a different Realtor, which one. She photocopies the many-paged contracts that Nellie and the other agents leave on her desk; she reads the new listings written by the active agents and says, *Looks good*. She uploads photos to the website: exterior a, exterior b. Largest interior downstairs room. Kitchen, bath, and so on. She doesn't have to think about George when she's working, and she doesn't have to think about money. She looks at listing prices all day, but these numbers are none of her business, abstract in their calm march down the page, unaware of her. (Unlike the bills at home, where the numbers are tiny hammers of doom or bad grades or angry eyebrows, depending.) At work, they are decorative and inscrutable as hieroglyphs, jaunty with their K: 750K, 500K, 275K.

She waited a long, terrible month for Bob to call her with news of their investment. Not that he didn't call; he's made a habit of calling her several times a day. At first, if George wasn't in earshot, she answered the phone as fast as she could. Had the money come through? But then Bob would say, "Hello, sunshine," and wouldn't mention the investment at all. When she asked directly, he'd say it was in the works and stay on the line to share stories she didn't care to hear. In a kind of reverie, he'd tell her how he'd wanted to be a baseball player, or what he thought about debt ceilings, or how much his father's death still shreds him, and that he never felt so comfortable talking to another person. Once he asked her to authorize a trade and she did, but nothing seemed to come of it. He talked about what he hoped for his sons, and how Martha wants another child but he does not. Once he left her a message that was three and a half minutes of the song "Let Go" by the Pist. He wanted to take her to this particular Korean restaurant, whenever she could get away. She murmured noncommittally, thinking, What a jackwad, but she was sorry for him too, once she recognized it was loneliness, as much as arrogance, that kept him talking. He took an excessive pleasure in what little she responded. He said they were really getting to know each other. She gave up believing there was any investment at all. She answered his calls less frequently and with more dread. When she didn't answer frequently enough, his messages grew long and hurt.

All she can do is get up and go to work and photocopy contracts. She'll ignore what she can't fix, which is everything else, until it falls down over her head. At least then she might be able to climb out and be free. For now, she's bound to try to make things better. She's not the kind of person who leaves her husband because the tides have turned. She won't prove CeCe right. Maybe George will recover and they'll start again. Maybe she can hold off the creditors. Maybe she'll stay in the house with the glass wall, grow old behind the wall, stay a Somner.

Still, it takes all her energy to be warm and ordinary with George as he saunters through the house, his eyes crossing and training on some distant phantom. To overlook how their life has changed. Prescription-pill bottles with the labels ripped off are in the sock drawer. George's skin hums beneath the surface when she can't avoid his petulant, eager embrace. Nights, he swishes and stalks from room to room in the Yale tracksuit he unearthed who knows where, littering handfuls of index cards and scribbled pages across their house like confetti. He says he's writing something new. Lately, he's begun listening to his opera, again and again. Often, he forgets to take off the puffy headphones and paces back and forth with the curl of the unplugged cord slapping along as he moves, a pen stuck in jaunty menace behind his ear. He's listening, he'd explained with guarded hostility, to the various earlier drafts of Vijay's scoring to root out the point they'd turned on him. What leaks out of the headphones, what at first had only puzzled her, now makes her shudder. She's given up trying to find out why CeCe will not speak to George or to her. She can guess. She's no longer curious to discover if, in her own heart, George's opera is as bad as they say. She no longer wonders about anything—the price she must pay for temporary peace of mind. She collates and that is all. She must order more flyers, without the laminate.

Until, one day, she supposes she's pregnant.

She has to wait. Two weeks. She is. At the doctor's office, she feels thrill and despair in equal measure. Too much of each, colliding out to nothing. How the door on her life might close if she has George's child—she still has time.

At lunch one day, she gets a decaf at the Starbucks on her way back to the office. A beautiful spring afternoon—the concrete walkway to the green umbrellas is lined with bobbing, sherbet tulips, just bloomed. She stands by her car in the parking lot, the one with the bank and the dry cleaner's and the deli. She balances her coffee on the hood of the car and works a scratch-off with a quarter. As she chucks the spent ticket into her bag, she hears a deep, urgent voice calling her name. For a moment she's afraid it's Bob, come all this way to press his face to hers, to maul her like a disoriented bear right in the lot. But it isn't Bob, it's Bill. Dear Bill! What a relief.

"Bill," she cries, "hello!"

His long frame seems to take the small parking lot in three strides. He's got a coffee in his hand. "Iris. I saw you inside. How are you?"

"I'm all right. It's good to see you. How's everything? How's Victor? I miss Victor."

"You can't guess? We're not so good."

"Oh, no, what's happened?"

"We'll be okay somehow, but right now it's tough." He speaks in the same soft, low calm she remembers from—could it be already? Last summer. The few times after the closing she'd suggested to Victor that Bill join them for a hike or a meal, Victor rolled his eyes and said, "Work, work, working."

"But what's wrong?"

"No idea?" he says. "No?"

She can think of nothing. "I'm sorry, I must be missing—"

"Been to Kingsgate lately?"

"I haven't. I'm mostly in the office."

"Any idea what you sold us?"

"What do you mean? Of course I do. Is there something wrong with the house? Victor said you painted. That you love it."

"It's not that we don't like the house, Iris. Liking the house is no longer the point. Did you look at the terms of the mortgage you urged us to get?"

"I did, absolutely."

"Half the apartments in the towers are in pre-foreclosure. Do you know anything about that?"

She doesn't remember hearing anything at the office. They don't talk about Kingsgate anymore. That's the cycle, she presumed. They made their sales and moved on. And she's been preoccupied.

"Where's the developer? Have you heard from them lately?"

"No," she says. "That was before I came on. I didn't really deal with them."

"They're not to be found. They're back under whatever rock they crawled out from, is where they are."

"But your house isn't like the apartments."

"Yes, our house is different. Our house is beautiful. But now our house is worthless because everything around it is worthless."

"I don't understand. It was a great deal."

"It was an unethical deal. Taking advantage of us like that—when you don't even have any need. What was that commission for you? Shoe money? Victor calls you a friend. You know how many people he considers friends? Not so many. It's our fault for trusting you. I'm not throwing away my own responsibility here. I didn't listen to my gut. Victor wanted it so badly."

"Bill, the towers are nice renovations! The office, they're professionals. I don't think they'd set up a bad deal. I'm so sorry. I don't know what to say."

"It was an okay loan, if it hadn't been on a misrepresented property. You're not the mortgage company, I know that. But you were the liaison. How could you not know? *Stated* income. What a fool I was. *I* should've known. The scandal of those loans. All over the news for years, but I assume we're different. I feel like a cliché and Kingsgate's a dump. You had no idea? You're on the sign, for Christ's sake."

"I didn't, I don't." Coffee flies out of her cup. "This is the first I'm hearing—I'd just started. I was new!"

A momentary confusion crosses his face. "You know, I almost believe you."

"The whole market's down. Everywhere, everything's down."

"Yeah, that doesn't help. But the market was already down. And the market's down because of deals people like you make for people like us. We were doing okay." He stops, and when he resumes, his voice is calm again. Iris feels as if he is looking down at her from a great height. "We were doing okay even when the payments jumped. Tricky fine print, there. Our fault, yes, our fault. Buyer beware. We were just able to handle it. We were scared, but what we didn't see coming! You know what doesn't do well in a recession?"

"I don't know. A lot of things?"

"Yes, a lot of things. One being nonessential luxury retail. Like, say, handmade artisan jewelry. I'm down sixty percent. I love what I do. I'll keep doing it. It'll come back, maybe."

"Your beautiful jewelry!"

"At least we had Victor's income. And then we didn't."

"What's happened? Has something happened to Victor?"

"*Has something happened to Victor.* Are you serious? He lost his job. Remember? You fired him."

"His other clients?"

"This and that. But, come on. He was at your house all week. *You* were the client, Iris."

"Bill, I'm so sorry! I thought it was a good deal. Maybe it still is, if you wait, ride it out? The senior brokers and I went through it at the office, I mean, it's a reputable lender! Nellie said the value of Kingsgate—"

"Someone in your position will not get this, Iris, but you can't wait if you can't pay. They don't let you wait. You understand?"

"Yes." She looks miserably at the tulips. "Will you sell?"

"That's the point. It's unsellable. You said, values will rise. Mortgages at all-time lows. When everything started to slide, I made a promise to myself I would never blame Victor. I would not be mad at Victor. But I can be mad at myself. And I can be mad at you, Iris. Every time I drive past those ugly towers with their little iron terraces good for nothing but suicide and bike storage, and every time I walk through that bullshit courtyard with the one remaining pansy letting us all know we're in the shitter, I'm mad at you and I'm mad at me. And when the rates go up again—I mean, that rate isn't fixed, of course it's not—and the boiler breaks and the mice nest in the oven, that is, if we can hang in there, if we're lucky, if we are able to stay with our tanked credit and our remodeled bathroom, it'll be on you, Iris. Iris, Victor's dear friend. Shame."

"I didn't know! I swear. Bill!" Her free hand covers her mouth.

He shakes his head. "I believe you. I can't believe it, that I believe you. Victor's right, I guess. You're like our beautiful little house with its pretty rainbow window that you can't see through. You really didn't notice what you chose to surround yourself with? What I can't put together is, you're not naive. That's not it. And you're not dumb. I guess it doesn't matter how we got here. Bad or blind, it's ended up the same, hasn't it?"

"I'm sorry, but I can't, I, what can I do?" She fumbles in her pocket and presses the button on her keychain. The car bleeps and unlocks. She steps toward it.

He touches her arm gently. "I wanted you to know. I saw you in there getting your coffee, and the thing I want you to know I still haven't said. I'm sorry I yelled. I don't do that. But what I want you to know is that we were at the beginning of our home study. Now they don't want us."

"Your home study?"

He shakes his head. "When you get close to the top of the list, they send a social worker to evaluate the fitness of your home. For adoption. Your financial stability and the safety of your environs. These are important factors. We were great candidates. Now, not so great. Now we're stranded on every wait list at every agency we registered with. It was never Victor's dream to have a child, but it was mine. You hardly know me, and look how much you've changed my life. I have no one to blame but myself. But I wanted you to know." He turns and strides back past the green awning, into the Starbucks.

In the car, driving the ten minutes to the office, she's glad her pregnancy is so early he hadn't noticed. She has and does not have everything he wants. It was a good deal, she tells herself, without any conviction, trying to argue her way out of the thrumming dread that she's destroyed a good family for a bad one.

They all told her what a good deal it was, Nellie and the mortgage broker and the inspector. Not the best deal in the world, but good for Victor, for what Victor had. Now she's in the office, has Paula in front of her, and she's asking Paula, *Is Nellie in? Paula, what happened with Kingsgate?* And Paula says, *I don't know, it was a good sales cycle for us, all around.* And later, Nellie, behind her cluttered desk: "Iris, we have no obligation to a client's experience after sale. That's not our function. Every home in the area has lost value this year. Mine, yours, theirs. You can't run into one angry client and absorb their anxiety and allow it to color your feeling about what we do. If that's how you react, maybe this isn't the game for you. You're not responsible for the future. We don't broker dishonest deals. We do broker deals in an up market and then the market goes down. Thirty years, I've seen it happen more than once. It's unfortunate, but it's not our responsibility. How could it be? Everything you did was standard and transparent and legal, period. You helped your client become a homeowner under the open eye of the law. Don't let some hysterical person who's mismanaged his finances get into your head."

On the way home that evening, Iris drives out of her way to Kingsgate and almost turns in, but does not. Instead she takes the narrower, siphon route running parallel behind it, where she's not driven before. On the one side is the pretty approach from the highway, but on the other, over the ridge of the bent, low metal guardrail, she sees a sprawling alien miniature city, a gridded maze of flaring pipes and steaming metal drums the size of houses. A waste-management facility, the hill sloping toward it littered with trash. She should've known it was there. Maybe Nellie Turner and the rest all knew it was there and sent her to sell because she was new to Stockport, and a fucking idiot besides. Maybe not. She'd never bothered to drive all the way around. She considers quitting, but she can't be at home with George. She must have somewhere to go during the day. They need the income.

She pulls into the driveway, sees the light in George's office is on. As she's assembling her face into a veneer of carefree greeting, she remembers Bob leaning across his desk, the vivid, violent painting behind him, and the serious, almost angry way he said, *I saw you first.*

34

Esme sits beside her in the backseat. Javier is driving. Esme is reading from a list pressed against her knee, written in pencil and ripped from a notebook, the corners of the page fluttering in the warm wind from the open windows. She's reviewing the staff's preparations at Booth Hill.

CeCe looks out the window, at the white line racing the concrete, the trees stretching by. *Let me not forget this day.* Where is this from, a hymn? Something she had to sing in school. *Let me not*—admonitory and sentimental at once—as good a definition of piety as any. No, thank you. She'll take forgetting. That morning, she made her thanks to the doctors and nurses and physical therapists, to young Orlow and the receptionists. Said goodbye to Yasser and to the lake. As they drove away, she turned her neck and watched the concrete portico and automatic doors at the main entrance recede. The clot of facility buildings shrank and lost all detail with the distance. The black road spooled out. The car turned. Oak Park ceased to be.

Esme, being wise and long-tested, has broken the house report into regular spring chores and chores particular to a homecoming after so long away. She's had the windows washed, the floors waxed, the silver and crystal polished, the mattresses turned, the drapery and rugs cleaned, the table linens counted and pressed, the lightbulbs and water filters changed, the alarms and intercoms tested, the lawn seeded and trimmed, the trees pruned, the outdoor furniture retrieved from storage, the path between CeCe's and George's houses cleared, and the gift closet restocked with all manner of hostess and holiday gifts, professionally wrapped and labeled as to the contents. Mr. Shoebridge, the expert long in charge of annually assessing the art for any necessary restoration or cleaning, is booked for next week.

Particular to this homecoming, the cupboards and refrigerator are restocked per CeCe's regular lists, but also per the new nutritionist's guidelines, who, to CeCe's displeasure, believes in nothing so much as dinosaur kale. The newspaper and magazine subscriptions are renewed. Her social diary and Rolodex have been put out on her desk along with the laptop she'd requested—"Someone will know the one I should get"—and a list of tutors in computer basics for her to consider. Esme had refused the task of interviewing and selecting a tutor as beyond the bounds of her duties. CeCe admitted she was right. Outside, the veranda awning is on order to be replaced, having been damaged in the same winter storm that broke the upstairs window. CeCe's hundred feet of beach have been re-sanded with three hundred tons of white sand, and this year with "an assortment of shells and corals for baby Douglas to find, like you asked." Esme sighs. "I put a copy of the shells invoice on your desk because it's too much. But house accountant"—Esme, having passionately loathed Mr. Pitt from the start, will not call him by his name—"has paid it."

CeCe's bed, her effects, and the rest of the furniture at Oak Park, are a half hour behind them on the road. The movers are tasked with restoring the larger pieces to their proper locations at Booth Hill in such a fashion as not to disturb CeCe's first day back home, having run a drill with Esme the week before. CeCe's everyday wardrobe, the five closets, has been laundered by Madame Relais in Manhattan and returned to the house by padded truck; the weekly standing order of flowers is reinstated. She doesn't like to pilfer her garden, nor can she or Esme arrange flora as well as good-natured Beth, whom they've never met but only spoken to on the phone, whose work they admire.

"I thought I couldn't get the flowers in time," Esme says. "The first order comes today. We had the boathouse cleaned. We didn't do anything with the boat. You want the boat painted?"

The road gathers into an expressway. Bleak, but to be moving fast, the air sweeping through the car, is invigorating. Esme clutches her list.

"Have it painted. Now why," CeCe demands, the wind against her cheek, "was the veranda awning damaged? Was it not rolled for winter?"

"One foot out all season. How I didn't notice, I don't know."

"We were distracted. Grounds isn't your job. Have you already ordered the fabric? I might want a change. What's your opinion of a wider stripe? And I'm thinking of rearranging the furniture in the living room. Tighter in, more friendly."

"The rugs. You'll be able to see the impressions from the chairs."

"You can't fix that?"

"It's a lot of years in one spot. I'll try. Can we do schedule? Tomorrow I'm making lunch for you and George and Iris? Shrimp salad? How is pineapple upside-down cake?"

Dread at George's name. She'd finally called, asked Iris when they were free for lunch in the most congenial tone she could muster. "The queen is back," she couldn't resist saying, as Iris hung up. That she was George's queen had not entered her mind until she'd read it in Esme's press clippings. To discover if she will be able to love and dislike her son at the same time—a heavy mission to hang on shrimp salad. Is an upside-down pineapple cake what one wants to contemplate at the conclusion of such an assessment? An assessment not of George, but her own capacity. If she can't, she's not sure what will become of them, or how they will go on.

"No cake. Fruit. Or, I could go to their house instead. A gesture. They don't always have to come to me. I'm worried, though. I might not be able to hold myself back."

"That won't be a problem."

"Why?"

"You'll see. They're having a hard time."

CeCe leans forward and puts her hands on the leather and mahogany of the open partition and shouts against the wind. "What do you think, Javier?"

"No way I'm getting involved in this conversation."

"You never get involved in any conversation. You're no fun, Javi."

"This is not my place of fun."

"The man never gives an inch," she says to Esme.

"No," Esme says.

Her iron gates. Javier punches the code. The gates swing back. They take so long to open. They drive up the hill, to the white house and the green lawn. The bright sea, rolling in below.

35

The next morning, CeCe decides that instead of driving around to Somner's Rest, she'll walk the path. But first, to business. At her desk, she opens the laptop, an alien slice of aluminum. Esme has unpacked it and charged it for her. CeCe considers the tumbling, three-dimensional letters in the middle of the screen, pulsing the word *welcome*. She closes the laptop and opens a drawer. She takes out a piece of stationery and makes some notes. She straightens her back and flips through her Rolodex. She calls Nan for leads on a new personal assistant, not liking the previous one enough to rehire. Still under the premise of looking for an assistant, she calls a few locals— Dana Barnes and Ellie Baker and the Rahvs—who she knows will gossip around town that they've had a chat with Cecilia Somner, same as she ever was. She ignores Dana's and Ellie's exclamations at hearing from her, ignores their inquiries as to how she's been. She schedules a meeting for Annie Mason and the foundation's staff to come to the house with presentations of all she's only nominally kept up with in the last year, and to expect to stay the day. She does not tell Esme that when she awoke she looked for the French doors and the bed crank and Round Lake and did not understand what was happening. But her calm was restored by breakfast: a poached egg and a croissant with orange marmalade in the sunroom off the veranda. A bright spring wind blurred the vermilion peonies and the lilac bushes and ragged the sea at high tide. After breakfast, she walked through the garden and along the beach, then visited each room to turn the small treasures of the house over in her hands, as she had the day before.

Esme brings a pot of bergamot tea to CeCe's desk. On the tray is a card with the number of the home-care nurse who is to check on her several times a week.

"Call," Esme says, and leaves her.

CeCe sticks the card in the back of the Rolodex. Instead, she schedules a house call with her lawyer and another with the woman from Ortez to come to do her hair and her nails. Ortez puts her on hold for two entire Billie Holiday numbers, disagreeably followed at a much higher volume by the opening to Bach's Prelude in C Major. She must find an assistant, posthaste. She's avoiding the only call that matters. It's time to see George. Yes, she'll walk the path and surprise them with how strong she is. Does she hope to see gladness spread across their faces, or to demonstrate she's well despite the outrage of their neglect? Both. It can't be more than a quarter mile. Shorter than around the lake. She finds Esme in the hall.

"Now? It's too early."

"I'm not getting anything done."

"You want me to call?"

"No. I want them to see. Don't look at me that way. Allow my mischief. Earrings."

"I'll get the box."

She listens to Esme trudge upstairs and down—Esme, who had the night before made one of CeCe's favorite meals, pecan-crusted trout in brown butter, with watercress. She'd eaten in the kitchen, asking Esme questions about how she'd handled difficulties with her own children, Esme answering opaquely as she liked.

CeCe chooses a pair of emerald studs that once matched her eyes. Soon enough they're on the path, Esme accompanying her for the uneven ground, the birds jabbering in the trees. They come out the other side. The house is as she remembered, a stack of rectangles ostentatious in its austerity. Iris is standing a hundred yards away under the ash, talking to a man in coveralls, kneeling at the base of the tree.

"Hello! Iris, hello!" CeCe calls, once she's passed the covered pool. Iris spins around. For once, her clothes aren't tight—jeans and a long, blue T-shirt, her hair in a ponytail, a look of surprise overtaking her fine features. The dog gallops over to CeCe, his maroon tongue flopping out. He's raced back to Iris by the time CeCe is upon them.

"CeCe! Esme, oh, hi, Esme. I wasn't—did you walk here? I wasn't expecting you until one." They embrace awkwardly. There's some change in Iris. Gaunter under the eyes. Her face more lined, though also more flushed. Yes, CeCe remembers how quickly it begins to happen at that age, the wear of the years arriving all at once. And something—a weary alarm. Iris's eyes flick up to the bedroom window. She's trying to hide where she looks, but the dog lifts his muzzle in the direction of the window and begins to bark.

"Am I interrupting? Should I turn around and go home? I can. As you can see."

"No, no, I'm so sorry. CeCe! That's wonderful!" This time Iris's hug is real, and unbalancing. "It's just, I haven't had a chance to clean the house. But that's not important. You're here. And you walked! I can't believe it!"

"Hello to you too, dog." CeCe pats the top of 3D's head. He wags in a circle. "Look! He thinks he likes me. He's forgotten. Maybe he and I will start anew."

"The situation is—" the man under the tree begins, rising heavily off his knees, his hand on the bark.

"I'm sorry, CeCe. It seems to be an emergency."

"I don't mind. Finish up. Esme, I'll call you if I need."

"Okay." Esme frowns and heads back across the lawn.

"The roots are strangling the septic," the man continues. "It's a mess down there. I wish you had me out a couple of years ago. You've got five, maybe six crushed pipes. First we replace the pipes, then we Vapo-root. Cauterize the offending roots, save the tree. We can do Monday."

"How dreadful," CeCe says.

"If it doesn't work?"

"The tree's got to go. Everybody looks sad when I say that. Also sad is right now you got no bathroom. Here, cards for Callahead and Handy Can. They're both okay. You'll want to book it for the week, in case."

"Monday!" CeCe says. "You need to fix this right away."

"Thank you, it's okay," Iris says. "Can I—can I call you later about pricing?"

"Sure thing. Have a nice day." The man gets into his van.

"Wasn't he the comedian," CeCe says, meaning to make Iris laugh, because Iris looks as if she's about to cry. "You should stay with me until it's fixed."

"Come in. George is asleep."

Inside, it takes CeCe a moment to understand what she sees. Despite the glass wall, it's dim: the vegetation on the other side has crept closer than she remembers, creating the unpleasant effect of being sealed in a giant terrarium. Below her, the fetid grotto is choked with leaves.

"Goodness, dear, turn on a lamp!"

"Yes." What a strange, drowsy way her daughter-in-law moves from one light switch to another. Something has changed. Something is wrong. The room is brightened.

"Have a seat. Let me wake George." Iris goes upstairs.

With the lights on, CeCe notices a copious streak of bird shit down the outside of the glass. She hears the door at the top of the stairs open and Iris murmuring. CeCe tries hard to see what she is seeing. A house missing half its furniture. There's dust and dog hair rolling in the corners of the room. Paw prints and footprints the color of gristle layer the kitchen floor. She peers into the mudroom. In a neat row, some ten heaping recycling bags sit uncollected. Back in the living room, she sees little rips of paper, scribbled notes, scattered on the floor. Clothes are piled on the far end of the sectional on which she sits, and an empty laundry basket is tipped on its side beneath. The dark, faint smell of the crushed pipes is unmistakable. A white rectangle on the wall marks where a picture must have been. No, a television—below is a console stacked with DVDs. She wanders to the kitchen area. *Area,* for the impractical democracy of these types of houses does not allow for separate kitchens. It seems altered, barren of appliances. All that's on the counter is a can of air freshener and a bag of dog food. She opens the refrigerator. Milk, sandwich bread, a door full of condiments, and the makings of what must be today's lunch for her—a bunch of arugula and a tomato and a wax-paper bundle with an expensive price tag that reads *Alaskan King Salmon.* She gingerly opens a cardboard box. A glistening, dense chocolate torte. Nothing else. She hears George's voice. Her son, his voice. She has missed him? This faint sound—she hears it more with her body than with her ears. She is his mother. Clearer is Iris's voice, rising in a hushed, desperate pitch: "But you *can't* use the bathroom." And, lower, but not low enough: "Don't make her wait. You should be the one waiting for her. Please get dressed."

"You know what, dears?" CeCe calls up the stairs. "You know what, George? I shouldn't have crept up on you like this. How about a rain check? I'll let myself out."

She'll make it back by herself. It will be fine.

Iris pads fast down the stairs. She overtakes CeCe at the front door, a crooked, unconvincing smile on her face. "I'm so sorry. Can I walk you? I'll walk with you."

Together, they cross the lawn. The path is dense and cool, with bright velvet moss and twigs under their feet. As it climbs the gentle hill, the sun shafts through the leaves. Soon they can hear the lapping of the tide going out.

As they step onto the lawn, CeCe takes Iris's hand. "We'll make it right. Do you understand?"

Iris lowers her eyes and shakes her head. Then she nods, but does not speak. CeCe leaves her at the edge of the path. When she turns, Iris is still there, nodding at the ground.

36

It's a strange kind of justice. Or a strange kind of injustice. Or, stranger still, justice and injustice have nothing at all to do with how the following week CeCe restores their finances. As if all the last months Iris has been inside a dream. It's seems as easy for CeCe as paying the hairdresser. The hairdresser is holding a white envelope and kissing CeCe goodbye when Iris arrives at the house. The accountant waits in the dining room.

"Iris," CeCe says, "you sit beside Mr. Pitt so you can read together, dear."

CeCe sits on his other side. Mr. Pitt gently takes the stack of battered, rubber-banded folders Iris is clutching to her chest. The folders in which she's tried to hold everything straight, keep both her and George's sanity ordered, keep chaos shut inside. Like trying to keep a folder full of dirty water. Mr. Pitt spreads the papers on the table. Bill by bill, she explains. At CeCe's insistence, she eats a dry piece of shortbread from a gold-banded tea plate painted with songbirds.

After a silence the accountant says, "I can manage it from here."
CeCe adds, "With the lawyers' counsel."

"Yes, and with your final." He slides the bundle into his briefcase.
It's all over in under an hour. Iris remains in her seat. The right thing
to do, to wait for the door to close behind Mr. Pitt so she can thank
CeCe, as properly as one can for such a bailout. But when no one
stands and she sees that CeCe and Mr. Pitt are staring at her, pleasantly and with the slightest puzzlement, she understands that it's she
who's been dismissed, that Mr. Pitt and CeCe have other business to
attend to. Empty-handed, she heads back home. She tries Victor as she
walks and hangs up at the voice mail. She's left enough messages—
four, five, six?—since running into Bill.

As if it were a dream. And she, the only one unconscious enough to
believe it real. By the next week their bank accounts are replenished.
Soon, most of the collectors stop calling. The lawyer instructs her
when any do call to refer them to him and not to give it another worry.
Without notice or comment, a housekeeping service is sent by CeCe,
to be supervised by Esme. (Esme explains that Erika is at a summer
essay-writing program in preparation for her first semester at Vassar,
Esme raising her eyes skyward to convey CeCe has had a hand in this
too.) The house is clean and stocked again. One morning, a large box
containing a new television is delivered. Appointments are made with
various psychiatrists and psychologists and substance-abuse specialists
for George, though he protests the last. Iris learns he is no stranger to
intervention. What is new, what has been different, the last years, was
George being on his own. Early on, he'd decided Iris was all he needed.
Without telling her, he had dropped away from the therapy and the
medication that kept him steady. Love required sympathy, he'd said,
and sympathy required suffering. But if he believes this, then why did
he hide who he was from her? How hadn't she seen?

When, in three weeks, the tree man returns to assess the Vapo-
rooted ash and tells her that they've hacked back the root structure
without endangering the tree, Iris finds, to the man's discomfort, she's
weeping with relief. "Ripped contact lense," she says. She's often in a
confusion of tempers, one hour crying in front of the tree man; the

next, carefree; the next, furious—though, with the exception of the breakdown under the ash, she's fairly good at keeping it to herself. Mostly, her fury and relief mingle and take the form of a continuous, boiling impatience. She is confused, some days, by the flickering reappearance of the George she'd fallen in love with. One day he said, "I'm sorry. I've been a jerk," and smiled at her with his old ease, shook the hair out of his eyes, asked her where she'd been all his life. It doesn't help that mornings now, she drifts along the sticky swell and ebb of nausea, corpse-limbed with exhaustion.

A month ago, they'd been bankrupt. Now they are safe. More than safe! To have plunged so fast and been bounced back up again as if she were on a trampoline. She must be an idiot. She felt like one, sitting next to Mr. Pitt! How smug CeCe is, sweeping back in! As if here is another rule about the rich no one explained to Iris—when they lose their money, they've only misplaced it, like a set of keys. Nothing isn't nothing. A rule written in invisible ink. And so her marshaling of resources—selling their things, battling the creditors, confessing to Bob, her certain panic that they would be turned out of their house—are, in hindsight, all a product of her stupidity and her misunderstanding. A madness of her own creation. One thing she's learned. She could've gone back to being broke. But not with George.

And how is it CeCe's restoration of their finances has cheered George right up? Back from the brink! Not all the way, but he's better. He's clean and well dressed. He's sleeping eight hours, and at night. Can money and sleep be all it takes? Is he so spoiled, he can exist no other way? He tells her it's because he's given up the concentration aids skittering around the backs of his office drawers.

"Concentration aids. It's just speed, you asshole!" she said.

He's no longer afraid to leave the house. Often she finds him outside, reading in the sun. He's stopped suggesting they hire private security. (A habit he'd developed toward the end of March, after claiming to have seen "a suspicious vehicle parked in the drive," and hearing "intruder noises in the garage," and another time, simply, on "good information that someone is watching." He'd snuck their last functioning credit card from her purse and used the balance to crown the house with cameras.) Seldom now does she catch his eyes flat with suspicion. She still doesn't know what he is doing, hunched at the computer all day. But he's begun cooking dinner for her in the evenings. Where he got this idea she doesn't know, but he is eager to learn how to dice an onion, to try to make her laugh. On her thirty-fifth birthday, he makes her tacos and apple pie and they eat at dusk by the pool. He calms more with each passing day. She's relieved. But she can't stand him. His well-being, determined by the state of his income more than by the love of his wife. Her devotion these past months, dirt. And how is it he is still barely noticing what happened to them?

Part of the dream was that she might leave. She wills herself to believe this won't carry over, that their life is beginning again. George hasn't detected the change in her shape. Her clothes still fit. She isn't showing and won't for some time. Why she can't tell him, she can't think. The last few days, he's been asking her tricky questions about where she's been, as if he knows she's deceiving him, but can't figure out how. It's something, probably something terrible, how forgetful she is of what she hides. Except when he asks for her to cook a pungent dish with him—lamb curry one evening almost did her in. But then the meal is done and another day passes without her confession.

She almost forgets one other shred of the dream, until the day she takes a call from a 212 number she doesn't recognize. Bob's office. Not Bob, but his assistant, the woman who sat at the smaller white desk. The assistant tells her 125K is to be transferred into the checking account Iris opened in March, per Bob's instruction. The funds should clear by the end of the week. Iris can't believe it, the ordinariness with which the woman delivers the news.

"Thanks so much. Bob, is he there?"

"Not at the moment. But I can take a message."

Two days later, at dusk, George is swimming in the reopened pool, keeping his head above the water, cautious of his ears. It isn't quite swimming weather, but he'd set the pool's thermostat to eighty-seven and waited all day for it to get there, marching several times across the lawn (once yelling at a robin in his path) to pull the thermometer out and check. Iris is making a salad in the kitchen, watching him through the window. The phone rings: CECE on the caller ID.

"Hi, CeCe. You want to join us for dinner?"

"Iris. It's Esme. It's okay, everything's fine okay. I know he saw her yesterday, but tell George it's time to come over. The drug's no good. Nobody gets it. They're taking her off. She found out this morning. She's mad at me for calling. She didn't want to ever say."

37

The taxi lurches through the warm, dark streets. They turn onto East Sixty-Third. While George pays, she leans against a large concrete planter at the entrance to the high-rise's courtyard. It was easier to convince him to take the trip into the city than she'd thought.

"Why wouldn't I?" he said, as if he hadn't holed up in Stockport all spring. She worries he'll be strange with strangers, too quick to defend himself against made-up barbs; it is his first trip since *The Burning Papers* closed. The doorman in his cap and long, gold-buttoned coat ushers them into an onyx lobby. They ride the elevator up to Bob and Martha's apartment.

How could she refuse Bob's invitation? How long since she and George have been to a party? Since the investment came through, she's no longer ignored Bob's calls but is again obligated to take each one. Again, she puts off his requests for them to meet. Whenever the phone jumps in her pocket, she hopes it's Victor. He's still not returning her calls. She needs to talk to him about Kingsgate. It's always Bob. The last time he called she was in Stockport, passing the church, its bell ringing the hour. He was more businesslike than the night before, when he'd called her from inside a whiskey bottle and told her a winding, indignant story about a fight and a movie theater. She'd had trouble understanding if the fight was in a movie theater or about a movie theater, if it had just happened or if he spoke from memory, or if he was recounting a movie with a fight in it. She'd crept down to the guest bedroom, to murmur affirmation, to hang up, but the movie bit turned into something about how Thierry was about to lose a front tooth, and she fired up the new second television on mute.

But when Bob called her the following day, he sounded bright and clean as morning itself and made no mention of the previous night's ramble. He invited them to come to his apartment, to kill Friday night as Friday night should be killed.

They can hear the party from all the way down the long, carpeted external hall. No one answers the doorbell. They let themselves in and do not find the dinner party she expected, but a fratty zoo—crowded, oppressively hot. Through the open balcony doors, cigar and cigarette smoke blow back into the room on a warm wind. In one corner, a red-mouthed woman with a braided topknot and black nails tends bar. In the other is a tattooed DJ behind a turntable in headphones and a short, glittering dress. To her left, through the door to the dining room, the table under an artichoke chandelier holds a lavish array of neglected catering, sushi on a lattice of banana leaves and lotus flowers. They shove in, George behind her, and see Bob across the room, in jeans and a polo shirt, his arms spread over the back of a couch, in shouting conversation with two louse-faced young men in suits. A man beside Iris untucks his dress shirt and pulls it off over his head, raising his balled fists in the air.

"You have blood," Iris shouts to the man, pointing at his nose.

"Aw, no!" He tips his head back and pushes toward the kitchen.

"This music is hurting my soul," George says, frowning.

"It's not bad, actually." She sees Bob shouldering toward them, an oversize diver's watch on the thick arm he holds high in the air to keep his drink safe from the crowd. A smile on his face, until he sees George.

"George-man. I didn't think you were coming."

"Why?" George yells, brushing imaginary lint from his white pant leg. "Should I leave?"

"No, it's great you're here. Let's go find you a drink. Hey! I want to show you something. Remember the Marilyn? The Marilyn I was trying to buy? I got the fucker. It's a fraud. Old bag grifted me good. I don't care. I love it. Life is all about how hard you fight for what you want, am I right? Come on." He puts his arm around George's shoulder, glaring at Iris.

"I'll give this to Martha," she says, prying the bottle of wine they'd brought from George's hands.

"You've got quite a trip. She's in Costa Rica with the boys. Come on, you reclusive fuckhead," Bob says to George, and escorts him away.

Three years have gone by since she answered her phone and the man on the other end said his name was George. They met at the club, he said. Did she remember? All that came to her was his linen jacket and the intensity of his eyes. She lied: of course she did! And as it happened, she was in the city. Why not meet for a drink the following day? She took a five-hour ride on a Coach USA that belched her into the dirty sleeve of Port Authority. It had been a bad year and she had nothing better to do. On the phone, he'd been so courteous and direct. He'd sounded like a grown-up. As she exited onto the blare of Eighth Avenue, having done something so weird and rogue, she decided she might as well get her money's worth, whoever this George might be. Over gimlets in a subterranean bar on Morton Street, she rallied their date to a pitch of genuine, hysterical fun, and their laughter carried out before them as they walked for many hours after, taking turns deciding right or left at the curb. As the night wore on she watched—with amusement and near disbelief—George fall in love. Too fast, like a man struck by virus. The next morning, as she was leaving his apartment, she rapped on the pointy, blue-glass sculpture by the door and made a face. He said they'd get rid of it when she moved in. And then, how she'd loved him too! But now she thinks maybe the truth is that at first, what she liked most about George was how much he liked her. How that night she'd pretended to be someone better than she was, and he'd believed her.

From across the room, the man with the bloody nose points to his cleaned face and gives her the thumbs-up. "Nice work," she yells, and begins jostling through the crowd as if she has someplace to be, the bottle of wine in her hand. She imagines getting back on the bus, taking her trip in reverse, finding her little bedroom at the foot of the college campus, with her roommate in the kitchen and 3D in the yard.

She's standing alone by the sushi. She smiles at some women picking at the rolls, women so young they are small-craniumed, almost girls. They smile wanly back but don't speak. She turns to a different group and says hello. They open up to include her.

"No, vegans can't have *anything*," one says.

"But milking doesn't hurt the cow."

"It does hurt the cow."

"It would be, like, if a vegan saw you milk a cow, as bad as you seeing someone milk your wife."

"Happy wife, happy life!"

Despite the smoke, she heads for the terrace, where she'll feel less like a flop for being alone. She's leaning over the rail, watching the cars below, when she hears her name.

"Martha hates my friends," Bob thunders into the back of her neck. "Do you hate my friends?"

"Bob, hey. When's the family coming back?"

"Nope. They've got the whole summer mapped out."

"In Costa Rica?"

"I'm paying a brick for them to save the turtles. Ecotourism, my penance. I suspect they aren't saving the turtles so much as *noticing* the turtles. Poor turtles hauling their wrinkled asses up the beach, and twenty feet away a bunch of pasty bipeds are appreciating the shit out of them. Must be fucking *baffling*. You know I'm a little in love with you."

How earnestly he looks at her. How little he needs to know her, to have convinced himself. "Don't say that," she manages, with a we're-just-kidding-around laugh.

"But I am. Even if you're not as nice as I thought you were."

"Look, where's George? I should find him."

"He's chilling in the den. Said the crowd's too much for him. Boy took a walloping, didn't he? But I think he can wait a minute. I want to talk to you. You owe me a serious talk."

He's placed himself between her and the sliding glass doors to the living room. He's swaying slightly, holding himself upright by staring at her. She starts to say something about how they can talk another time, but he cuts her off.

"You don't care about other people, huh? I thought you were the sweetest gal. You're very convincing. But you don't play by the rules. Why'd you bring him? I invited *you.*"

She steps forward. He blocks her. She looks up at the glittering lights of the surrounding buildings and at the clusters of guests, blowing lovely streams of toxic mist up into the air, oblivious of how Bob is now holding her by the waist, of how she's twisting to get away.

"I thought you were inviting both of us."

"No, you didn't."

"It's your and Martha's apartment."

"Martha's leaving me."

"Why wouldn't she?" she says, anger in her voice.

"Now that hurts. Like your shit's going so well. Stuck with Mr. Time-Out-Chair."

"There's no stuck. I love George." But it sounds hollow. She can tell, wasted as he is, that Bob hears it too. He laughs. He jabs his stubby index finger at her, and vowels out something like "Ah-haaaa," twice, three times.

"Fuck off, Bob."

"Hey." He stops laughing with the abruptness of the very drunk. A look of bewilderment passes over his features. "Hey, you owe me."

She tries to step out from between him and the rail.

"Not yet. George and I just had a chat. A real heart-to-heart-to-heart. Want to know what he confided?"

"If you don't get off me, I'll scream."

"Said you guys got into a whole mess of unmanageable debt. And I was whistling at the ceiling, pretending it was the first I've heard of it, keeping our secret nice-nice. But then! He made up with Mama and everything's all fixed. That true?"

"It's none of your business." She goes still under his hand.

"I go, 'What a help Iris must have been before the family dough came through.' And you know what he says? 'Iris? How? Her little admin job?' So, I ask myself. What has Iris done with all that money I gave her? Why hasn't she told her George about it? Maybe she's keeping it for a rainy day. Maybe she's thinking about making a break for it. Maybe I have a chance with the lovely Iris after all."

"Gave me?"

"Made, gave. Whatever. Let me show you something."

Before she knows what's happening, he's yanked her around the corner of the wraparound terrace, past a man and a woman sitting on a deck chair smoking, who smile and wave hello as she's trying to pull free, even as she's saying "Let go!" and dragging her feet.

"Listen. Don't you like me, a little?"

She sees another set of sliding doors on this, the darkened, side of the apartment. "Sure, Bob, I like you. But I don't like this. Please, let's go back in."

"I didn't take a risk for you? I did. Oh, I did. You pretend it's nothing."

"You're his only friend. You're his only friend left!"

"And you're scamming us both. Digging more than one fellow at a time? Are you so incapable of seeing what I've done for you?"

She hears—she is pleading. It is her voice so it must be her: "It's true, okay, it's true. I didn't tell George but it isn't what you think, and please let go of my wrists, Bob, too tight, I had the idea to give the money to my friend, now it's for my friend, not for me, Kingsgate was a mistake and I feel so bad and Victor won't answer. If you want it back, you can have it, it's sitting in the bank not doing nothing! All of it. Let go, let go!" She hears herself, louder: "You're not nice, you're the one not being nice!" She gives up caring if he tells George. She sputters, "I'm not—I don't give a shit what you do! You going to push me down now? That's the type you are? You try. You dare try it and see."

This startles him. He lets her wrists drop. He looks around the balcony. "You like me. I know you do. You don't like me?"

"No."

"But this isn't how I wanted it to go," he says, with a wild, despairing laugh.

"Why?" She is stepping back, once, twice.

"You know? I don't know. I don't."

She takes a breath, hides her shaking hands. "Forget about it. Let's go inside."

"In a minute."

She finds George in a corner of the kitchen, staring into a cupboard full of spices.

"I've been looking all over for you," George says. "Let's go home."

38

Astrasyne may be relevant for tomorrow's patient, reads the letter that comes two days after the call from the doctor, *but for the safety of today's patients, usage should be stopped with the supervision of your coordinating physician.* The rest is written in the most general terms, presenting neither cause nor resolution, excepting the phrase *systolic dysfunction.* Most likely meaning, her doctor says, an unanticipated and statistically significant incidence of heart attack in the wider study. *NewGenA will hold a conference call at 8:30 a.m. EDT to discuss the clinical hold. Participants can access the conference call live via telephone by dialing 866-502-6497. The passcode is 43937228. An audio-only webcast of the conference call will be available for replay approximately one hour following the live broadcast.*

Maybe Astrasyne is to blame for Dotty's death, CeCe thinks. Maybe it is not. The other therapies on the market she's already tried. Here she is, going off the drug. Already she's tying back into a knot. Already the fatigue's returned. She can feel the tremor is getting close, coming soon, warm, warmer, hot—the ticking down of her wrong-wound clock. This time, she does not doubt, to tick her down to zero.

"—because Iris will be more comfortable in here," she is saying to Esme. CeCe's sitting at the long wooden table in the kitchen, the sun coming through the window. "Can you busy yourself elsewhere this morning?"

Truth being, she's in the kitchen not for Iris's comfort but her own. Since the news, she's inclined most to the kitchen, with its warm feeling of everyday use. More often than to her sitting rooms or the library—unnerving, lately, the grand lengths of tapestry and upholstery rolling and lurching away from her, the haughty, gilded backs of the chairs. Unwelcoming, as if their assemblage is no longer for her. The height of the rooms makes her uneasy. An expanse as in a cathedral. Too much air between the top of her head and the ceiling, room for her thoughts to float and gather to the corners, to strengthen one to another until she finds that by dusk, that loneliest hour, the ceiling is fear-coffered. Try as she might, she can't read or write a letter or even watch television for the dreadful weight of the translucent hoard of herself above. The kitchen, on the other hand, smells like baking. She's had Esme make blueberry scones and the plain shortbread Iris seemed to enjoy the last time she was over. Esme arranges the breads in a basket on the table. What will CeCe say? How will she say it? Uncertainty—it is unlike her. She feels unlike herself.

For it has occurred to her—she was in a corner of the vast library, turning distractedly through a volume of Keats she's had since college—that she needs the girl. She'd read . . . *I behold, upon the night's starred face / Huge cloudy symbols of a high romance*, and she couldn't go on to the next line. She slammed the book shut. The line echoed in her head, so she chucked the book to the rug. Why not, with nobody to see? Because, how can it be? If she goes—if she fails, at present, she can count on no one but Iris. To protect, to preserve—her house, her son, her name. To manage the people who will manage the future. To insure her foundation continues to be run honorably by honorable people, not ransacked or folded to slow incompetence. To guard her written instructions against the greedy world. Iris. Directionless waif.

No. She isn't ready. To will, to be well. She will be! But in case she is temporarily impaired, to be sure everything remains in order until she, or George or Patricia—maybe Patricia, who is coming to see her, but who knows how that will go?—until then, she must make friends with the girl. Not girl. The wife. Lest what she's made of her life be undone. Lest she be forgotten.

"Leave the pot, leave it!" she says, accepting a parting tray of tea from Esme. She sounds hysterical. Come along, it's only Iris! She must remember, Iris will do whatever she asks, being of malleable virtue, having that eagerness for instruction common to people who do not belong. And Iris has proven her devotion to George. CeCe saw it when Iris brought over that ridiculous stack of bills, looking miserable as a cashier turning in a short drawer. Still, how to begin? What are Iris's interests? Is it possible she doesn't have any? What do she and Iris have to talk about? George's collapse? Local real estate? Energy policy? A dismal project, new friendship. She's eating a fourth shortbread when she hears Javier directing Iris to the kitchen.

"Hello, you!" CeCe exclaims, thinking—Why, she looks worse than I feel!—with a little leap of delight, golden and shameful at once. "Goodness, are you tired? Come, have a cookie."

"I had a rough night. You?" Iris sits beside her and takes a scone, revulsion fleeting across her face.

"I'm exhausted," CeCe answers, observing common experience, that universal shortcut to friendship. Except, she hadn't expected it to be a relief to say. For a moment she can't say anything else. They watch Esme through the window, crossing the lawn to the garden and stopping far enough away she could be a mouse among the flowers, round in her gray uniform, her hands clasped against her chest. She is explaining something to CeCe's new gardener. He's kneeling on a bright foam board, turning soil. CeCe can tell from the angle of Esme's head that he's not yet won her confidence.

"Yasser," CeCe says, pointing. "He drives two hours to get here. We became friends at Oak Park. He's a good man. I've made it worth his while."

"I—" Iris leans forward. "I met him the day we visited. Anyway, our debt, everything's pretty much straightened out. Let me show you what I've done with the budget. Our gratitude—"

"Is that why you thought I wanted you over? No, no. What's family for? " CeCe waves the unsavory subject of money away, its mortifying claim to desire and need. "It was nothing. Don't waste another thought on it. How are *you*?"

"Oh. Fine, excited for summer. Any new pictures of Douglas?"

This is irritating. Or, *something* is irritating. Iris looks weary. These last months have been hard, but why does Iris seem worse? Defeated, as cheerful as lead. Anguished where before she'd been anxious. What is irritating, CeCe realizes, is that a feeling of real care is springing up inside her. When she was getting better, it was tolerable to experience the occasional soft emotion. Not anymore. Her mind turns to Dotty shouting, when CeCe asked if the Astrasyne was working, "I don't know!" Gently, despite herself, she says, "Don't put me off with talk about babies. Are you fine? I don't think you are."

Iris looks at her sharply. "It's not your right to ask." Iris's voice— something unfamiliar. It stops CeCe's breath. Hatred. It is hate.

"Oh, no?"

Iris shoves her untouched scone away. "No. You ask me how I am and tell me I'm not fine when the answer around here is always supposed to be 'I'm fine.' It's nothing to you, to help us? Then why didn't you help us earlier? You didn't want to be embarrassed. That's why. Now you pour money on our heads for the same reason. What is my life? How should I know, one day to the next? How can I, if it's not up to me? I'm not like you. I'm—" She raises her arms wildly, oddly pointing, it seems, to Yasser. "You take it all away by giving it back. Without once think-ing what it cost. What it cost *me*. It's enough to make a person insane."

Well! Ingratitude is not what she expected. Fine, and fine arrives the steely, old feeling, the bracing calm of fighting with Pat, of break-ing Pat, of being the one who is right. "But I didn't know, Iris. How could I help you if I didn't know?"

"Huh. I guess you got me there." Iris begins to cry.

"I told George I had reservations about you, enjoying your new-found advantage. But complaining about it, I never anticipated!"

"Yes, *where* is Iris from? No one's heard of her. Attractive, a little stupid! In it for the money, of course. For the money, money, money." Iris puts her face in her hands. "Next time you want an update on George, pick up a phone and talk to him yourself."

How brutal, how lucky, to be a woman that the world still sees. "You aren't stupid," CeCe says.

"I didn't think I was, until I met you all. Oh, maybe I did. I'm sorry. I'm not getting along with anybody these days."

"How is he?"

"The same. Better. Not great."

But then, had Iris meant—*enough to drive a person insane*. Is Iris blaming her for what George has become? And she, sitting here feeling sorry for *Iris*! Sorry, for a young woman grousing about a windfall! Complaining about the unknown, about possibility, about the future rolling out ahead of her, but a bit foggy? It's as if someone's put a blazing candle right behind her ear, the flame encircling her skull. She would like to take Iris's life, take it and inhale it. To take, to breathe the breath Iris is so ungrateful for. To suffocate the world into herself—and then, her fury leaves her as quickly as it came. Iris, wiping her wet cheeks and scowling at the table. To be saved by the girl. It can't be done. All, lost. But when all is lost, what is not?

"My husband strung some ducks together and they died," CeCe says.

"Huh?"

She can only continue. "Walter tied a piece of steak to the end of a long string. Ducks will eat meat, but do not digest it. It comes out whole. He fed the piece to the first duck. When that duck passed the meat and the string, he fed it to another and another, until they were all bound by the string, mouth to tail. You see it? Shredded their intestines, trying to pull away from each other. It took days. I discovered them too late. They wouldn't die and they couldn't live. I had them killed. Walter said their wretchedness was *interesting*. He was in a fit of misdirected admiration for Beuys, with that coyote."

Iris was already queasy when she arrived. Whatever CeCe is talking about—disgusting. "That's disgusting," she says.

"What I mean is, I understand what you are going through, more than you might think."

"Okay. Can you tell me what's wrong with George?"

CeCe shakes her head. "When you met him, he'd been doing well a long time. A decade. I hoped it was the end and not the eye."

"I'm not with him for the money."

"Of course not."

"What should we do?"

"I don't know. I've never known. You are allowed to have your own standards. As to what is acceptable, for what you will accept."

"Is that right?" Iris laughs a pitiable laugh.

"What is it you like to do? What would you like your life to be?"

Iris can't think of an answer. She senses—memory or imagining, she can't tell—a high ceiling, a place quiet but full of people, dim but full of light, a square of bright color.

"No idea. I guess that's the problem."

After Iris leaves, CeCe sits at the table and looks out the window. Esme's no longer in sight. Yasser is digging a trench around the spoon mums. She'd tried to protect her son. She should not have. All those years. Instead of fading, one particular had gathered truth unto itself until she knew as if she'd known all along. Gravel, embedded in the young woman's palms. The uninvited guest wasn't Iris, has never been Iris. She'd been wrong about that. It isn't George, or even George's disgrace. The uninvited guest has all along been waiting inside, the spider hiding in each of her cells, plotting by the light of her neurons, knitting time until time. The uninvited guest, always and only her own self in the mirror, scuttling through. Come on already, she decides, reaching for the stick, standing to go to her desk, to take care of what is left, to take care of whom she must. Come on in. Here we are. It's a good house. It's been a good house. Make yourself at home.

39

It rained in the night. A wet blade of grass is stuck to the bottom of George's foot from collecting the newspaper when the phone rings.

"You get it, Iris!" he calls down the stairs. He's putting on a suit, to meet with Annie Mason and the other foundation managers in the city. They're considering making him a consultant, a favor he's considering accepting.

"Iris!" he calls again. "If it's Pat, tell her I'm too busy to see them today." Then he remembers. Iris has gone to an early showing. Nellie's finally giving her clients. Iris will be back by lunch to meet Victor. After that there's dinner with Pat and Lotta and CeCe again, at Booth Hill, assuming he can survive another crap round of family bonding. He can tell this lunch with Victor has preoccupied Iris—by how often she's brought it up and yet how little she will say. Seems Victor's been avoiding her. If she wants to hire him again, well. George will see about that.

"Yes?" he says, picking up the phone and sitting down on the unmade bed, his tie hanging around his neck.

"George, Pete Scott. Have a minute? I'd like to discuss Robert Barrow-Woods's indictment." His lawyer.

"Bob? I saw him a few weeks ago. What did he do?"

"He hasn't necessarily done anything. It's an indictment. But we should set up a meeting to discuss what kind of counsel you'll need. Today, if you can."

"Counsel? I'm Bob's friend. We went to school together."

"Yes, but your investment with him—the SEC hasn't contacted you?"

"What are you talking about?" George looks around the room as if he might find clarity in the unmade bed, the open curtains, the crack in the skylight—since when is there a crack in the skylight? His neck goes hot.

"Ah, I see. Caution on the phone, is, well, we all watch a lot of television. But it isn't necessary. Attorney-client privilege. Please speak freely. It's only an inquiry, in your case. With little sustainable cause, I should add. Can you take a look at the news?"

"Everything's downstairs. I'm trying to tie my tie. Just explain it to me."

"All right. The indictment, for securities fraud, suggests that Mr. Barrow-Woods had a contact at the FDA furnishing him with information re pending drug approvals. There are other counts, most of them unrelated to drug development, but that's the one we need to focus on."

"Why? Does Bob need our help?"

"One of his more recent trades was a short sale of NewGenA, which you have a personal connection to. And because you have an account with him that recently saw a profit—"

"I don't have an account with him."

"We can discuss it, George."

"But I don't."

"Okay. Let's just say, if you did, Barrow-Woods shorted New-

GenA, possibly knowing their main treatment was about to lose FDA approval. Let me be clear. This point isn't even in the indictment. Indictments take years to build. What he's being investigated for is earlier, dates most recently to 2008. But, going forward, they'll look into all his transactions. Government's still on a bit of a publicity rampage with Wall Street. Suffice to say, your mother was in a public drug trial. I'm confident you had no access to information beyond her experience. Which means, legally, you're in fine standing. But it looks unusual. There's a chance it'll show up in the complaint."

"I don't understand what we're talking about. What's NewGenA?" Something's happening. He runs to the window and pulls the curtain.

"The biotech that was testing Astrasyne. Astrasyne was their main development. Meaning, no Astrasyne, the company tanks. This is not like a Glaxo or a Bayer. NewGenA's eggs are in one basket. Remember ImClone? Like ImClone. Don't forget, this is one of many of Mr. Barrow-Woods's trades that will be looked at. It's unfortunate that your family, being somewhat high profile—if you get enough press, the SEC will look negligent if they *don't* investigate. I thought you'd know by now. When the SEC does contact you, refer them to me."

"Look, I don't understand what you are saying. You have to believe me. No one ever believes me!" George clears his throat. His voice is trembling.

"No need to panic here. Let me explain another way. Because you have an account with Mr. Barrow-Woods and that account recently saw a profit right around the same time as his trade against NewGenA, there will be scrutiny. By investing short, he made a profit, you understand?"

"I've never done that stuff with Bob. We have drinks once in a while. That's all! I don't do the finances around here."

"George, this is the appearance of malfeasance causing your family a headache. Not actual wrongdoing. But I do have that on May 3, Tryphon Capital deposited one hundred and twenty-five thousand dollars into a joint account controlled by you and your wife. Some of which could have come from the trade against NewGenA."

George racks his memory. "This is a mistake!" he shrieks. Who could have done this? What is their plan? How does Pete know so much? "How do you know more about me than I do?"

"There can be years of back and forth between Barrow-Woods—between anyone—and the SEC before an indictment comes down. Requests for documentation, clarification, etcetera. Indictments are not out of the blue. This also gives Barrow-Woods's representation time to make its own investigation, to prepare. His lawyer and I—I'll just say we were D-I squash together. We still play. So, doing his audit, your trade looked unusual, unusual enough to give pause. Even though it's outside the timeframe Barrow-Woods is currently in the soup for. Don't ask me more. Could you go back over your accounts? Personal finances are complicated. Can you look online while you have me on the phone?"

"I don't know how to do that."

"Okay. Hey, take a breath. It's kind of a pain. You need to register and set up a password. What about your financial manager? Your wife? Or, I can walk you through it, if you're comfortable with that, and we can look together."

George says something that sounds like *fine*. He races to his office. Doing as the lawyer tells him, he finds his checkbook; with the account number and many failed passwords—numbers and letters, numbers and letters—he registers online. Yes, there's a newer account. There's their primary joint checking, their secondary checking, the trust his mother has restocked, the mutual funds, the retirement accounts, and, and! A new joint account opened in March, registering one deposit: 125K, made May 3. But how can he trust what he sees? He tells Pete the login and password and immediately regrets doing so. He races back up to the bedroom. Safer in the bedroom.

"Okay, George? Hey, George? Yeah, it's a personal trade in, one second, here we go, in your wife's name."

He sits on the edge of the bed, stands, sits again, puts his hand in his hair, looks under the bed, looks out the window from behind the curtains, bites his thumb, locks the bedroom door, unlocks the bedroom door.

"May third. My wife?"

"Can you come by today? This is a fish-caught-in-the-net scenario, you understand? It's a red flag for the SEC, that's all. I'm confident none of it will hold water. But you and your wife do need to come by. I have two other attorneys, in finance law, financial crime specifically, I'd like to bring in. Can you come down?"

"Financial crime?"

"That's the territory."

"I mean, we mentioned my mother to Bob but—but why does that matter? He's a friend. Are you telling me that's a *crime*? I keep saying, he's never handled our finances. And they trade all kinds of things all the time, right?"

"Yes, exactly right. Maybe your family situation made him aware of the trial. Maybe it's a coincidence. Nothing wrong either way. We'll discuss any conversations you and he have had on that subject. Again, it's because of the timing, because you've recently been in the news, the SEC most likely can't *not* pursue an inquiry. How will it look when the *Journal* makes the connection and points out the SEC never bothered to investigate? We want to be prepared."

"I'm trying to tell you, I've never fucking invested with Bob."

"George, you have. All I can say is, you have. How's three o'clock? Can your wife make three o'clock? We'll need to talk to you both."

"Wait! How did he make money if the drug went bad? This is bullshit. This is because of *The Burning Papers*, isn't it?"

"George, no. One thing at a time. As I said, Mr. Barrow-Woods bet against NewGenA a few days before the study shut down. The profit on that specific trade was not significant, not compared to what he's indicted for. But they'll look at how he got his information. Again, this is not part of the current indictment. We're trying to kill it early here. As far as we know, he could have simply gifted much of that one hundred twenty-five to you. It's your only transaction and you never transacted back to him and that's in your favor. I don't think there's a case. But you understand there's an inquiry and there may be an investigation, evidence or not. A bumpy ride, press-wise. We're working on strategy. Three o'clock? I'll need you to approve additional counsel. I'm general counsel, you understand?"

"I see! I'm the joke of the world! Who's trying to ruin me? You might be one of them. How would I know? What have I done that's so bad?"

"This is a shock. But please, we're your team, here."

"Fine, I'll see what you have to say. My wife. Even my wife? I have to be in the city anyway. I'm dressed and everything."

"Very good. See you soon."

Now he understands. He thought his humiliation was over. But it was never over. They'd waited until his guard was down. A mistake he won't repeat! Three o'clock. He won't go to the city at three o'clock. He won't—Iris. Even Iris! He'd thought if the world was against him, it was against them together. Somehow she's betrayed him. He's suspected her for some time, but how he wanted to be wrong! He can't figure it out. How many times Iris said, "You're being paranoid." It makes him want to cry! It makes him choke! He *is* choking, he *is* crying, he's careening across the bedroom, clutching his own throat. He'd done a decent job, hiding how decimated he is, manning up, while talking to the lawyer. He'd thought that he and Iris were almost happy again. He'd tried to ignore his suspicions. He'd told himself he *was* only being paranoid. Things were getting better. Better and better and better and better. Now what will happen? What happens next? Will they throw him in jail?

Suddenly, he remembers Iris asking him to open the account with her. She'd come home late, said she'd been shopping in the city. So this is why she took over the credit cards and the banking those months, exerted such control! Is the screen a lie or is the lawyer a lie or is Iris—to be fooled by—it was Bob who convinced him to talk to her that day at the golf club. It was Bob who insisted he go that day, insisted he talk to the tall, pretty woman with the dog. Back to the office, ducking low! He googles Bob. He races over several articles, only a few hours old, confirming that yesterday Bob was indicted on fourteen counts of securities fraud along with two employees at the FDA.

He'd resigned from Tryphon Capital, entered federal court in Manhattan, surrendered to federal authorities and was arraigned, pled not guilty to all counts, and was released pending trial.

Released! He dials Bob's number from the home phone and is surprised to see—only more evidence, why should he be surprised?—seventeen recent calls attached to the number on the phone's display.

He *is* surprised, however, when Bob answers the phone. He was planning on leaving a scathing message, he didn't know what, or on terrorizing Martha.

"Hey, man," Bob says, "I'm totally ripped up about your name getting into this."

"You. You and Iris."

"Listen, it's not in your best interest to talk to me. I picked up to say I'm sorry, okay? I'm sorry."

"You're fucking Iris and you fucked me!"

"Never. It's a good girl you've got there. Aboveboard. All of it. The money was for you. Her heart's in the right place."

"For me? Then why am I learning about it today? I'll kill you," George hears himself say. "I'll ruin you. You tell me, who I am and what is happening."

"All right. All right, calm down. You want to know the truth? The truth is, everything's clean as a whistle, which is why I took your call. And I *am* sorry you got roped in. Deeply."

"I don't believe you. You've been calling my wife? You paying my wife? You sleeping with my wife? You know what she calls you? Mr. Pig. Smug Mr. Pig. A cover, I guess. Oh, she's clever. How long have you known each other? Everything's a cover-up."

"George, I'm—Mr. Pig?"

"Fat, fucking Mr. Pig."

"Yeah? Hmm. Okay then. Listen, I don't want to speak ill of another man's wife. But, Iris, you know what? She tricked *me*, man. She said you were broke. You want me to explain the money? I was trying to help you out. You, not her. She came to my office and she said, George needs this, George needs that. And then, after. After, man. I mean, weeks after, at my party, remember? She lets it out that it was for somebody named Victor. I never touched her. And that's the truth. You're looking at the wrong guy."

George throws down the phone. When he trusted no one, he'd trusted Iris. When he hadn't trusted Iris, the clearer part of him had. When his mother was cold to Iris, those early days, when his mother had said, "You met her where?" and "She's a coat checker? A bartender?"—every question of Iris's motivation for marrying him was right. His mother, always right. Oh, to have thought he was loved. Every memory, black. Every memory, burned.

Where will he go? He has to go. Maybe he'll go to the south of France and find his father, who probably *is* dead, but if he's not dead, George will kill him, tell him how he's ruined his life and then throw his old ass off a cliff. Or maybe he'll go to Buenos Aires, change his name and buy a new face, become a man none of them can find. Maybe he'll go—anywhere!—and come back when everything's sorted out. If it's safe. Whatever, three o'clock, he won't be there. He'll have to miss his meeting with Annie Mason. Bullshit gig, anyway.

He googles Iris and finds nothing.

He googles himself and finds the malicious old things, nothing new. He googles NewGenA and Astrasyne and his mother, but there's no connection. He googles his mother's foundation. The result is an unending list of articles about all the ways she's made the world better—bah. He shuts the laptop and finds his briefcase and shoves in the laptop. He opens the desk drawer—what does he need? He needs his watch and his passport and his wallet and a copy of the libretto and his notebook and his good pen and his checkbook and his integrity and he's already wearing a suit and he'll buy clothes on the other end, and he finds everything but the watch, where is his watch? He still isn't wearing shoes. He swipes the blade of grass from his foot and takes the bag and drops it on the living-room couch, next to the dog. The dog eyes him, chews on its peanut-butter grenade. If there were any justice, he would bite the dog, but he'd never bite the dog, he is kind and he is just, a good man in a bad world. Instead, he pets the dog, somewhat frantically; then he's up the stairs to fetch his shoes and socks, down the stairs wondering where Iris keeps the keys to the second car, to the Lexus he never drives, but drive it today he will, and he's just spotted them, right on the hook with all the others, when the doorbell rings and here is Victor, holding the blue leash.

"Hi, George. How's it going? I've had this in my glove compartment forever. Um, are you okay?"

"Iris isn't here." He's dimly aware that he is shaking.

"I can wait. Or, should I come back?"

"I've lost my watch." George's voice shakes with the rest of him. "Maybe when I was getting the paper this morning. Somewhere in the grass, maybe."

"You want help looking?"

"Yes." They step outside. Victor bends over and squints into the grass, his hands on his thighs. "Here's something!" he cries, turning his back to George. "No, it's only—" George slugs Victor with all his might, a sideways blow that half misses, cuffs him at the throat. Victor staggers, blinking with surprise. He steps backward, his gold medallion swinging. His foot catches in the exposed roots of the tree. He twists at the waist and falls. There is the satisfying sound of his head knocking against the trunk, but also the unsatisfying truth that he fell because he tripped, and not from the strength of the blow.

"What the fuck," Victor says.

The dog, inside the house, begins to bark. Bark, bark, bark. His nails drag against the inside of the door. Victor is lying on his back as if he were looking for bunnies in the clouds, next to the glinting bullet of a sprinkler head poking out of the ground.

"Victor," George whispers, squatting down, putting his face beside Victor's face, "I know why you're here." The grass tickles George's nose, smells sweet. As if the world has slowed, the life teaming around him reveals itself—an ant climbing an emerald blade beside Victor's ear. Victor's closing eyes. Two squirrels, chasing each other up the ash, into the rustling leaves. A gleaming black beetle on the cuff of George's light gray pants. The bright sound of the crickets and the dark sound of the cicadas. The dog barks through the window and the bees rise heavily from the purple-flowered weeds, not so many bees, anymore, and the mosquitoes float and somewhere hopping the lawn are sweet field mice and adorable chipmunks and hawks and starlings and the asshole blue jays rocketing the sky and once Iris told him about a skunk hiding by the pool and once Iris told him a pair of box turtles live behind the artificial waterfall but he's never seen them and he never will and he hears himself saying, "Victor, Victor."

Victor's eyes snap open and he touches the back of his head. "What did you do that for?" He gets unsteadily to his feet.

"You can have her." George springs up. "Don't hit me!" He leaps away. He dashes back into the house and slams the door. Through the plate glass over the flagstone beside the door he shouts, "Know what I think? I think *you* stole my watch. A lot of things have gone missing! You think I haven't noticed? What else of mine have you taken?"

"You people are unbelievable," Victor says, his hand on the glass. Or, George is pretty sure that's what Victor says. Louder, so there's no doubt George can hear, Victor says, "I could but I won't." He points at George. "Not worth it."

"Now I know everything!" George screams, pounding his fists on the glass. "I've figured it out! Thief!" The dog is a fury of sound behind him.

"I didn't steal anything from you, you ass."

"My watch has been missing a long time!"

"I was trying to help you find it." Victor seems about to say more. He shakes his head.

"What?" George says, holding his hand to his ear. "Speak up!"

"Never mind. I don't need this shit." Victor turns, and with the care of a man who is injured, he walks down the driveway, against the high, howling pleas of the dog.

George dashes upstairs and yanks his cell phone charger from the wall socket beneath the night stand. He returns, grabs his bag and keys. He looks cautiously out the window. He doesn't see Victor, though Victor's car is still parked out front. Whatever, what the fuck, asshole, George thinks, as he fires the Lexus to life and scrapes out of the garage. He swerves around Victor's car and is on his way.

40

Pat's arrival at Booth Hill, three days before, did not encourage in CeCe much hope for the rest of the visit. As Pat climbed out of the taxi with Douglas nestled against her, CeCe cried, "Let me have him!" stretching her arms out toward the baby, over the gravel.

Instead of handing her the boy—almost five months—Pat shrank back against the taxi door, her big-lidded eyes, round and sparsely lashed, blinking, a lattice of wrinkles above her brow. Wrong, that her daughter had aged, that her children would ever age. Pat's style certainly hadn't changed: her hair was in a high bird's nest of a straw bun. A hook of silver curled at the top of each ear. Her dress was a sleeveless, billowing tent, hemp or burlap, with a pattern meant to evoke the word *indigenous*, solemn and festive, but likely indigenous to nothing. "Do you know how to hold a baby?" Pat asked.

"*Meu Deus*, Patricia!" Lotta said, stepping around the suitcases at the back of the cab, closing her wallet. "Where do you think you came from? Of course she does!"

Lotta whisked Douglas from Pat's arms and pressed him toward CeCe. But Pat had the truth. *Did* she know how to hold a baby? CeCe wasn't sure, and now she might topple over if she tried. So she took Douglas's socked feet in her hands and pumped them up and down, saying, "Hello, young sir." She petted the top of his head. Without meaning to, she scowled at him, because Pat had been right. His eyes grew wide and fearful. He began to cry.

"Leave the bags," CeCe said, feeling dull and dreadful. As they entered the house, she caught between the women a private glance, Lotta's brows raised. But once they were arranged in the morning room and had dispatched with pleasantries about the flight, Pat said, "I'm sorry. *Would* you like to hold him?"

Her daughter! She remembers her daughter at eight, carrying an orange cat across the lawn, who knows where she found it. A private, sentimental child. She remembers Pat's look of stony tolerance when CeCe made infrequent passes at doing the mother things—pulling back the hair only to find she could not make a braid; tugging the sweater over Pat's head without seeing the neck was too tight. Only occasionally would Pat give in and curl up against her, silently handing over whatever book or toy she clutched. There was the year after Walter left that CeCe woke each morning to find Pat, her strapping, bare feet poking out from the long nightgown, sleeping wretched on the floor at the foot of CeCe's bed.

Seizing on the word that had caused them trouble so long, CeCe answered, "I'm sorry too." It hung in the air—too soon, too much feeling, and Pat looked away. "Well, aren't those practical," CeCe continued quickly, appraising Pat's shoes, a pair of felt boulders lumping out from under her voluminous smock, tapping the silk Persian as Pat bounced the baby on her knee. Worse footwear even than the pair of oiled pilgrim's hats buckled to Lotta. "I hope the pregnancy didn't give you flat feet?"

"I guess that's a no." Pat sighed and grumbled something about being thirsty, mumbled and grumbled as she had as a teenager. She handed Douglas to Lotta and clumped off in the direction of the kitchen.

"You might wait for Esme! On its way, with a moment's patience!" CeCe called after, to no effect.

"An extraordinary house," Lotta said. "I can't believe your family called this a cottage. Custom is crazy, wherever you go. My work's informed by a different history, but incredible, this ceiling!"

CeCe looked, with her eyes but not her stiff neck, to the gilded vaulting and the circular medallions, the central octagon of pale blue mosaic, the chandeliers like sprayed ice at regular intervals. When she lowered her gaze, she found Lotta was upon her, plunking the baby into her lap.

"Do you mind?" Lotta, already across the room, was inspecting the scrollwork above the door, a droll smile on her face. CeCe clutched Douglas by the armpits. He squirmed but didn't look unhappy.

"He's tired." Lotta said. "Turn him face in. Send him up the mountain. Rub him on the back." CeCe did, and Douglas tucked his heavy head into her neck. It didn't take much to learn. To learn or to remember, she wasn't sure.

They grew easier by the end of dinner, on the wisteria-wrapped end of the veranda, Yasser's stick hooked over CeCe's chair, the table facing the dark ocean. Douglas asleep, tied to Lotta's chest in some kind of felt Chinese puzzle.

"Look at how strong your mother is," Lotta said, putting her hand on CeCe's shoulder. "Fierce. A fierce woman." Lotta, unmoved or unaware of the Somners' inexperience with spontaneous encouragement.

"Thank you." CeCe pulled her back straight as she could at the word *fierce*. Comforted, despite herself, by the weight of Lotta's hand.

Their stomachs full, they talked about Pat's work supporting the microeconomies of the favelas and about clean-water access. On her phone Pat showed CeCe photos of narrow streets and water pumps. The word *proud* did not occur to CeCe, but she saw how Pat had made a family, simple instead of complicated. They insisted she tell them about Oak Park. "Tell us one good thing and one despicable thing," Lotta said.

For good, CeCe described Yasser's garden. For despicable, she said, "That nurse, Jean—I was trapped! Every day, summarizing at length—*television*." She did not trust she would maintain her composure if she told the truth, if she described getting her hopes up and trading away a year for nothing. The pneumonia, George's evil Queen, Dotty, all the days in a row she was alone.

Pat laughed. "Did you give the nurse that eye of yours?"

"I did."

"The American health system is criminal," Lotta said.

Douglas woke and arched in the sling. "No," Lotta said to Pat. "Sit. We have the bottle." She took Douglas inside.

Pat looked glum again and poured herself half a glass of wine. "It isn't fair."

"What isn't?"

"You. What's happening. I can't stand it."

"Nothing's fair. Children complain of unfairness, not adults."

"You're right. I'm right too. Hold on, we brought you a present."

Pat fetched a box from inside. In the tissue paper was a thick earthenware pitcher, brown with blue polka dots and a heavy base.

"This?" CeCe tipped it and looked inside. "Why are you giving me this?"

"We know the woman who makes them."

"I hate it."

First she, then Pat, burst into a laugh.

Now, three days later, and what a fine morning she's having with the baby! Even if she's tired and the previous day's visit to George was as grim as it was brief. (On the drive back from Somner's Rest to Booth Hill, Pat looked out the window. "Shit, shit, shit," she said softly and to herself. To distract them, CeCe asked Lotta her opinion of George's house. Lotta raised an eyebrow above her glasses and said, "I understand what it's trying to be.") A fine morning, even if none of them—

not Pat or Lotta or CeCe—is looking forward to having George and Iris for dinner. Even if CeCe woke with her head pinned sideways to her shoulder. Even though Pat and Lotta will return to Seattle in four days and are making plans for São Paulo.

After breakfast, they help her down to the beach, her folding chair and umbrella under Pat's arm. Lotta arranges the chair in the sand, arranges CeCe in the chair, and puts the baby in CeCe's lap. Pat angles the umbrella over the both of them and slathers the baby in suntan lotion. Douglas bobbles and babbles and grabs at CeCe's cheeks and pats stickily at her neck and takes her fingers into his mouth, staring at her placidly from under his white sunbonnet, or with a wide and curious alarm that passes as soon as it has been expressed. Pat sits in the sand beside CeCe's chair, wrapped in a dry towel, holding Douglas's kicking foot or resting her hand on CeCe's arm. Once or twice, CeCe asks herself if Pat has been kind the last days only because she's never seen her mother in such a pitiable state. She doesn't know the answer. But then, she doesn't know if it matters.

"Mind if we swim?" Pat asks. CeCe watches Pat plod away through the sand, plump like an apple in a maroon suit, the boy in her arms. Lotta, in a black two-piece they explained was called a tankini that CeCe can only think of as a 1920s men's bathing costume. Pat takes Douglas into the shallows, where he pets the water's surface and leans forward with alert caution as his mother dips his feet. CeCe watches Lotta swim out, watches the baby splash himself, burst into tears, and recover. Lotta, chopping slowly back to shore. CeCe has to rest. She's sleeping short intervals a few times a day, to gather energy for dinner. Pat walks her up to the house. They are shy of each other still, without Lotta.

She wakes an hour later but out the window sees no one on the beach. She makes her way to the veranda. Shading her eyes, she sees her chair is still planted in the sand. Likely they're taking a walk, or swimming farther down. Not knowing which way they might have gone in the unsteady sand, she decides she'd rather stay up at the house. She fixes herself a sandwich with the egg salad Esme left, this being one of Esme's days with her own family. CeCe fetches her stick and her tortoise sunglasses with the green glass and settles herself on the veranda. It's peaceful, to eat a sandwich in the sun and watch the billowing hem of the waterline, to scan the foundation's quarterly report, and then open the book Pat's left on the table, a Brazilian novel translated as *Monster and Hero*. The novel begins with the discovery of a set of university lecture notes in the back of a drawer. Their author has gone missing. She finishes her sandwich and is watching a sailboat knock along when something at the corner of the lawn catches her eye. For a moment she thinks it's a doll. But Douglas is too young for dolls. She hasn't gotten the distance right. A pair of legs, could it be?

Squinting, she sees it *is* a pair of legs, splayed under her willow tree, the willow weeping so low as to obscure the man they belong to. On the beach, no sign of Pat and Lotta. Should she go inside? Call the police? Something about how the legs are flopped—is he sleeping? Pointless to be afraid of a trespasser at her age, in her condition. He isn't here to tear off her clothes and leave with the tea service. She isn't afraid. She collects her stick and pushes out of the chair and takes the three veranda steps down onto the lawn. Not a cloud. Only an airplane contrail, splitting the blue.

She crosses the lawn. Harder than this morning, harder as the day goes on. She jerks along, jamming the stick into the ground until she makes it to the willow tree. Its branches dip to the ground; she must part a section to discover the man. She lets the heavy green lock fall back behind her. She and the man are in a soft sort of tent together, the light falling in as by a prism. The ground is dirt, in the shade where the grass hasn't grown. The man is not asleep. He sits with his back against the trunk. His eyes are open.

"Hello, this is private property. What is your business? You can't stop here. Do you know your way to the road?"

He looks at her, uninterested. His hand rests on a thermos attached to the belt of his cargo shorts.

"Are you lost? Move along please," she says, louder. "Have you been drinking?"

"No, no drinking."

She looks more closely at his face—a sweet face, she sees—dark eyes set with an open and youthful mildness above a strong jaw. "I didn't recognize you. It's Victor, isn't it? Are you all right?"

"I'm okay."

"Well, what are you doing here?" One of his shoes is half off his foot. "Do you mind if I come closer?"

When he doesn't answer, she leans forward, her stick in the soft dirt. A fly buzzes between them, its iridescent wing. A purple bruise is on his calf. A red crosshatch around his ankle as if he's scraped through low bramble. Nothing more serious than what a child might acquire in an afternoon outside.

"Where are you coming from?"

"No, I want to stay here."

Something in the way he's looking—at the air over her shoulder, as if he were addressing a person behind her—makes her heart snap in her chest. She *is* afraid. "Have you hurt yourself?"

"Wasn't me. I do have a headache."

"You have a headache. What else? Feel this?" She reaches down and squeezes his hand.

"Sure." He squeezes back.

"Can you get up?"

"I don't want to."

"But can you? Can you try?"

"Pull the shades up."

She peers frantically behind her, as if the apparition might help. There's only the soft, folded wings of the willow tree and the green lawn racing away, so bright she squints. The sliver of sky between the branches, a lovely blue.

"Yes, we are in the shade. But I think we should try."

"No, thank you."

It is difficult, but with the help of the stick she comes down onto her knees. She wants to push the hair off his forehead. She hesitates and does so, gently. His forehead is smooth and warm under her hand. His eyes seem fine. Except—it's only the eyes looking back at her. The eyes, but not the mind. She moves one hand unsteadily to the trunk of the tree, the other to his chest. His heartbeat is strong and regular. She looks at his neck, his hands, the sides of his head, his black hair against the bark of the tree. Nothing wrong. But something is wrong! She reaches her hand, his hair thick and dark; it could be, yes, blood. Behind his ear, in the hair. So little she wouldn't have noticed had she not been looking—a matted patch, sticky, no bigger than a penny. It doesn't seem enough to matter.

For this to be Esme's day off! Of all the days! She needs Esme! No one she can call for. She shouldn't leave him. Yet she must get to the house. She's about to wrench herself up when she remembers what everyone carries.

"Victor. Have you got a cellular phone?" She rifles in his pocket. It's on! She presses its only button and holds it to her ear. "Hello? Hello?"

She lifts it away from her ear and pushes the button harder this time, twice. Nothing. She holds the phone up to her eye. At the bottom of the screen—the screen, good God, a picture of 3D—are the words *slide to unlock*, lighting up and going dim, letter by letter. She follows this instruction but it does not unlock. She tries again. If both her hands were free, maybe she could get the angle, but she can't let go of the trunk.

"Victor, can you unlock this?"

"What?"

The phone buzzes to life in her hand. The word IRIS appears on the screen with a green bubble containing the words U HERE? Iris! Answer, answer! She presses the phone to her ear. "Hello? Iris dear, hello?" The phone buzzes once more, stops.

Now Victor's hand is shaking. What to do? No, it isn't his hand, but hers. Of all the unwelcome times, it's her hand thrusting the phone into his hand that's shaking, it's she who's shaking, she who's kneeling over him in the dirt, he who's slumped against the tree; she who's in charge of bringing this situation to a better conclusion than the one she fears; he who's looking at her with an unnatural generality. He, with his borrowed tremor that banishes all thought from her mind so she hears herself cry, "Esme!" And, to Victor, "Can you hear me?"

"I can hear you."

"Can you stand up with me?"

"Motor." He flicks away her shaking hand. For the first time he looks up, into her eyes directly. "Motor!"

"Oh, dear, oh, no." It slips out, she hadn't meant to show him her alarm. She must get to the house.

"My head."

"Don't worry. What's wrong with your head, young man, is you need a haircut. Here we go, please. Up!"

"It's okay, I have a headache."

"Yes, yes. How about I'll be right back."

Suddenly she's aware of the cool dirt packed under her knees and how impossible it will be, shaking as she is, to pull herself up with only the stick, but she must. She's only two halting steps onto the lawn when here are Lotta and Pat and Douglas, the baby's pudgy legs dangling from the crook of Lotta's arm, the baby's white bonnet flapping as the women, wet and wrapped in towels, hike up the lawn toward the house, Pat slouching as she always has, and CeCe cries, "Pat! Pat! Lotta!" Pat's dull-blond head turns in the sun, and though Pat's far away, CeCe knows her so well, she is her mother, she can see her daughter's focus shift, and the women turn and break toward her in a fast walk and then a run, Lotta dropping the chair but holding the child tight, and as the women hurry toward her, she turns back to Victor, and she becomes aware she is frozen, her knees are locked, that the one hand is clutching the strong, low branches of the willow and the other is wrapped around the stick and she is as rooted to the ground as the willow itself but no matter, they're coming, and she twists best she can back toward Victor and calls, "Don't you worry, we've got you some help," and he looks at her as though he understands.

41

Iris is halfway home from showing James and Eleanor Reed a falling-down Victorian, thinking about the conversation she'd had with CeCe, when her phone rings. Two weeks, and what CeCe said won't let her be. Whenever she is alone, it vaults to mind and sits on her other thoughts, heavy and noisy as a frog. It's as if with that creepy story about Walter and those ducks her mother-in-law was telling her to go. Two, ten times a day, she remembers the sound of CeCe's voice as she said, "Before it's too late," and how CeCe's eyes were scary and caring, black and green. But CeCe hadn't said "before it's too late." The memory is as vivid as it is false. CeCe left not one marriage but two. What did she do with her freedom? What did she become? Frail as a chip of salt. Iris's thoughts, now so often a confusion: Here is CeCe, saying, or not saying, "Before it's too late," getting mixed up with what she *did* say yesterday, that unending afternoon she and Pat and Lotta came over. When George greeted them by asking sulkily, "What's new?" CeCe answered in a lively, unruly voice Iris had never before heard, "No more new! The life I am living is the life I will live!" And later: "To be thirty-five again! Thirty-five, but not twenty. Twenty is the pits." She'd laughed as she said it, but her eyes, on Iris, were serious.

The phone. Iris hits accept and puts George on speaker. His voice fills the car. "A hundred and twenty-five grand! A hundred and twenty-five grand!" She has betrayed him. She is a whore. Does she know Bob is going to prison? That he's a criminal? A *financial* criminal? Does she know her treachery will likely land him in prison too?

"Where are you? Where?" she insists, but he ignores her and howls when she tells him to calm down and howls when she says he is delusional, not about the one twenty-five, okay, but about whatever else. He continues—she's a slippery, golden snake, untrue from the first. He's leaving and never coming back. As he blares through the car, a stillness falls around her. He hangs up abruptly. She drops the phone on the seat. Where he is or what he is planning to do is no longer a question for her to ask. The road is shady and cool air gusts in the window. It's done. The Reeds hadn't liked the house.

"I agree," she'd said, to their obvious surprise, "what a dud."

In the driveway, she pulls up behind Victor's car. She sees the garage door is open, the never-used Lexus gone. George, save them, must be on the road. But she can't figure where Victor is—not on the lawn, not at the pool. "Victor?" she calls, opening the front door. The house is quiet. To her text—U HERE?—she gets nothing back. 3D shakes himself, jumps down from the sofa cushions, and comes to her with the big beg eyes. It's time for a walk. She'll take him out and have a think. Maybe Victor went walking to pass the time until she arrived. Maybe they'll run into him. She takes 3D through the mudroom and heads down past the grotto, along the trail to the meadow. Victor isn't there. She throws the ball. Once, twice, ten times. She sits on a rock, looking at her phone, George's howl in her ears. 3D gallops back to her, panting, and rolls in the grass at her feet.

"You're a good dog. What are we going to do, you and me? Where do you think we'll live? No idea? Me neither." She stands and stretches her arms up, looking at the trees. She touches her toes, rubs 3D's hot armpits. "You want to know something, dog? That opera was the ugliest heap of ugly I ever saw. Maybe our friend's at the house by now. Come!"

3D is at the grotto's trickling waterfall, Iris just behind, when she catches sight of something moving on the other side of the glass wall. No, through the glass wall and across the room, through the large windowpane by the front door. Three police officers, cupping their hands to the glass, looking in. Thick-necked, bulky at the waist. Two cruisers are parked beside her and Victor's cars. These are not the graybirds who walk the beat in town, post office to church. Someone is knocking and ringing the bell: a fourth officer, a sallow, freckled woman, her face tight as a nut under her uniform hat, steps away from the door, into the frame of the window. What had George said on the phone about Bob, about prison? Without thinking, Iris drops into a crouch behind the bushes at the edge of the glass. She pulls 3D close, holding his collar and the scruff of his neck. 3D at attention, straining forward.

"Hello," an officer calls. "Hello?"

"Going around," another says, and disappears.

The three remaining stand idle by the door. She can't read anything from their expressions. They've quit squinting into the house. The woman tries the bell again. Iris jumps. 3D barks, deep and sure.

"No!" Iris whispers. "Shhh!"

It's as if she's stumbled into a nightmare where everything George makes up comes true. Was he right? Are they here to arrest him? To arrest her? For what? What had George called Bob? A financial criminal? What has she done! 3D barks again.

"Hey, somebody's home. C'mere, boy!"

"You going to interrogate the dog?" The female officer's voice. Another laughs. Iris muzzles 3D. He closes his mouth on her palm. The pain isn't bad, but it startles her and she lets the collar go. He springs forward and takes off, not around the house as she would expect, but back from where they came, down the lawn and into the trees. She can't think why—is he on the scent of the cop who's no longer in sight? Could it be Victor? Could it be George? The doorbell rings again. "3D,

3D," she whispers. She stands. She steps out after him, light and fleet as she can down the hill. The three officers are coming around the house. Where is the fourth? They talk casually among themselves. She ducks down. She whispers, "Come, 3D. Please." She reaches the edge of the woods and with all thought traded for panic, she breaks into a run. She's in the trees. Left, no right. She only needs time. To understand what's happening. To understand what is meant for her. Time to think, time to get the dog. She pleads with her body, *3D, come, come, come.* Farther in, she sees him! Careening up the narrow path to Booth Hill. She chases him to the break in the trees. The ocean fills her vision. What if—if she's really in trouble—what will happen to her baby? The cops will testify she ran away. That looks bad, doesn't it? Could they lock her away from her baby? They do, they lock women away from their children. They do it all the time! Her child! But she's done nothing wrong! She calls to 3D once more, hears nothing. She'll get him later. She turns from the ocean and hurries back out onto the lawn. She lifts her face to the officers. She greets them with a wave.

42

The airport! Destiny's steely armchair. Infinity's featureless foyer, tedious antechamber—the air as refreshing as thinned glue, the pattern of the long concourse's carpeting rolling out before him simultaneously dull and frenetic, static and busy as a lost language. Here in the Fortress of Boredom and Becoming, he strides to his gate. Or not quite strides, as he must first wade through security, taking off his shoes and putting them in the gray plastic bin, wondering, briefly, if they can glean anything from the laptop that might be used against him. He finds a seat at Gate 3, but he can't sit still. He calms his nerves by rushing several times around the departure area. He thinks of his mother, the word she used, how for so long she called JFK by its old name, Idlewild, and he thinks, Ha-ha! She was right, she's always right, in some intricate, useless way, for this is exactly how he is, idle-wild, and what else can a person be, waiting for takeoff?

Freedom. It's free to be rash, to speed to the airport with no particular plan, to call one's treacherous wife with one hand on the wheel.

Freedom to tell her he's no longer a fucking dupe and hang up, though really he hung up because he'd hit congestion on the perilous Van Wyck, stopped short, and was rear-ended with a neck-jolting thunk by a yellow cab. He hadn't seen the traffic ahead of him, distracted as he was, shouting and also maybe crying. Freedom to simply drive on, even as in his rearview mirror he watched the cabdriver climb out on the litter-strewed shoulder and wave his arms in the direction of George's Lexus, picking up speed. No, he would not be delayed. He found the hulking ramp to the terminals, chose one at random, parked at a rakish angle in the lot, hurried in to buy a ticket, got lost in the crap-faced and anemic swarm of what was apparently a line, cut the line, was shouted at, was escorted to the proper counter. He was exasperated to discover he couldn't, at the last minute, book a direct flight to Rome or Paris. The ticket agent explained (and how well George comported himself, how politely he contained his wrath! His upbringing good for something, after all) that he could go to Montreal and then Milan, or Montreal and then Rome, or Logan in Boston and then Paris. A variety of other destinations were available with a first stop in Geneva or Reykjavik. Logan to Paris, he said, because it was the flight leaving soonest, so soon the agent only allowed it because George didn't have luggage to check. She told him to proceed directly to the gate. Paris! A dignified escape. It's been many years. Yes, he'll stay at Le Meurice and go to the opera and, maybe, he'll bring to them *his* opera. His opera, to which he has in secret been making no small revision! He'll take a meeting. America's too stupid, too young, and at the same time too washed-up. He should have seen this all along. Maybe then he'll take the train south and look around for dear old dad, dead or alive.

As the plane hauls into the sky, he thinks about what Walter might say to him. He thinks of Iris's beautiful face, her hand on the back of his neck. Iris! Oh, Iris, we might have sat side by side in the cooling hours of a peaceful summer, so many years from now. I would have taken your hand as we watched our children, doing whatever it is we'd helped them discover they liked to do. We'd hold so many stories between us by then, belonging to us alone. I waited for you there in the dream of our becoming. You saw me waiting and you changed your mind.

Well, fuck her. Fuck them all, he decides. He orders a tomato juice and watches the daylight bounce against the dingy curve of the overheads in the shape and pattern of the windows. He'll become someone new. Make a new life. A better life. But then, something dark without words, some light without sound, some heartbreak, tells him he won't. Tells him this is not the trading of one chance for another but the loss of all chance, and beneath him he sees the outlines of other lives he might have had, the shadow of a different wife who never betrayed him, stretching out languid against the clouds, the sweet ghosts of the children he'll never have. The shadow of himself, taller than he is. The rest of the flight he spends with his head in his hands, trying to convince himself it can't yet all be over.

As they taxi in at Logan, he turns on his phone. The twelve calls are from Iris, from his mother, from the lawyer, from several numbers he doesn't recognize. He puts the phone to his ear to listen.

"Sir, not yet, sir," the passing flight attendant says. "The rules apply to everyone."

She's right, he decides. Not yet. He doesn't want to hear a word from them. He turns off his phone. They hold the plane at the gate long enough the air grows hot and stale and the passengers begin to grumble.

A steward from another section approaches his seat. "Mr. Somner? We need you for reticketing. There's a ticket issue. If you would follow me."

"Me?" He looks around the cabin.

"With Preferred Circle, advanced deplaning—"

"Okay, okay." Sweat blooms along his collar, for the eyes of all the passengers are on him, and why has no one else been told to get up? He disembarks. At the end of the breezeway he sees three officers, not quite idle. A German shepherd, wearing a kind of security overcoat, stands leashed at attention. Again he hears his name. He is told to step to the side please, Mr. Somner. Mr. Somner, right over here.

43

"Esme," CeCe calls from the sunroom into the kitchen. "Could you please hold lunch? I think I'll lie down. Then we'll visit George. We'll need sweaters, do you think?" 3D lifts his head and emits a whistling sigh. There's the stack of books and the newspaper, her chair turned to face the ocean. The sun is in the russet coat of the dog. She reaches down and strokes the top of his head. He is always by her side. "Don't fuss, Dog." She only calls him Dog. "I'll be back. Why don't you go investigate what's left of the flower beds? Maybe Yasser has brought you a treat."

Almost a year ago and out of the blue, the sheriff delivered 3D to her house. He'd been found by a family near Poughkeepsie, some sixty miles northwest, but brought to the pound when one of the children proved allergic. Animal Control scanned him for the address chip. It seemed he'd followed some mysterious course—the smell of an animal, the sound of a car. As it happened, a neighbor had that same day lost his dog, a jittery, drip-eyed Maltese who was later found near

Booth Hill. Maybe the Maltese had set 3D going. But why he kept on, they'd never know. His first week back, Dog remained by the kitchen door at Booth Hill, by the kitchen door or the kitchen window or the front door, but always leaning in the direction of Somner's Rest, forlorn. He whimpered for Iris and wouldn't eat the food Esme put in his bowl. To coax him, CeCe fed him bacon from her hands. When they took him for walks, CeCe watched from the veranda. Two months back, Dog still couldn't be let off the leash. Quick as he was free, he'd race into the woods, down the path, and circle the locked and darkened house, crying for all pity.

She and Esme discussed it, and Pat, on the phone, agreed. CeCe would keep him until they heard from Iris. They couldn't understand why she didn't call them back, if only to arrange for the dog—the year before, when 3D hadn't turned up after a day, a week, six weeks, Iris told CeCe she couldn't bear to continue looking. She went ahead with her plan to move back to the college town in upstate New York where she'd been living when she met George. She filed for divorce the day she left. She asked for no settlement and did not contest their prenuptial agreement, which left her almost as before the marriage. George granted the divorce quickly, remotely, and without trouble. She promised to be in touch when she was settled, but as the months wore on, CeCe came to think of her and the dog's vanishing as one, as if they had disappeared into the trees together, like something out of a book. CeCe understood. Iris needed a break. But she didn't understand about 3D.

After the sheriff drove away, CeCe suggested they crate the dog and send him to Iris's forwarding address. "No," Esme said. It was a PO box. "Dog misses her, but what happens with maybe no one to collect him on the other side?" Hard to believe Iris didn't want him, but so was everything else that had happened. They'd contemplated the dog, drinking water with loud and sloppy gusto from his bowl. CeCe said, "We'll hire someone to find her if we must. For now, let the poor girl be. If she wants us, she knows where we are."

"I liked her," Esme said. "But I don't think she's coming back."

"I liked her too. Do you hear?" CeCe said, to the red backs of 3D's ears. "Make the best of it, Dog. She's not coming. We'll do for you as we can."

He couldn't have understood. But he looked at her over his shoulder and lowered his head to the floor and seemed to accept his new situation.

George's lawyers argued for bail, citing his clean record and the Somners' prominence in the community. But a defendant apprehended trying to make a connecting flight off U.S. soil was, as the judge put it, not a good beginning, and the request was denied. George awaited his trial, for manslaughter, three months in jail. While the prosecution gathered its case, George's lawyers organized their defense, principally that Victor's death, by epidural hematoma due to blunt impact to the head, could not definitively be linked to George's blow. On the advice of counsel, George agreed to a bench trial at Stamford Superior Court, his appearance in the tabloid news too recent and negative to risk a jury.

Still, the lawyers said he had a good chance. CeCe was hopeful. Each day, she watched her son's quivering back as he sat beside his lawyers, facing the judge. She listened to the lawyers argue that a definitive timeline could not be established. Victor might have arrived at George's door already injured, with blood already leaking into his brain. The defense noted that Victor had a felony record of driving under the influence, and individuals with a history of alcohol abuse are potentially at higher risk for hematoma formation. The prosecution countered with testimony from the hospital; Victor, a few hours from death, in what the expert witness called a *lucid interval*, was able to describe his encounter with George. The prosecution followed this with footage retrieved from the security camera George had installed above the front door. It was in George's favor that, watching the footage, the judge could see the punch was not impressive. George was exonerated of prosecutable intent to kill. Less helpful to the defense was that George's attack appeared unprovoked, and despite the lack of audio, it was obvious he'd taunted Victor as he lay on the ground. The case proved simple and took less than a week at trial. CeCe looked to the courtroom's high, narrow window as the judge read the sentence. Fifteen months.

She did not exactly think it was wrong. When she saw in the paper a photographer had caught her in the quick moment the umbrella was pulled away from her face, as they lifted her into the car, her eyes wide, she felt no stake in the world's opinion and was not ashamed. Since then, no matter her failing health, she's gone to visit George every day the prison has allowed, with Esme and the strongest of her three nurses, an able, burly giant, graceful as a dancer, good at swooping her through the narrowest of doorways, up and down stairs.

Toward the end of his term, George told CeCe why he'd gone to the airport. He'd thought he was being charged with insider trading. For nothing—the SEC's investigation discovered Bob's gift to Iris was one of the altogether-legal transactions he'd made. "I am always afraid," George said, as they sat in the corner of the visiting room that was wide enough for her chair, "of my own mind. I was so certain."

Another visit, CeCe brought the envelope that had arrived at Booth Hill without a return address. Two photos, one of the baby in the delivery room, in Iris's arms. Iris, looking down at the baby through a thick pair of glasses CeCe had never seen. The second, taken from above, of the baby sleeping in a bassinet, with no glimpse of the room or anything beyond. After looking at the photos a long time, George said he did not want to keep them.

Today, when Esme comes to wake her, to go see George before visiting hours expire (it takes them a good hour and forty minutes to make it through the prison's three security checks), CeCe does not get out of bed. Esme calls the doctor. The doctor comes. The doctor calls Pat and Lotta. They fly in two days later. They drive straight to the hospital. The stay at the hospital is short. The pneumonia has returned, fiercer. Pat and Lotta and Esme and the giant nurse bring her home, her head on her chest, her eyes not quite closed but closed. "Oh, Esme," Pat cries, "I don't think she can hear us anymore!"

For many days, Lotta keeps Douglas out of the house with elaborate excursions around the lawn. Douglas, almost two, totters speedily through the cool grass in a tiny Windbreaker, his fists full of vegetation, while Pat remains inside. They call Iris. She finally calls them back. She's moved again. It would be a long trip. She isn't sure if she can come. But she'll e-mail more pictures of the baby. They offer to send the dog. She says she can't keep a dog where she is living, not yet anyway. She's sorry, she's so sorry, she says, and abruptly hangs up. Later in the week, Lotta hands Douglas to Pat, and Pat holds the boy up to CeCe, hoping he might wake her. Later still, they hold up the photographs of Iris's baby that they've printed from the laptop on CeCe's desk. They say, *Can you see? Do you see her? She's beautiful, take a look.* They hold photographs of CeCe's garden in high summer, bright smears of color, right up to her eyes. They say the names of the flowers and point to the ocean behind the flowers and Pat tells her mother the stories she can remember from her childhood that include the flowers and the ocean.

On a soft October day, there is a service in the churchyard in town.

A public memorial will be held some weeks hence in the city, where the mourners will fill the Cathedral of St. John the Divine—so many beneficiaries of Cecilia's generous endeavors—and afterward spill out onto Amsterdam Avenue, to shake hands and take out their phones. But here, at the churchyard, the orange and yellow leaves still in the trees, there's only Pat, and Lotta, Esme and Javier and Yasser, the rest of the staff, and the friends Esme instructed Pat to invite. Nan Porter and Annie Mason and Clifton Franks sit in the front row beside the family. Dana Barnes is there, and the Rhavs and the Bakers and the Becks and the Conrads and a tall man with white hair from Arizona whom no one knows. Esme said she was certain they should invite him. George, beside Pat, only just released. Thinner and harder, with the unexpected posture of a soldier, his hair cut close, the guests trying not to look at him too much or not enough, having heard that somehow he was already again engaged. They wondered if it indicated his general malevolence that throughout the service he did not cry, until the moment he bent his head and could not stop.

During the service, 3D lies on the grass at Esme's feet. His neck flat to the earth, his ears flat to his head. Douglas alternately sits and lies on the dog, sinking his fists into the red fur, slap-patting at the dog's back with both hands. *Dog! Dog! Dog!* he says, tugging 3D's ear, which 3D endures. Lotta crouches down and says, *Shhh.*

Where Iris lived was by then known to them, though they could not persuade her to come to the funeral. The private investigator Pat hired, for reasons of dispensation of inheritance, found her in less than an afternoon. She was living once again in Nova Scotia, with an aunt of advanced age, her father's oldest and last remaining sister, in a town called Great Village, which, the investigator said, at the 2010 census, claimed five hundred inhabitants. The residence was listed as a bed-and-breakfast. They imagined she might be helping the aunt run it.

But they couldn't know what in those last days came to CeCe's mind. Shut away from sight and sound, in the first vanishing that is the vanishing of time, in the dream that is not a dream, CeCe was sitting under the willow, and why are you looking over here? Why are you looking at me? I'm sitting, is all. Entertain yourself somewhere else, please. I own this land. I sit where I please. I sit under my tree. I am sitting under my tree and it was hard to get down here. The trunk caught my sweater. Sweater, I need to visit George. Caught on sweater is the woods. The woods, a poor man's overcoat, and cleverness is cheap is what I think of that. I am in the woods, and in the story the witch says don't go into the woods and in the story the mother says you must journey though the woods. Mother says you can't stay where you are forever and the story says that too. Tell me, lesser sex, how was your day? Tell me, what do you like? What matters to you? Dragged myself down the trunk of the tree like a bear with an itch so I may sit my bony in the copper leaves and feel the leaves mulching as I sit them, black and soft. I see my house. Over there is my lovely white house. Rain or yesterday's rain gusting off the leaves. Rain, rain. Run is shouted when a girl. I was a lucky person never on a dark street, never under the hand behind the wall across the bed never anyone the boss of me I am I was always tempted but never the car going anywhere they wouldn't wait, knees together under trees girls I do remember picking up a black button from the lawn it had rained or there was dew and then it was my button that I had lost so long before. I was picking up the button and my heel sank in the earth. Strange word. Earth, earth, what does it mean? Once when George was a boy he was confused he said sprawled eagle and I laughed he can laugh at me now if he wants maybe he will laugh his wish at me. Did he mean spread or bald? No one knew be-

cause no one was listening to what he was saying and then he ran
away? My heel sank in the dirt and made a little hole like a golf tee
very short heels as we had then and the feeling is satisfying in a way
but I complain to the woman who is with me having tea with lemon
slices and I complain to the man who once loved me and I say my heel
is ruined so she can say yes yes yes you are right and he can say I miss
you, I miss you, I miss you, everyone's missed you, and missing is
without a friend and poor Cecilia does not deserve to be called poor
and I am missing something like a button, not a button, some convenience that one forgets one is missing until it is needed something
nagging something at the back of my head where I can't turn to see it
that I can't quite remember but there are those fine many days one
million thousand days with the sun and that woman bending crooked
over me and over me, close and closer until I cannot see the house can
only see her face and will it, be—

44

Dear CeCe, the letter began.
Dear CeCe, Pat read again.

Last week we visited Great Village. It reminded me of running out of Stockport and of how hard that time was. When I lived in Great Village and my mind was still full of George and you and everything that happened, once or twice a day I would say to myself, I'll write CeCe, but I never could.

I applied to college. Can you believe it? I'm in my junior year.

I think you would like it how Cecilia pretends to study with me. We make piles of books side by side. When I pick up my pen, she picks up her crayons. The house is filling up with books for both of us. We have a garden. It's kind of a mess. Mostly vegetables. C likes to help by dragging the basket and by bothering poor 3D, who is old and puts up with her. Last spring, I made a secret winding path through the part of the garden where the plants are taller than she is. When she disappears

inside the plants I pretend I can't find her and then I find her, that
oldest game of mothers and children. We are alone, but we aren't lonely.
It is because of you, what we have. I think about that all the time. She's
five. When did that happen? Old enough to know where she gets her
name.

　Love,
　Iris

"I don't understand. Why write a letter to a dead person?" Pat says, frowning at the postmark, flipping over the envelope that Esme forwarded to her, that the post office at Stockport had forwarded to Esme. "To a house nobody lives at anymore?" And because she wasn't sure what to do with it, she folded it back up and left it on the table.

ACKNOWLEDGMENTS

My love and gratitude to the McManuses: Deborah, Jason, Alan, and Mage. Mattie Miller, I love you. Bridget Forster and Eleanor Murphy, always.

Bill Clegg invented this book twice, first with editorial vision and then by finding it a home. He took extraordinary care, every step of the way. Thank you to Shaun Dolan, William Morris Endeavor, and Chris Clemans.

Courtney Hodell edited *The Unfortunates* three comprehensive and compassionate times. Her standards were higher and her perceptions keener than mine. It is how it is because of her brilliance. Thank you also to Mark Krotov.

My heartfelt thanks to Eric Chinski for his generous and wise care in guiding *The Unfortunates* to print. Thank you to Peng Shepherd for her excellent and tireless help and direction. Thank you to Lenni Wolff and Steve Boldt for making an elegant book out of a stack of pages. Thank you to Rodrigo Corral and Emily Bell for this most brilliant cover. Thank you to Katie Kurtzman. Sarita Varma, I'm very lucky it's you taking her out the door. Thank you to Ken Holland and Steven Pfau.

Advice from kind and gifted readers is woven though each page of this book: Thank you to Peter Cameron, Sarah Dohrmann, Fredi Friedman,

Elaine Kim, Valerie Martin, Leslie York, and my fellow writers at Sarah Lawrence's MFA program. Josh Henkin read the first eight pages of *The Unfortunates* and suggested it might be a novel. He read the rest ten years later. My deepest gratitude to Sam Leader. Thank you to the genius and generous Amanda Coplin, Jaimy Gordon, and Christine Schutt. Thank you to Janet Benton, who helped me learn how to be. Emma Ortega, thank you for your love and care.

For their advice and expertise on various matters of law, finance, and business, I am indebted to Marshall Beil, Elizabeth Egan, Micah Kelber, and Alexa Kolbi-Molinas. Special thanks to Alex Chachkes for his illuminating e-mails about drug development. I am grateful to Steve Almond for lending his beautiful line about why we need books to Victor, unattributed on page 53. Thank you to Kyle Smith, of whose style I made inferior imitation in the form of a fake *New York Post* article. Bradford Louryk loaned me his scarf.

Multiple system atrophy is a disorder I learned about while writing *The Unfortunates*. I took narrative liberty with its symptoms. I thank anyone who reads this book and suffers from MSA for tolerating my interpretation of the experience. I am grateful to the MSA Coalition for their informational video *Sophie's Search for a Cure*. Learn more at www.multiplesystematrophy.org.

I owe a turn of plot each to *Howards End*, by E. M. Forster, and *The House of Mirth*, by Edith Wharton. For the customs and tribulations specific to an American industrialist dynasty, I am indebted to *Mrs. Astor Regrets: The Hidden Betrayals of a Family Beyond Reproach*, by Meryl Gordon, and to Gloria Vanderbilt's works, particularly *It Seemed Important at the Time: A Romance Memoir*.

My life was forever changed by the Fine Arts Work Center in Provincetown. Thank you to Elizabeth McCracken for extending my time there. Thank you, Roger Skillings. Washashores make the greatest captains. I am grateful to the Constance Saltonstall Foundation for the Arts and the Jentel Foundation for time and space to write early on.

Salvatore Scibona, I learned more from you about how to write in five hours at a pizza place than I did in the preceding ten years. For that, and for the many other good and bighearted turns you've done this book and writer, thank you.

Rob Strauss, dear friend. Thank you for so much, going way back and forward. This book wouldn't exist without you.

Jason Mones, life of my life, maker of days. You made it so I could make it. All thanks and all love. You too, sweet V.

A Note About the Author

Sophie McManus was born in New York City and received her MFA in creative writing from Sarah Lawrence College. She is a recipient of fellowships from the Fine Arts Work Center in Provincetown, the Constance Saltonstall Foundation for the Arts, and the Jentel Foundation. Her work has appeared in *American Short Fiction* and *Tin House*, among other publications. *The Unfortunates* is her first book.